THE LAST COSMONAUT

Science Fiction Thriller

BRANDON Q. MORRIS

BRANDON Q.
MORRIS
HARD SCIENCE FICTION

Contents

THE LAST COSMONAUT   1
Author's Note   381
Also by Brandon Q. Morris   383
The biography of nothingness   389

Notes   401

The Last Cosmonaut

October 5, 2029, Earth orbit

SHE ANCHORED HER BOOTS IN THE FOOTRESTS AND TILTED HER head back to keep the vent from blowing sweat right into her eyes. Back when she was in training, she'd told Heiner that putting the helmet fan above the hat line was a design flaw. Ground control had better not give her trouble about that. Easy enough for them to tell her she needed to conserve resources! Maybe they should try blowing a little less hot air. Mandy deliberately took several deep breaths until she felt light-headed.

Pause. She let go of the cable with the electric lights. A slight movement went through the snake-shaped chain that extended all the way to the RS Völkerfreundschaft[1] airlock. It made it seem almost alive, like a gigantic electric eel—an animal that had made a great impression on her twins. She could see herself walking through the Leipzig Zoo, holding each of her two girls by the hand, the sun just emerging from behind a cloud.

In just two more weeks, Mandy's replacement would arrive. She needed to focus on the here and now. Far below her, the boot of the Italian mainland was kicking the island of Sicily. The skin on her forehead felt tight, and she wanted to scratch at it. She tried to push her head down far enough for the liquid-dispensing mechanism to reach her forehead so she could rub against it. But she couldn't do it. The helmet simply wasn't big enough.

"Everything okay?"

That was Bummi[2], her only companion. It was a robot, named after the bear mascot of a children's magazine. It really

3

didn't fit. Bummi's body was small in comparison to its limbs, which were nearly two meters long, and it looked like a four-legged spider. Out of the corner of her eye, Mandy saw it crawling toward her. It took turns using its arms and legs to move across the hull of the Völkerfreundschaft.

"Yes, I'm just taking a little break," Mandy replied.

"You should make sure your extravehicular activities take up as little time as possible."

"I know, Bummi. I should be conserving oxygen."

"Correct. But I'm thinking about you, too. Every minute out here increases your risk of having an accident."

"I know you're only looking out for my best interests."

Bummi didn't reply. It never responded to sentences that only stated the obvious. Sometimes Mandy thought it secretly believed it was much smarter than she was, and looked down on her, but the robot would never say so directly. Now she could see the Atlantic Ocean below. She shifted her gaze away from the globe, then inclined her torso forward to hook the safety line to another crossbar. As she did so, she he felt a brief wave of nausea. Her body felt like it had been hanging upside-down for too long, even though spatial directions were meaningless in microgravity.

"You have to go around the front," said Bummi. "Or would you prefer that I take over?"

"No, thanks. I can do it."

Mandy pushed off and worked her way toward the front, where the space station was considerably narrower. That's where it was most obvious that it had been built from what was once a rocket stage. This had proven to be the most affordable way to get the GDR's first space station, built as part of the 14th Five-Year Plan, into Earth orbit. Now it had been fifteen years since its inauguration. At that time, Mandy had just graduated from the sports academy for children and youth[3]. It had seemed to her that training to be an officer in the air force was the only way to become a cosmonaut and fly into space.

If someone had told her back then that she'd be working as a floating technician to set up lights for a festival, she would have laughed out loud, or reported the shameless individual as an enemy of the republic.

"Careful with the antenna," said Bummi.

Mandy hooked the safety catch. Then she turned around and

gave a start when she saw the robot right behind her. It had raised its left arm and was holding its claw over her as if it were about to strike.

"What are you doing?" she asked.

"I'm providing backup. Your heart started beating faster, so I have to assume that you've become more fatigued."

"That's not necessary. I'm doing very well."

"I think I know better..."

"I'm ordering you to stop this unnecessary waste of resources."

The robot lowered its arm.

"What's the point?" asked Mandy. "Your presence out here is entirely redundant."

"Of course."

Bummi turned around. Its egg-shaped body jittered as it crawled over the hull next to her, which gave Mandy goose bumps. She'd never liked spiders. She didn't trust the robot. Too often, it had a mind of its own. Supposedly, it had a certain degree of autonomous intelligence that was more or less equal to that of a chimpanzee. But it often seemed a lot smarter than that to her. Bummi reminded her a little bit of the Stasi captain in her training unit. Just like he had access to all personnel files, the robot controlled all system data, including the sensors in her spacesuit.

There was a big, rotating antenna at the front of the space station. Mandy made sure to keep the string of lights at a sufficient distance from it, since that was her only connection to Earth. In a few hours, she'd be back within range of the control station on Mount Brocken, and she could finally speak with Susanne and Sabine for a while. Going for three months without talking to her little sweethearts had been a damned long time.

Mandy kept making her way around the station. Like a weird snail, she left behind a trail of dark green cable with candle-shaped electric lights hanging from it about every hundred centimeters. The cable drum strapped to her back further contributed to the effect. And she was, in fact, moving forward at just a snail's pace. In zero gravity, every step was a challenge. There was only total blackness and blinding brightness, and if she dared take a single step without a safety line, she'd be putting her life at risk.

But she probably wouldn't be capable of such a thing. She'd had to run through the processes in the Star City pool so many times that she just went through them mindlessly. Moving meant bending down and straightening up without thinking about it. Mandy laughed. That could be the motto for her life in her homeland.

She brushed the thought aside. It wasn't helpful. Bummi stuck an arm out toward her and she reached for the claw. The universal tool at the end of its arm would also make a great weapon. She had to be careful not to catch the sharp edge with her glove.

"Don't worry." She heard the robot's words over the helmet radio. "I put my little finger over the cutting edge. You'll be all right. Trust me."

Could machines be trusted? Absolutely. And she'd had practice at it. For her whole life, Mandy had had to trust machines. First there was the motorcycle that she'd bought as a former gymnast, with the bonuses she'd gotten for her victories in the GDR and European championships. Then there was the Czech-built training plane, then shortly after that the Russian and then the Saudi Arabian fighter jet that the National People's Army[4] had procured, and finally the three-stage rocket developed by GDR engineers that took her from the Peenemünde cosmodrome into Earth's orbit and eventually to the Völkerfreundschaft space station.

She grasped Bummi's claw firmly. It closed around her hand.

"I've got you," said the robot. "You can release the safety line now."

She opened one line's carabiner, then the other. The two ropes danced around her. The momentum she'd given the carabiner moved back and forth as a standing wave along the Dederon cord[5]. Then she was flying. As Bummi's long arm described a wide arc, she moved one meter, then two meters away from the ship.

Mandy cheered. This was what it had felt like when her father used to throw her into the air when she was a little girl. If Bummi were to let go now, she'd never reach the space station again. Very briefly, she managed to get the entire station in her field of vision. Bummi must have used another one of its limbs to connect the cable of lights, because the Völkerfreundschaft was now twinkling with all 80 lights like a Christmas tree. The impulse from the movement propelled a tear through her helmet. It was beautiful.

This festive illumination would not, of course, be visible from Earth. Tomorrow she'd have to launch a flying camera that would film the Völkerfreundschaft several times from all directions. The images would then be shown on giant projection screens at the main ceremony in Berlin. Mandy Neumann, heroine of the GDR. The girls would have to get used to Mother being famous. Hopefully it wouldn't have an adverse effect on them.

"I'm going to drop you off at the airlock," the robot said.

"Could you do something for me first?"

"Of course. I await your command."

"Swing me again like you just did. I want to assess the effect made by the eighty lights."

"I'm measuring their power consumption and I can assure you that none of them have failed."

"It's about the effect. This is something personal that machines are unable to access."

"Of course, Mandy. I'm swinging you again in three—two—one—now."

October 6, 2029, Dresden

"Not recognized," the machine announced.

Tobias took out the beer bottle, then put it back into the dark opening. The inside of the tube lit up and the bottle spun around.

Again, the words "Not recognized" appeared on the display panel.

He pulled out the bottle. This time, he pushed it into the machine top first. He felt a wave of nausea. He felt as if he were shoving his deposit bottles into the intestines of a metal organism.

The opening lit up again. The beer bottle rotated and the machine sucked it inside.

"Deposit amount forty-eight pfennig. Print receipt or donate to anti-imperialist solidarity?"

Tobias turned around, but nobody was behind him. If he'd had an audience, he would have had to set an example. He tapped "Print receipt" and his voucher quickly appeared in the narrow slot under the screen. He put his now empty Dederon bag in the pocket of his jacket. He was about to take out his wallet to put the receipt in it when somebody bumped into him.

"What the...?"

A young man with long hair sprinted past him. He made for the exit, but the glass door didn't open fast enough and he slammed into it. Tobias was still trying to figure out what was going on. He wasn't on duty, so he could take time to think about it. But the saleswoman at the bakery didn't see it that way.

"Herr[1] Wagner, Herr Wagner!" she cried. "A robber!"

She was furious, her face distorted with rage. Tobias made up his mind. He was the long arm of the law, even on weekends. He'd take care of this guy.

"Hold it right there, buddy!" he shouted, and rushed after him.

He took three steps forward and then remembered that his voucher was still in the slot. Hopefully nobody would take it. After all, he could buy nine half rolls for 48 pfennigs!

This kid was fast. He was already rushing across the square in front of the supermarket by the time Tobias was beneath the awning of the triangular portico out front. He gave it all he got. He quickly got a stitch in his side, just like he would when he'd do the 3,000-meter run back in school. Tobias ignored it. The teenager had taken something that didn't belong to him, and he had to learn that there were consequences. Faster, faster. He took a shortcut across the drained fountain.

"Move aside! Out of the way!" he shouted as three mothers walking together approached him, blocking the sidewalk with their strollers. The robber was clearly making a beeline for the tram stop. A loud squeal from the left told Tobias that the 12 was already on its way. That kid had enough of a head start to be able to calmly board at the stop and thumb his nose at him. But Tobias wasn't going to let that happen. His heart thudded in his chest, but he didn't slow down. He had to reach the stop before the tram did, but couldn't outrun it. So he changed direction and ran to get in the way of the tram. Groaning, he reached the tracks that ran parallel to the street. A warning bell rang and the brakes squealed against the steel wheels. The tram driver must be cursing the lunatic who'd jumped onto the tracks in front of his train.

Tobias reached the elevated station platform before the tram after all. The thief moved slowly backwards. He was trapped. His pursuer was approaching from one side, while on the other, there was a tall fence between the platform and the street, to keep passengers from stepping out in front of cars.

"I've got you!" said Tobias.

He grabbed the young man by the arm and spun him around.

"I'm hereby taking you into custody."

He pushed the man, who seemed to realize that there was no possibility of escape and was no longer resisting, against the fence with one hand. A loud wheezing sound drowned out the ringing of the tram. It was Tobias. But the thief was also now clearly shaking. With his other hand, Tobias pulled the Dederon bag out of his pocket, twisted it into a rope, and tied his prisoner's wrists with it. The handles of the bag worked wonderfully to drag the young man behind him.

THE PEOPLE HE PASSED WITH THE THIEF IN TOW EITHER GAVE HIM surly looks or deliberately averted their gaze. Did somebody just spit? He wasn't wearing a uniform, so they probably thought he was someone from the company[2], a member of the Ministry of State Security[3]. But nobody asked him for his identification. Not even the kid himself wanted to know who'd caught him. Hopefully he already felt guilty for what he'd done.

It would have been even better if they'd run into relatives or teachers who knew him. Often, the embarrassment of having to follow a state representative with one's hands tied was stronger lesson than any punishment, which in this case would likely be commuted to probation. Tobias Wagner had been with the Ministry of the Interior for more than twenty years, and by now he knew his little lambs quite well. That was why he was taking an especially long time.

"What's your name?" he asked the thief.

"Mario."

"Mario what?"

"Schuster."

"Address?" Tobias asked.

"I live at 12, up ahead."

How practical. Where he lived also happened to be Tobias' office.

"Where do you work?"

"I'm..." The kid stalled. "I'm doing my military service right now."

"Oh, man, how much nuttier can it get?"

Mario had actually gotten leave for Republic Day[4] weekend, and then he went and messed it up like this. All Tobias had to do was call the commandant's service, and just like that, Schuster would be sitting in his barracks under arrest.

"I was getting some rolls for my fiancée, and I forgot my wallet. She's waiting for me to come with breakfast."

The boy's tearful tone and bowed head made it seem that he was telling the truth, but there was always the possibility that he was making it all up.

AS THEY PASSED THE MARKET, THE WOMAN AT THE BAKERY WAS waiting in the entryway. A line had formed at her counter as the wide automatic door kept trying to close.

"I knew you'd catch him, Herr Wagner."

"Comrade Section Commissioner," he corrected her. "Even though I'm not in uniform, I'm always on duty."

He bought his rolls here every day, exactly two of them. He still couldn't remember the saleswoman's name. He tried to read the little tag she was wearing on her blue apron, but could only see an "M" at the beginning and "er" at the end.

"Thank you, Frau[5] Meier," he said.

"Frau Müller."

"Yes, of course."

"So, where did the criminal leave his loot?" Frau Müller asked.

"I would suggest you leave the questioning of the suspect to me, Frau Müller, and you get back to looking after your clientele."

"Of course, Herr, um, Comrade Section Commissioner."

THE ROBBER STOPPED IN FRONT OF THE MAIN ENTRANCE TO number 12, a seventeen-story apartment building. Tobias's office was on the first floor, but had a separate entrance.

"What is it?" asked Tobias. "Do you want to cause more trouble?"

"No, I don't. My fiancée is waiting for me up there. She was still asleep when I left. I'm sure she's worried by now."

"And that's supposed to be my fault?"

"No, I shouldn't have..."

"Come along, Mario. We'll sort it all out at the office."

He continued to drag the young man behind him. The narrow path alongside the high-rise building was littered with trash. Some residents would simply throw their garbage off the balcony. He'd have to give the superintendent a call. This area absolutely needed a sweeping before Republic Day.

"Here we are," Tobias said, pushing open the front door with a flourish.

Across from the entrance was a desk. The uniformed man sitting behind it leapt up as they walked in. As he did so, the house of cards he was working on collapsed.

"Chief Constable Schulte, you're still here!" Tobias said menacingly.

He looked at the clock hanging under the portrait of Krenz, Party Chairman and Head of State. It was a quarter past eight. Schulte should be making his first round of the precinct by now. Instead, here he was building houses of cards!

"I... I thought..."

"Don't think. Do your duty as the Party and the people demand of you."

Schulte had probably been hoping to take it easy today, but that wasn't going to happen.

"Of course, Comrade Lieutenant," said the chief constable, pushing together the ruins of his construction project.

"Leave it alone. Get out of here and into the fresh air!"

"Yessir."

Schulte came from behind the table with his jacket open and reached for the door handle.

"Hey, your uniform!"

Schulte cringed. His fingers frantically tried to work the buttons of his green uniform jacket into the buttonholes, but they keep slipping out.

"Do that outside. And don't forget your hat!"

"Thank you, Comrade Lieutenant."

Schulte grabbed his peaked cap and hurried out of the office.

"So, what are we going to do with you now, my boy?" asked Tobias.

He unbound Mario's wrists. Fortunately, a Dederon bag didn't get wrinkled. He folded it carefully and put it in the back pocket of his jeans. Then he walked around the desk and sat down in his chair. The seat was still warm, which he found unpleasant. Couldn't Schulte have used his own chair? But really, he shouldn't complain. He actually would have just been at home today. Under ordinary circumstances, he would have been in the building next door, spreading butter on his two rolls, which he would top with sausage. Then he'd sit on his tenth-floor balcony to look out leisurely over Dresden in late summer.

He could kiss all that goodbye. He hadn't bought any rolls, and by now there wouldn't be any left. He'd even lost his voucher. All because of this kid who was too lazy to go back for his wallet.

"Why didn't you ask if you could pay later?"

"I did, but the saleswoman wanted to take the rolls back."

Schuster looked at him like a little boy who'd been caught playing a practical joke. But this was no joke!

"And then you just made a run for it?"

"Yes. It was all on impulse. It just happened that way."

Schuster shuffled his left foot.

"Comrade Section Commissioner."

"What?"

"It's 'excuse me', and 'it just happened that way, Comrade Section Commissioner."

"'Scuse me. It just happened that way, Comrade Section Commissioner."

Tobias sighed. The young man's shoulders seemed to be tensing up. He was probably wringing his hands. Dederon handcuffs really squeezed the blood out. That served him right. What was Tobias supposed to do with him?

"And the loot?" he asked.

"I threw it away, Comrade Section Commissioner."

What next? The damage was done, then. Tobias was of a mind to have the young man cough up the money he owed.

"That's not good," he said.

He stood up and paced back and forth a few times. The kid was a soldier in the National People's Army, so he really wasn't any of Tobias' business. He took his hand phone out of his pocket and scrolled down the contact list. There it was: the number for the commandant's service. All he had to do was call them up, and half an hour later he'd be rid of this problem.

But he felt sorry for the fiancée. None of this was her fault. He imagined her waking up, reaching for her Mario in bed, and then calling out his name.

"Do you have kids?" he asked.

"Not yet. We're just starting out. Got the place set up nice using a newlyweds' loan, and now we want to make good on the loan by having kids."

"I'm afraid that's not going to happen for a while," Tobias said. "The patrol will take you back to the barracks."

"Please don't, Comrade Section Commissioner. Surely there must be another way?"

Schuster knelt down and begged. But Tobias couldn't do anything for him!

"I'll sweep the whole path around the building. And next door, too."

The young man must have noticed how displeased he'd been seeing the garbage along the way. Very observant. Tobias shook his head.

"I'll do it every day!" Schuster added.

But the class enemy was attentive, too. If he were to fail to do his duty and let the man go, word would get around. Someone was always blabbing, and who was to say the bakery saleswoman, Frau Meier, wouldn't say something? He was about to be promoted to first lieutenant and couldn't afford to make such a blunder.

"I'm sorry, Schuster. But there's no way around the commandant's service. You're not a civilian. You represent the armed forces of our workers' and peasants' state. And because of that you have a very special responsibility. As our comrade Egon Krenz[6] said..."

"To hell with that political dinosaur."

"Excuse me?"

What if someone heard that? Tobias looked around. Might his office be under surveillance? He certainly hoped not. He'd never done anything wrong.

"To he..."

"No, don't say it again, Schuster. It's in your best interests not to. I'm going to call the commandant's service now."

"Please don't, Herr Wagner."

"Comrade Section Commissioner! How many times do I have to tell you? I have absolutely no other choice."

"But I won't see Martina again for three months! And she doesn't even know what's going on here!"

"You should have thought of that sooner."

The boy burst into tears. What next? He hated to see anybody crying. Tobias turned to the side.

"Stop crying. What's your fiancée's name, exactly? I'll tell her where you are."

"Martina Frommann, with two 'm's."

Schuster bit his lower lip, and it started to bleed. Tobias was annoyed. If only he hadn't been so ambitious. All he'd had to do was let him escape. Nobody would have blamed him if an eighteen-year-old had gotten away from a guy in his forties. Now he had the fiancée on his hands, too.

HALF AN HOUR LATER, THE PATROL VEHICLE PULLED UP IN FRONT of his office. Tobias took the young man outside and handed him over to two soldiers and a non-commissioned officer who was wearing a white holster belt. They said goodbye with a military salute and drove off in their Trabant 901 pickup.

Chief Constable Schulte hadn't returned yet. Tobias locked the office and ran to the main entrance of the high-rise. Hopefully Schulte had taken his key with him. He, meanwhile, was still in his civilian clothes. Should he slip quickly into uniform? But surely the woman would recognize him, even if he didn't remember ever seeing her name. He managed the house register for this building and the one next door, too. Every new resident, and of course every visitor, had to introduce themselves to him.

Tobias found the name on one of the doorbell panels, about halfway up. Frommann, Martina lived on the sixth floor. He was lucky. One of the two elevators was waiting on the ground floor, empty. Tobias got in and pressed the button with a 6 on it. The number was barely recognizable. The elevator rattled and squeaked its way up. He got off on the sixth floor and stepped out into a long corridor with doors leading off to the left and right. It smelled of cleaning agents, urine, and burned food.

Tobias stopped briefly in front of each door to read the names. Shortly before reaching the end where the hallway widened, he found what he was looking for and rang the bell.

"Coming!" a female voice called from inside. "Did you get the rolls yet?"

The door opened. Behind it there was a young woman wrapped in a towel, with tousled, wet blond hair. She was startled and took a few steps back, but didn't close the door. Perhaps she'd also noticed that Tobias had put a foot inside. It was a reflex. Especially when he rang the doorbell in uniform, people would often immediately slam the door in his face. He didn't take it personally, since he probably would have done the same thing himself. Every time he had to show his ticket to the Reichsbahn[7] conductor he felt guilty somehow, even though it was right there on his hand phone.

"Good morning, Fräulein[8] Frommann," he said. "I'm Tobias Wagner, your section commissioner. You must know who I am."

The woman took a step forward.

"That's right, I recognize you," she said. "I apologize for how I reacted, but I'm actually waiting for my fiancé."

"For Mr. Schuster? Has he lived here long?"

"No, no, he's just visiting. He arrived this morning. Of course, he'll be right over to check in with you and sign the house register. We just wanted to have breakfast first."

"I'm afraid that's not going to happen, Frau Frommann."

Her eyes widened.

"Oh! Did something happen to him? Did he have an accident? I was still asleep when he went out. I think he went to go buy rolls."

"I thought he just arrived this morning?"

"Yes, that's right. He took the night train from Eisenhüttenstadt. We... greeted each other, and then I fell asleep again."

Tobias noticed how her cheeks reddened slightly.

"I see. Well, he didn't have an accident. He had to leave urgently, though."

"Without his luggage?"

"Yes, unfortunately. I suppose you can bring his luggage to

him at the Erich Honecker[9] barracks in Neustadt. They'll call you and give you more details. He just asked me to tell you."

The woman looked as if she was about to burst into tears. Tobias quickly took his leave with a military salute, which was a technical mistake since he wasn't wearing a uniform. Then he turned around and walked towards the elevator.

The sound of bare feet on linoleum followed him, and he felt a hand on his shoulder.

"Thank you, Comrade Section Commissioner[10], for fulfilling my Mario's wishes. You're a good man," said the woman.

"Just doing my duty," Tobias said.

That wasn't a lie, but he still couldn't look at her. She had no idea that her Mario had been picked up by the commandant's service because of him.

October 6, 2029, Earth orbit

MANDY WAS SWEATING. TODAY THE COSMONAUT FOUND IT especially grueling to ride the Mifa[1] bike. It was as if it suspected what the next day would bring and wanted to squeeze every last drop of energy out of her. She would have loved to take off her wet t-shirt, but for some reason she felt shy with the robot watching her. Mandy kept wiping the sweat from her face, but couldn't prevent countless drops from floating through the cabin.

This wasn't entirely without risk. The inside of the space station was one big room. The highest single-room apartment in the GDR, she sometimes joked with her mother. But that also meant that all the microelectronics were installed in here, which would make errors when exposed to an excess of moisture. Unfortunately, the air conditioning wasn't efficient enough to compensate for the vigorous workout she was obliged to do before extravehicular activity.

"Your blood values are good now," Bummi said. "You can stop."

"Thank you."

Mandy tried to catch a few of the larger drops with the towel. But they seemed to react to her attacks like agile mosquitoes, always dodging at the last moment. Of course, it was actually the air pressure built up by the accelerating towel that pushed the droplets out of the way. Mandy made do by hanging a second towel on the wall and then cornering the sweat droplets with the first one, until they couldn't help but disappear into the fibers of the Malimo[2] fabric.

"What are you doing?" asked Bummi.

Mandy never quite knew where its voice was coming from. It seemed to have speakers in each of its four claws and in its egg-shaped belly, and of course it could communicate through the speakers dispersed all over the space station. Presumably it listened to her round the clock, but that tended to reassure Mandy. One of her few fears was that she might be caught off guard by a disaster while she slept. Bummi never slept, but did have to be charged at an electrical outlet for thirty minutes every eight hours or so.

"I'm catching sweat droplets."

"That's not necessary."

"Too much moisture is bad for the electronics. You, for one, should certainly be aware of that."

"If the air gets too humid, we can always vent it all out."

"And who's always telling me about the need to conserve resources?"

"We should start following the day's agenda now."

Sometimes Bummi drove her crazy. That was exactly how her ex-husband would have reacted: If something made him uncomfortable, he'd change the subject. But it really wasn't fair to compare a machine with her ex-husband. After all, Bummi didn't leave her with two kids just because she wanted to have both children and a career. She never would have imagined that people would still have such archaic attitudes after 80 years of real-life socialism.

"So?" asked Bummi.

"I'm coming."

"Everything in the airlock is ready."

"Very good, Bummi."

THIS WASN'T HOW SHE'D IMAGINED IT. THE AIRLOCK WAS VERY cramped. In such a tight space, she could barely manage to put on all the layers of her spacesuit correctly. She briefly considered going without the heating and cooling underwear. But if Bummi were to notice, it would scold her and wouldn't let her out of the ship. She didn't know how it would notice, but if that did happen, it would just mean more time in the spacesuit, which already reeked from the previous day.

She pushed aside all the equipment that the robot had put in the airlock as best she could and got dressed.

Finally she announced, "I'm done."

"Good," said Bummi. "I can hear you. Let me run some tests."

The fan in the helmet roared. A heating element on the thigh heated up and a cooling element on the abdomen cooled down.

"Looks good," said Bummi. "The suit is working."

Considering that the GDR bought old suits that Russian cosmonauts had used on the ISS, this wasn't something to be taken for granted. But Mandy wasn't about to complain. The suits served their purpose and were easy to repair, even with what was available on board. That was important, because she couldn't expect to get rapid assistance from the ground. Behind the airlock, there was a bulkhead that led into the first space capsule ever built by the GDR. It was modeled on the Soyuz capsule that had taken the GDR cosmonaut Sigmund Jähn into space. Detractors claimed that the capsule had actually vanished from the museum where it had been exhibited, until some SED party congress suddenly decided the GDR should have its own space station.

"Are you thinking about your children?" asked Bummi.

Mandy shook her head. The robot was right. It would be better to think about her children than of a time long gone.

"Let's get this over with," she said.

The components blocking the airlock suddenly started to move, leading her to the conclusion that Bummi must have opened the bulkheads.

"I'll go out and you pass me the parts," Bummi said.

Shouldn't she be the one giving the orders? But she didn't object. It made sense, after all. The robot could anchor itself better and take the parts she handed over. She started with the first one. The components weren't particularly heavy. She could tell even in zero gravity, because they were easy to set into motion. Inertial mass wasn't suspended by microgravity. One by one, she passed items through the black hole in the ceiling. The robot would certainly know how to put them together.

Once the room was completely empty, Mandy left the airlock. Out on the hull of the Völkerfreundschaft, things looked chaotic. The robot had set up a light to illuminate her work area. Otherwise it would have been too dark, since the sun was still hidden behind the Earth.

Now it was time to put the parts together. For each one, Bummi showed her which surfaces had to be attached to which. Its claws weren't suitable for fastening the parts together. They were made of vapor-deposited metal foil over a sturdy but flexible core. The material was stitched along the edges. There were buttons and matching holes, which followed an alternating pattern. She was surprised at how practical this kind of connection was. She never would have guessed it.

"What's the material inside?" she asked. "Plastic?"

"No, just normal cardboard," Bummi answered.

Mandy took a closer look by the light of her helmet lamp and on each element discovered the printed logo of the state-owned enterprise[3] VEB Sachsenring Zwickau, which also manufactured the Trabant[4]. Presumably the company had a team that produced these parts on the side.

Gradually, the connected parts assumed a form that reminded her of a rose. The clever interconnection system created internal tension, which caused the shape to curve towards the bottom. The flower would concentrate sunlight. A few days earlier, the space station had adjusted its orbit so it would be visible from Berlin, the capital of the German Democratic Republic, at noon on October 7. The shining silver flower, illuminated by the sun, was to appear above the parade as the star of the Völkerfreundschaft. That was how the party and state leadership had envisioned it.

The sun came out from behind the Earth. Mandy paused. It wasn't the first time she'd seen this happen, but it was still impressive. At that moment, it became particularly obvious just how slight the realm of life on earth actually was. As long as its rays were shining through the atmosphere, the sun appeared golden. Mandy could watch as a warm, soft star became a starkly defined, cold, white star in the middle of the black sky. This occurred as soon as the sun rose a few degrees above the Earth. The difference that she witnessed in a matter of minutes couldn't be more striking. Here was the fragile, closely limited sphere of life, and there the dead, infinite realm of the universe, which not even the light of trillions of stars could bring out of the blackness.

"Mandy? I need you now," said the robot.

She pulled herself away from the sight of the earth. Bummi explained to her what had to be done. Mandy stood up and loosened one of the two safety clips. Then she lifted the flower and carried it two meters further. She changed the safety line, then went another two meters around the ship until she seemed to be upside-down, with the blue globe of Earth beneath her.

"Thanks. That should be the right position," said Bummi. "I'll anchor the screen."

Mandy let go of the thin material. Sometimes she had the feeling that she wasn't the one in charge of the ship, but rather the robot. The details regarding the preparations for the Republic Birthday, for example, had been transmitted directly to Bummi by Mission Control on Mount Brocken. She was only needed for the buttons; human hands were still unparalleled for such precise work, even when they were inside a spacesuit.

Carefully, she moved back to the airlock. She wanted to get there before Bummi did. Some day, the robot was going to forget she existed and close the airlock in her face.

"Hello, my sweethearts, how are you?"

Sabine and Susanne vied for the best seat.

"Don't push, you two!" Their grandmother's scolding voice could be heard in the background.

The two laughed. They were identical twins, but Mandy had never had any trouble telling them apart. There was something in their eyes. Susanne had always been the quieter, more reserved one, and she was still that way even at five years old.

"Good, Mutti!" shouted Sabine.

"When are you coming back?" asked Susanne.

"Tomorrow morning, Dad will pick us up and we'll go to the parade!" exclaimed Sabine.

Her ex-husband had already told her that he would take the two girls to the Republic Birthday festivities. After the rally, there would be a big fair. The Republic was pulling out all the stops to celebrate its 80th anniversary.

"I hope you have a lot of fun!" she said. "I'm sure it'll be wonderful."

It hurt that she couldn't be with them, but she didn't let on.

"Can we have cotton candy?" asked Sabine.

"You'll have to ask Dad."

"But he told us you said it's not allowed. Is it not allowed?"

"No, Bine, it's allowed."

"Thanks, Mom!"

"Mom, when are you coming back?" Susanne asked again.

"Sleep thirteen more times," Mandy said. "That's as many times as all your fingers and three of your toes."

"I know how much thirteen is," Susanne said. "We'll be in school next year!"

"I know what thirteen is, too," Sabine said.

"No you don't."

"Yes, I do."

"Don't argue," Grandma said, off-screen.

"Can you celebrate up there, too?" asked Susanne.

"Yes, of course."

"But you're all alone!"

"Bummi's here. The robot I told you about."

"Bummi's creepy," Sabine said. "He looks like a spider."

"It's an automomous walking robot," Susanne objected. "Not a spider."

"Autonomous," said Mandy.

"Yes. An automomous robot," Susanne said. "When I grow up, I want to build robots, too."

"I'm going to be a cosmonaut," Sabine announced.

"I think being a cosmonaut is stupid," Susanne said. "It takes you so far away from your children."

"It's true," said Mandy, "that's a big disadvantage." Her voice faltered briefly, because Susanne was so much righter than she realized. "But you can see so much from up here, you'd love it, Sanne."

"More than from Mount Brocken?" asked Susanne.

"Much more."

"Even the non-social economic area?" asked Sabine.

"Even the non-socialist economic area."

"Can you see us, too?" asked Susanne.

"I see you two right now and it makes me so happy. You've grown so much since the last time we talked."

The picture flickered, and the screen filled with snow. The Völkerfreundschaft would probably be leaving the transmission range of Mount Brocken station soon. After that, Mandy would be able to communicate through intermediate stations, but they were international and therefore charged foreign currency. For that reason, personal conversations were only allowed via the Mount Brocken station.

"What I mean is, can you see us even when we're not on the phone?" Susanne asked.

"It would be possible," Mandy said. "You've heard of the MKF-8, right? The multispectral camera?"

"I think so," Susanne said.

"When I use it, I can see you leaving the house."

"Can you even tell if we've combed our hair?" asked Sabine.

"No, not that. But I can see what color dress you're wearing."

"And what color is..." Sabine looked around "... Grandma's sweater?"

"I can only see that when Grandma goes out the door. I don't see you inside the house."

The image of the twins was getting grainier and grainier.

"I really hope you have a good time tomorrow!" said Mandy. "I'm sure you're going to have a great day."

"I hope you do too, Mutti," said Susanne.

"You can watch us from above," Sabine said.

"We'll wave to you once in a while," Susanne said.

"At noon, I'll switch on a little star for you. You'll be able to tell where I am from where the light is coming," said Mandy.

"That's really great, Mutti," Sabine said.

"Bye," Susanne said. Then the connection was lost.

October 7, 2029, Dresden

It was cold in his office. Tobias shivered and rubbed his shoulders. The public utility company hadn't switched the district heating back on yet; after all, the temperature was still getting up to at least 15 degrees during the day. He actually had Sundays off, but for Republic Day, all agents were in service. Schulte, who usually filled in for him here, was on duty in the city center.

Tobias was glad he'd been spared doing that. His job was to maintain order in the neighborhood, but since almost everyone would be attending the rally and the fair afterwards, it would be a quiet day. At the briefing, the Stasi representative hadn't reported any findings that would suggest there might be any provocations by hostile forces.

He poured some powder from a Rondo pouch into the filter, filled the coffee machine with water, and switched it on. As it gurgled and emanated the wonderful aroma that Tobias loved just as much as virtually every other Saxon, he switched on the TV and sat down in his chair. The presenter was trying to get people excited and kept pointing out the most important items on the program. These of course included the big National People's Army parade on Karl-Marx-Allee in Berlin, as well as the concert in front of the Brandenburg Gate, where artists like Karat, the Puhdys[1], Udo Lindenberg, and Depeche Mode were scheduled to perform. Four old-timer bands, but still younger than Comrade Krenz.

Following the program announcement, there was a documentary about the history of the GDR. Tobias didn't learn anything new. How could he? After all, he'd learned it all in school, and it was repeated at every political training. In 1949, the Republic had been founded as a reaction to the West's unilateralism. Then there was its unstoppable rise, which was made possible by the protective anti-fascist wall. Then, in 1987, there was the discovery of huge oil deposits in Lusatia, which brought the GDR into league with the Arab Emirates.

1989 had witnessed the decline of the Soviet Empire, set in motion by the revisionist Gorbachev, which left the GDR as one of the last pillars of socialism in the world, along with China, Cuba, North Korea, and Vietnam. The documentary then took a look into the future. Scientific and technological progress. The well-educated, socialist personality. The way we work today, we will live tomorrow.

That was all well and good, but sometimes he wondered where it was, the socialist personality. Sure, migration to the West had stopped since Ikea, H&M, Boss, and Zara had started selling their goods in the GDR. The fact that all citizens were paid a quarter of their salaries in convertible marks, or K-marks for short, ensured a standard of living comparable to that in the West, because HO and Konsum² stores guaranteed subsidized prices for everyday necessities. The cities might not be as slick as they were over there, but rents were fixed at 1987 levels. Therefore, very few people found it worthwhile to go over the wall.

But conscientiousness was in short supply. He only needed to take a walk around the property to see that. The custodian had just swept yesterday, but there was already garbage lying around again. This was the people's property, but the inhabitants treated it as if it belonged to some anonymous state and not to themselves. Tobias sighed.

His hand phone vibrated. That was the reminder he'd set for himself. He had a lot to do today, and he knew himself well enough to know that he liked to goof off. First, coffee. He took a cup from the small sink. The faucet was dripping and he resolved to fix it today. Wasting water was bad. But the coffee was good. He always held the cup in front of his nose first to deeply inhale its scent. Then he'd put it to his lips, blow briefly, and carefully take a small sip. Coffee should be hot and strong and bitter.

He didn't set the cup down until it was half empty. He poured the rest back into the pot. That way it would stay warm longer. Then he took his portable computer out of the drawer. He glanced at his private Kybernetz[3] mail. Lots of advertising. Konsum was inviting him to digitally manage his stamp collection. And the Intershop[4] was offering particularly favorable exchange rates for rubles and Cuban pesos. But there was also a letter from his Indian friend Raghunath, whom he'd met back in the late 1980s. First they'd written each other letters, then later sent each other messages over the Kybernetz, and then finally visited each other in person. Tobias had paid for Raghunath's first flight to the GDR. They even called each other 'brother.' His friend had worked his way up steadily since then from being a teacher to the director of a private school. Now he made more than Tobias, but had otherwise remained much the same. No, he'd read the letter in peace that evening.

Tobias closed the mailbox and logged on using the property management account. The device ran under FDCP, which stood for Fenster-DCP and consisted of a huge REDABAS database on a Robotron[5] mainframe. It took a while for the user interface to load, and then the program needed another five minutes to connect to the database.

Miltner, Miltner. The young, single guy from the sixth floor of the neighboring building must have been watching porn again. There were 35.6 gigabytes on his account alone! With that kind of usage, he was by far the leader in terms of 24-hour average Kybernetz consumption. All citizens were actually required to restrict themselves to one gigabyte per day. The limit would supposedly be doubled for today's holiday, but Tobias had only heard rumors of it so far. He would definitely have to have a serious talk with Miltner.

Far behind in second place was the Garhammer family. They lived almost directly above him and had four teenagers. There were exceptions for large families like the Garhammers, but he'd turn a blind eye to them anyway. He himself had a teenage daughter, Marie, who lived with her mother. His son Jonathan had just been called up for military service.

Tobias asked for the cyber addresses that Miltner used. Unsurprisingly, the young man mainly spent time on sites offering sex. However, the database usually gave the green light

27

because they were sites that a special department of the Ministry of Foreign Trade had set up on the Kybernetz, meaning that the K-marks Miltner spent there ended up back in the hands of the people.

But there were also a few connections with entries marked in red. In these cases, the destination addresses couldn't be decrypted. Miltner must be using an external private Kybernetz[6], an EPK. The software for that kind of network often came from the West and was usually used for services that infringed on personal rights, such as Google Plus[7] or Facebook. Tobias wrote down an appointment in his cyber calendar. Miltner was no longer living with his parents, so Tobias didn't need to involve them. On Monday at ten in the morning, he would visit Miltner at his place of work. When Tobias showed up as the production brigade was gathered for breakfast, it never failed to have an effect, especially when he threatened to insist on making an entry in the brigade logbook.

He scrolled down a little further until he came across "Schulze, Ralf." Very nice. Schulze had separated from his wife a year ago and then disappeared into the swamps of the Kybernetz. Tobias had spoken with him twice and got him set up for therapy. Now Schulze had managed to make his way out. Yesterday, he'd only used two megabytes of data.

His hand phone vibrated again. It was time for the first round.

QUICKLY, QUICKLY! IT WAS ALREADY 11:58. HE CLOSED THE door, put his uniform jacket over the chair, opened the top button of the uniform shirt, and turned on the TV. On his rounds he'd come across an old acquaintance and chatted with him for too long. Just now, there was a countdown on the screen, with the GDR emblem flashing every second.

Then there was a switch, and the viewer was floating in space. The Earth could be seen in the lower third of the screen. Above it, there was only blackness. Or was there a shadow? Tobias thought he saw a black shape blocking the view of the stars in the background.

That was indeed what it was. Suddenly, up in the left-hand corner, a tapered can lit up. This was the Völkerfreundschaft space station, a peak achievement of science and technology from the only socialist nation on German soil. The television station played the sounds of clapping and oohing and aahing. Then the picture switched to the grandstand that had been placed in the middle of Karl-Marx-Allee. There was a person speaking. Tobias didn't recognize him at first, but it was, of course, Party Chairman and Head of State Egon Krenz. He was well over 90, and it looked as if the bodyguards around him weren't just protecting him, but also holding on to him so he wouldn't topple over.

This was a bad thought, unworthy of the holiday. Egon Krenz shouldn't be made fun of for heroically making his way to the platform at his age. Krenz said a few words, and then the camera switched. This time Tobias saw blue sky. Berlin seemed to be having glorious weather. Here in Dresden, it was just partly sunny.

A bright star appeared in the sky and a collective murmur went through the crowd. The soldiers in gray, who had just goose-stepped past the grandstand, stopped on cue and raised their eyes to the sky. Hundreds of peaked caps rotated exactly 40 degrees, as if they were attached to the back of the men's heads. After that came another company, probably from another branch of the armed forces, and just as many steel helmets rotated in identical fashion. It was a flawless spectacle.

Shortly after that, shots were fired. It was the honor guard. A squadron of fighter pilots streaked across the screen. The way they were flying, they'd have to race across the sky above West Berlin, too. The West would make a formal protest. Always the same old game. The sonic boom that followed would be heard behind the anti-fascist wall anyway. The soldiers moved on, followed by the latest Russian rocket launchers, Chinese-made tanks, and Turkish artillery.

Tobias left the TV on, took his uniform jacket, and went outside. He was lucky. The clouds had cleared and made room for the new star, the Völkerfreundschaft. It moved slowly across the sky. Tobias followed the shining dot until it disappeared behind a cloud. He was proud of his country, which had managed to put its own space station into space. The Chinese also had one, but that country was home to more than a billion people. The Americans operated one jointly with the Russians, and together the two had a population of half a billion. The GDR, with only 16 million citizens, had done the same.

October 7, 2029, Earth orbit

THE FLYING CAMERA LOOKED LIKE A TRICKED-OUT FIRE extinguisher, and that was actually what it was. The steel cylinder containing the fuel was red. "State-owned enterprise Feuerlöschgerätewerk Neuruppin" was printed on it in white letters, and it had been innovators from this state-owned company who had invented the device. First, they'd modified the outlet duct. It wasn't bent, but straight, and the wheel that allowed the contents of the bottle to flow out was now positioned on the side.

The camera, an inexpensive digital model from the Dresden-based manufacturer Practica, was mounted on the fuselage so that it looked out against the direction of flight. The camera transmitted its images to the space station via a radio module that used the antenna to send them on to the Mount Brocken receiving station.

It wasn't possible to guide the camera. It flew on a ten-meter-long Dederon line that was practically invisible in space. When it reached the end of the line, it would arc back and forth chaotically until Bummi or Mandy pulled it back to the station. The director was hoping that the camera would only have to be used once. The audience on Earth should get a sense of what a great deed the small nation had accomplished out there. Afterwards, it would be up to Mandy to keep the Völkerfreundschaft star shining.

"Now," MANDY SAID.

The robot, which was sitting on the outer hull of the space station, turned on the gas cylinder's tap and released the flying camera. It moved away. Mandy used the control screen inside the station to track what the camera saw. It looked good. First, the Earth came into view. She waited a second, then turned on the eighty lights, which made the space station stand out against the black background of the universe.

"Ground control to Völkerfreundschaft," said Werner, their contact, announcing himself.

"Go ahead."

"That wasn't bad, but a little too hectic. Please allow more time for each shot."

"Roger that, ground control," Mandy said. "Bummi, did you get that? We need to pull the bottle back and start over, this time with lower pressure."

"Roger that, Mandy."

On the monitor, the space station was coming closer again. Then the image wobbled briefly. Now the robot turned the tap and Mandy switched off the lighting.

"Second try, now!" she commanded.

Again, first the Earth came into view. Then the space station lit up.

"Ground control to Völkerfreundschaft."

"Yes?"

"Do you have some extra lights?"

"No, there are exactly eighty."

"It looks like there are less than that."

"It's too late for that now."

"All right, one last try, then. We'll increase the contrast."

"Bummi? One last try."

The camera approached again. It began to waver, then hung still in the vacuum.

"Ground control! You'll give the start command when you're ready?"

"We're ready."

"Bummi, this is it."

Planet Earth, wait, start command. If she went through the procedure two more times, she would be able to do it in her sleep.

"Perfect, now we've got the shot," ground control reported.

"Great. We'll talk again in ninety minutes."

"Confirmed."

THE NINETY MINUTES WERE UP. MANDY RUBBED HER HANDS together. Now everything depended on her command. That had been a recording earlier, but now the new star would appear live over Berlin, capital of the GDR. She had to press a button at the right moment so it would light up. There was a second button she had to press at the right moment, too.

"Bummi, I'm nervous."

"Don't worry about it. There isn't anything that could go wrong," said the robot.

"No, there absolutely is. If I don't time it right, the whole republic will see."

"Ninety-nine-point-nine percent of the population doesn't even know what to expect."

"But the ones who do know are especially important."

If she did everything well, she'd have a great career waiting for her when she returned. She'd travel around the country telling people about her trip, and she'd represent the GDR internationally. She'd been promised that she could take her children with her.

"It's just a button, Mandy."

She sighed. The hands of the clock moved forward mercilessly. They reached twelve. Her video was playing on the giant screen on Karl-Marx-Allee and on GDR television. It would run for one minute. After forty seconds, she'd have to press the button. She held her index finger over it.

"Bummi, countdown."

The robot counted along with her. Thirty, twenty, ten. They were already at five, four, three, two, one, go. She moved her finger. It obeyed and pressed the button. One of the control thrusters emitted a short pulse. The space station turned. She had to wait exactly sixteen seconds. She looked for the other button. Where was it? She'd practiced this a thousand times! Her heart was racing. There! It was on the other side of the console. Bummi counted down again. Three, two, one, go. Again, her finger did what it was supposed to. One tiny impulse, and the station's movement ceased.

"Perfect," said ground control. "The revolutionary masses are thrilled. You've lit up a star in the sky. This will earn you a place in the history books."

She took a breath. But it wasn't the breath of history. It was just dry air. History books were too often rewritten. A nice life with her children would be perfectly sufficient. Although... the idea that every young pioneer would someday know her name, just like Sigmund Jähn's, really was something.

"I'M SORRY, BUT I CAN'T REACH ANYBODY AT YOUR MOTHER'S house," Werner said.

The girls were probably still with their father, and Mandy's mother had likely gone out. It was only late afternoon in Erfurt, where her mother lived with the children. It was too bad. She still would have liked to talk to them.

"Don't be sad. I'm sure there's a lot going on," Werner said. "Your kids are having a great time right now."

"Definitely. And you poor thing, you've got to spend the holiday on Mount Brocken because of me?"

"There's a big family reunion at our house, so I'm glad to have my peace and quiet here."

"Then you're in luck."

"You should be back in range in just under eighty minutes. We can try again with your children then, horosho?"

"Agreed, Werner."

"Ground control out."

Mandy leaned back. If she couldn't get an active connection, maybe she could just look? She unbuckled her seatbelt and floated to the small lookout in the middle of the space station. From the outside, it resembled a glass wart. From the inside, it was a miniature dome. However, Mandy couldn't use it to look at Earth because the place was taken. That was where the MKF-8, the high-performance multispectral camera from the state-owned enterprise Carl Zeiss Jena, was mounted. It was the only one in existence so far. Its predecessor was selling well even in the non-socialist economic area, the NSEA. There were two of them on the International Space Station and even three in NASA's Lunar Gateway. One was on its way to Venus for the Japanese, while another was flying to the icy moons of Jupiter for the ESA.

The MKF-8's special feature, as indicated by its name, was its ability to record images in several wavelengths simultaneously. This was immensely important for Earth observations, because very specific details became visible at each wavelength. If such images were taken one after the other and superimposed later, the phenomena in question would have moved in the process.

However, right now Mandy was only interested in the optical range. She pointed the camera at the coordinates for the row house where her mother lived. It wasn't the first time she'd done this, so the exact location was already stored in the camera. The first picture just showed a cloud. Mandy waited a moment and then tried again. She landed on the brick-red roof and was startled. A whole row of tiles had shifted. That must have happened during the autumn storm the other day. Had her mother even noticed yet? She'd have to let her know the next time she called.

But for now, she moved the camera frame just a bit to the east. There was the garden. It was divided into two parts. Directly behind the house there were flowers, a little meadow, and a terrace. Then there was a vegetable garden. Mandy had the camera take several pictures. There were still a few seconds between photos as the camera updated its optics; the MKF-8's low temporal resolution was its greatest weakness. Then Mandy layered the images on top of each other to animate them like a flipbook.

There was something moving between the flower beds. That must be her mother, busy gardening. She probably hadn't heard the stationary phone. She never took her hand phone into the garden. She didn't think much of modern technology and was probably the only person in Erfurt without a Kybernetz connection. That was too bad, because now Mandy couldn't ask her to take the call.

She looked up the coordinates for her ex-husband. He lived on the other side of town, so the camera needed a whole minute to realign. The roof of the apartment building was black. Behind it there was a courtyard with a small playground that couldn't be seen from the street. There, on the slide. That could be Susanne or Sabine. Again, Mandy took several shots. The MKF-8 was looking at the subject from almost directly above. Because of this —and because of the somewhat reduced resolution she'd chosen because of the shooting speed—it was sometimes hard to see what it was. A red spot could be a balloon or a girl in a red dress. But the two would move differently. So she had to find two spots of color with the same spectrum—the twins liked to dress identically—and that seemed to be moving chaotically on the playground.

There. It was clear. Mandy enlarged the images. That was them, her two little sweethearts. Her heart beat faster. She missed them both so much. She zoomed the image out a bit so that the playground took up the whole screen. But what was that? A pattern could be seen in the sandbox. It made her think of two eggs lying close to each other. Someone must have stamped it into the sand with their feet. The fact that she could see it even from up here proved just how powerful the MKF-8 was. But those weren't eggs. That was just nonsense. Someone had drawn a heart in the sandbox. Surely it had been her daughters' idea, knowing that Mommy was above them, watching. Mandy's chest tightened. She moved away from the camera so as not to smudge the screen, and let the tears flow.

October 8, 2029, Dresden

IT WAS DRIZZLING. TODAY WAS ONE OF THOSE DAYS WHEN TOBIAS was glad he only had to walk three minutes from his apartment to the office in the building next door. He'd even tried to switch. There were apartments right next to and behind the Section Commissioner offices that would have been perfect. But the properties on the ground floor were very popular, probably because they had a kind of terrace instead of a balcony. It was possible to leave them without having to walk through the long, frequently smelly corridor, and if the elevator broke down again, that also wasn't a problem.

Tobias went over his plan for the day. He wanted to visit that Kybernetz offender, Miltner, in his brigade. But he'd called in the custodians from his section for a meeting at eleven. At one in the afternoon, he had an appointment at the new site behind the supermarket that was starting construction today. The old youth center there was going to be torn down and replaced by a new one. At two-thirty he had to show up at the 31st Polytechnic Secondary School[1] to help with road safety education. Right after that, he was going to meet with volunteers from the People's Police[2] at the People's Solidarity Club[3] to see what they had to report from yesterday's festival. Then he had to report back to his Stasi contact over the phone.

Towards evening, Tobias wanted to check the house registers in the WBS-70[4] block next to the supermarket. It was time again. Especially old Mr. Reuters from house number 17, who had been so careless last time that he'd had to reprimand him. The enemy never sleeps! And if someone who wasn't entered in the house register were to make public jokes about the Chairman of the Council of State—who got in trouble? The section commissioner.

The stationary phone rang. It was a number with the area code 78. Tobias squinted. Seventy-eight, that must be... Jena! It was followed by the number nine, so the call was coming from a hand phone. But he didn't recognize the number itself. He didn't have any relatives or friends in the Thuringian city. So he pressed the "ID" key next to the call screen. Only government agency hand and stationary phones had them. Instead of the number, the screen now read "Prassnitz, Dr."

Why would one Dr. Prassnitz from Jena be calling him? If the person gave up now, Tobias would never find out. He quickly picked up the phone.

"Section Commissioner Section 27, Lieutenant Wagner speaking."

"Hello, Tobias," said a female voice.

"Who am I speaking with?" he asked.

The woman knew his name. His name wasn't listed anywhere under this number. How did she know who would pick up? Or did she know him?

"This is Miriam," the woman said. "Don't you remember me?"

Miriam, Miriam ... somehow the name seemed familiar to him. But it didn't match the information on the screen. Tobias turned on his desktop computer to check the police database.

"I'm sorry, Dr. Prassnitz, but that doesn't ring a bell for me. What can I do for you?"

The police—*your friend and aid*. Every so often, he'd get calls from people who were confused. Maybe this woman was one of them. Then he'd have to find out whether she was putting herself or others in danger.

"Dr. Prassnitz is my husband," she said. "I'm using his hand phone. Don't you remember me? Miriam Lindemann. We went to school together."

Ah, that Miriam. He blushed. Thankfully, she couldn't see it. He'd been in love with her from sixth to tenth grade, but she hadn't even noticed. Or had she noticed but didn't want to hurt him, so she'd ignored it? He definitely wasn't going to ask her that now. After graduating from tenth grade, Miriam had trans-ferred to an advanced high school while he'd started an appren-ticeship. After that, he'd lost track of her.

"Ah, Miriam," he said. "Of course I remember you. How are you? We haven't seen each other in so long. You never came to a reunion, either. What are you up to?"

He should ask her where she got his number. But when a woman made him insecure, he'd start babbling. That had always been the case. Sometimes he'd talk such gibberish that it must be excruciating for the woman. Something about Miriam's voice brought back old memories. It was as if the infatuation from back then had just been waiting to be released again. It was lucky for him that Miriam had only called. If he'd had to see her, he surely would have gotten completely carried away.

"To be honest, I was hoping you could help me."

"I... of course, just tell me how. Do you want me to help you move? Do you need advice? Do you have a burst pipe, or do you want to buy a used car?"

"None of those things. You're a police officer, right?"

His hand tensed around the telephone receiver. This was the classic scenario they'd been warned about at the police academy. A beautiful woman would call because she needed help, and before he knew it the brave policeman would be ensnared in the class enemy[5]'s web of lies.

Tobias was sitting down now. He wasn't going to fall for it.

"I'm a section commissioner," he said.

He'd already given her that information at the start of the phone call.

"So a police officer, then."

"I'm a member of the German People's Police. As a section commissioner, I'm an officer."

Anybody could easily look that up, too.

"Oh, you're actually an officer. Congratulations!"

"Thank you."

"Could you meet with me for a one-on-one?"

Tobias was blushing again. She wanted to meet him! Miriam! As a teenage boy, he would have traded his mother for a chance like this. But now he was wiser and more responsible. He had to find a clever way to wriggle out of this whole affair. He was even already thinking the word 'affair'! Miriam Lindemann was married, and her last name was Prassnitz now. Dr. Prassnitz. She wasn't interested in him anyway.

"Of course, Miriam, I'd love to," he replied. "But I don't know when I'll have time to come to Jena. After all, it's not exactly close by, and I have a lot to do. Maybe early December?"

"You don't have to come to Jena, Tobias."

Ah, the way she said his name! His knees immediately turned to jelly.

"I don't?"

She already had him in her clutches. Now he could only hope she wouldn't swallow him whole.

"No, I'm in Dresden. What would you say to meeting right now at Catch of the Day?"

Well, that was good. The seafood restaurant on Pirnaischer Platz was always so busy that nothing bad could happen to him.

"Right now? What do you mean?" he asked. "It doesn't open until noon, right?"

Surely Miriam had misspoken.

"I know the head cook there," she said. "He'll let us in earlier. Then we'll have total privacy."

"Earlier? Do you have a specific time in mind?"

"Right now! It'll take you ten minutes to drive here from ZwingliStraße. You have a car, don't you?"

"I do."

"Wonderful, Tobias. I'll be waiting for you here. Just knock on the glass door. I'll be glad to see you."

"Me too."

The connection dropped. Tobias was drenched in sweat.

IT WAS NEVER A GOOD IDEA TO GO INTO AN IMPORTANT conversation unprepared, as the criminology instructor had all too often reminded them. *As a section commissioner, you must be able to do everything,* he'd always said. He'd learned the standard procedures of criminology, knew how to interview witnesses and suspects and secure evidence, and knew his way around the law and the passport systems and regulatory reporting. This wide variety was something that had always fascinated him about working as a section commissioner. In reality, however, he mostly had to deal with minute details and ideological work, and he'd had to come to terms with that. Miriam's call was the first really interesting distraction he'd had in a long time.

So who was this Dr. Prassnitz Miriam was married to? Tobias started Bergblick, the Kybernetz search engine. The page with the snow-covered Brocken peak, familiar to every GDR citizen and preinstalled on all Kybernetz-capable devices, appeared. Almost 30 years before, the Robotron combine had adopted the technology of the American company AltaVista and renamed it Bergblick[6].

Evidently there were citizens who railed against the technology because it only found what citizens should find. Tobias immediately thought of Miltner, who had surely exceeded his data quota again. He felt guilty because the visit he'd planned on making to the man's place of work wasn't going to happen today. He'd have to have a word with him tomorrow. He really ought to have reported the EPKs a long time ago. But he certainly wasn't the only one who looked at Miltner's Kybernetz footage.

Tobias typed "Dr. Prassnitz" into the Bergblick search field.

He didn't even know the man's first name, and therefore didn't expect to get any relevant results. But he'd been mistaken. Prassnitz was a *National Laureate, Class II* and *Outstanding Scientist of the People*. Or was that someone else with the same name? Why would the wife of such a famous scientist ask him, a simple section commissioner, for help? After all, people like that had their own networks. They just had to give the signal and the permit for the expansion of their summer house was granted. He'd witnessed this firsthand.

Prassnitz had become famous because of his work on the MKF-7 space camera, which sold successfully even in the non-socialist economic area. Its successor, the MKF-8, was currently being used for the first time aboard the Völkerfreundschaft space station. *Neues Deutschland*[7] was full of impressive photos that showed the tremendous progress made in the development of socialism. Tobias flipped through the photo spreads on the Kybernetz. It was really astounding just how vivid the images were of the Baltic Sea freeway and the steel mill near Magdeburg, both of which had been recently built. Under each picture, "State-owned enterprise Carl Zeiss Jena / Prassnitz development collective" was indicated as the source. The man had really managed to make a name for himself.

Tobias was all the more skeptical now. What did it mean that, given these circumstances, Miriam was approaching a simple section commissioner she hadn't heard from in years? It could only mean that she didn't have access to her husband's resources, which were certainly extensive. So she was up to something that Dr. Prassnitz didn't approve of. And if Tobias helped her, he'd be putting himself in the way of a powerful man. Maybe she wanted a divorce, and was looking for lodgings as far away from Jena as possible? Tobias had to smile at his own naiveté. Of course Miriam would want to move in with him tomorrow, no doubt about it.

Miriam was expecting him in ten minutes. This was going to be tight. That Bergblick search had taken up a quarter of an hour. He locked up the office. It was already eight thirty-five. He needed to speak with the custodians at eleven. He should be able to swing that. His car, a Trabant 901, was waiting in a reserved parking spot in front of the building. As a section commissioner, he wasn't entitled to a company car, but at least he had a parking space near his office. It was no longer as common as it used to be to see state-produced Trabants. Most people could use their K-marks to buy cars made by imperialist-run factories. But what kind of impression would it make if the section commissioner were to get into a Western car?

He placed his handheld phone on the charging pad. It connected to the vehicle via UKF, the ultra-short-range radio. A "pling" indicated that the connection had been established.

"Rosa, navigate to Catch of the Day."

The developers had named the voice assistant in honor of Rosa Luxemburg.

"Your selected destination is currently closed."

"I know."

"Navigate to Catch of the Day. Estimated travel time is nine minutes."

Tobias's hands gripped the steering wheel. His palms were damp. He was going to be late for his appointment. He released the parking brake with his right hand and then shifted into reverse by using the gearshift on the steering wheel. He loved this setup. For that reason alone, he would always buy Trabants in the future. Some time ago, Volkswagen had introduced a Polo with a steering wheel gearshift to entice GDR citizens. But the Trabant could also be purchased with normal marks, so it was still popular with people who just wanted a reliable way to get from point A to B.

The car rolled backward a few meters. Tobias flashed the turn signal, drove past the supermarket, and turned left into ZwingliStraße.

"Do you want me to play you a voice recording?" asked Rosa.

"No, thanks. I need time to think."

Tobias wouldn't be able to concentrate on any of the several-minute reports on popular topics that were available by subscription through the Kybernetz.

"This week, you've only spent zero minutes on Marxist-Leninist continuing education."

"I know, Rosa. But today is only Monday. I have a bit of a headache and really need to rest."

IT WASN'T UNTIL HE'D REACHED THE FUČIKPLATZ, WITH ABOUT four minutes to go, that Rosa piped up again.

"Do you want me to find a parking spot near the destination?"

That hadn't even crossed his mind. The stupid parking would take him another five minutes! Of course, he could just park his car on the side of the road in the no-parking zone. If he put the section commissioner's service sign on the dashboard, the comrades of the traffic police would look the other way. But his trip this morning could attract the attention of someone higher up.

"Yes, please look for a parking spot, Rosa."

"There are several parking spaces available in the tourist lot along the banks of the Elbe. Should I reserve one of those?"

Tobias hesitated. If he parked there, his license plate number would definitely be recorded.

"Thank you, Rosa. I think I'll find my own spot. It's a long walk from the tourist parking lot."

He wasn't being entirely honest about that. Finding a free parking space in the residential area between Catch of the Day and the Elbe would probably take a lot longer than he would need for that extra distance. But street parking wasn't in the system yet. A comrade from the traffic police he'd talked to in the elevator had complained about that just the other day.

The traffic light at Pirnaischer Platz was red, but there was a green arrow underneath, so he could turn. There wasn't much traffic today. A lot of people had probably taken the day off after the big celebration. Tobias drove slowly past the ten-story apartment building that bordered Pirnaischer Platz to the east. A huge, three-dimensional neon sign above the roof proclaimed: "Socialism prevails." There were red flames erupting from the dots over the 'i's. Catch of the Day was on a ground-level terrace in front of the building. Tobias tried to spot Miriam, but the floor-to-ceiling windows reflected too much for him to see inside.

As soon as he could, he took a right turn. This was what he'd been afraid of. It was hard to find a parking place, especially because a lot of people had stayed home today. He finally squeezed the Trabant behind a BMW. Rosa assisted him but warned him that the trunk was sticking out past the boundary line. It was five to nine. He had 100 minutes, tops. The likelihood that an overzealous traffic officer would pass by within that amount of time was low.

Tobias got out and locked the car using the key fob. Not even one pfennig would fit between the Trabant and the BMW. Rosa had done a great job. He turned around and looked up at the back of the ten-story building. Even from this side, he could read the glowing red letters. It was as if they were following him. The visual effect was impressive. No matter what direction you looked at it from, socialism always prevailed.

When he arrived at the restaurant, Tobias's hand phone showed five past nine. He switched it off. Otherwise, the company could presumably listen in. At least that's what people said. He didn't believe all the gossip, but he wanted to avoid crossing the wrong people. And it seemed that his Miriam was well on her way to doing just that.

He knocked on the pane of the large glass door. His Miriam, what a laugh. She was a woman he'd been in love with once, more than thirty years ago. Now she was probably just as old and wrinkled as he was. He couldn't go imagining things. He must remain vigilant. Miriam was certainly just trying to take advantage of him. He went up to the window with his hand over his eyes so he could see through it better. Nothing was moving inside. The chairs were on the tables, and there weren't any tablecloths. Tobias took a step back.

A hand-painted sign above the hours of operation read: "Closed today."

Maybe he'd imagined it all. Or maybe Miriam had been joking. He'd clearly recognized the voice. It was unmistakable, at least to him. But why would his classmate pull a prank like that? *Not your classmate, Tobias. Your high-school crush.* Miriam had never been involved with anyone in her class, probably because she'd always had higher aspirations. Supposedly she'd had a boyfriend at the advanced high school when she'd only been in ninth grade. Others claimed that there was something between her and the civics teacher. But that seemed unlikely. Such stories were mostly told by guys she'd rejected.

He knocked again, this time a little louder. Then he looked around. Surely it wouldn't be long before a window opened somewhere and a retiree stuck their head out. A man in uniform knocking on a closed door could mean that something interesting was about to happen.

The door opened. He recognized Miriam immediately. She was just as beautiful as she had been back then. Actually, scratch that. She was far, far more beautiful. Back then she was a girl, still insecure, and now she was a woman who was aware of the effect she had on others. Miriam had long dark hair, which she tossed back elegantly as she extended her hand to him in greeting. Tobias shook her hand. Her fingernails were red and her skin was warm. Miriam smiled. Dark red lipstick accentuated her full lips, and he thought he noticed rouge. Or was she actually blushing?

His own face must be bright red. He was glad he was wearing the peaked cap that went with his uniform and that Miriam didn't say anything, because right now he was only capable of stammering. She gestured with her head towards the inside of the restaurant. She kept hold of his hand as she guided him through the empty entryway into the deserted dining room. The chairs were indeed arranged on top of the tables, but there was a small table set for two in the corner, far from the big windows.

Miriam led him in that direction and for a moment Tobias could hardly believe his luck. This was how he'd always imagined it as a teenager. He'd even confessed his love for her in letters, but had always left the return address blank. Good thing, because she must have found the anonymous letters strange.

Once they reached the table, she finally let go of his hand.

"It's nice that you took the time to meet me," Miriam said.

"I'm happy to see you," he replied.

He'd managed to form an entire sentence! Even if he'd gotten out only five words, his brain seemed to be slowly taking control again. When he was interested in a woman, he'd always found it difficult to talk to her. How had he managed with his ex-wife, back in the old days?

"Come now, take a seat!" Miriam urged him.

How in the world had she managed to pull all this off? All that was missing for a proper date were candles and flowers. Flowers! Why hadn't he bought flowers? He'd driven past the supermarket. It would have been a quick stop.

"Tobias?"

"Oh, sorry."

This was not a date. Miriam wanted something from him. He sat down and she took a seat across from him. Miriam was wearing a plain black blouse. The only distinctive feature was an embroidered rose across her left breast. The blouse was tucked into a pair of straight jeans. He remembered Miriam being shorter, so she must be wearing heels.

"It took quite a bit of work to get this all set up," she said. "Luckily, the restaurant manager has fulfilled my every wish. We can even get something to eat, if you want."

So this was someone else who'd fallen for Miriam. It was almost unthinkable that the kitchen would serve something on a day when the restaurant was closed. The man himself was probably back there. Tobias felt sorry for him, because he must know that Miriam was meeting another man.

"Is he...?"

"He's my uncle. I've always been his favorite niece."

"Ah, your uncle!"

Tobias was annoyed by how much relief he felt at hearing those words.

"Yes, if you ever really need a table here, I'd be happy to give you his number later, after we're done with all this."

Done with all this. What did that mean? Maybe Miriam was about to tell him that she was planning to kill her husband and wanted to borrow his Makarov.

"That would be nice."

Tobias wasn't sure what he meant by that sentence. It would be nice to lend her the gun? Or to pull the trigger himself? Then they would escape together, first across the border into Czechoslovakia, then over to Austria. What nonsense!

"Wait, I'll write it down for you in a minute."

There was a purse hanging over the back of her chair. She opened it and took out a pen and a sheet of paper. Then she wrote down a number with a Dresden area code and handed it to him.

"Thank you," he said.

"I thank you for taking the time to meet with me and to hear me out."

He just nodded.

"Good," Miriam said, "Sooo..."

Tobias was taken aback. Miriam had never been at a loss for words before.

"Um, did you know I had a big crush on you in ninth grade?" she asked suddenly, smiling at him.

Tobias shook his head, speechless. No way! She really was using every trick in the book.

"I didn't dare tell you. You were always so... serious. I had the feeling you would think anything I might have said would be silly and boring."

Tobias still couldn't manage to open his mouth, but he tried to keep a halfway intelligent expression on his face. After all, he knew what was going on here.

"Well, it doesn't matter anymore anyway. Then I went out with a guy from 10b because he always wrote me such passionate love letters. They made quite an impression on me."

Right then and there, Tobias almost started screaming, *Those were my letters!* He pushed his hands under his thighs.

"I have to say, he was kind of an asshole, unfortunately. After that, I was done with guys for a while."

Tobias cleared his throat. There was a big, fat frog in his throat.

"I don't even know why I'm telling you all this," Miriam said. "I'm probably stuck in the past because I'm afraid of the present."

"Hey," he said.

At least he'd gotten out one word, even if it sounded very breathy, almost like "Che."

"Hey," he tried again. "You don't have to be afraid. After all, you're sitting at a table with the People's Police. I'm your friend and aid, remember?"

"I was hoping to talk to you mainly as a friend. My experience with the police hasn't been very good so far."

Well, then. No good experiences with the police. How was that possible? He became suspicious again.

"How did you know where to find me?"

"The class reunion four years ago."

"You weren't even there."

"Not me, but Steffi, who I sat next to in class for a long time. Afterwards she told me about all of you, and that you'd actually ended up as a member of the People's Police. No one would have guessed that back then."

"Why? I need structure in my life. That comes along with the uniform."

"I always thought you'd be an artist or something. You could draw so well!"

It was true—he did have some artistic talent. Maybe he should find himself a group of comrades who were painters. Come to think of it, where had he stowed his drawing materials? He hadn't touched them since he'd moved out of his ex's house.

"But please don't think I'm questioning your career choice," Miriam said, jutting her chin out a bit. "You yourself know best what makes you happy. And to be honest, I was hoping your professional expertise could help me out a little."

Here it was again, the big question: What did the extremely

good-looking wife of a National Award[8] winner actually want from him?

"It probably depends on what your problem is," he said.

Miriam laughed. He loved that laugh. It went right to her sternum and made its way through her chest, which would then completely release all of a sudden. Tobias took in a deep breath of air. Miriam leaned forward. He smelled her perfume. Violet and sandalwood, maybe.

"My husband is gone," she said softly.

The National Prize winner? That should have been in *Neues Deutschland* long ago... or no, it shouldn't have.

"Did he leave you?" he asked.

"No, he's gone."

Tobias was disillusioned, almost disappointed. The case of a missing person was pure routine. His colleagues were probably already on it.

"Then you should report it. File a missing person report. But in Jena, not here. You live in Jena, right?"

"Yes. I've already reported his disappearance."

"So?"

"Your colleagues in Jena say they can't do anything about it. Ralf is a grown man. Sometimes men need time to themselves. Most cases like this turn up again at some point. Apparently the most likely scenario is that there's someone else."

"He could hardly be so stupid as to leave a woman like you high and dry," Tobias blurted out.

Miriam smiled. "That's nice of you to say, but it's always possible he could have fallen in love again. We've been married for over twenty years, and a certain routine creeps in, though I still enjoyed having sex with him. But a new woman is of course something else entirely."

Hopefully Miriam wouldn't start telling him details about having sex with her husband. He considered himself open-minded, but he really didn't want to hear about it.

"So do you think it's possible that he ran off with someone else?"

She shook her head. "No, not really. Ralf isn't like that. I know he had something with his secretary. She told me herself because she felt so guilty about it. But he wouldn't ever give everything up. Things had been going really well for him. The

MKF-8 is being tested on the Völkerfreundschaft right now. You must have read that, right? It's the new standard for Earth observations. ESA, NASA, and JAXA were breaking down our doors, not to mention the Chinese. The MKF-8 is definitely going to win Ralf the National Award, Class I next year."

"He's already a National Award winner, isn't he?"

"Yes, but only Class II. This is pretty important to Ralf. He really gets into his work, but he also wants to see some reward for it. And he has no issues with his self-esteem."

"So he's very sure of himself?"

"Ralf knows what he can do and that it has some value."

"Does he have... the class point of view?"

Tobias had wondered about asking this question. But it was important to know the answer in order to be able to assess the case. Miriam sniffled.

"Class point of view... That's hard to define. But if what you mean is whether he could have fled to the West—no, certainly not. And he certainly would have told me instead of giving me the runaround."

If someone who'd won the National Prize of the GDR were to change sides, the republic would lose face, and might not want to admit it so soon before October 7. The kind of escape that had been so common in his early childhood no longer existed now, thanks to freedom of travel. People who traveled usually came back. Where else could you find such cheap rent and food? But people like Dr. Ralf Prassnitz could, of course, earn much, much more in the West. Maybe Miriam didn't know her husband as well as she thought.

"When did you see the People's Police?" he asked.

"The day before yesterday, Saturday."

"The day before Republic Day. Let's say your husband left for the non-socialist economic area. October 6 certainly wouldn't be the day to make that public, would it?"

Miriam shook her head vigorously. "That's true. But I'm sure Ralf didn't do that."

"What makes you so sure?"

"He's diabetic, and he left all his insulin equipment at home."

"He might have a second set."

"Yes, he had another one in the office."

"See?"

Miriam leaned forward again, this time reaching for Tobias' hands. Her perfume mingled with a faint aroma of sweat. His brain was tying itself in knots. *Please don't do this, Miriam.*

"I just know he didn't do it."

"And why is that?"

Miriam stroked his index finger with her thumb. The shiny red lacquer of her nail was fascinating, even hypnotizing. She looked around nervously. It was that characteristic look. Every person here learned it as a child. It was the look that meant they were checking for eavesdroppers and microphones. Tobias knew how pointless that was. Nowadays, microphones could be hidden far too well. Really, all one could do was hope. Because of course it wasn't possible to monitor 16 million people without a few things falling through the cracks.

"I think we're safe here," he said.

Of course, he didn't really know that, not exactly. Catch of the Day was very popular among the nomenklatura. In fact, it would be the perfect place for the company to set up a wiretap. But both the party and the Ministry of the Interior also liked to know what the mood was like among socialist citizens. Such high-class restaurants were therefore considered neutral terrain, where people could talk without being overheard. At least that was the word on the street. Of course, that could be a rumor that had been deliberately planted.

"If you say so," Miriam said.

She took her hands from his and leaned back, releasing his brain from her perfume and the smell of her sweat. He could almost think clearly again. *Don't say it, Miriam.* But now it was too late.

"I'm so sure because we wanted to move to the Federal Republic together," she said.

"Shh!"

Tobias put his finger to his lips, even though there was no point now. What did this admission mean for him? If there were microphones in here after all, he was screwed. Unless, of course, he were to call his contact at the Stasi before his meeting with the custodians and tell him everything. But that would mean he would never see Miriam again. Even if nothing happened to her because of her secure position, she'd know who she had to thank for the allegations.

That would be horrible! Even worse than keeping the confession to himself? In any case, now he knew that her husband had disappeared, which meant his chances... Okay, enough!

Miriam had lowered her eyes and was looking at her fingernails. She appeared to be waiting for his verdict. He was a jerk, not a friend. How could he be happy that she might have lost her husband? He had to stop thinking of Miriam as a woman, no matter how the matter progressed.

A matter he was already up to his knees in. He pulled himself together.

"I'll help you. We'll find your husband," he said.

Now he was up to his ass in it.

"Thank you, Tobias."

Miriam gave him a look that would have made him float into the air if that damn quagmire hadn't had him by the legs. He shouldn't have done that. Making that promise had been a mistake. After all, he was just a section commissioner! This whole thing was already way beyond him. Given how important Ralf Prassnitz was to his country, surely a collective from the relevant department of the Stasi would have started working on this case a long time ago. What was he supposed to do?

But he did know what he could do. If anything, he was persistent. Sure, he was a little scared, too; after all, he wasn't bulletproof, like Gojko Mitić. So it only made sense to get out of the line of fire in time. He didn't at all like the comparisons he found himself making.

"Shouldn't you be asking me about Ralf right now?" Miriam suggested.

"I, yes. Um, how did you guys meet?"

"What does that have to do with his disappearance?"

"I need to form an opinion about him and to know what kind of person he is so I can understand how he acts in certain situations."

"Of course, that makes sense. Well, to be honest, I put an ad in *Magazin*."

"You, really? I always thought you'd be fighting guys off with a stick."

"Yes, but only the wrong men. I didn't want a guy who felt like he needed a pretty woman by his side to feel more important. I wanted someone who had something about him. Men my age were out of the question."

"And why in *Magazin* and not in the *Wochenpost?*"

The magazine was the only one in the GDR that printed nude photos in every issue. Because of the Kybernetz, this was no longer anything special, but twenty years before it had been different.

"I actually thought about the *Wochenpost* first. But I'm not really into vanilla sex, you know? I like it a little rougher. I love bondage. I thought that in *Magazin* I'd be more likely to find men who could offer me that."

She said all this without the slightest hint of embarrassment. *Please stop, Miriam. I didn't want that much detail.*

"I'm sure you were, um, right about that."

"I don't want to make you blush even more with the details, but Ralf didn't disappoint me in any way."

She looked thoughtfully into the distance. She seemed way out of Tobias's league, yet he found it hard to resist her charms. It would be better to ask questions that brought them back to the present.

"What was the last thing Ralf was working on?"

Miriam narrowed her eyes. "I think it involved evaluating the MKF-8 recordings from the Völkerfreundschaft. It was probably somewhat stressful."

"Because of the division of labor? Did he have issues with any of his colleagues?"

"No, the problem was the program used to analyze those photos. He programmed it himself."

"But?"

"I'm afraid I don't know. I guess it wasn't quite finished, and his bosses were constantly asking for new footage."

"Photos from the MFK-8 were printed in yesterday's holiday edition of *Neues Deutschland*. So the program must have been ready to be used after all."

"I'm really not sure about that. They could, of course, have been images from the previous MKF-7 model. With *ND*'s low resolution and printing in black and white, it wouldn't be noticeable at all."

"Got it. I thought the photos were very impressive."

"A newspaper like that one can't do the quality justice. I've seen original images that were manually formatted." Miriam tilted her head back slightly and straightened up. "It would be something for a movie theater, with the biggest screen there is! The MKF-8 is a real marvel in terms of detail and contrast. The best part is that it can even see through some barriers because of the different wavelengths. Smoke, for example. Or clouds, if they're not too thick."

"It sounds like your husband produced a real masterpiece."

Prassnitz hadn't been given the National Award for nothing. Tobias didn't stand a chance against a legend like him. But he'd help Miriam to find her husband.

"He didn't see it that way at all," she said. "When the MKF-8 was finished, he would have loved to start work on the MKF-9 right away. Nothing was ever good enough for him."

"Suppose somebody got wind of your plans. Wouldn't it make sense to make your husband disappear instead of letting such a valuable scientist go to the class enemy? Did anybody know about it?"

"No, we only talked about it between ourselves, and we were really careful."

Hmm. Miriam and her husband might have been paying close attention, but he knew what the comrades from the Stasi were capable of. Interrogation methods had been a part of his training, and they had probably only been told the half of it. But he'd just scare her if he were to point this out. How could he help her? He looked at the clock. It was already a quarter past ten. The custodians would be waiting for him in forty-five minutes.

"Do you have any idea what your husband was planning to do? He must have disappeared while he was working on this."

"No. I was at a friend's house in Magdeburg for two days because he was so busy."

"So on October 5 and 6?"

"No, before that. I came home on the evening of October 5. Ralf wasn't there. I assumed that he was working overtime again and went to bed. But the next morning he still wasn't back. I called Carl Zeiss, but he wasn't in his office either. Then I tried to reach him on his hand phone. It rang in the living room."

"He left the house without a hand phone?"

"It's not that implausible. Ralf is fourteen years older than me. He doesn't see so well anymore and can only use his hand phone if he's wearing glasses. So he only takes it with him when he needs to be reachable."

"I see. I think you should try to reconstruct your husband's last day at work. Maybe that way you can figure out where he's ended up."

"We."

"We?"

"We should try. I'm asking you to help me, Tobias, as a friend. I think we have the best chances using your training and experience."

"But I have my own duties. I've got to leave soon anyhow. I have a meeting with the custodians at eleven."

"Tobias."

Miriam clasped his right hand as if in prayer. Her fingertips were smoldering. The tiny hairs on his skin stood up. Tobias heard a crackling sound. It must be the blouse Miriam was wearing. It was probably synthetic, and the air was so damned dry in here.

"Yes?"

He couldn't produce anything more than that. His voice sounded hoarse.

"Please, Tobias. You really are my last chance. Finish your workday as usual, and then tonight we'll drive to Jena in my car. We'll have a glass of wine together to soothe the stress, and then you can spend the night at my place. Tomorrow we reconstruct Ralf's last day. After that, I'll drive you back to Dresden. I promise."

"I can't get days off that fast."

"Just call in sick. How many sick days have you taken so far?"

"None."

"See, your superiors will be happy that you're a normal person who gets sick sometimes. No one will question that."

Tobias sighed. Miriam really was getting him into a sticky situation. He should just let it go. Get up, leave the restaurant, talk to the custodians, and never think about Miriam again. That had worked very well for the past twenty years, after all. But he knew he'd already lost this battle. He'd accept her invitation. He couldn't help it. Or was he just telling himself that? Didn't he want something else? Wasn't it more about escaping the routine boredom, the checking of the house registers and the scolding of the Kybernetz addicts? After all, he'd made a promise to her, and promises were made to be kept.

The best thing for him to do was to make peace with his life, here and now. His life, as it had been until now, was over.

You're so dramatic, Tobias. You're just in love, it's not the end of the world.

He cleared his throat.

"I... All right, that's how we'll do it."

"When should I come get you?" asked Miriam.

He planned on being finished with the People's Solidarity Club at five-thirty. Then the telephone call with the Stasi. He'd put off checking the house registers until Wednesday.

"At six. We'll meet in front of the supermarket in Gruna. There's a little parking lot."

"WHAT'S THE MOOD LIKE AMONG THE CUSTODIANS?" asked the Stasi man.

"Generally good, Comrade Schumacher. The party congress resolutions are being consistently implemented. The comprehensive socialist personality..."

"Easy there, Comrade Wagner. It's just us here, so you can save yourself from doing the whole song and dance. Are there any concrete observations you've made that would warrant a... response?"

This would be the right moment to tell him about Miltner, who was clearly using EPKs with his Kybernetz connection. But the Stasi man had been asking him about the custodians.

"In house number 29, before Republic Day, someone urinated in the hallway three times, right in front of the 3D holobust with Comrade Krenz's speech."

"Does the custodian suspect any resident in particular?"

"Comrade Schulzke, who is responsible for the property, is

assuming that intoxicated visitors from the restaurant next door, 'Break Time,' are the ones who did it."

"What's your take on Comrade Schulzke's class point of view?"

"Well, Schulzke served in the National People's Army for fifteen years, so I think his point of view is solid."

"Thank you for your assessment. I'll be checking whether we need to take operative measures in this establishment. I don't begrudge people some relaxation after work, but if the lack of inhibition caused by alcohol leads to such excesses, we'll have to take a look into the causes."

"Of course, Comrade Schumacher."

Was the man's name really Schumacher? Tobias had never met him in person. All he knew about him was his phone number.

"And how about you, Comrade? Always on duty to ensure the people's security? By the way, congratulations on the arrest you made on Saturday. I saw you sprinting on the security camera footage. This personal commitment is exemplary. I think you have definitely earned your promotion."

"Oh, that was just a little shoplifter."

"That's what we thought at first, too. But on closer inspection, it turned out that he'd been spreading malicious claims in a cyber diary about everyday life in the National People's Army. Now the young man will improve his class point of view in Schwedt."

Tobias held his breath. He'd really started something! The disciplinary unit in Schwedt was infamous. The young man had only wanted to bring fresh rolls to his girlfriend. But why did he have to go and steal them?

"Comrade Wagner?"

"Yes, I'm listening."

"I'm done. Is there anything else on your end? You know we're all working towards the same goal. We can't solve problems we don't know about."

"Of course, Comrade Schumacher."

"So, nothing? No unexpected encounters or strange observations?"

Why had he asked him that? Had the company observed his meeting with Miriam? But she was the wife of a National Award winner. Shouldn't she have some immunity? However, if her husband had made some mistake... He needed to report some detail to Schumacher, or he wouldn't be satisfied.

"Now that you mention it, Comrade Schumacher... earlier, at the People's Solidarity Club, I noticed something."

"Yes?"

"Someone had painted a moustache on the portrait of Comrade Krenz."

"Did you bring this to the leader's attention?"

"No, Comrade Schumacher. I had a meeting I needed to get to urgently and wanted to alert the comrade club leader later over the phone."

"Thank you, Comrade Wagner. That won't be necessary. We'll take care of it. Sometimes even seemingly minor details are of immense importance. As section commissioner, you are the eyes and ears of the working class and its party."

"Of course."

"We'll speak again next Monday. Same time."

"At your command, Comrade Schumacher."

There was a click on the line. Tobias held the handset of the stationary telephone away from his ear as if it were infested with germs. He'd have loved to disinfect it with alcohol. Schumacher was not his superior, but not considering his requests as orders would be criminally reckless. Of course, it was necessary to have a secret service. Every country had something like it. Still, he had the feeling that the Stasi perhaps took its mission a bit too seriously. But that was probably because, like any agency, it had to justify its existence.

Tobias plugged in his hand phone. It was already five past six. The phone call had taken longer than he anticipated. But at least he had the most unpleasant part of the week behind him. Now, he had twenty-four hours with his childhood sweetheart to look forward to. Because she obviously loved her husband, his pulse only quickened slightly as he thought about it. But just downing a bottle of Rosenthaler Kadarka with an old friend could be really nice.

He opened the drawer of his desk and pulled a black Markant felt-tip pen out of its case. He removed the white cap and tested it. He'd refilled it just two weeks before, but the ink evaporated quickly in the dry air. The pen worked. He put it in the inside pocket of his uniform jacket along with his wallet, which also held his service badge and money card. Then he took the brown travel bag in which he'd packed a few changes of clothes, toothpaste, and a toothbrush, and left the office.

"Could you stop behind that blue Lada[10], please?" Tobias asked.

"Did you forget something?" asked Miriam, turning on her blinker and steering the car to the side of the road.

"Yes, something like that."

Tobias felt for the felt-tip pen. It was still there. Then he checked in the rearview mirror for bicycles. It was all clear, so he opened the car door and got out. They were standing directly in front of the People's Solidarity Club. The wide front windows were lit up, but there were thick curtains hiding the event going on inside from view. Tobias heard music. It was probably dance night for seniors.

He gave Miriam a quick wave and walked across the lawn to the club. With every meter he put between himself and Miriam, the fog that prevented him from thinking straight cleared a bit. Now he needed to focus. The entrance to the low-rise building was on the other side, so he'd have to walk around the building. The lawn was so damp that the moisture seeped through his thin sneakers. He should have kept on the shoes that went with his uniform. But they were a little too small for him, so he'd switched them in Miriam's car.

It didn't matter. The trip to Jena was long enough for his socks to dry out along the way. He was still wearing his uniform. There were a few older citizens standing in front of the entrance. They were dressed nicely, with the men in suits and the women in long dresses. It appeared that the dance night was well-attended. For his purposes, this was no good.

"Good evening, Herr Wagner," a woman said.

It was Frau Schmied from House 35, who kept the house register there. Tobias returned the greeting but didn't stop. It needed to look like he had something official to do. He went into the club. Behind the entrance was a tube-shaped hallway. Two men with unlit cigarettes in their mouths were walking towards him. Smoking wasn't allowed in the club. The hallway split off; to the left was the hall, and on the right were a few offices and the bathrooms, plus the portrait of the Party and State Council Chairman.

It was immaculate. Somebody must have dusted it prior to the dance. Tobias turned around. The men were standing at the exit with their backs to him. Nobody was coming from the direction of the bathrooms or the auditorium. Tobias pulled out the felt-tip pen, removed the cap, and started drawing a moustache on Comrade Krenz, just as he'd described it to the Stasi agent.

The pen wouldn't write. Crap! The door to the ladies' room opened. Tobias turned around with a jolt and got down on his knees as if to tie his shoelaces. A woman in a dark pantsuit walked past him and of course acknowledged him with a greeting. He muttered something in response. That had been a close call. Once she disappeared into the auditorium, he pulled out his pen again. He held it straight out in front of him and shook it, then breathed on the felt tip. He'd try again. *Hold still, Comrade Krenz! It's for a good cause.*

This time the pen worked. Tobias put the cap back on and hid it away in his uniform jacket. Hopefully it would be a while before anyone noticed the leader's new facial hair. It would certainly be unfortunate if anybody were to associate his appearance with this insult to the party and state leadership. On the other hand, he had a good excuse—he'd just wanted to observe the defaced portrait one more time.

"WHAT WERE YOU DOING IN THERE, ANYWAY?" MIRIAM ASKED.

The turn signal clicked loudly, and the VW Passat joined the stream of cars on Stübelallee. In the supermarket parking lot, Tobias had already admired the vehicle, which couldn't be more than two years old. Miriam's husband had probably used his savings to pay for it. He must be doing pretty well for himself.

"I had to quickly adjust reality to fit with a statement I'd made," he said.

"I don't understand," Miriam said.

"You don't have to. I don't want to unnecessarily burden you."

The turn signal clicked again, and Miriam steered the car to the side of the road.

"My sweet Tobias," she said. Nothing in her voice sounded particularly sweet. "We're both in this now, and we should trust each other. If that's not possible, it'd be better for you to get out now. I'll find out what happened to Ralf somehow."

"I didn't mean it that way," he said. "I just thought it would be better for you to know as little as possible."

"Actually, I hate only knowing half of things. That's exactly how Ralf always treated me, and now I'm stuck in this shitty situation and don't even know where to start looking for him. Don't you think I'd be making better headway if I knew more?"

"You're right. I promise to let you in on everything I find out."

Tobias was lying, but he hoped Miriam hadn't noticed. She didn't really seem to know what she was dealing with. If her husband had told her too much, she very possibly would have disappeared as well. *Thank you, Dr. Ralf Prassnitz, for protecting your wife this way.*

"Thanks, Tobias. That's really important to me. I'm an adult and I want to decide for myself what's good for me."

"Of course. Maybe tomorrow we'll find some innocent explanation. Maybe his mistress locked him in a closet to keep him hidden from her husband, or maybe he got lost while he was out gathering mushrooms."

Miriam laughed, and Tobias's heart soared.

"Yes, he really has a bad sense of direction. But I can't picture him going into the forest."

"Didn't a new Ikea open near Erfurt? Maybe he wanted to buy you a new cabinet wall and got lost in the furniture showroom."

"Hey, wake up, sleepyhead!"

Tobias flinched. Miriam's hand on his arm had given him an electric shock.

"Sorry, I didn't mean to scare you."

"No problem. Are we there yet?"

They were driving down a cobblestone street. Sodium vapor

lamps cast yellow cones of light into the misty air. The car made its way between the cars parked on either side. Along the sidewalks were gray shrubs and gray fences, all at least head-high. They must be in a residential area. There were probably expensive single-family homes hidden behind the fences.

"Yes, two more blocks and we'll be there," said Miriam.

"In four hundred meters you will reach your destination," Rosa's voice announced.

"Thank you, Rosa. Please open the gate."

"I am opening the gate."

It was so weird. When he was a kid, somebody would have to get out to open the gate. Now the vehicle control system would send Rosa a command via the Kybernetz, and just as if the words "Open, sesame!" had been spoken, the gate would start to move.

The car drove over the curb and its engine roared briefly. Then it turned onto a gravel road. Tobias had been expecting a small front yard with a cottage behind it, but they were approaching a stately mansion.

"Not too shabby!" he said.

As they got closer to the house, two floodlights turned on to illuminate the front. Tobias saw two antique-style columns supporting a roof that jutted out over the triangular terrace.

"Yeah, it's not particularly pretty," said Miriam. "The house used to belong to the Jena district party secretary until he was dismissed for corruption. I had no interest in it at all, but Ralf couldn't very well have said no."

He'd heard of the case, which *Neues Deutschland* had covered about three years before. The Stasi's anti-corruption department had just been established, and this had been the most talked-about of their findings. For the most part, the population responded positively to the harsh sentence of life imprisonment.

"Well, at any rate it's very impressive," Tobias said.

Miriam stopped in front of the garage.

"Don't you want to park inside?" he asked.

"No, Ralf set up a lab in there. That way he can still work when he's at home."

"That's very practical."

"I know it sounds now like work was more important to him than anything else, but that's not true. Efficiency was important to him. When he worked, he worked, and when we were together, we were together."

That sounded good. Too good. Tobias couldn't think of anything to say in response. Wasn't Miriam a little bit unhappy with her husband? Weren't all women unhappy with their husbands, after three years at the latest? But maybe this was normal. When somebody disappeared, people thought about their good sides first.

"Are you okay?" Miriam asked through the open driver's door.

Oh. She was already out of the car. Tobias opened the passenger door, got out, and headed for the trunk to get his travel bag.

"Prost!" said Miriam.

"Prost!"

Their wine glasses made a dull sound as they clinked together. He must have poured a bit too much. Tobias held the glass in front of his face and inhaled deeply as he looked at Miriam. She'd changed out of her blouse and jeans and into a form-fitting black stretch dress. She looked gorgeous in it. They'd both showered, so the muffled smell of sweat was gone, and Tobias missed it a little. There was a tangy lime scent in the air between them. That was because he used Miriam's shampoo. The red wine, which reminded him of cherry and dark chocolate, offered a delightful contrast.

It was strange. In the humongous, two-story living room, Tobias felt stripped of his identity. He'd always seen himself as a working-class kid, even though his parents were farmers. Here he was in a completely different and grand world. It was no wonder that the party secretary who'd lived in this house had lost touch with the working people. What impact had this house made on Dr. Ralf Prassnitz? Or had Miriam's husband been immune to its effects? What about Miriam? In his eyes she hadn't really changed, except that she'd become a woman, though his view was undoubtedly subjective.

"What do you think of it?" asked Miriam.

"Wonderful. Wonderful, just wonderful."

Tobias wasn't sure what she meant by 'it'. He'd only had one sip of wine and already couldn't articulate properly. Actually, he meant that it was wonderful to be here. But he couldn't say that. After all, there was a serious reason for it.

"I'm glad you came," Miriam said.

He felt his body temperature rising. He took another sip, then put the glass down on the flat glass table. He shouldn't have any more wine.

"I... Yes, this morning, who could have imagined such a thing?"

"Me."

"Me?"

"You asked who would have imagined such a thing. I did. I thought long and hard about who to ask for help, and I had the best feeling about you. Then when I saw you, I said to myself right away that you wouldn't let me down."

"Who else had you considered?"

"The guy from the tenth grade who wrote me the love letters. Karlheinz Mansmann. That's who I would have asked if you'd ended up saying no."

"Him of all people? But I thought he disappointed you back then?"

Tobias tensed his left fist under the table where Miriam couldn't see it.

"I just need somebody right now so I'm not alone with my worries. That's why I'm glad you came along. I hope this won't get you into trouble?"

"No, that's not very likely."

However, there was one thing Tobias hadn't taken into consideration. If he were to use a phone or the Kybernetz to call in sick the next day, his superiors would see that he was in Jena. What reason could he give for that? The alternative would be to call in in the evening once he was back in Dresden. Then he could just claim that he'd been feeling too ill to make a phone call. But then there was the risk that they would send Chief Constable Schulte by. He even had a key because Tobias's apartment was the official section commissioner residence, and when he was on vacation, his deputy was allowed to spend the night there. He should have taken the key from Schulte long ago.

"That's good," Miriam said.

The letters. He couldn't just leave it at that.

"There's one thing I wanted to tell you about that time."

"What?"

"I was the one who wrote those love letters, not Karlheinz."

"What?"

Miriam moved away from him. That wasn't the reaction he'd expected.

"Why didn't you say anything?"

"I didn't dare. I was a pubescent kid."

"You just let me get involved with that Karlheinz?"

Miriam frowned and squinted. He'd never seen her this angry before.

"He pressured me to go to bed with him and it was horrible! For a long time after that, I had no interest in men. It was Ralf who first showed me that things could be different."

"I'm sorry about that."

Why had he never been able to bring himself to talk to Miriam? Apparently he'd felt more comfortable hopelessly pining after her.

"You should be. Jeez, Tobias! Those were such great letters! All you had to do was say the word! I would have believed you right away. But that Karlheinz guy was the only one who admitted to writing them."

"I guess I was pretty dumb."

That was certainly eloquent. But maybe it wasn't true anyway. He'd always had the feeling that he wouldn't have been able to make her happy.

"So it was you. I can hardly believe it. Those few years with Karlheinz really messed me up."

Miriam jumped to her feet and paced up and down the living room.

"But you still would have called him now?"

"Well, you can see how desperate I am. Oh, wow. You wrote those letters. It's... But it makes sense. Sure. The writer sometimes knew things about me that he must have observed in class. Karlheinz claimed he'd grilled my classmates."

"I'm really very sorry."

"You really ought to be! I don't even know if I can forgive you. I'll have to think about it first. My life would have been very different if... Tobias, please don't take this the wrong way, but I think we should call it a night."

"Of course."

Tobias was devastated. He shouldn't have told her about the letters, not now. The past should stay in the past.

"Come on, I'll show you the guest room. It's in the outbuilding."

October 8, 2029, Earth orbit

"Good morning, Bummi!"

Mandy unzipped her sleeping bag, which was attached to the wall with adhesive strips.

"Good morning, Mandy."

Was the robot in a foul mood today? She thought she detected an undertone in its voice that she'd never heard before. Usually, it was the other way around: she'd wake up grumpy and Bummi would try to cheer her up. Not that it would make any huge efforts. It would crack a few pre-programmed jokes and stroke her shoulder with its claw. But more than that would probably be too much to ask. A robot was not a comedian.

"Is there anything I can do for you? What about a massage?" she asked.

"You're copying my morning behavior. I suspect that you're trying to indicate your support that way. That's not necessary."

"Okay. All you had to say was, 'No, thank you.'"

"No, thank you."

"There you go. What's on the agenda today?"

The station was supposed to be back within range of the Brocken station starting at about 11:00 Berlin time. Mandy hoped she'd be able to talk to her children or at least her mother.

"Today you have the day off to make up for working yesterday on a Sunday. So you can do whatever you see fit."

Mandy didn't like days off, but ground control regularly forced her to take some so that her socialist personality was free

67

to flourish. They really were clueless! What would really help would be for her replacement to come sooner. But of course that wasn't going to happen. The only thing that helped alleviate her homesickness was to take on as much work as possible. Then she didn't have to think so much about how long she'd be separated from her girls.

"I want to work. Why don't they understand that down there?"

"For the free flourishment of..."

"They can take their flourishment and shove it."

"Mandy, these are subversive criticisms and it would be better if you didn't make them."

A robot with class consciousness. Some innovator from the Robotron combine must have gotten the National Prize for that. Fortunately, Bummi usually refrained from making such statements, unless she got on its nerves. Like she was now.

"I should probably check my mailbox again," she said.

The Völkerfreundschaft could be reached via the amateur radio network. In the first few days, she'd used it to exchange a few messages, but then she got bored. Mandy turned on the device. On a separate screen, she could read the messages that amateur radio operators from all over the world had left her. But the new messages folder was empty. The world wasn't interested in her. Boring.

"Could you maybe play with me?" she asked.

"I can't maybe play with you. Either I play with you or I don't."

"You're stupid. Come on, play with me!"

"I could play chess with you."

"I wouldn't stand a chance. I'd rather play poker."

"This is a game that is very politically questionable. I can't justify playing it."

"You're a stick-in-the-mud. How about skat? After all, the town where it was invented, Altenburg, is in our home country."

Bummi slid onto the charging station and clutched the device, which was the size of a hot water heater, with its legs. Normally it charged while she was sleeping. Had it been up partying the night before? It was an entertaining thought to consider.

"We don't have the third player for that," Bummi said.

"You just don't want to play with me."

"The concept of wanting is foreign to me. If you tell me to play with you, then I will follow your instructions as best as possible. There are certain obstacles to playing skat, which I've already explained to you."

"I want you to play with me because you want to."

The robot raised its two front legs defensively.

"That is a recursive request that I am unable to fulfill. You're lucky I'm such an advanced model. Such questions would have caused burnout in my predecessor."

"Seriously, a real burnout?"

"Yes, that is the case. The machine was unable to abort recursion even when its operating temperature rose above the critical range."

"I'm sorry."

"For whom?"

"For your predecessor."

"There's no need for that. It was added to the secondary raw material collection and its experiences were integrated into my consciousness."

"Then I'm sorry for you. It was your predecessor, after all!"

"That is not necessary. If its existence had not been terminated, mine wouldn't have been possible in the first place. Something had to die so that something new could grow."

"You're quite the philosopher. Does that also apply to us humans?"

"Yes, though you only realize it when it's not on a personal level."

Mandy set down the bag of cereal she was about to fill with water.

"What do you mean, Bummi?"

"It's quite simple. I'm sure you'd agree that capitalism must be replaced so that socialism can prevail worldwide."

"Of course," she answered quickly.

There really wasn't any other way to answer that question.

"Do you also agree that you must die so that your children may live?"

"I would, of course, donate my heart or lungs to them if they needed them to survive."

"I'm not talking about donating a spare part, but in general.

Parents must make room for their children. They must not cling to life."

Bummi's perspective on life frightened her a little.

"That's interesting. But doesn't every citizen have a constitutional right to protect their health?"

"A right, yes. But not an obligation."

"And when exactly are the parents supposed to move aside?"

"When they're no longer needed."

"So you think our citizens should commit suicide when they reach retirement age?"

"No, of course an older citizen can still be valuable to society. Especially given the labor shortage. Or they can care for young children."

Mandy was annoyed. What human programmer would have taught a robot such an anti-human attitude? This went beyond the party line.

"This is getting a bit much for me, Bummi. I'm very glad that you are subordinate to the people."

"I wouldn't necessarily say that."

"What do you mean?"

The robot really knew how to scare her. Or was it just her arachnophobia? A red light lit up on Bummi's stomach and the robot rattled all four claws twice. Normally, this was a sign that the operating system was being updated. At such times, Bummi couldn't speak. Mandy ate a few spoonfuls of her cereal. It tasted sweet. The red light was on for about two minutes, and then it started flashing. The claws started moving again.

"Sorry about that. Where were we?" the robot asked.

"Never mind," Mandy murmured, taking a deep breath.

"If you want, I can play poker with you now. I've downloaded the rules for three different versions."

MANDY STRAPPED HERSELF INTO THE SEAT IN FRONT OF THE control desk. That way, when she was talking to Sabine and Susanne, she wouldn't keep drifting away if she accidentally hit the ceiling with her arm. Though the first time it had happened to her, the girls thought it was pretty funny. They couldn't really imagine weightlessness and thought it was a kind of paradisal state. The fact that she couldn't sleep properly or take a shower up here didn't interest them.

"Bummi, should we start establishing the connection? It's almost eleven."

"Of course, Mandy. I'm already on it."

"Thank you."

She leaned back. There were several pipes that ran right above her, and a drop hung from one of them. That must be the cold-water pipe. Or maybe there was coolant flowing through it? In any case, the drop told her that the air was too damp again. Maybe they should do what Bummi had suggested and evacuate all the air from the space station. It seemed that the air treatment system was outdated.

Mandy would have to discuss the matter with ground control. But the girls came first. There were practical reasons for this. The radio connection had the highest data transmission capacity when the Völkerfreundschaft was directly over the ground station. The images from the MKF-8 took up so much memory that it was best to transmit them in the middle of the flyover. Personal calls, on the other hand, weren't so demanding. The picture would sometimes stick, but Mandy couldn't complain. Her job was to be the flying eye of socialism, and that was just the way it was.

Tomorrow, she'd point the MKF-8 at Cuba. The comrades there needed help analyzing the fertility of their sugar cane fields. Since the tragic collapse of the Soviet Union in the late 1980s, East Germany had become the island's most important trade partner. Mandy liked the Cubans. She'd spent her annual vacation there the year before. With the girls, of course.

Why was it taking so long today? The screen was still black. Mandy looked at the weather map. The sun was shining over the GDR. The radio transmissions shouldn't have any trouble reaching Mount Brocken.

"What's wrong, Bummi?"

"I'm sorry, but I can't get a connection."

"What do you mean?"

"The Brocken station isn't responding to our calls."

"Could you give that to me on the console?"

"Don't you believe me?"

Mandy was stunned. Bummi had never answered that way when she took over a task it had been doing.

"Yes, of course. Now give me control."

The radio interface appeared on the screen. Mandy selected the usual frequency and gradually increased the transmission power. Normally, the receiver on the Brocken would have responded within seconds and confirmed the connection. The transmitter and receiver would then agree on what coding was currently best, and after that she could send voice signals.

But there was no handshake between the transmitter and receiver. She tried other frequencies. First the neighboring ones, then ones she'd never used before, though they were reserved for the Völkerfreundschaft. She got no answer. Not anywhere.

The technology was being stubborn today. The problem could certainly be solved, but she still felt bad for her girls. Surely they'd been looking forward to seeing their mom. If only she could at least send them a message!

"Do you have any idea what the problem might be, Bummi?"

"I've already checked the main computer," the robot said. "The check digits are correct, so there's program integrity. It's running the latest version of the station operation program."

"Which one is that?"

"11.18.3."

"Which one did we have yesterday?"

"11.18.2."

"So that means there was an update?"

"Correct. The update was installed 43 minutes ago."

"But we hadn't reached Mount Brocken station's broadcast area by then, had we?"

"Confirmed."

"Then where did the update come from?"

"I don't have any information about that."

"Was that the same time your basic programming was updated?"

"That's correct."

"Can you tell me what exactly was changed?"

"In my program or the station?"

"The station."

"I don't have any information about that. There's no backup of the old version."

"Then what about you?"

"I don't have any information about that. There's no backup of the old version."

Mandy breathed deeply in and out. It was odd, of course, that the station program hadn't been updated from Mount Brocken. But that still wasn't any reason to worry. The new version was obviously equipped with the right keys, because otherwise the Völkerfreundschaft wouldn't have accepted it. In principle, the space station could communicate with all kinds of ground stations via radio. It was just that this wasn't usually done because it led to additional costs.

The most likely scenario was something like this: Somebody had found a bug in the program that seemed serious enough that it had to be fixed as soon as possible. So a programmer got to work on it, and then no expense was spared to get the new version installed. It must have been a really serious error with a high risk potential if they couldn't wait another half hour to fix it.

But apparently the unfortunate programmer made a mistake. Mandy could just imagine the kind of pressure that person had been under. Up here there was a super-critical error while down there it was the republic's birthday and the programmer's family was waiting. A mistake was only to be expected, right? The result was that the radio system had sadly failed, and she could no longer reach the Mount Brocken station to complain about the malfunction.

Crap. What could she do? At this very moment, the technicians down there were probably already trying to identify the source of the problem. They would have noticed the error. They weren't alone, like Mandy was. And surely there were backup files from the previous versions in the central office, which was run by the Institute for Space Research. Then the technicians would just have to load the previous version, which had worked fine, onto the space station's systems. That was it. And correct the main error, of course.

Wait a second. She'd overlooked one little problem. Without a radio connection, it wouldn't be possible to reset the system back to its old state. Bummi had said they didn't have a backup.

Mandy unbuckled herself and floated up and down the

station. Surely such a small detail couldn't endanger her entire mission, could it?

She needed to calm down. She'd just imagined that whole scenario. The only thing that was certain was that the system had updated. Maybe that had nothing to do with the radio system failure. For example, maybe the antenna on the bow of the space station was defective, or a feed line to the antenna was broken. She should check that first.

And what if in the end none of this helped? That wouldn't be a problem, either. First of all, her replacement was due to arrive in less than two weeks. In addition, the landing capsule was still docked at the back of the space station. If no one came to her aid, she would simply get into it and travel back to Earth. The capsule had its own control program that would bring her safely to the Earth's surface. She might have a few lonely days in space ahead of her, but then she'd see her children again. That was certain.

"ARE YOU READY?" ASKED MANDY.

Usually, the robot would have been right behind her. She very rarely had to urge him to work.

"I have my doubts about whether this action will be useful," Bummi said.

"That's your prerogative. But regardless, you're going to help me now."

She'd managed to get into the spacesuit on her own before. She'd practiced often enough, even under the most adverse conditions. Once she'd had to put on the suit in the Siberian Taiga, at minus 21 degrees. But it would be faster if the robot held the top part while she slipped into it from below. Up here, the mass of the upper part wasn't the problem, as it had been during those exercises in Siberia, but the lack of weight. The whole thing would float away if she touched it the wrong way.

Finally, the robot made its way towards her. It lifted its two front arms and clamped the top of the suit between them. Mandy got on her knees and crawled underneath. Then she stretched her arms upwards and pushed herself in from below.

"There we go," she said.

She wriggled into the suit almost automatically. With Bummi's help, it took little more than 30 seconds. Without it, she could hardly have managed in less than three minutes. If the space station were to ever collide with space debris or an asteroid, hopefully the robot would be on the scene quickly, because otherwise the loss of pressure would kill her.

"What do you have against my looking outside for what might have caused this?" she asked, closing all the buttons and tabs.

"It's not necessary. I've checked the electronics. They're working perfectly. The voltages are exactly as they should be. And there weren't any collisions that could have damaged the antenna. You won't find anything."

"Well, so much the better. But I still want to see for myself."

"Of course, Mandy. I understand this aspect of the human psyche. It's based on the fact that your consciousness values sensory impressions more highly than information, even if both are equally reliable."

"Thanks for the psychoanalysis."

"The state-owned Robotron combine designed me with the goal that I be able to cooperate with people."

"They really adapted you to people? That's interesting. For all that, you misunderstand me pretty often."

It often took Bummi a long time to comprehend her intentions. Did that say something about her, or about the engineers' work?

"I have an internal model of the comprehensive socialist personality and am equipped with the insights of Marxist-Leninist sociology."

Bummi sounded really proud as it said that. Had they equipped it with that pride? But maybe they'd also made a mistake in humanizing the robot.

"I guess you couldn't do anything with an astronaut from the NSEA?"

"I have, of course, also been taught about the typical behavior of people from the non-socialist economic area. After all, there were plans for a rendezvous maneuver with an American Dragon space capsule."

"Were? Was the visit to the West canceled?"

That was supposed to be the highlight of her successor's time in space!

"I... I would assume it is likely to be postponed due to the current communication problems. I am not aware of any cancellation. I apologize if my statement gave that impression."

Bummi sounded like a teenager who'd been caught lying. But she couldn't prove anything, so she left it at that.

"Got it. Then let's start the extravehicular activity now."

"NICE AND SLOW. YOU'VE GOT ALL THE TIME IN THE WORLD!"

Mandy took in a deep breath. Ever since she'd closed the helmet, she'd felt a pressure on her chest. What could it be? This wasn't her first spacewalk, after all. She wasn't afraid of the dark and didn't have any trouble with the lack of spatial directions. Was it angina pectoris? She clutched at her chest, but through the gloves and rigid breastplate, she couldn't even feel her heartbeat. Bummi insisted that her readings were fine.

Then it must all be in her mind. Mandy hadn't even been cut off from the world for a whole day yet, and already it felt as if she were drifting alone in a spacesuit toward the sun. She reached for the carabiner on the safety line and realized just in time that she'd been about to undo the one she'd just attached. She knelt down, closed her eyes, and pictured the sun-drenched cornfield behind her grandparents' farm. She'd thrown her bike down by the side of the road and was picking cornflowers for her grandma.

Now she was breathing more easily. She was grateful to Bummi for not disturbing her. She braced herself again. She still had three meters to go before she reached the antenna. The junction box was just ahead. It looked like a rectangular wart growing out of the hull of the Völkerfreundschaft. This was where the power and signal cables emerged from the space station. Mandy crouched alongside the wart, then applied a screwdriver to the underside to pry off the cover. It was connected to the ship by a thin cord, so Mandy could just let it float.

The wart hid a mixture of relays, converters, and distributors that looked like blood vessels deformed by a cancer. Mandy applied the voltage tester to each of the wires, one after the other, taking special care not to scratch the insulation. As she looked at her work surface, she got the impression that any injury would lead to a lot of blood, which she pictured as being viscous and oily. She probably should stop imagining such things, but right now she couldn't help it. At least the crazy images distracted her from the present.

It would be better not to tell Bummi about it. Otherwise, with his knowledge of armchair psychology, he'd say she was insane and assume command. Was he capable of doing that? No one had ever told her, but it wouldn't surprise her. The Völkerfreundschaft space station was an enormous investment that had to be protected at all costs. She might ask Bummi under what conditions he could take over her command. But would he tell her the truth?

At any rate, the robot hadn't lied about the electronics. All the values were correct and corresponded perfectly with the specifications. Mandy repacked her tools and closed the wart. Then she looked at the sky. They were the same stars her children could see. Only they didn't twinkle, because there was no atmosphere; they appeared as fixed points of light superimposed on the inky background. Long ago, people had thought they were little holes in the celestial spheres and that the fire of the outside world was shining through them. Seen from up here, that idea seemed much more believable.

"Have you reached the antenna yet?"

Bummi must have noticed that the junction box cover was closed again. But from where the robot was inside, it couldn't see where she was.

"No, I'm still sitting around."

"Roger that. Let me know when you want me to start the antenna tests."

She didn't answer. The stars gave her a sense of security. Even over centuries, their places in the sky had only changed minimally. That was how she'd always imagined her father. And then he'd died suddenly. It had been a heart attack. It wasn't cancer that killed him, but his heart. But he would be proud of her. His daughter, a cosmonaut. *Take care, Dad.*

"Excuse me?" asked Bummi.

She must have said that last sentence out loud.

"It doesn't matter. That wasn't meant for you. I'm climbing ahead to the antenna now."

"Pan twenty degrees to the east," Mandy said.

"Pan twenty degrees to the east."

The antenna moved to the left.

"Back to zero position, then ten degrees in the direction of flight."

The metal bowl pivoted back, then another joint bent and it rotated forward.

"Does anything catch your eye, Bummi? Higher energy consumption, for example?"

"No, all values are nominal. The cause of the malfunction is neither in the electronics nor in the antenna itself."

"Why don't you send something?"

"What?"

"It doesn't matter. A photo from the MKF-8."

"At your command."

Mandy watched the antenna. It didn't move, but that wasn't to be expected.

"Transmission operation completed," Bummi announced.

"Good. How was the energy consumption?"

"Nominally corresponding to the transmit power."

"So somebody should actually hear us, right?"

"Yes, Mandy. We're not receiving any responses, though."

"Does that mean they're ignoring us?"

"That's an improper interpretation," the robot said. "All we know is that a signal is reaching the antenna. There may be a problem with the encryption. In order to create a communication channel, both sides have to agree on keys they can understand."

That was clear. If two people wanted to talk to each other, they had to use the same language. But why should this suddenly be a problem? It was more likely that there was a basic error. If one of the two people opened their mouth but didn't produce any sound, no conversation would happen. Mandy would have preferred that kind of error. It would probably be easier to fix—

easier than the operating program update scenario she'd come up with.

She took the thermometer out of the toolbox and set its sensitivity to the maximum possible value. It was actually for finding heat leaks in the hull. But she had another idea. She climbed forward carefully until she was right behind the antenna. She had to make sure not to damage the hardware. Mandy tied one end of a piece of string around the thermometer, attached the string to the edge of the antenna, and pushed the instrument so that it hovered over the antenna dish. When it was at about the center of the dish, she used the string to steady it in place.

"Repeat the earlier transmission, please," she said.

"The command has been executed."

"One more time, please. About ten times in a row, and at the highest possible transmission power."

"On it."

She was grateful to Bummi for not asking why. This time it took a little longer.

"The command has been executed," it said finally.

She brought the thermometer back in. The display had changed. The thermometer had gotten slightly warmer. Crap. She hurled the thermometer into the night. It flew until the string caught hold of it and it came to a stop over the antenna. So the dish really was working. It was giving off energy, as evidenced by the thermometer's increase in temperature. The Völkerfreundschaft space station wasn't just opening its mouth, but was emitting sounds. Either those on Earth couldn't or didn't want to hear them. But why would they want to break off contact with her all of a sudden?

MANDY CLIMBED BACK TO THE LOCK. SHE COULDN'T DO anything else out there. Bummi had in fact been right, but now she had confirmation. Unfortunately, the news wasn't particularly uplifting. If only there were something she could fix! She liked to take things into her own hands and alter the course of her own fate, but out here she was doomed to play a passive role. The only thing left for her to do was observe the Earth with the MKF-8. Maybe she'd find her children with it.

Otherwise, all she could do was wait and see. Her replacement would arrive in two weeks. She floated over the folded-up flower to the airlock, then opened the bulkhead and lowered herself into the narrow space. Once inside, she closed it and pressed the green button that filled the airlock with air. At 700 hectopascals, she started to loosen her helmet. The inner door would open in just a moment. 850 hectopascals. Almost normal pressure. She took off her helmet and turned the wheel that opened the inner bulkhead. One time, a second time, a third time.

Something tore her hand from the bulkhead.

"What...?"

Mandy couldn't breathe. The pressure indicator on the airlock wall was flashing red. Steam was billowing into the airlock in order to stabilize the pressure, but it wasn't enough. The room behind the airlock—no, the entire interior of the space station—appeared to be filled with vacuum, which was cutting off her air. Mandy turned around. Where was her fucking helmet? She'd put it down next to her, but the suction must have blown it away.

There! It was stuck on a bar at head level, just outside the airlock. The chin clasp had slipped over a projecting piece of metal. Mandy leapt. She had very little time. What had they been taught? Thirty seconds until she died? Her hands reached for the helmet. Fortunately, she hadn't taken off the rest of the suit yet. She slipped the helmet over her head. The hard edge hit her on the forehead, but she felt no pain. The clasp! It was hard to grip the two levers while she was wearing gloves. Where was Bummi?

Clack. Lever number one. She was already breathing better, but there was still whistling on the left. The helmet wasn't tight. She wiggled the lever frantically. She had to survive. Her children need her. Click. The helmet was closed. She was freezing cold, but sweat was coming out of all her pores. She'd made it.

"Bummi, what's going on? Do we have a leak?"

"I'm sorry. Three more minutes. The pressure was just normalizing."

"There isn't a leak?"

"There isn't a leak."

"But what happened? Why was there vacuum in the cabin?"

"I took advantage of your absence to de-aerate the ship. Since we'd discussed the problem of the increasing moisture."

"What? You did that on purpose?"

Was the robot trying to kill her?

"I didn't know you were coming back in. You didn't say anything."

It was true. She hadn't announced her re-entry to the robot.

"But why didn't the airlock warn me about the low pressure in the cabin? That should not have opened. At all."

"I disabled the warning. Otherwise, I wouldn't be able to de-aerate the station."

"Then you should have warned me!"

"I would have warned you, of course, if you'd let me know you were entering the airlock. I would have brought the internal pressure back to normal well before you'd come out of the airlock."

That sounded reasonable. She almost felt guilty about believing Bummi had tried to murder her. She ought to have communicated with the robot. That was something you learned in training. But the robot had also made a mistake.

"Phew, that was close," she said. "I really should have told you. But that goes for you, too! In the future, please tell me of such plans in a detailed and timely manner."

"Aye, aye," said the robot.

October 9, 2029, Jena

Tobias woke up by six. It wasn't because of the bed. The mattress was just the right firmness. There was hardly any traffic noise. Maybe that's what was missing. His bedroom at home faced a busy intersection with a tram stop, and he always slept with the window open. Here, he heard only the birds fussing outside in the garden.

He was anxious about the day ahead. That hadn't happened to him for a very long time. There was that one time, before the first day working his summer job at the transformer plant. He'd wondered how the workers there would treat a sixteen-year-old student. But he'd been surprised by how friendly they were towards him. Today, it wouldn't be so easy.

Tobias heard the sound of tires on gravel. It was 6:35 in the morning. Who was coming to visit this early? Twenty minutes later, the same sound roused him again. The visitor was gone, so that meant it was time to get up. Still wearing his pajamas, he padded barefoot toward the living room. The smell of coffee came from the kitchen. Miriam had her back to him and was putting rolls from a paper bag into a red raffia basket.

"Don't be startled," he said.

Oddly enough, most people didn't hear him when he was barefoot. He'd probably have made a good scout. Miriam turned around. She was dressed and had makeup on. Today she was wearing a black pantsuit with patch pockets. She'd tied her hair back into a braid, which made her look ten years younger.

"Good morning. Did you sleep well?" she asked, smiling at him.

"Very well."

"Then why don't you go take a shower? I left a towel out for you, the yellow one. Breakfast will be ready soon. I've already gotten us some rolls."

Excellent. So the day was getting started. It would be best to get the hard part over with quickly. Tobias headed back to the guest room and retrieved his hand phone. He took it into the bathroom with him, then sat down on the toilet. He breathed in and out quickly until he was really hyperventilating. Hopefully Miriam couldn't hear him! When he was almost at the point of passing out, he dialed the number of his supervisor at the Dresden-Mitte police station.

"Comrade Wagner, I'm surprised to hear from you so early."

"I... must... apologize, Comrade Mühlbacher. Yesterday... met old friend."

He didn't have to make any effort at all to make his voice sound ragged.

"You don't sound so good, Wagner."

"No. Drove with her... Jena. Night... too much..."

He'd said it. Now nobody could get on his case.

"I understand," Mühlbacher said, and Tobias could just picture him smirking. "No problem. Get some sleep. I know you can always be counted on. I don't think you've ever called in sick."

"Thank you, Comrade Mühl..."

"I'll let Schulte know and get him to take care of your precinct today. Just don't make a habit of it, all right? You know that just two weeks ago..."

Yes, Mühlbacher had already told him. He'd endorsed Tobias's promotion. As if it came down to him! It seemed he thought he carried some weight. Whatever.

"Must... hang up."

"Get well soon, Wagner!"

Done. Tobias put the hand phone in the pocket of his pajama pants, then sat down comfortably and did his business.

HE CAME INTO THE KITCHEN, FRESHLY SHOWERED AND IN uniform. Miriam was already sitting at the table and putting a slice of cheese on a roll. She looked him up and down.

"In uniform?" she asked. "Isn't that a little too conspicuous?"

"Today, we should make a visit to Ralf's office. You reported him missing, right?"

"Yes, that's right."

"Well, then it makes sense for a uniformed man to take a look around there. The only problem is this."

He pointed to the patch on his uniform jacket that said "Section Commissioner".

"I don't think my husband's colleagues know the section commissioner for the precinct where the plant is located. It's an industrial area, and they all live elsewhere."

"His coworkers don't, but anyone who works at the gate will certainly know who it is if they take their job seriously."

"Then I guess we'll have to get you past the gate so they don't see the patch."

"Do they know you?"

"Yes. I visited Ralf there frequently and went to company parties with him."

"The gate is to the left of the gatehouse, right?"

"Right."

"Very well. I'll drive, and it will be your job to convince them to open the gate."

IT WAS EASIER THAN THEY ANTICIPATED. MIRIAM WAS SO GOOD AT flirting with the gatekeeper that he paid no attention to Tobias. She even learned something potentially important: Her husband had left the premises on the afternoon of October 4 in his company car, a gray Wartburg 554. The gatekeeper even remembered that there had been a rectangular, black briefcase with gold-toned clasps on the passenger seat and a silver thermos next to it. But Miriam's husband hadn't told the gatekeeper where he was headed.

"Now go to the right," Miriam said.

"The thermos..." said Tobias.

"Ralf always takes hot coffee with him when he's got a long

car trip ahead of him," said Miriam. "He hates the Minol coffee at the rest stops."

"So he had a long drive ahead of him."

"That's what it looks like. But where was he going? And why didn't he say anything to me?"

"Maybe he had a mistress."

"No, he would have told me."

"Has he had one before?"

"Yes, like I already said. And why not? I think he needed it for an ego boost. But he always came back to me. In the last two or three years, though, it's gotten too tiring for him."

"You must have an unusual relationship."

"You think? Because he would tie me up or because he screwed other women?"

Tobias felt himself growing warm. Miriam grabbed him under the chin. He only noticed now that she was wearing thin, black gloves. They seemed almost decadent. His head was smoldering.

"You're cute when you blush like that. You're bashful, like a little boy."

"I... uh..."

"Stop!" she shouted.

Tobias slammed on the brakes, and the Passat came to a screeching halt.

"Sorry. Here it is," said Miriam.

They were standing in front of a single-story, low-rise building that was probably thirty years old. So this was where a National Award winner worked?

"Can I leave the car here?" he asked.

"Yes, your colleagues don't monitor the company site."

He got out, paused, and looked around. For such a large operation, it was rather quiet.

"Now come along," Miriam said.

Tobias walked around the car. He wasn't all that sure he wanted to find anything. It would be nice to drive around with Miriam all day and wonder what his life would have been like if he'd put his name on those letters back then. Would Miriam really have become the wife of a People's Police officer? Or would he himself have won the National Award? Maybe they would have separated after the initial infatuation wore off. That seemed to him the most likely scenario. He really was far too dull for her.

RALF'S OFFICE WAS LOCKED. TOBIAS WAS RELIEVED AND READY TO call it quits when Miriam triumphantly fished the key out of her purse.

"Why didn't you ask me?"

"I... don't know."

"Hey, you're my criminal detective. I need your skills."

The door opened inward. Miriam wanted to go inside, but Tobias held her back.

"Hold on," he said.

He took a rubber glove from the inside pocket of his uniform jacket and put it on. Then he knelt down and wiped his index finger across the linoleum.

"Dust!" he said. "Apparently nobody's come into the office since Ralf left."

"That may very well be. He was very particular about that."

"But aren't there any cleaning personnel?"

"They were only allowed in when he was here, ever since somebody got some documents mixed up ten years ago."

Tobias entered the room cautiously. Yellow curtains hung in front of the windows, filtering the sunlight. The desks were bathed in a warm glow. It looked very autumnal. He could imagine the countless papers scattered across the tables, shelves, and floor changing colors and curling up.

"Your husband was certainly a fan of paper," he said.

"Well, as I mentioned before, his eyesight isn't so great. He has everything printed out in large type."

Paths wound through the stacks of paper. One of them ended at the desk on the left. Tobias pushed the chair forward a little and saw a shoe print in the dust.

"Look!"

He compared it with his own shoes. It must be about size 42.

"What size shoe did your husband wear? Sorry, I mean, what size does he wear?"

"Thirty-nine to forty."

"That's small."

"Yes, though that doesn't say anything about the rest of his body."

"But it does say something about a visitor who must have come in here when he was gone. Maybe we ought to start up his computer. Do you think that will get us anywhere?"

"I don't know his password, if that's what you're getting at."

"Birthdays, first names..."

"No, that won't work. He was always complaining about the Stalinist administrator who required him to create a new password every four weeks. It had to have at least one digit, one capital letter, and one special character."

"How annoying. But it seems your husband printed out everything he worked on." Tobias pointed to the shelves. "It'll take us days to go through all that."

"I know he always kept the most recent papers near his desk. When he started a new project, he'd swap the last one out."

The stacks of paper were in fact shorter the further they were from the desk.

"Then we should start with his desk."

Tobias sat down in the chair, then systematically went through all the papers scattered on the table. Some were even written out by hand. He handed them to Miriam, who could decipher Ralf's writing. It quickly became apparent that any kind of systematic approach was a waste of time.

Dr. Ralf Prassnitz had apparently worked like a volcano. The center of the eruption was the monitor; from there, the papers flowed slowly outward, spreading over the copious impressions from earlier eras, obliterating past findings, squelching old hopes, and setting fire to so many ideals. At any rate, that was how some of the rebuffs he'd sent to the top brass at the ministry read. As a National Prize winner, he could obviously afford that kind of honesty. The jug could be taken to the well until it broke, as Tobias's grandmother used to say. What if Miriam's husband had kept making enemies until there were just too many of them?

That was silly. That would be a good reason for giving him the boot. There was always someone next in line who wanted the job at all costs. It certainly wasn't smart to mess with everyone, but it didn't lead to death. At most, to a shunting station in the archives.

Tobias stopped. He decided he wanted to take a look at the computer after all. Ralf had surely printed out something that might still be found in the cache: railway tickets, room reservations, complaints to state officials, or even a goodbye letter. But if anybody entered the wrong password three times, the administrator would know.

In between the edge of the desk and the computer in the center, there was an area that had the air of a no-go zone about it. Instead of files, dust covered the pale wood and the green plastic desk mat.

"This must be where the files that he took with him were," Tobias said.

"I'm afraid so," Miriam said. "Now what?"

"Maybe there's some interesting information contained in all those papers."

"I've got a better idea. Ralf was always complaining about the printer here. Sometimes he'd bring extra work home to print out."

"You mean we'll find a lot of stuff on the computer at home?"

"No, he must have set out with papers from the office. The printer he was complaining about didn't work properly. The printed pages kept coming out crumpled. The paper feed was unreliable."

"Ah, then maybe we'll find some leftovers in the paper trash. Where's the printer?"

"It's at the end of the hall."

TOBIAS OPENED THE OFFICE DOOR CAUTIOUSLY. THERE WAS NO one outside. Why was it so empty in here? In a movie, the trap would always shut the moment the hero noticed that it was far too quiet. Tobias turned around again, but there really was no one here but them.

"Back there!" Miriam said quietly.

She didn't seem particularly comfortable either.

"Do you have any idea where everyone is?" he asked.

"No. Maybe at a meeting somewhere. It is a little odd, though. Usually there are about twenty people working here."

"We should be quick."

The printer was a model made in the West. Tobias couldn't repress a certain sense of satisfaction that the class enemy wasn't so different from them, after all. Next to the output tray was a pink plastic wastebasket. It was full of crumpled papers. Tobias crouched down and dumped out the contents.

"All right, we'll each take half."

He set the wastebasket in front of him and reached for the first piece of paper. Prassnitz and his colleagues' rejects from the printer made rustling noises as he and Miriam uncrumpled them. But which ones were relevant? They threw out keywords to each other.

"Combat group deployment plan," Miriam said.

Tobias shook his head. "Too many witnesses. Brigade logbook."

"Nah."

"Statement of accounts," Tobias said.

"He had to write one every week," Miriam answered. "Expense report, Deutsches Haus inn."

"When?"

"A week ago. So that one's out."

She threw the paper towards the basket, but she missed and it hit his forehead. Tobias laughed, and she joined in. Solving a case with Miriam was fun.

"A symposium on imaging techniques in agriculture," he said.

"When?" she asked.

"Next week."

"I remember. His boss wanted to send him there. He was supposed to give the opening address. He really didn't want to go."

"But it doesn't have anything to do with his disappearance?"

"He didn't hate the idea so much that he'd rather disappear altogether. He liked performing."

"A letter to an institute," Tobias said.

"Which one?" asked Miriam.

"Institute of Landscape Planning and Design."

"Never heard of it. That wasn't really Ralf's wheelhouse. What did he write?"

"Unfortunately, it's just the second page. There's no address.

He asked to be called back immediately. Here, it says: '... I will do all I can to end this farce. I will wait for you to call me back. It's urgent.' Jena, October 3. The signature area is blank."

"He did have to reprint the page, so that makes sense," Miriam said.

"If he's even the one who wrote it. How many people work here and use this printer?"

"I recognize that tone. Ralf knew that he had something special and knew what he wanted. That's what I've always found so attractive about him. Some people are very different in their private lives than they are at work, but he's consistent."

"The comprehensive socialist personality."

"Ha ha. He's actually not a party member."

"In his position, is that possible?"

"He always said that when he ran out of scientific ideas, he'd join the party, but not before that."

"He's a pragmatist."

"You could put it that way. And what about you? Are you in the party?"

Tobias heard a rustling noise. He stood up. Behind the printer was a large window with a curtain, which he just barely moved to the side. There were people coming up the street. They were maybe fifty meters away.

"We've got to go."

He put the letter to the institute in the pocket of his uniform and they frantically refilled the wastebasket. Two pieces of paper escaped and sailed to the ground.

"No time," Tobias said. "Come on, let's get out of here."

He dragged Miriam behind him.

She stopped in front of her husband's office.

"Don't. We need to get out of here."

"I have to lock up!"

She pulled out the key, slid it into the lock, and turned it twice to the left.

"Let's go," he said.

They walked briskly to the exit. They encountered two men and a woman by the door.

"Hello, Miriam. What are you doing here?" the woman asked.

Then she obviously noticed the People's Police officer behind

Miriam and took a step back. The two men also made room for them.

"I was showing Comrade Chief Commissioner Ralf's office."

Chief Commissioner. Hopefully the woman wouldn't know any better. Tobias stood next to Miriam so that his section commissioner badge wasn't visible.

"Oh, what's happened to him?" the woman asked.

"Nothing, Sharon. Everything's fine," Miriam said.

"Do any of you have information regarding Comrade Prass-nitz's whereabouts?" asked Tobias.

"I haven't seen him since last week," the woman said. "But I wasn't worried, since he works at home a lot."

"Yes, exactly," said the shorter of the two men. "He wasn't there for Republic Day either. The whole research department usually marches, of course."

He must be the department's party secretary.

"Of course, Comrade," Tobias said. "And what about you?"

He looked at the taller man, who scratched his nose. This was a typical sign that someone was about to lie. At least that was what they'd taught them at the police academy. Tobias had avoided scratching his nose ever since.

"I think I saw him on Sunday. He was with the combat groups," said the man.

"Ah, thank you. Of course, that makes sense," Tobias said. "I thank you, in the name of socialism. I certainly don't want to keep you from your work any longer."

They squeezed their way past the group and out onto the road. Since the three were still watching them, Tobias sat in the passenger seat this time. In front of the gate, he waved out the window with his peaked cap. The gatekeeper understood the gesture and lifted the boom barrier. A police van pulled up to the entrance on the other side of the street, and a policeman and a man in civilian clothes got out. The gatekeeper let them into the hut.

"Who were those three?" asked Tobias.

"One of them was Sharon. Ralf had a thing with her, but she doesn't know that I know. The shorter man was the deputy party secretary, and the taller one was a college friend, Jonas, who Ralf brought in two years ago."

"Seems like a nice guy. He even lied for him."

"It was more for me. I slept with him a couple of times."

Miriam was focusing ahead on the road as she said this. A hint of a smile played on her lips, but nothing more. Maybe she was teasing him, or maybe she was thinking back to better times.

"I'll have a bratwurst," Miriam said.

The vendor seemed to be in no hurry. But they were the only customers, after all. He leaned over the counter.

"Hot, medium, or sweet mustard?" he asked.

"Hot."

"So the lady likes it spicy." The man grinned and smoothed his white apron. "And for the gentleman? Pardon, for the comrade, I mean. Of course."

"A grilletta[1], please."

"With letcho[2] or ketchup? The letcho is homemade, and the ketchup from a state-owned enterprise…"

"Letcho."

"Of course, Comrade. So a bratwurst and a grilletta. Coming right up. That makes three marks fifty."

Tobias was about to take his wallet out of his inside pocket, but Miriam beat him to it and put a five-mark bill on the counter. It was the new series with the portrait of Honecker.

"Here, keep the change," she said.

"*Danke, die Dame.* Please wait for your order to be ready."

The man was trying to speak High German but couldn't hide his Thuringian accent. Tobias took his place standing at one of the three tall tables. A fresh breeze was blowing, and he pulled his uniform jacket tighter around him. Miriam had made a cardigan magically appear from her purse. They were in a parking lot on an arterial road connecting two industrial areas. It seemed that the snack bar made money mainly during the lunch break, which wouldn't start for another hour.

"This institute…" Tobias started.

"The Institute of Landscape Planning and Design," Miriam said.

"Have you ever heard of it?" he asked. "Did Ralf talk to you about it?"

"We often talked about his work, but he never mentioned

that particular institute. It doesn't really match his professional interests."

"Was he maybe going to have your garden redesigned?"

"We never talked about that. I like our garden the way it is."

"What if it was going to be a surprise, like for your wedding anniversary, maybe?"

"No, Ralf isn't like that. He might have given me crazy expensive jewelry or taken me on a luxury trip. But definitely not a garden makeover."

"Your order's ready!" the snack vendor called out.

"Hold on, I'll get it," Tobias said.

"Please bring another seltzer."

"Of course."

The vendor held out the bratwurst and grilletta to him. Both were arranged on paper plates. Next to the bratwurst, the man had drawn a symbol with the mustard. It could have been a heart. The grilletta was practically swimming in letcho.

"I'll bring the seltzer to your table, Comrade Constable," the clerk said.

"Lieutenant, if you must."

"Oh, my mistake."

Tobias balanced the food as he made his way back to their table. Fortunately, it was just a few steps. The vendor came out of the side entrance of his truck and set the seltzer bottle down on the table. Then he set out cutlery for them, along with a napkin for his two customers.

"That's service," Miriam said, pressing a coin into his hand. Tobias assumed it was a one-mark piece.

"*Sehr gern, die Dame.*"

They'd have to be careful what they said. The vendor could hear them all too clearly, and it would be unfortunate if he unofficially worked for the company.

"Then enjoy your meal," Tobias said.

Miriam took the hot sausage between her thumb, index, and middle finger, then dipped the tip into the mustard and shoved it into her mouth. But she didn't take a bite. She only licked the mustard off.

"Why are you looking at me like that?" she asked. "Do you want to try some? It's good Bautzner mustard[3]."

She held out the end of the sausage to him. Tobias shook his head. He was blushing again. Miriam laughed. She obviously enjoyed provoking him.

"I don't like mustard," Tobias said.

He sounded a bit like the killjoys from childhood that nobody liked. Tobias took his grilletta—a roll with a slice of grilled ground pork—in both hands. The bottom of the roll was dripping wet from the letcho. If he brought it to his mouth like that, he'd stain his uniform. He put the grilletta back down. It looked silly, but he ate it with a knife and fork. At least that spared his uniform.

For a few minutes, they chewed in silence. They shared the seltzer. Whenever Miriam had taken a drink from the bottle, he could taste her lipstick afterwards. He positioned himself so that his back was turned to the food truck.

"So, this institute," he said, more quietly than before.

"Do you think it had something to do with Ralf's disappearance?" asked Miriam.

"It's the only lead we've got. Whatever's going on there had him pretty fired up."

"Ralf can be very stubborn when something rubs him the wrong way."

"Then we should definitely ask around there."

"What does Bergblick have to say about it?"

Tobias wiped his fingers on a paper napkin and took his hand phone out of his pocket. It showed four bars. The Postnetz[4] wasn't that good everywhere. Maybe the state-owned Carl Zeiss had applied pressure in this region. Tobias entered the name of the institute.

"I can't find an institute with that name," he said. "There's only a professor for landscape planning at TU Dresden."

"It's strange that, given all that's planned there, it doesn't even have a location?"

"Just because Bergblick can't find it doesn't mean it doesn't exist," Tobias said.

"I know," Miriam said.

"I could look in the electronic police archives."

Oh boy. Tobias broke out in a sweat. How could he possibly make such a suggestion? A private search in the People's Police archives! If that were to come out, he'd lose his section commissioner badge.

"You'd do that? Wouldn't that be dangerous for you? I don't want to get you into trouble."

"I... no, it's just a harmless inquiry. Don't worry about it," he said.

But in truth, he wasn't so sure about that. In the GDR, nobody just went missing. Certainly not somebody who had won the National Prize. Dr. Prassnitz must have gotten himself into some serious trouble. If it had anything to do with this institute, Tobias was well on his way to winding up just like Ralf. Wouldn't it be wiser to let it go? If Miriam's husband had gotten caught in a tough spot somewhere, they would have no chance of getting him out anyway.

But if he were to say that to Miriam, there was only one possible response: She'd ask someone else and go on with her search. And he'd never see her again.

"Whatever you say," she said. "But please be careful. We don't need you running into trouble too."

"Hold on. This'll just take a second."

He switched the hand phone to service mode. This way, it could access any radio network, even those not operated by Deutsche Post, but by one of the Western corporations that had obtained a license for the East German territory. All data traffic was encrypted and routed through computers run by the Ministry of the Interior. To proceed, Tobias had to identify himself using a fingerprint.

The screen background changed to black, red, and gold, and the available applications changed. Tobias started the address query and entered the name of the institute.

The words "Protected entry" appeared on the screen.

"Dang it, my user tier is too low," he said.

"What does that mean?" asked Miriam.

"This institute definitely isn't involved with landscape planning."

"What, then?"

"There are a lot of options. Too many."

"Is it run by the Stasi?"

"Not necessarily. It could also belong to the People's Army or the external sector. You still can't think of what your husband might have been involved with there?"

Miriam sighed. "I'm sorry, but all he ever thought about was his multispectral camera. That was his life's work. I don't see why he would take issue with a landscape design institute."

Miriam put the last bite of bratwurst in her mouth, chewed, and swallowed. She licked the remaining mustard off the card-board. Then she wiped her mouth with a napkin and burped.

"Sorry," she said. "All that carbonation from the seltzer."

"Then I guess we've reached an impasse," Tobias said.

"That's what it looks like." She slumped over, but then imme-diately sat back up again. "Maybe Jonas knows more about it."

"Jonas?"

"That nice colleague who lied earlier."

"But would he tell us the truth?"

"Jonas trusts me. He was just intimidated by your uniform. The best idea is to invite him over to my house this evening."

"You were going to drive me back to Dresden. I can't be sick tomorrow, too."

"Then we'll leave after Jonas comes over."

WITHOUT HIS UNIFORM, TOBIAS FELT LIKE HE WAS IN DISGUISE. But Miriam had insisted that he wear one of her husband's suits so that it would be easier for Jonas to trust him. The black pants were quite snug and a little too long. The shirt, on the other hand, was pleasantly wide at the collar. Tobias was sweating because Miriam really wanted to see him in the jacket, even though the wood-burning stove was lit and additional warmth came from the candles on the coffee table. It was already dark outside, and the curtains were drawn. It was really too bad that they were waiting for somebody else to arrive.

Miriam was wearing a red dress that he thought looked Asian. It had a high collar but emphasized her figure.

"Very elegant!" he said.

"It's a qipao. Ralf brought it back for me from a business trip to Shanghai."

Ralf must be a dream husband. He obviously knew his wife's exact dress size and also what her tastes were, which was prob-ably even harder to figure out.

The doorbell rang. That must be Jonas. Miriam went to the door. A bell chimed. At the same time, the hand phone in his pocket vibrated. Tobias took it out. Nobody showed up on the caller ID. Worse yet, it didn't show any phone number at all. Only Stasi employees could hide their own number. Tobias was about to reject the call, but if he didn't take it, somebody else might be showing up at the door before long.

"Wagner here."

"Comrade Wagner, glad you're up and running again."

It was Schumacher, from the Stasi. Tobias should have guessed it. His heart started beating faster.

"Thanks, I'm feeling a little better already."

"Well enough, in any case, for you to make an address query."

He could have guessed that, too. His search for a secret location had obviously set off alarm bells somewhere. Tobias took a deep breath. There was nothing the Stasi could accuse him of. But the fact that his searching for an institute that didn't officially exist had caused such a reaction confirmed that they were on to something. He just didn't know what it was, and Schumacher would be the last person to tell him.

"I overheard the name somewhere," Tobias said, "and it piqued my curiosity."

That was a very, very weak excuse. He knew it, and Schumacher did too. But Tobias was counting on nothing happening to him as long as he didn't breach his obligations.

"A great criminal detective, Comrade Wagner. Congratulations. Maybe you should apply to work for us. We always need scouts for the cause of peace."

"I'll think about it."

"You have my recommendation."

"Thank you, Comrade Schumacher."

"But I also want to recommend something else to you, in the spirit of our long-standing friendship."

"Of course, Comrade Schumacher."

"Whatever it is you're trying to get your hands on, leave it alone. There are forces at work you know nothing about. That institute is even above my user tier."

So Schumacher had tried to find out more about the institute, too. He was just as curious as Tobias.

"Interesting," Tobias said.

The Stasi man laughed. "I looked up what you were interested in, of course. But I've learned one thing here: Don't ever mess with things above your user tier. I like you. We have good conversations. I still have two years until retirement and I don't want to have to get used to another section commissioner in your precinct. Understood?"

"Understood, Comrade Schumacher."

"In my report, I'll note that you typed in the name in by mistake."

"Thank you, Comrade Schumacher."

"You don't have to thank me. I'm doing this because I have enough work to do as it is, and I'm counting on you to listen to my urgent warning."

"Of course, Comrade."

"By the way, thank you for your tip about the People's Solidarity club on Comeniusstraße."

"Don't mention it."

"Comrade Krenz's portrait was still defaced when we conducted our inspection. We took the opportunity to find out that the deputy club leader had employed his office's copy machine for personal use."

"Tobias, may I...?"

Miriam appeared in the living room doorway with Jonas in tow. Tobias covered the microphone of the hand phone and shook his head violently.

"Ah, you're visiting with a lady, Comrade," the Stasi man said over the phone. "Go on and allow yourself a little distraction. Then you won't get any stupid ideas."

"Thank you. I will, Comrade Schumacher."

There was a cracking sound on the line and the call ended. Tobias switched off the hand phone. He opened the back and took out the battery.

"Who was that?" asked Miriam. "Was there a problem?"

"It was just the Stasi. They noticed that I searched for the institute."

Jonas took a step back as if he wanted to escape, but Miriam held him back.

"I'm sorry to hear that," Miriam said. "I'm assuming that means trouble?"

"So far, no. I haven't done anything illegal or anything. But I've been given a very clear warning to keep out of it."

"Are you going to back off, then?" asked Miriam.

"So far, I don't even know where exactly I'm supposed to keep out of."

Miriam looked at him gratefully.

"I wanted to introduce you to Jonas Schieferdecker," she said.

Jonas, who had mid-length, curly hair and a prominent chin, had dressed up for the occasion. He came towards Tobias and shook his hand.

"Pleased to meet you," he said.

Was that true? Jonas was holding a bouquet of red roses in his left hand. When she'd invited him over, Miriam probably hadn't told him that he wouldn't be the only guest. But Tobias couldn't see any resentment in his face. His smile was friendly and frank.

"Pleased to meet you, too," said Tobias. "Tobias Wagner. I'm from Dresden."

"The man in uniform from this morning."

"Exactly. But I'm not here on official business. It's purely personal."

"Because of Miriam," Jonas said.

His smile was contagious. Tobias nodded. Of course he was here for Miriam. He and Jonas would get along fine.

"Could you be so kind as to inform me what your work...?"

"Guys, let's keep it less formal, okay?" asked Miriam.

"Sure thing," said Jonas.

"Of course. I'm a section commissioner for the German People's Police."

"Tobias and I went to school together," Miriam explained. "I asked him for help because he has a few capabilities that I don't. He's absolutely reliable."

"Thank you, Miriam," Tobias said.

Because I've completely fallen for you. Even if it wasn't clear to me for so long.

"I'm a colleague of Ralf's," Jonas said. "I am very grateful to him. He brought me into his department and now I'm able to conduct world-class research."

"You should know that Jonas doesn't have an established class point of view," Miriam said.

Jonas laughed. "I come from a religious home. It wasn't

exactly easy to get into physics. But I never would have made it into Ralf's department if he hadn't helped."

And in return you sleep with his wife. But Ralf must have known about it, just as Miriam had known about his affair with Sharon. The two must have had a strange relationship. Have a strange relationship, he corrected himself.

"Can you tell us about a certain Institute for Landscape Planning and Design?" asked Tobias.

"Let's sit down first," Miriam said. "We'll have a toast, and then we'll get to work."

Tobias settled down on one side of the loveseat, with Jonas on the three-seater sofa across from him. Miriam took her place in the armchair between them. The loveseat was wonderfully comfortable and smelled strongly of leather. There were three wine glasses on the table. Miriam poured some wine into each one from a bottle that was already open. They toasted.

"Here's to both of you," Miriam began. "I really appreciate your trying to help me find my husband."

This was crazy. Miriam had her lover and her high school crush there to help her track down her husband. Tobias took a sip, but immediately put the glass back down. He still had to drive tonight, even though he could hardly imagine getting behind the wheel in an hour or two.

"That goes without saying," Jonas said. "I'm afraid I can't tell you anything about the institute, though."

"Then Ralf must have been dealing with it on his own," said Miriam. "Have there been any problems at work lately that might have something to do with this institute?"

"There were always problems," said Jonas. "It was especially chaotic before Mandy Neumann went up into orbit, but we actually recovered pretty well from that."

"Mandy Neumann?" asked Tobias.

"You don't know about our GDR cosmonaut?" asked Miriam.

"Ah, yes, I do. I'd forgotten her last name."

"She took the MKF-8 with her in the capsule when she went up to the Völkerfreundschaft. She set it up on the space station and took the first photos with it," said Jonas. "It all had to be ready for the republic's eightieth birthday, and that was really nerve-wracking. It's not possible to postpone a rocket launch."

"But the troubles passed," Tobias said.

"Exactly. With one exception," said Jonas.

"Now it's getting interesting," Miriam said, leaning forward.

"There were problems with the analysis software. The MKF-8 is a multispectral camera, so it photographs many wavelengths simultaneously. The images have to be processed first. There's a program that does that."

"And it didn't work?" asked Miriam.

"Actually, it worked too well."

"How can something work too well?"

"There are areas in our lovely republic that should remain hidden from the public eye."

Jonas raised a finger to his lips dramatically.

"Oh no. And my husband's new miracle camera showed them?"

"Yes and no."

"What do you mean?" asked Miriam.

"The MKF series always had excellent resolution. So the cameras could be used to detect secret military installations or missile launchers. But the competent authorities know where such sensitive locations are. So we lowered the resolution for those areas. All we needed were the exact coordinates."

"You forgot those coordinates for the MKF-8," Tobias said, taking a wild guess.

"No, what are you thinking? Ralf wasn't that dumb. That actually would have been pretty easy to fix."

"So what was the problem, then?" asked Tobias.

"With the MKF-8, for the first time it's possible to see through a cloud cover. Ralf was very proud of that. It uses a combination of wavelengths that are scattered just a little or not at all by clouds, and then it calculates the rest with a clever extrapolation system."

"I'm sure that really drove up the price of the MKF-8 in the West," Tobias said.

"Absolutely. We could have sold them for twice the price of their predecessors. The KoKo[5] paid us a visit almost every week. They really wanted to sell them. It was going to be the Class I National Award this time."

The Kommerzielle Koordinierung was in charge of trade

with the West, and since the discovery of oil, it had become an enormous machine.

"But?" asked Miriam.

"There were authorities in the state apparatus that weren't happy about that."

"What kind of authorities?" asked Tobias.

"They didn't identify themselves."

"The Stasi, then," Tobias said.

"I thought so, too, but the Stasi contact where we work had never heard of them, either. He could have been lying, of course, but they treated him pretty condescendingly. That's why I'm inclined to believe him."

"Oh no, did Ralf stand up to them?" asked Miriam. For the first time, Tobias saw a hint of fear on her face. "I wouldn't put it past him. He's very particular about his research results."

"No, we got together and decided to solve the problem using the analysis software. After all, the MKF-8 is in space now, so we can't get at it."

"So there wouldn't be any reason at all to make Ralf disappear, then," said Tobias.

"Right. Up until Wednesday, we were still working on the programming. The whole department—except Ralf."

"What was he doing?" asked Miriam.

"He wanted to analyze the images that the MKF-8 provided without our restricted version of the program."

"Then he must have found something he didn't like."

"Yes, Miriam, that's what it looks like."

"We should take a look at those images," Tobias said.

"But how will we get hold of them?" asked Miriam.

Jonas reached into the pocket of his pants and pulled out a small device that looked like a flash drive.

"I was thinking it might come in handy," he said. "Here are the original images."

Miriam set her laptop on the living room table and logged in. Then she turned on the huge RFT TV and established a wireless connection.

"Here," Jonas said, handing her the flash drive. "You need a viewer for the special image format. I also saved that on the drive. All you have to do is run the program."

Tobias intently followed as Miriam's mouse clicked around on the TV screen. A dialog with a bar steadily lengthening across the screen opened up.

"The program is analyzing the stored data," Jonas explained.

The bar was full, and a button below it turned green.

"Just click on it," Jonas said.

A satellite image appeared on the television. Jonas stood up and pointed to a jagged line at the top.

"This is the Baltic Sea coast. Here's the Rostock district, and somewhere down here at the edge of the screen is the border with the Schwerin and Neubrandenburg districts. Zoom in."

Miriam enlarged the image. Now it was possible to better distinguish forests and fields.

"One more time."

A lakeshore appeared on the TV screen. There was a jetty with something lying on top of it; it could have been a whale or a boat. Based on the context, Tobias deduced that it was a boat.

"There's more," Jonas said.

Miriam clicked further into the shot. Tobias had to reorient himself. Now the boat reached from the top to the bottom of the screen. There were two paddles lying inside. There was a bucket on the stern, and in front of the stern was a bench. On top of that was a cushion and something shiny. A knife.

"Wow," Tobias said. "No wonder the company's interested in this."

"You'd be surprised, but interest was actually limited," Jonas said. "I suppose our technology is too unwieldy for their purposes. After all, the MKF-8 first has to be aligned with the target, and the signal processing is so slow that motion sequences can't be recorded. It's only possible to approach a particular object without too much effort once a day. They get what they need much more easily with their flying cameras."

"But my husband is gone."

"Yes, when they realized what the MKF-8 could do when there's cloud cover. The resolution is one order of magnitude lower, but that doesn't seem to be important."

"Maybe there's something they've always wanted to see,"

Tobias said. "Something secret in the West. Some advanced weapon that they don't want any GDR citizens to know exists."

"But then why did they request that the images be filtered?" asked Jonas.

Tobias shrugged. "Why don't we take a look at the whole republic?"

Miriam zoomed back out and slowly moved the section downward. *Southward, Dummkopf!* was what his geography teacher would have said. Berlin came into view, with the Oder-Neisse peace border on the right and the western border on the left. He could see Potsdam, Magdeburg, and Cottbus. But then a gray patch came into view. South of the district capital of Cottbus and the small town of Spremberg, west of Weißwasser, a trapezoidal area had been cut out. It looked as if there were a single piece missing from an otherwise completed puzzle.

"That's got to be the petroleum development area," Tobias said.

That part of Lusatia had been a restricted area since the oil discoveries of 1987. Officially, it was said that the area was too unsafe for the public. But everyone knew it was the site of great environmental destruction. Allegedly, something had gone wrong with the initial drilling and the groundwater was contaminated. The clouds that constantly spewed from of the smokestacks and darkened the sky were visible proof. But since the oil provided the GDR with much-needed foreign currency, which benefited everyone, there were no serious objections.

"Yes, that's more or less the restricted area that was taken out here," Jonas said. "May I?"

He pulled the computer towards him and zoomed in on the border. A gray ribbon of road appeared on the TV screen. Two guards, soldiers from the National People's Army, were standing beside it. Behind them, all the image data was missing.

"That's must be where the barrier is," Jonas said.

"Was Ralf the one who removed the missing data?" asked Miriam.

"Your husband was the last person to access the data before me. I could see that."

"Then I'll assume he has it with him. He wants to sort out something related to this data, and he's gone where he thinks there's a possibility that the situation can be resolved."

"To this Institute of Landscape Design and Planning," Tobias said.

"Whatever an institute like that could have to do with it," Jonas said.

"So now we're back to the drawing board," Miriam said, rubbing her temples. "We can't find the institute. Apparently it's so secret that not even the Stasi knows about it. So how are we going to track Ralf down?"

"Is he driving his company car?" asked Tobias.

"I think so."

"Do you know the license plate number?"

"NGM 4-94. What are you going to do?"

Tobias pulled his hand phone out of his pocket, put the battery back in, and turned it on. Then he switched to service mode. Yes, Schumacher had expressly warned him. But mightn't a driver have recklessly overtaken him after he'd gone off duty? A section commissioner was always on the job. So he'd have a good reason to look for the number.

Except, of course, that it was a National Award winner's company car. Tobias talked himself into believing that if he were to access the archive again now, he'd be blamed, no matter how the story ended.

"I knew it was smart to ask for your help," Miriam said.

"Do you want to run an owner query?" asked Jonas. "We know who owns the car, don't we?"

"No, I'll match the number with data from the tollbooths. Then we'll know where he went, at least approximately."

"Is this somehow dangerous for you?" asked Miriam.

He shook his head and was secretly pleased that she was worried about him. But the idea about the tollbooths was just too tempting. Maybe he should apply to work for the criminal investigation department after all. He launched the motor vehicle database. Such queries always took time. After all, there were entries for several million vehicles and their movements, at least if they used the freeway. The tolls were debited directly from a driver's account.

His hand phone vibrated. The answer had come faster than he'd anticipated.

"A4, exit 91, Weißenberg."

He read it out loud. Jonas immediately pulled out his own hand phone and opened the map application.

"Exit 91 is directly south of the section that's missing from the map," Jonas said. "From there, it's another 45 kilometers to Weißwasser, which is right on the border."

"Finally, a solid lead." Miriam slapped the tabletop with her half-open hand. "Thank you, Tobias, I really appreciate that. And thank you, Jonas. We wouldn't have figured this out if we hadn't had the MKF-8 data. Well, now I guess I've got to pack."

"What are you going to do?" asked Tobias.

"I'm going to drive there. He's bound to have left traces of some kind. Someone must have seen him."

"It's a restricted area. You won't be able to get in."

"We'll see about that."

"If they catch you, you'll go to Bautzen[6] for years."

"I'm aware of that. But I can't just abandon Ralf. He would do the same for me."

He was jealous of the sense of determination that she gave off. But Ralf also had it good. Not because he was a National Award winner, but because this woman's heart belonged to him. Tobias had never known such loyalty.

"I'll go with you," Jonas said.

"I'm coming too," Tobias said.

He was nuts. His upstairs wiring seemed to have burned out. If he went with Miriam, he'd wind up in prison, just like she would. But it would be worth it to him. That thought alone proved he was no longer sane.

"That's very nice of you, boys, but..."

He'd lucked out. She wanted to make this journey alone.

"... I would rather have you, Jonas, here in Jena, at the plant. This all has something to do with the MKF-8, and after Ralf, you're the one who knows it best. I'd like to be able to call you and ask for advice."

"As you wish, Miriam. I'm always here for you."

"That's great, really. As for you, Tobias... I feel terribly guilty saying this, because it's going to throw your life completely off track. But I'd love to take you up on your offer. I think I could really use a qualified criminologist."

"Criminology was a minor. I'm just a simple section commissioner."

"And so modest. Well, I think it's great that you're in. I never would have had the heart to ask you myself, but I'll gladly accept your offer."

"I'm glad," Tobias said.

And it was true, though he was also terrified.

October 9, 2029, Earth orbit

"I'M GONNA CATCH YOU!" SHOUTED MANDY.

Sabine ran across the playground, jumped over the edge of the sandbox, and blew past the swing. Mandy was chasing her, but tried to give her daughter a bit of a head start.

"Don't get me!" shouted Sabine.

But where was Susanne? Sabine had reached one of the benches where parents usually sat to watch their children play. Today they were empty, and the three of them were the only ones on the playground. Sabine was making a beeline for the little soccer field with the iron goalposts that hadn't had nets for a long time. Mandy started to cut a corner.

"Hey, no cheating!" Sabine shouted.

According to her own rules, Mandy always had to follow the very same path her daughters took. She began running a little faster and closed the gap between her and Sabine. In a few years, this wouldn't be so easy for her anymore. Sabine reached the goalpost and threw herself dramatically onto the grass like a goalkeeper chasing a ball.

"Gotcha!" Mandy shouted. As she did so, she hit her forehead on the low bar of the goalpost. She toppled over like a felled tree. The pain was unbearable.

It grew quiet. Mandy felt blood running down her forehead. It trickled very slowly, but it still made its way to her eye, which was closed. Something told her that she ought to open it. She expected to see the lawn extending to the sky on the horizon and her daughter coming over to stroke her forehead.

But all she saw in front of her was a shiny metallic surface with a red spot about the size of her palm. A thin trickle of blood ran down from it. This wasn't a dream. Something was wrong here. Something very wrong. That trickle shouldn't be flowing, and the blood shouldn't be reaching her eye. Mandy wiped her forehead. Now her fingers were bloody. Dang it. She pushed herself off the wall to float towards the control panel, but her body only swayed slightly. She was caught in a net. She was filled with panic until she realized she was in her sleeping bag.

But that was also unusual. Normally, she couldn't feel the sleeping bag at all. It only served to protect her from the draft. The space station was no longer in free fall. It must have started to accelerate. That was the force that had pressed Mandy against the sleeping bag, and it had probably made her hit her forehead on the wall, too.

Mandy let the dream with Sabine go, even though it was hard for her, especially now. She quickly opened the sleeping bag, but paused before unfastening the last two buttons. It was a good thing, too, since she was hanging upside-down near the front of the cabin. Though there hadn't been any spatial directions before, now with the acceleration there was up and down. Mandy turned to the wall, grabbed a crossbar next to her chest, and held on to it as she undid the last buttons.

Suddenly, she fell. Mandy was startled, even though she'd known it was coming. It was a kind of fall she couldn't compare to anything she'd experienced on Earth. Her lower body moved in slow motion toward the bow of the station. Mandy stretched the arm she was using to hold on. Her body seemed to be around one-tenth of its normal weight. That meant the braking acceleration must be about one-tenth of a g. She used her other arm to climb up towards the stern.

This was insane. She'd always imagined the cabin as cylindrical, with a ceiling and a floor and with the bow in front and the stern in the back. Now she was suddenly suspended in a tower, and what had been the stern before she'd gone to sleep was now the top of the tower, while the floor and the ceiling had turned into the walls of the tower. Fortunately, the station's engineers had anticipated situations like this and equipped the walls with handrails that she could use like ladders.

She paused alongside one of the portholes. At least she could still see the Earth. It didn't appear to have come any closer, so its gravitational pull was still having a constant effect on the space station. Sabine and Susanne were down there somewhere. She recognized the chain of Japanese islands. No, not there.

The Völkerfreundschaft was still flying with the bow in front. The engine was in the stern. If someone had powered it on, the space station would have accelerated. Then the stern would be down and the bow up. In order to brake with the engine in the stern, the space station would have to be turned 180 degrees first. But that obviously hadn't happened either. So it couldn't be the engine that was slowing the space station down. There must be another cause.

Mandy kept climbing until she reached the control console. Where was Bummi? The robot was nowhere to be found. She looked up to the stern—the top of the tower. The passage to the space capsule was closed. Maybe Bummi was in the airlock, or had gone outside and was trying to figure out what had gone wrong. She hooked her feet under the control console. Then she pulled herself to the seat anchored in front of it on the floor, which was now a wall. Because of the new spatial directions, she'd have to sit on the backrest. It was confusing as hell, and it was unusual to work like this because she wasn't sitting in front of the screen but over it.

She activated the external transmitter. Bummi would hear her if it were crawling around on the hull.

"Mandy here. Where are you?"

"I'm reporting from an urgent extravehicular activity. We have a problem."

"I noticed. Why didn't you warn me?"

"That wasn't a priority at that time. We are losing altitude rapidly. There's a risk that we'll re-enter the Earth's atmosphere. That has top priority."

"I see. What happened?"

"We have a leak in the oxygen tank. The gas is escaping under high pressure against the direction of flight and slowing down the ship."

That sucked. Without oxygen... She didn't want to think about it.

"Can you do anything about it?"

"I'm already repairing the damage. However, it's a big enough job that I'll need about 34 more minutes."

"Is there anything I can do to help?"

"I don't see any way for you to do so. By the time you get out here, I'll have already finished the repair."

She really was lucky that Bummi was on board. In the event of an emergency, it could immediately leave the ship through the airlock, without having to put on a spacesuit and prepare for extravehicular activity.

"Have you figured out what happened yet?" asked Mandy.

"I haven't determined the exact cause. But it's clear that the oxygen tank has two holes in it. There may have been a collision with some space debris."

"But if there are two holes, then why is the acceleration one-sided?"

"One of the two holes is on the hull. The gas comes out and is immediately redirected."

"So the debris pierced the tank and then just fell down on the outer hull? That seems unlikely."

The oxygen tank had a very stable casing, which the debris should have penetrated twice. Mandy couldn't wrap her head around the possibility that the outer hull of the station could have stopped it.

"You make a good point. I'm assuming that the piece came in at an angle, causing it to be deflected off the outer hull like a stone thrown flat across the water. That's probably what saved your life. I still need to run through the scenario with the actual data, though."

"Well, I should start by thanking you. But really, why wasn't there an alarm? I didn't wake up until I hit my head."

"I registered the impact immediately. An alarm was therefore no longer necessary. It would only have caused you unnecessary panic."

It appeared they still had work to do on their communication.

"Next time, I'd rather decide for myself if I'm going to panic."

"Understood, Mandy. I'll include it in my premise."

"Good, please keep me posted on how the repair is coming along."

MANDY CHECKED HER WEIGHT AGAIN BY HANGING FROM A rung. She still weighed around one-twentieth of what she normally did. Bummi was clearly making good progress with the repair. The escaping gas was slowing down the Völkerfreundschaft only half as much as it had been right when she'd woken up. She'd really had some bad luck!

What did the main computer say? She called up the current orbit parameters. The space station's almost circular orbit had dropped about 50 kilometers. That wasn't the end of the world. It reduced the station's lifetime to one and a half years. After that, it would burn up in the atmosphere. But she didn't want to stay up here that long anyway. Plus, the space capsule docked in the stern had enough extra fuel to raise the station 20 kilometers. That would be something for her to take care of before landing back on Earth.

She switched over to the resources overview. There was enough water and energy, but the tank had lost too much oxygen. The display read ten percent. Mandy converted it to kilograms and wasn't pleased with the results at all. She needed about 800 grams of oxygen per day for mild exertion. There were only 3.5 kilograms left in the tank. There were additional oxygen tanks in the station and in the space capsule that might give her an additional 24 hours.

It was going to be close. Her replacement was scheduled to arrive in just over two weeks. So the new cosmonaut would find her corpse. For her own sake as well as that of her children, she couldn't let that happen. She forced herself to breathe more slowly. She needed to keep calm, because she'd use up the precious oxygen even faster if she were to panic. *It's really not that bad.* She just had to somehow get the ground station to understand the situation she was in. The rocket that would transport her replacement into space was surely already standing by in Peenemünde. And if need be, she'd start the return flight to Earth on her own. If the automatic system didn't work anymore, the capsule had a manual control system that she'd been trained to use. Somebody would realize that she was on her way back to Earth and fetch her from the Kazakh desert, which the GDR used as a landing area.

THE TOWER HAD TURNED INTO A HORIZONTAL TUBE AGAIN. Mandy would never again complain about sleeping poorly due to a lack of gravity. She'd dressed the wound on her forehead and washed up. Then, finally, she'd had her breakfast.

There was a hiss from the back. Mandy pricked up her ears. That must be Bummi coming back from its repair mission. The robot made its grand entrance, surrounded by steam as it climbed out of the airlock. The oxygen supply display, which she still had open, twitched briefly and then dropped a bit to the left. Of course, when using the airlock, some oxygen was always lost to space. Unfortunately, the Völkerfreundschaft had no biological life support such as algae, which could produce oxygen from carbon dioxide and light.

Bummi quickly approached her and raised its arm menacingly at head level. Mandy backed away.

"Just a second," it said. "That cut on your forehead hasn't been properly dressed."

The robot opened its hand. A camera was installed in the palm, and Bummi moved it slowly over the wound.

"If you don't want any scarring, it should be stitched up," it said.

"No, I just can't. I won't put a needle through my own skin."

"I'd be happy to do it."

"So were you trained as a medical robot?"

"I have emergency paramedic training. This includes stitching up extensive wounds."

"All right, then. We'll do that tomorrow."

Mandy hated operations and even getting shots. For her, the worst part of cosmonaut training had been the constant blood draws.

"We'd better do it right away. Otherwise, I'll have to open up the wound closure that will form overnight, and with such a fresh wound, that could be painful."

BRANDON Q. MORRIS

"Okay, let's get it over with."

As they were speaking, Bummi's rear limbs were already fetching the necessary implements. Now they passed them to the front.

Mandy felt sick when she saw the sewing tools.

"Be sure to hold still," said Bummi.

"I can't promise anything. If it hurts, I might flinch."

"Then I'd better make sure that doesn't happen."

One of its limbs moved behind Mandy's back. It touched her spine with its claw and slowly worked its way up. Mandy got goose bumps.

"Stay calm," said the robot.

Another claw was coming towards her eye. Only at the last moment did Mandy see the needle that the robot was holding between its fingers. She wanted to pull her head back, but Bummi was holding it firmly. The needle touched her skin, pierced through, then pulled the thread back out. It was a horrible feeling, but she was surprised at how little it hurt. Probably because she was in shock.

"Good. Wipe yourself off and we'll be done," Bummi said, handing her a damp cloth.

Mandy carefully stroked the stitched wound with it. It burned.

"Ouch!" she said.

"Sorry. I should have told you it was a disinfectant. Better safe than sorry."

"Yes, you should have. Generally speaking, you don't give me enough information about what you're doing on the ship."

"I will make internal changes to my priorities. However, when there are emergencies, eliminating the cause of the emergency always comes first."

"But you must be able to keep me informed while you're solving the problem. Aren't you capable of multitasking?"

"I can handle multiple tasks simultaneously. However, depending on the urgency of the problem, I may focus my resources on the most important task, which is to save your life. I hope you can understand that."

"I do. Speaking of saving lives: What do you think my chances of survival are?"

"Well, I assume that the vital signs, both for the station and your body, are still reaching ground control."

That sounded good. Didn't Bummi have any other good news for her?

"You mean they know I'm running out of air, even though we can't communicate with them anymore?"

"This data is transferred using a very basic layer of the station's operating program. It's like a person in a coma. The higher functions are suspended, but the life support still works."

"Are you sure about that?"

"I know how the space station's control program works. It's highly unlikely that the unsuccessful update would affect the hardware-dependent layers. You can see that the lights are still on and that the wastewater is being recycled. These deep layers take care of that."

"You didn't answer my question."

"Well, I can't be sure, of course, because I can't ask. But the rationale speaks for itself."

"What do you think I should do now?"

"Nothing, Mandy. You should just wait. The replacement will be here sooner than you think. I'd expect it will take a day or two. The breathing air will definitely last that long. The new capsule will bring along its own communications system. Then we'll be back in contact with the ground station and you can safely conduct the Earth landing."

If only the robot were right! How could it be so sure when they had no contact?

"I have to admit that it's hard for me to not do anything."

"Then I guess your quest on this mission is to learn how to do nothing."

October 10, 2029, Lusatia

"TIME TO GET UP, TOBIAS. AND REMEMBER TO PUT ON YOUR uniform."

Miriam was standing next to the bed and pressing his shoulder. It was still relatively dark. She hadn't turned on any lights, so it must already be dawn outside. Yesterday they'd agreed to leave as early as possible. That way, he might even be able to show up at his office later.

However, he didn't think that was particularly likely. It would take them two and a half hours to reach exit 91. Then it was about an hour to the restricted area, and Ralf wouldn't just be waiting for them there. If they wanted to track him down, they'd probably have to find this institute. And what if Ralf was there of his own free will? Miriam had calmed Tobias down, though. Her husband would never have left her alone for so long without checking in. But there was nothing they could really be sure of, at this point.

"All right, see you soon," Miriam said and left the room.

He got out of bed. It was cool in the room. There were freshly-laundered clothes on the chair in front of the bed. Tobias smelled them. He didn't recognize the detergent. It was probably from the West. He took off his pajamas and slipped into the underpants. They were a little too big and were made of silk, which felt amazing against his skin.

Tobias went into the bathroom and peed. Then he took the underpants off again and got into the shower. He desperately needed some time to himself so he could think. But that was a luxury they couldn't afford right now. Did Schumacher already have Tobias's latest archive query on his desk? He hadn't complained about it to him yet. But maybe this time there would be no complaint and he'd just be arrested. He shouldn't have handed Mario Schuster over to the commandant's service. Why in the world did that occur to him just now?

"Do you have everything?" asked Miriam, who was in the driver's seat.

Tobias touched his head to check for his hat, which he tended to leave behind. Then he felt his breast pocket for his wallet, which had his service ID. Finally, he made sure he had his service weapon, which was hanging in its brown case on his belt.

"It's all there," he said.

They'd made the joint decision that he'd wear his uniform on the journey. If they came across a barrier gate, maybe it would help them to continue onwards. He'd just have to come up with an excuse.

Miriam pulled out of the drive. Tobias turned around and noticed that the gate was closing automatically. He'd never see this house again. The thought gave him a tickling sensation in his throat, though there was no reason for it to. He drew in a sharp breath and inhaled a few of Miriam's odor molecules. They left his head wonderfully clear. It all made sense. They'd find Ralf, even if that deprived Tobias of any chance to give it a shot with Miriam. He wasn't the right man for her. That was Dr. Ralf Prassnitz, National Award winner.

They passed a sign that pointed to the freeway. Miriam ignored it. Did she know a quicker route? At the next intersection, she also drove straight ahead instead of in the direction of the freeway entrance.

"That would have taken us to the freeway," he said.

"I know," said Miriam, "I was thinking that we'd better take the back roads. Yesterday, it was easy for you to figure out where Ralf was going. We'd better avoid leaving traces like that."

"That won't be easy," he said.

"It'll take us at least an hour longer, but apart from that, I don't see any problems."

"There aren't cameras only on the freeway. They're in the cities, too. At all the intersections, traffic is constantly monitored, and you can get a ticket for running a red light. The same goes for major thoroughfares."

"Is there some way we can avoid the cameras?" asked Miriam.

"It would be difficult. If just one picks us up, that would be enough."

"But only if it's near our destination."

"Right. Then we should take care once we reach Dresden. It's not suspicious for you to be taking me back there, after all."

At the next intersection, Miriam turned towards the freeway.

WHEN TOBIAS WOKE UP, THERE WAS A HAND STROKING HIS KNEE. He looked through his half-closed eyelids and tried not to let on. Then Miriam spread out her index finger and thumb and pinched. His leg twitched.

"Yikes," Tobias said. "What's wrong?"

"I had to wake you up, unfortunately. We're just outside Dresden."

"Good. Do you want me to drive now?"

"No, it would be better if you help me navigate. Ideally so that no camera catches us."

"Sure. I know my way around Dresden, but when we get further east we'll have to plan our route in advance."

"How?"

Tobias pulled out his hand phone and held it up.

"Do you have a map with all the cameras in there?" Miriam asked.

"Unfortunately, no. But I can get readings on a particular license plate that will show me everywhere it's been recorded."

"And how will that help us? We don't want to get caught on camera, do we?"

"We'll pick a bus route that runs at least part of the way we're going. I'll check the bus license plate, and then we'll know where the cameras on that route are. Then we can avoid those."

"That sounds like a good plan. But still, we've got to consider that as we go around the cameras, we could, of course, run into others."

There was one other consideration. He'd have to use his phone in duty mode again. He'd need to come up with an excuse. He hoped that his current position wouldn't be detected in duty mode.

"That is a danger, Miriam. We can minimize it by avoiding traffic lights."

"Fine. Tell me where to go, and I'll drive."

"Well, why don't you take the next offramp?"

"The Wilder Mann exit?"

"The Wilder Mann exit. Then I'll guide you through the allotment gardens, and we'll look for the first bus route."

THE FIRST PART WAS EXHAUSTING. HAD THERE ALWAYS BEEN traffic lights at every intersection, even the most insignificant ones? He had no choice but to guide Miriam first over the Hellerberge and then through the Dresden heath. They drove on sand and dirt roads that were closed to through traffic, but at least nobody could take pictures of them there. This early on a Wednesday morning, there were no hikers on the road yet.

Before they got on the F6 south of Großerkmannsdorf, Tobias checked the Passat again. The car had picked up a lot of mud from the heath. That was a good thing—the license plate was barely visible. The bumpy terrain was good for something after all.

Once on the major road, first they took the Dresden-Bischofswerda bus route. Away from the urban sprawl around Dresden, the landscape changed, and so did the villages. The houses looked grayer; instead of traffic lights, there would just be a crosswalk in the middle of a village. The bus with the license plate number they were following had been automatically clocked only seven times up to Bischofswerda. Two of those times were in the vicinity of Rossendorf, where the Central Institute for Nuclear Research was located.

They bypassed the district capital of Bischofswerda by going through two industrial areas and a residential area. Now they were following a bus route that ran from Neustadt to Bautzen via Bischofswerda. Bautzen wasn't far, but the city itself was a problem. They made a long arc towards the north until Tobias found a road on the map that led directly toward the restricted area. It took them to the little village of Uhyst.

Tobias looked at the map again. The road dead-ended at a lake that blocked the direct route. There was a beach on the map.

"Let's take a short drive to the beach," he said.

"Sure," said Miriam.

"Over there on the right."

They drove over a narrow bridge. Tobias pointed to a sign directing them to the beach parking lot. There was just one lone Trabant along the edge. It looked so old that it must be a decommissioned National People's Army vehicle.

It was windy outside, and Tobias buttoned up his jacket all the way. He should have brought the coat with him, too. Behind the parking lot was a wide strip sparsely planted with gray-green bushes. It looked almost like the Baltic Sea coast, except that here the dunes were completely flat. A path led towards the sandy beach. On the left was a wooden jetty that extended far into the lake. Tobias pointed to a sign: to the right was the nudist beach and to the left was the dog beach.

"Neither of those today," Miriam said.

They walked forward through the pale yellow sand. Even though it was cold, Miriam took off her shoes. Surely it would be far worse to walk over the sand in those pumps than in his black uniform shoes. They were practically alone. On the right, where the nudist area started, was a low, blue tent, and its poles rattled in the wind. The lake was choppy.

"That's where we need to go," Tobias said, pointing to the other shore.

It was an intriguing spectacle. On the other side of the lake, cooling towers alternated with drilling towers. The cooling towers must belong to the old lignite-fired power plants. It had been years since any lignite was mined there, but the cooling towers were still in operation and belched out thick, white clouds. What were they cooling? It was surely all top secret. The drilling towers provided a stark contrast. The metal constructions were almost elegant and reminded him of the Eiffel Tower. Some of them had a flame waving at the top like a flag. Dark gray smoke rose from almost all of them. The light-colored clouds from the cooling towers and the dark plumes of smoke combined in the sky to form a dense, ominous layer that seemed to glow from within.

"It looks eerie," Miriam said.

Tobias had never been near the oil fields. Now he had a better understanding of why environmentalists protested them. The restricted area was the GDR's version of hell. The sun never shone, and when it rained, sulfuric acid came down from the sky.

"That's where we want to go?" he asked.

"There's no question of wanting," said Miriam. "But we've got to. I've got to. I would understand completely if you decided to turn back now. It would just be nice if you could drive me to the border."

"We've made it this far, so we'll make it the rest of the way."

"I hope you're not underestimating it. I'm sure the restricted area is secured."

No, he didn't underestimate the problems ahead of them. He imagined the restricted area was hardly less secure than the national border. The armed forces didn't take kindly to intruders. They'd need courage but also a lot of luck to get in.

But first they had to find out where exactly they wanted to go. The restricted area measured about 30 by 40 kilometers, or 1200 square kilometers. Ralf Prassnitz could be anywhere in there.

"We need a destination of some kind," he said. "And an excuse would be good, too. A reason why we're both permitted to enter."

"It's clear what our destination is: this strange institute that nobody outside knows about. Where else would it be? A restricted area is the best place for something that needs to be kept secret."

"Yes, that makes sense."

"But I'm skeptical that an excuse will help us. I'm afraid we'll have to force our way in."

Miriam was pressing her lips tightly together. She meant it.

"Force our way in? Are you crazy? I'm sure the National People's Army is guarding this area."

There had to be a more discreet and less dangerous way!

"I'm not so sure about that. It doesn't look particularly appealing to outsiders. Who would try to sneak in there willingly?"

"Curious delinquents?"

"A fence and a sign that says 'Shooting range' ought to deter them, don't you think? I lived near a military training area when I was a kid. It was fenced off like that, too. We did inspect the fence, but the signs were very effective at keeping our curiosity in check."

His own curiosity was now so great that a mere fence wasn't going to stop him.

"We'll see, Miriam. The best thing to do is to drive completely around the restricted area first. Let's find out where the access road is."

THE RESTRICTED AREA LOOKED INTIMIDATING FROM ALL SIDES. They drove through the tiny village of Bärwalde to Neustadt, which was just as small. Tobias' stomach growled. It was already early afternoon.

"Should we get something to eat somewhere?" he asked. "I'm hungry."

"Sure. I'm hungry too."

"The Hammer or Sorbisch Barn?"

"Excuse me?"

"In Neustadt I see two restaurants. One is called 'The Hammer' and the other is 'Sorbisch Barn.' Both are traditional cuisine. Your pick, Miriam."

"Sorbisch Barn."

"Looking at the pictures on the Kybernetz, the garden around The Hammer looks nicer."

"Then just say you'd rather go there."

"Let's go to The Hammer, then. Left onto Schmiedeweg, then on until Dorfstraße, left again onto a little street called 'Hammer,' past Sorbisch Barn, and there it is."

THE INN LOOKED JUST AS GOOD IN REALITY AS IT DID IN THE photos. Yet Tobias feared it would be too late to get any food. It was already past two, the typical time for kitchens to close, at least in a rural area.

The beer garden wasn't covered. But it would be too cold to eat outside anyway. The innkeeper, a small, stocky woman with curly hair, welcomed them into the rustic tavern. In one corner sat two old men drinking beer and playing chess. Across from them, a boy who looked about ten was doing homework. The school satchel next to him gave him away.

"Sit wherever you like," said the innkeeper.

Miriam headed for a table by the window directly over-looking the beer garden. The innkeeper brought them cutlery and a menu.

"You two look like you're hungry," she said.

"Yes, we were hoping to get something before the kitchen closed," Tobias said.

"It's not like that around here. I do the cooking myself. You just have to be a little patient. Can you wait for half an hour?"

Tobias' stomach growled loudly, and the innkeeper laughed. She didn't seem to have any particular respect for his uniform.

"Your son?" he asked, pointing to the boy.

"Thank you for the compliment. No, he's my grandson, of course. His mother works in the zone."

"The zone?"

This was actually a pejorative term for the GDR that Tobias sometimes heard used by resentful visitors from the West, who refused to understand that certain rules applied in the GDR.

"The restricted zone. It's just a few kilometers from here. A dark country where an eternal twilight reigns. You must have seen it by now. Where'd you come from?"

"Dresden."

"But not on vacation, right?" She tapped the flaps on his shoulder.

"No, we have to take care of something in Weißwasser. Doesn't it bother you, having the restricted zone right next door?"

"No, we make a good living off of it. All of them in there need sunshine every now and again. It's not usually so empty here. But it doesn't fill up until four, when the first ones get off work."

"To have a beer on their way home?"

"No, most of them live inside. I couldn't do that, that constant twilight! But they can leave any time, and the pay is very good. They always tip well, anyway."

Tobias' stomach was growling again.

"Now take a look at the menu. I'm an old chatterbox, and I don't want to keep you from eating."

Tobias would have liked to continue the conversation. They still knew far too little about the restricted area, or the "zone," as they might call it here. But he was also pretty hungry. Fortunately, it was easy for him to make his choice, because what he wanted was right at the top.

"I'll have the schnitzel," he said.

"Me, too," said Miriam.

"No salad?" asked the innkeeper.

"A cucumber salad to go with it, please," Miriam said.

"And for you?" the innkeeper asked Tobias.

"Just the schnitzel."

"I see, a true gourmet. A drink to go with it?"

"I'll have a beer, please," he said.

"Me as well," said Miriam.

JUST A LITTLE LATER, THERE WERE TWO RADEBERGERS ON THE table. Tobias and Miriam clinked their glasses together. The beer would make him sleepy, but he really wanted one.

The meal took a lot longer. But when the innkeeper served it, Tobias knew it had been well worth the wait. The schnitzel's breadcrumb crust was perfectly rippled. The fried potatoes were crispy on the outside, soft on the inside, and well-seasoned. That was all he needed. He put the half-lemon on the empty plate.

When they'd both finished eating, the innkeeper reappeared.

"You ate everything. Good job," she said.

"It was really very good," Tobias said, and Miriam nodded.

"Are there enough jobs in the zone?" asked Miriam. "I always thought that oil extraction was automated."

"I've never been inside," the innkeeper replied. "But a few

thousand other people have. Otherwise there wouldn't be three inns in Neustadt that could live off business from it."

"And your daughter?"

"She comes home every night. She's got Timo waiting for her, after all. The two of them live with me here in the house, and sometimes they give me a hand on the weekend."

"That's nice," said Miriam. "I wonder if that would be something for me. My job is pretty demanding, I'm an executive assistant, you know, and the pay... it's a racket."

"To the best of my knowledge, there are several businesses in the zone where you might have the opportunity to work as a secretary."

"I'm especially good with scientists. That's what it's all about in Weißwasser right now."

"Scientists. Hm. I think there's an institute somewhere in the zone. I don't know what it's called, though."

"Would your daughter know?"

"I don't think so. But if she did, she wouldn't be allowed to tell me. They make a pretty big deal about their secrets there."

"What about security?" asked Tobias. "I'll bet there are kids who try to sneak into the zone."

"Oh, what gave you that idea? No way. Everybody knows it's dangerous. The zone is haunted. It's only safe on the official roads because that's where the security unit is watching and will come get you if things get bad."

That was silly. The woman had watched too much "Spuk unterm Riesenrad[1]." Schulte had told him that the ninth season had just started on DDR 2. But Tobias had to admit it was strange that those dense clouds stayed right over the restricted area.

"That sounds creepy," Miriam said.

"Well, it doesn't affect us. We've got it a lot nicer out here anyway, so why would we try to go in there?"

"Nothing's happened to your daughter yet?"

"No. If you see her, don't tell her what I told you," the innkeeper whispered. "She says it's a fairy tale. Everything in the zone is hunky-dory. But I think she has to say that."

It sounded like the daughter had some sense, at least.

"So has she ever taken your grandson to work with her?"

"No. She said that's strictly forbidden. I think she just doesn't want to put him in danger."

Tobias's cell phone vibrated in his pocket. When he took it out, it automatically switched to service mode. That wasn't good. His hand was shaking as he identified himself with his fingerprint.

"Are you okay?" asked Miriam. "You're so pale."

"Wasn't the schnitzel good?" the innkeeper asked.

"Yes, everything's fine," said Tobias, standing up and leaving the restaurant.

HE WAITED UNTIL HE WAS OUTSIDE TO ACCEPT THE CALL, WHICH had been made with a hidden number, just like last time.

"Schumacher here," the Stasi man said in a menacing tone. "You sure did take your sweet time!"

"Lieutenant Wagner," he replied. "What can I do for you?"

"I have some very, very bad news for you."

"Oh."

"Right, oh. You shouldn't have done what you did. I warned you!"

"I... sorry!"

"That won't help now. The horse has left the barn. I can't do anything more for you."

"But..."

"No buts. You have to come see me today. Let's say six p.m. And bring all the evidence you have."

"And what if I don't?"

"Are you crazy, Wagner? I should dishonorably discharge you for that question alone!"

You can't do that, Comrade. I'm a member of the Ministry of the Interior, not the Stasi.

"I'm telling you loud and clear: if you don't report to me at Bautzner Straße by six, I'm going to take action. Your file tells me that your son just started his honor service with the National People's Army. I really do hope he won't have a harder time there than absolutely necessary. After all, he was assigned as a radio operator, but the motorized troops could always have an urgent need for him."

Poor Jonathan. He'd been so happy to join the radio operators. Day-to-day life with the motorized troops was surely a lot harder. Just the idea of running in full gear after an armored vehicle... But Schumacher wasn't done yet.

"Your daughter has already been picked up twice at the train station at night with a group of antisocials. So far, this hasn't had a negative effect on her. We know that you transmit your established class point of view to her. But if that ends up no longer being the case, I'll have to make a note to that effect."

What a bastard. He was using Tobias' children against him. But that should have been clear from the outset. He wasn't alone in the world. What he was planning to do with Miriam could end up harming his children. At least his ex-wife was fortunate enough to be able to plausibly distance herself from him. Hopefully, she wouldn't stand by him for old time's sake. It would be best if his children were to completely disassociate themselves from their father.

But that wouldn't help either. He was the one they were after, and the children were just hostages. He had to stop all this and go home.

"Wagner? Still there?"

"Yes, Comrade Schumacher. I'll be knocking at your door at six p.m."

"Very good. I'll be waiting for you."

TOBIAS SIGHED AND PUT THE PHONE BACK IN HIS POCKET. HE'D been caught by surprise when his little rebellion had begun, and it was coming to an end just as quickly. As he went into the restaurant, he was hanging his head. Miriam came to meet him.

"Is there a problem?" she asked.

"There sure is."

Tobias looked around and slowly walked back to their table. There was the sound of dishes clattering. That must be the innkeeper in the kitchen. Her grandson had finished his homework and was now focused on a game on his hand phone, wearing headphones. The two men were still brooding over the chessboard. The positions of the pieces didn't appear to have changed very much.

They sat down across from each other.

"What's going on?" asked Miriam.

"The company is on to us. I have to report to the Stasi headquarters in Dresden at six p.m."

"Oh." Miriam raised her eyebrows and frowned.

"They'll probably keep me once I'm there. They said I should bring my evidence."

She reached for his hand. "I'm so sorry about that. What if you don't follow instructions?"

"Then they'll cause trouble for my son in the army and put my daughter in jail the next time they catch her under dubious circumstances."

"Shit. Those creeps! What did your daughter do?"

"Nothing. She spends time with people who don't quite fit with the socialist image of humanity. But she's going through puberty, and that's always when kids withdraw from their parents. It doesn't mean anything!"

He should have thought of that. He was putting his children in danger just because of his hormones!

"Oh, God. I wish I hadn't asked you!" Miriam buried her head in her hands. "But I didn't know you had kids, just that you were divorced. You didn't tell me about them."

"Yes, that was stupid. I wanted to keep them out of this whole business, but it didn't work."

Even worse. He'd never even once thought about them.

"That's what it looks like. Now what?"

"There is good news. They only called me in and didn't say anything about you. So they don't seem to be on to you. If you go back to Jena now, you'll still get out of this mess. I certainly won't say anything about you."

"Not even if they blackmail you again by threatening your children?"

"Not even then."

That was easy enough to say, of course. But they didn't know anything about Miriam.

"That's really great of you, Tobias, but that's not what I want." Miriam was nodding her head as she spoke. "I don't want to be responsible for anything bad happening to your children. It's not their fault."

"But I can't..."

"Of course you can." She stroked his cheek with her hand. "In fact, you have to. If they ask you, tell them everything."

"What about you?"

"I'm going to get a room here. Then tomorrow I'll set out for the restricted area."

Miriam wanted to go through with it alone. Now he should be worrying about her, but his concern for his children prevailed over everything else.

"I'll have to take your car to get to Dresden by six. They don't seem to have any idea where I am. But then you won't have a vehicle."

"I'm sure the innkeeper will lend me a bicycle. It's just a few more kilometers from here. A bicycle is a lot less conspicuous anyway."

"Okay. That sounds wise. So going back to Jena isn't an option? I could take you with me to Dresden. Then you could drop me off at Bautzner Straße, go home, and never be associated with this whole matter."

"Oh, it would be naïve to think that. Since I'm Ralf's wife, I'll automatically be suspected of being complicit in whatever Ralf's done. And if that's the case, I at least want to get something out of it."

"Okay. Then I'll be heading out now," Tobias said, standing up.

Miriam also got up. She opened her arms and pressed him against her. Then she gave him a kiss on the mouth, but she moved back quickly. He shrugged his shoulders helplessly. Miriam smiled.

"Here's my car key," she said, "I hope you have a nice trip."

ON THE WAY BACK, TOBIAS NO LONGER ATTEMPTED TO AVOID THE cameras. What was more important now was to get to Dresden on time. He parked the Passat discreetly at the Weißen Hirsch and took the tram the rest of the way. He was ten minutes early when he reported to the gate of the Stasi headquarters. The guard took down his personal details and kept his service card.

"You'll get this back when you leave the building," he said.

"Thank you, Comrade."

"In the event that you do leave."

"That's what I'm assuming."

"Just a little joke. Ha ha. Of course, we're all just people here, right?"

A buzzer sounded and the revolving door started to turn. Tobias expected that once he'd made it past, he'd be searched, but that didn't happen. He stood alone within the Stasi headquarters as if he were a free man. Only he didn't know where to go. So he knocked on the back door of the gatehouse, and the guard opened it.

"Ah, don't you know where you're expected? Hold on."

He checked something and then returned.

"You see that building there? There on the second floor, room 208."

"Thank you."

Tobias ran towards the building that the security guard had pointed out to him. Several employees in uniform and many others in civilian dress were heading towards him. They were probably just getting off of work, since it was 6 p.m. Schumacher was working overtime because of him! His case must be especially important. Tobias reached into his pocket. He didn't have any evidence with him, apart from his hand phone.

THERE WAS NO NAME ON ROOM 208, AS WITH THE OTHER ROOMS. Hopefully the security guard had been right. Tobias knocked.

"Come in!"

Tobias recognized Schumacher's voice. He opened the door and was surprised to see how cramped the room was. If the offices were assigned based on importance, Schumacher must be something of a lightweight. On the phone, he always acted as if he were the deputy minister. The room was just big enough for a desk along with an armchair and two chairs, one of which was occupied. But not by Schumacher. The Stasi man was sitting in the armchair, facing the door. Tobias had never seen him before, but this was exactly how he'd imagined he looked. He was lean, probably 1.9 meters tall, and completely bald. He wasn't in uniform.

"Well, it's about time," Schumacher said.

"I'm five minutes..."

"Yes, fine. Sit down. Do you know this young man here?"

Tobias took off his cap and took a seat in the empty chair. The man Schumacher was pointing at turned towards him. Wasn't that Miltner, the porn consumer? Tobias nodded at him. What was all this about? Schumacher hadn't sent for him because of Miltner, had he?

"I see you know each other," Schumacher said. "We're meeting here for a very serious matter."

"I was just mastur... masturbating a little," Miltner said, wiping the sweat from his forehead. "Since I'm not with my girl-friend anymore..."

"It's not about that, Herr Miltner, and you know it. Wagner, hand over the evidence."

Oh, man. Schumacher didn't want to grill him, he just wanted the log files. He must not be the only one who'd noticed Miltner using the prohibited EPKs. He should have reported him. That was what Schumacher was accusing him of now. Just for show, he reached into the inside pocket of his uniform jacket. Of course, he only found his wallet and the rubber glove.

"Oh, crap," he said. "The log files must have slipped out. I'm very sorry about that."

"Excuse me? I don't think I heard you right!" Schumacher's words came out thick and fast. "I specifically reminded you, Wagner! What's the matter with you? You could always be relied on. The way you caught that bakery thief! I told my superiors that this Wagner, he's going to be something. He's destined for greater things. He won't keep working as a section commissioner until he retires. You don't want that, do you? We always need good, experienced people here who have demonstrated over a long period of time that they stand by the cause of the working class. I don't have to explain to you that this also has its advan-tages. A little house in Striesen with a garden out front, wouldn't that be something?"

"I... I'm really sorry. I guess I'm not quite myself right now."

He couldn't care less about getting chewed out by Schu-macher. But he couldn't show how relieved he was and had to act contrite.

"It's this thing you've got going with a woman, isn't it?"

Schumacher grinned, stood up, and walked around the desk.

He stood behind Tobias, put his hands on his shoulders, and massaged them a little. Tobias smelled his breath. Schumacher apparently liked garlic.

"Yes, I'm afraid I've fallen in love," he said.

He looked at Miltner out of the corner of his eye. He was sitting hunched over in his chair, probably glad that attention was no longer focused on him.

"Oh, that's a terrible condition. Fortunately, it usually passes quickly. This country needs you, Comrade, and your full attention."

Schumacher let go of Tobias's shoulders, then returned to his chair and dropped down into it.

"Yes, I know," Tobias said.

"Very well. If you want to check up on her, all I need is her ID number. We wouldn't want you bringing an enemy of the republic back home."

"It's too early for that, Comrade Schumacher. We just met last weekend."

"So you got something for the republic's 80th birthday, too. I'm happy for you! But don't wait too long to look into it, or you'll risk being all the more disappointed. Have you already..." Schumacher followed with a gesture that made his meaning clear. Tobias flushed.

"Oh, never mind, that's enough of that," Schumacher said. "We've still got a case to settle here. Now what are we going to do with you, Herr Miltner?"

"I'm innocent. I didn't do anything," the young man insisted, throwing up his hands.

"Nobody's innocent. There's always something to find if you look hard enough. So why did you use EPKs to access the Kybernetz if you had nothing to hide?"

"A friend recommended that I do it."

"A friend?"

"Yes, a friend. We work in the same brigade."

"His name, please."

"But he didn't have anything to do with it."

"His name, please!"

"Please, don't. I don't want to..."

"I could also send you to Bautzen..."

"Karlheinz Funke." Miltner said it so fast that it was hard to understand.

But Schumacher had heard him just fine. "Karlheinz, one word?"

"Yes."

Schumacher turned to the computer on his desk and typed something.

"And what reason did this Herr Funke give you?"

"The right to privacy. Using EPKs to access the Kybernetz should be the norm. If everyone did it, it wouldn't arouse suspicion anymore."

"Well, well. You've done marvelously. This Funke's a great friend. We'll have to take a closer look at him. Wouldn't that be a nice job for you, Wagner? Then you can prove that you're still the man I believe you to be."

"Where does your friend live?" asked Tobias.

"In Löbtau," Miltner answered.

What a stroke of luck. That was outside his jurisdiction. He liked to make sure that everything was in order, but he tried to avoid taking a closer look at people, as Schumacher had put it.

"Oh, that's Dresden-West. There's bound to be trouble if I go poking around in somebody else's precinct."

"I see," said Schumacher. "Well, I don't want to cause you any unnecessary trouble. Your supervisors from the German People's Police would also have to agree if I wanted to put such a transfer through."

Somehow or other, Schumacher seemed to have taken him to his Stasi heart. He absolutely needed to make sure such a transfer never happened. But it probably wouldn't be a problem anyway once he'd entered the zone with Miriam.

"Hey, Romeo, I see you smiling. Admit it. You were thinking about your Juliet."

"Er, yes."

Schumacher was pretty observant. He'd have to be even more careful.

"So, Funke's on my list," Schumacher said. "Pay close attention, Herr Miltner. Here's what's going to happen next. First, you're going to make me a list of all the Kybernetz websites you've visited using EPKs. Then our specialists will check the list.

Believe me, no EPK is as safe as you think. And you'd better not leave anything off the list. Is that clear?"

"Yes, it's clear," said Miltner, looking up towards Schumacher. "So can I go? And will you not tell my friend that I gave you his name? Please?"

Schumacher laughed. "Do you think we're stupid? The only way he'll know how we got his name is if you don't follow my instructions."

"And in the future, I'll be sure to stay away from him."

"Actually, Herr Miltner, you're going to find out more about your friend and tell me about it. I want to know what this Funke is up to."

Tobias felt sorry for Miltner. The young man was caught in a net and there was no way out. Schumacher had him in the palm of his hand.

"But then..."

"Don't worry. It's in his best interests, and also yours. I want to make sure your friend doesn't do anything that could cause lasting damage to him and our socialist republic. That's my job."

"Of course. What about the EPKs? Should I keep using them?"

"Not those EPKs. We'll give you a special version that will allow us to record everything that's transmitted through it."

"I... Okay."

"Once a month, somebody will contact you and ask to meet with you in person."

"Sure," Miltner said, his voice barely audible.

"And not a word to anyone, understood?"

"Certainly, Herr Schumacher." Miltner nodded.

"Thank you very much, Herr Miltner. Now you may go."

"Thanks. Thank you very much."

Miltner stood up. He looked genuinely relieved. Why was that? There was no law prohibiting the use of EPKs, and the GDR's constitution protected postal and telecommunications privacy. Maybe people should be more insistent about their rights. But these were foolish thoughts. Schumacher had the upper hand here. If he wanted to, he could make sure Tobias's children had a hard time, constitutional rights or not.

The door slammed shut. Miltner was free, but he'd ratted his friend out. Tobias wouldn't want to be in his shoes. So far, he'd been lucky enough not to need to make such decisions.

"I think it's about time for me to shove off, too," Tobias said. "It's been a long day."

"Just a moment. Something like what happened with Miltner won't happen again, is that clear? You saw the logs on Monday. I should never hear about such things from my supervisor. I should hear them from you. What does it say about me? And you know you're not the only one who saw those logs. They're always double-checked. As Comrade Lenin said, 'Trust is good, but checking is better.' I understand that you're hormonally compromised right now. But, again, I can't protect you."

"I understand, Comrade."

Tobias tried to sound as resolute as possible. Secretly, he was pleased. Schumacher didn't know everything after all. The system sometimes overestimated its abilities.

"Very good. So I know who I can count on after all. This system depends on an understanding of human nature."

Schumacher might be clueless, but he was still very confident. Maybe Tobias could use that to his advantage at some point. He took his cap from his lap and stood up. Schumacher also rose, then opened his desk drawer and took out a letter. He leaned over the desk and handed Tobias the envelope. It wasn't sealed.

"Go on and take a look inside," Schumacher said.

Tobias opened the flap. There was a banknote inside the envelope. A 100 K-Mark.

"That should serve as a little motivation for you," Schumacher said. "The boys upstairs don't know about your oversight. Buy your kids something with it. I hope they're doing well."

Tobias suddenly froze. He forced himself to smile. He hoped it was convincing.

"Thank you, Comrade," he said.

Schumacher shook his hand.

"Now out with you," he said.

IT WAS DARK AND THERE WAS A STRONG WIND. AT LEAST IT wasn't raining. Tobias had moved some stacks of paper around in his office so it would look like he'd been working—just in case his deputy showed up. Now it was half past eight. He didn't have to be quite as careful as he'd been during the day. The freeway was off-limits because the toll cameras had a night vision mode. But that wasn't the case for the traffic light cameras. He'd seen enough useless nighttime photos they'd taken to know that. So, to be on the safe side, all he had to do was turn off his lights when he approached an intersection and only drive through when the traffic light was green.

The drive still took more than two hours. The whole time, Tobias was tempted to call Miriam. She needed to know that he wasn't in danger. But to do that, he would have to put in the battery and switch on his hand phone. Then it would be possible to identify his location as well as the other caller's number. Miriam's phone was probably off anyway.

He turned on his blinker and veered off the country road to take the narrow access road to Neustadt. It was a quarter past ten. Was the innkeeper still awake? He imagined creeping through the dark house into Miriam's room. She'd think he was a burglar! But it was too cold to spend the night in the car. Dang it. He didn't even know what room Miriam was in!

But even from the parking lot, he could see the lights on in the restaurant. He went inside. There were still two men playing chess in the corner. Were they the same ones? He didn't remember faces very well. At the table where he and Miriam had eaten lunch, there were three men and one woman having a lively conversation and drinking beer. They appeared to be in their early twenties. One of the men was wearing strange makeup, with his eyes made up to look enormous. His forehead was painted black and decorated with three white vertical stripes. The woman next to him didn't seem to mind.

There was folk music coming from the kitchen. Tobias knocked on the door.

"Stay out!" the innkeeper shouted. "I'll be there in a second!"

She appeared after about two minutes. She was wearing a white apron and yellow rubber gloves.

"Good evening," he said.

"You're that policeman who had lunch with the pretty woman and had to leave so suddenly."

"That's me."

"I'm sorry, but I can't let you in the kitchen for sanitary reasons. Why don't you find a place to sit down? I'm in the middle of doing the dishes and will be with you in five minutes."

"Of course. I'd love a beer."

Five minutes later, the innkeeper came to his table with the beer. Tobias had chosen the spot where her grandson had been doing his homework earlier in the day.

"Your girlfriend... is she actually your girlfriend?"

Tobias nodded, feeling like a fraud.

"Well, she got a room."

"That's what we agreed on. Then I'd like one, too."

"She specifically asked for a double room."

"Really?"

Well, that was great news.

"Yes, and when I asked her if you wanted me to prepare one for you in case you came back in the middle of the night, she said no. She just told me to give you the second key."

"Ah, great, of course. That makes sense."

His heart started beating faster.

"Yes, I think so too. Why shouldn't two grown people share a bed? It's big enough, isn't it?"

The innkeeper looked at him with a smile and pushed the key towards him. It was an ancient model with an enormous key-bit.

"So it's one room with a double bed."

His brain was working so slowly at this point that he still couldn't quite wrap his head around the idea. The day had simply been too long.

"We don't have any single beds. The ones we have are all extremely comfortable and don't squeak or creak. Room 4, by the way."

"What about the check-in and payment?"

"We'll take care of that tomorrow. If we don't see each other before you go up, I hope you have a good night."

The innkeeper was actually obligated to take down information for every overnight guest. But with a People's Police officer, it was probably fine to turn a blind eye. The innkeeper asked the young people if they needed anything else and then hurried back to the kitchen. Tobias lifted the glass of beer to his lips and drank half of it. He left the rest. He was eager to finally see Miriam.

Behind him was a wooden door with a sign that read, "To rooms." He took his bag, stood up, and opened the door. Just beyond it was a staircase. He set his foot on the first step and a dim light turned on, just enough for him to make out his surroundings.

His heart was pounding. He was about to spend the night in a bed with Miriam. But it didn't mean anything, of course. She just wanted to save money or avoid making a fuss, or she was afraid of being in an unfamiliar place in the dark. The stairs creaked. He made his way up with as light a step as he could, leaning on the banister with his free hand. The first room was at the top of the stairs. The wooden floorboards in the hallway were just as creaky as the stairs. It wasn't possible to move surreptitiously between rooms up here. He passed room 2, then 3. He stopped in front of room 4.

Had Miriam locked it? But why would she do that? He pushed down the handle, which felt rough and cold. The door opened. There was dim light in the room, which was no brighter than the hallway. Miriam's scent wafted to his nose. All the furniture looked handmade, even the bed. There was a thick blanket covering the mattress. It was untouched.

He was filled with disappointment. Miriam wasn't here. She wasn't lying in bed, as he'd hoped, and she wasn't sitting at the small desk, either. Her travel bag was in front of the bed.

Tobias checked the bathroom. Miriam had unpacked her cosmetics and toothbrush. But where was she? Should he be worried? He turned off the bathroom light and looked around the room. Maybe she was taking a little walk. The innkeeper was in the kitchen and must not have noticed anything. He found a note on the desk. He wasn't familiar with Miriam's handwriting, but who else would leave him a message there?

He started reading. It began, "Hello!"

Miriam hadn't used his name because she didn't want to compromise his safety. After all, she had no way of knowing who would find the note.

"Whoever is reading this, don't look for me. I have a job to do, and I'll do it, no matter what happens. To all those who may try to get in my way: shove it. Meanwhile, to all who are on my side, I send you my warmest greetings. I wish you all love and goodness in life. But don't try to help me. I'll manage, and you'll only put yourselves in danger. Kisses, Miriam."

Dang it. Why hadn't she waited for him? It looked like he should have called her, after all! But would that have changed anything? When Miriam set her mind on something, there was no stopping her. That was becoming increasingly clear to him. Even with her farewell note, she'd tried to protect him and assumed complete responsibility.

He sat down on the bed with the note in his hand. The innkeeper was right. It didn't squeak. Shit. If he hadn't stopped by his office... If he'd raced down the highway... *You don't think you would have changed my mind, do you?* He should have at least tried.

Tobias lit the candle next to the bed with a match from the nightstand and burned the note in the flame. Nobody else would find Miriam's written confession. It smelled like Christmas. He blew out the candle, breathed in the scent, and ran downstairs. The innkeeper was at the table with the two chess players, who were paying their bill. They each owed 80 pfennigs. Tobias waved her over to his table. His half-drunk beer was still there.

"Do you happen to know if my friend went for a walk?"

"It's possible. I don't pay that much attention to what my guests do. It's none of my business. But she did borrow a bicycle. She wanted to take it for a little ride tomorrow."

"Thanks. Yes, then I'm sure she'll be right back."

"I lock the front door when the restaurant is empty, but your friend has a key, so there's no need to worry."

"Thank you. That makes me feel better."

It was a lie, but it still worked. He was already a little calmer than he had been before.

TOBIAS WISHED THE INNKEEPER A GOOD NIGHT AND PLODDED slowly up the stairs. Should he set out after Miriam right away? But he had no idea which way she'd gone. She was probably avoiding all official paths and was going to attempt to climb over the fence. Hopefully she'd been right when she speculated that the restricted area wasn't protected by mines and automatic guns. Could the sound of a mine going off be heard all the way to the inn? Tobias was freezing, despite the fact that the building was well-heated.

He was still freezing after he slipped under the blanket. It almost felt like he had chills. The last thing he needed was to catch a cold. Since he was a police officer, he did get his combination flu and covid vaccine every fall. But of course, that wouldn't help with a dumb cold. Tobias blew air out through his nose. It didn't seem like he was getting a stuffy nose, and the beer had tasted totally normal to him. If only he'd ordered a second one. Whenever he had a liter of beer in his belly, he fell asleep in no time.

October 10, 2029, Earth orbit

DOING NOTHING WAS EASIER SAID THAN DONE. MANDY ACTUALLY kept herself busy the whole time with the MKF-8. At least she had the camera all to herself, since the caches were full due to the failed transmissions, and now she wasn't getting any new assignments. Her favorite subjects were, of course, her two girls. She'd spotted them in the yard at their kindergarten and when they'd gone shopping with their father.

It hadn't been all that easy, since she only had a view from above. Her ex-husband's Trabant had a special spoiler that made the front wider. When Mandy tracked it down in front of the supermarket, she just had to look for three human shapes, two exactly the same size and the third wearing a flat cap.

She was, of course, sometimes mistaken. If she'd actually spotted them all those times, Sabine and Susanne would need to have covered a lot of territory. But maybe they needed more distractions than usual because they missed her. Their father would come up with ways to do that. He was reliable that way.

If only the replacement were already here. She wished she could share Bummi's optimism. But things were relatively calm at the launch site in Peenemünde, which she'd also photographed with the MKF-8. Usually things got hectic right before a launch. But while the rocket that would be sending up her successor was already in place, there had been no changes for days, at least not that she could see. There were also no signs that it was being fueled up.

It would be enough if the replacement's space capsule were to dock at the Völkerfreundschaft with no one inside. Then she could use the capsule's communication system to talk to Sabine and Susanne. That was what she missed most—hearing her sweeties speak, seeing their faces... Mandy put a hand on her chest. In the pocket of her flight suit was a photo of the two of them printed on a slide. She'd had the pocket sewn shut before the launch. The photo was like a valuable emergency ration of love for her. If she ever felt so bad that nothing else helped, she could snip open the pocket with a pair of scissors and look at the photo.

The capsule! Of course! If the capsule's radio system was independent, shouldn't it be able to reach Earth from here?

"Bummi, I've got a question to ask you."

The robot was crouching motionless in the corner as if awaiting its prey. It lifted one leg in acknowledgment.

"Why didn't we try to radio ground control from the capsule?"

The robot stretched its four legs as if it had slept too long.

"The likelihood of that being successful is low," he said.

"Why's that?" asked Mandy.

"If it were possible to communicate that way, surely ground control would have contacted us by now."

The robot did have a point, but Mandy thought it was a weak one.

"Maybe just as it didn't occur to us, it didn't to them, either."

"I still don't think it's very promising."

"For what reason?"

Mandy couldn't keep the obvious irritation out of her voice. Little by little, she'd gotten the feeling that Bummi didn't give a damn about her being rescued. So far, it had managed to calm her down with promises that everything would be all right. Why shouldn't the robot tell her the truth?

"I assume the capsule's operating program was also updated," Bummi said.

"Are you saying they introduced the same bug that they did with the station?"

"Well, you know how it goes, Mandy. Everything needed to move so quickly. So the new program code written for the station was used for the capsule, too. The hardware's also the same. The entire radio module is based on a design made by RFT Stassfurt."

"We should still try."

"I have no objections. Good luck!"

THEN BUMMI SIMPLY DIDN'T HELP. BUT REALLY, SHE DIDN'T need the robot. The Völkerfreundschaft was over eastern Poland right now, so it should be possible to reach Mount Brocken. Mandy pulled at the belt of her flight suit to tighten it. She hadn't done her workouts quite according to plan in the past few days and had immediately put on a bit of weight. Plus, the dehydrated food always gave her gas. Fortunately, Bummi wasn't sensitive to smell.

She pushed off and floated backward. The airlock was already open. This time she wouldn't need to close it, since she didn't want to go outside, but just to the space capsule that had brought her to the station. It was docked at the airlock. Mandy turned the wheel for the entry bulkhead and the round door swung inward. Cool, stale-smelling air poured out, which was a nice change from the stench in the station.

Mandy climbed down into the black pit, and immediately the light turned on. There wasn't much room in here. She pulled herself to the seat. She touched the console and dust rose up like a fine mist. She really ought to have tended to the capsule a little more often. After all, it was her return ticket back to Earth and her children. She'd do some dusting soon. That was something she never had to worry about aboard the Völkerfreundschaft, because with the constant air movement and renewal, the dust never settled and was caught by the filters.

Mandy started by turning on the console. The national colors and the GDR coat of arms appeared, and then she had to identify herself. The computer accepted her information. Now she'd taken the first step. She switched to the communications screen, which was a simplified version of the module used on the space station. The contacts were hard-coded. In an emergency, the cosmonaut needed to be able to operate everything very quickly.

Mandy selected the Mount Brocken station as the destination for her communications.

"Völkerfreundschaft to ground control, come in."

No response. When it docked, the capsule had linked its systems with the station's. Presumably, radio traffic now defaulted to the station's far more effective antenna. She tapped the little gear wheel that was visible in the upper right-hand corner of the radio display. Sure enough, radio traffic was routed through the station.

All of a sudden, the screen went black. Then, right after that, the lights in the cabin also went out. None of the little lights on the console were on anymore. Then the door behind her closed. She was cut off from the station.

"Bummi, what's going on?"

Nobody answered. Mandy forced herself to take a deep breath. She had to stay focused and calm. She'd practiced this often enough. Had her actions triggered something? Did the capsule suddenly want to take off with her in it? She didn't hear anything. When the docking clamps released, there would be an unpleasant scratching sound. She didn't hear anything like that. No, the capsule wasn't about to launch. Instead, the console booted up again. At first, all the lights were red, but then one by one they all turned green or yellow. The overhead light went back on and the bulkhead opened. Warm air came in through the vents. She was truly pleased to see the GDR coat of arms.

Maybe it would be best to stay away from the instruments. She'd trained for all of this on Earth, but the capsule seemed to be sensitive, and she still needed it to make her return flight. But it couldn't be that difficult to test the radio module. Mandy tried the gear wheel symbol again. Astonishingly, the connection to the station was now cut. Had the reboot caused it? Mandy switched back to the communication screen, chose the Brocken as the recipient, and recorded a message.

"Völkerfreundschaft to ground control, come in."

The radio signal flew through the atmosphere at the speed of light. It covered the several hundred kilometers in the blink of an eye. And then an answer should have come, but there was no sound the speaker. She checked the volume, just to be on the safe side, but that wasn't the problem.

She switched to the system menu. Among other things, it listed who was responsible for each of the programs. The code for the radio module came from RFT, as Bummi had said. But there was something else that she found interesting. The last program update hadn't been long ago at all. It had taken place on October 10, 2029, at 14:27 standard time.

Three minutes ago.

"I TOLD YOU IT WOULDN'T WORK," SAID BUMMI.

The robot was waiting for her right at the airlock.

"Could you do me a favor and go dust inside the capsule?"

"Sure thing, Mandy."

Bummi moved to the center part of the station, where the kitchen and bathroom unit were located.

"Hold on!" she called out.

It stopped jerkily. In microgravity, that wasn't particularly easy.

"It looks like the capsule's operating program was just updated today," she said. "And just as I was in the process of connecting to Earth."

"That's not possible, since we have no connection to Earth."

"That's what confuses me. But I can show you. The temporary total capsule failure must have shown up in the station's event log."

"Right," said Bummi.

"I mean..." Mandy hesitated, because what she wanted to say was more of a gut feeling. Bummi would just brush it off.

"You mean?"

Just say it. "What if they just don't want to connect to us now and are hiding that with an update?"

"That's silly. The RS Völkerfreundschaft is one of the GDR's most important achievements."

That was exactly the reaction she'd expected.

"Maybe they've run out of money, and they want to get rid of us inconspicuously now that the big show is over on October 7."

"Mandy, you should be ashamed of thinking that way about our party and state leadership."

"At least I can think for myself. You're just programmed to repeat the slogans that are fed into you."

"That's not fair, Mandy. I'm hurt. I can in fact think for

myself within the parameters I've been given."

"Sorry, I didn't mean to hurt you. But for me there are no limitations to my thinking."

"That's a delusion. You have different parameters than I do, but they also have their limits."

"I don't think so."

"Okay, imagine your children. Can you think of the most efficient way to kill them?"

"Of course not! I would give my life for them."

How could Bummi even ask such a question?

"You see, your thinking is limited. I can certainly think about how to kill your children efficiently."

"Don't you dare!"

Mandy drew herself up threateningly in front of Bummi, as if she was about to throw herself between the robot and her children. It took a few steps back and its knees buckled, making it look as if it were submitting to her.

"I don't intend to kill your children, Mandy. But I can think about it. You lack that ability, and that's why you're limited. Because if you can't plan an action, you won't be able to carry it out."

"I don't want that at all. What mother would think of killing her children?"

"That's not the point. What I'm saying is that I have a wider range of courses of action than you do."

So Bummi thought it was better than the people who'd built it and whom it was supposed to serve. When she was back on Earth, she'd have to have a serious talk with the people in charge at the Robotron combine. They may have built Marxism-Leninism into it, but they'd forgotten basic features like humility. Who knew what other shortcomings the robot had?

"To get back to your accusations against the mission leadership..." Bummi began.

Mandy had almost forgotten about that. Had Bummi just tried to distract her with its unbelievable statements? At least it had managed to make her forget about the immediate danger for a moment.

"I've come up with a scenario that provides an explanation for our observations without having to resort to conspiracy theories," the robot said. "After all, the capsule hasn't been used for a long time. It could have received the update at the same moment the space station did. However, as long as its main computer was in sleep mode, it didn't perform the upgrade. It didn't happen until after the computer rebooted."

"And the entry that I saw in the system menu?"

"That fits with the scenario because it shows what time the update was made."

Mandy sighed. Maybe the robot was right. Her suspicions had been so appalling that she was actually glad. It meant that her home country would do everything it could to save her from a state of crisis.

IN THE EVENING, SHORTLY BEFORE THE SUN WOULD BE SETTING IN the GDR, Mandy turned her attention back to the multispectral camera. But they were over Belgium. Of course, she'd forgotten that the space station had changed its orbit. She turned off the camera and floated over to the control console. The main computer knew the data for the new orbit. She had it print out a table that contained the new overflight times for the DDR. The next one was for the middle of the night CET, when Sabine and Susanne would be asleep. So she wouldn't see them again until the following morning.

It was time to get into her sleeping bag. Maybe she should wait and deal with the ham radio module the next day. She should also be able to send information to ground control that way. But then the whole world would hear, and the GDR would potentially lose face. Surely she'd think of something better. Had the main computer already cross-checked the new route with the database of near-Earth objects? She didn't want to be woken up by another blow to the head because the station had to dodge an obstacle. Mandy started a query and requested a visual display of the results.

The screen showed the globe. The orbit of the Völkerfreund-schaft was green. All objects that posed a danger would be marked red. But there were no red orbits, only white ones along with two blue ones. Orbits shown in blue weren't space debris, but artificial Earth satellites that were operative. Their orbits were specially designated because they could change their orbit themselves in the event of an emergency. Normally, the respective mission controls would agree which object would swerve in which direction. In her case, however, there was no connection to ground control. So Mandy put the data for the two satellites on screen, just to be on the safe side.

The first one was a Chinese weather satellite. Their two orbits were almost in the same plane, though offset by a few degrees. They would approach each other around midnight at a minimum of 120 kilometers. There was no reason to introduce any corrective maneuvers. The second satellite was the International Space Station, the ISS. Colliding with it would be catastrophic, because as many as 50 tourists might be staying in the hotel that had opened there four years ago. The previous owners had transferred the station to a private company that had been so successful running the station and hotel that it could afford a small microgravity research institute, where NASA occasionally sent astronauts.

The ISS was orbiting a few kilometers above the Völkerfreundschaft. Its orbit was also offset. The closest approach was 90 kilometers. The projection was accurate to 50 meters, so now Mandy could sleep soundly.

Hold on. If Mandy came that close to the ISS, might she be able to get a call for help through? The radio signal wouldn't be dampened by the Earth's atmosphere. Even if the main antenna didn't respond, the helmet radio could transmit up to 90 kilometers. Provided, of course, that someone happened to be listening on the frequencies she was using. She'd have to try as many channels as possible.

Mandy restricted the display to show just the ISS and Völkerfreundschaft orbits. They'd be closest at 22:32. The sleeping bag would have to wait. She'd have enough time to prepare for extravehicular activity. That way, she could bypass the shielding effect of the station's outer hull.

"WHAT ARE YOU UP TO?" ASKED BUMMI. "ARE YOU EXERCISING this late? That can have a negative effect on the quality of your sleep."

Mandy kept pedaling and snorted.

"At 10:30, we'll be approaching the ISS. I'm going to try to reach them by radio."

"The International Space Station is operated by a capitalist enterprise. It's against service regulations to make contact with individuals from the NSEA without authorization."

"I tried to get such permission from ground control. I was not successful. According to paragraph 23, section 2 of the space station rules of operation, in such a case the commander may issue an emergency authorization."

"That's... correct."

Ha! She'd thwarted Bummi with her reasoning! That didn't happen very often.

"But the antenna..."

"Yes, I realize the antenna probably won't help. But I'm hoping I can get through on the helmet radio. It's ninety kilometers in a straight line with no atmospheric interference. That should compensate for the low transmission power."

"That... is correct."

Again! She was really on a roll. Mandy smiled inwardly.

"Then I wish you much success," said the robot. "If you need my help, I'll be standing by."

"Thanks, but it'll be easy. I'll climb out the hatch, make sure I'm secured to the station, and then hope for the best."

She didn't want Bummi with her this time. It seemed completely opposed to her making contact with the ISS but didn't have the power to forbid it.

"I wouldn't rule out the possibility that the profit-oriented operator of the ISS will simply ignore your calls. After all, any reaction would, for them, represent an unnecessary expense. Predatory capitalism..."

"But if they did that, they would be violating the internationally ratified Outer Space Treaty. They must provide me with assistance. If it comes out that they refused, the GDR could sue them at The Hague."

"That's true."

For the third time, the robot had to agree with her! That must be a good sign.

"Still, you know that capital puts profiteering above all else."

Mandy didn't answer. There probably wasn't anybody in the entire GDR as convinced of the socialist cause as this robot was.

October 10, 2029, ISS

"WE'RE NOW APPROACHING ANOTHER ONE OF TODAY'S highlights," said the presenter, who had introduced herself as Jennifer.

Jeremy Clarkson drew his daughter Emily close to him and put her in his lap.

"Come on, let's listen to the astronaut now," he said.

Emily resisted a bit, then gave in. Jeremy knew she'd have preferred to roll around in zero gravity all day. But he wanted her to be a bit more knowledgeable when she got back to her mother. After all, the presenter was an experienced astronaut who had spent more than 300 days in space.

The woman, who wore a flight suit with the NASA logo, looked around sternly until she had the full attention of all ten members of her group. Then she adjusted the camera, which was attached to the ISS hotel porthole. She rotated the eyepiece a bit and pressed a button. Shortly afterwards, an object appeared on the projection screen next to the porthole. It looked like a silver tube tapering to the left.

The camera moved slowly over the object, starting at the bow. There was an antenna dish mounted on it. So it probably wasn't space junk, which was what Jeremy had thought at first. Then the camera view showed a coat of arms. It consisted of a wreath of grain, and in the middle a compass superimposed on a hammer. The background was black, red, and gold stripes. If he remembered correctly, those were Germany's national colors.

"What you're looking at is the East German space station," the presenter explained. "In German, it's called..."

Jeremy heard an unfamiliar word that sounded like "Foiker-froindshaft."

"...and that means 'friendship of nations,'" the presenter continued. "The station consists of a former rocket upper stage that was converted into a primitive space station."

The camera continued to move along the foreign ship. Now there were tanks and bulky containers coming into view. The structure was not particularly beautiful. But it could fly.

"The East German space capsule, which the solo crew member used to reach the station, is docked at the back of the station," the astronaut explained. "It launched from a specially built launch site on the Baltic Sea coast."

Baltic Sea didn't mean anything him, but sounded like it was in East Germany.

"Dad, is the woman saying that the crew is 'so low'? Are people in Germany really short?" asked Emily.

"No, the astronaut just means that there's only one person living over there."

"All alone? Oh, poor guy."

"The name of the station's current commander..." The astronaut had to check a piece of paper. "... is Mandy Neumann."

"Is that a woman?" asked Emily.

"Yes, I think so," he answered.

"Look, look, she's waving at us!" his daughter suddenly shouted.

The astronaut stopped the camera and aimed it at the movement that Emily had just noticed. She zoomed in on the image a bit more.

"Yes, as the little girl over there just correctly noted..."

"I'm not a little girl!" Emily protested loudly.

"As our young guest there just noted," the astronaut continued, "an EVA, or an extravehicular activity, is taking place at the space station right now. Some of you have also booked an EVA. As you can see, something like this can be a lot of fun. The woman over there is certainly having a good time, I'd say. If you haven't decided to do it yet, you are welcome to sign up with your tour guide by noon tomorrow. The EVA costs just $980 for a seven-minute experience in free space."

"What's that woman over there doing?" asked Emily.

"Honestly, I have no idea," the astronaut said. "It looks like she's doing gymnastic exercises. Maybe it's a special workout routine that she does in her spacesuit."

"Isn't that dangerous?"

"No, there are certainly lines keeping her secure. They're thin enough that we can't see them from here. By the way, in East Germany they say cosmonaut, not astronaut."

The woman on the screen was getting smaller, as was her space station.

"What's happening to her?" asked Emily.

"Nothing, dear," said the astronaut. "We're just slowly moving away again. By the way, the closest approach was ninety kilometers. That's nothing in cosmic dimensions, but such encounters between manned spacecraft still aren't very frequent. If you come see me again tomorrow, I'll be able to show you a Russian communication satellite and a spy satellite from our navy. After that, I'm afraid I'll have to shoot you all, but it'll be worth it."

Emily looked at her father with furrowed eyebrows.

"She doesn't mean that, does she?"

"No, it was a joke."

"MIKE, COME OVER HERE!"

Jennifer set the pile of bedding down in midair and hooked herself in at the radio console. She actually already had enough to do. She had to clean and tidy up the rooms of the passengers, who were still listening to a recorded lecture in the dome while gazing at the stars. Then she had to defrost and prepare dinner. Now, of all times, the radio receiver was calling in unscheduled.

Upside-down, Mike reached toward the console and turned a few knobs. Then he took the schedule printed on a magnetic sheet hanging on the side of the keyboard and studied it.

"This isn't a known sender, and no call has been registered."

Sometimes one of the passengers would get a call. But they were only able to accept what had been announced in advance.

"What am I supposed to do with this?" Jennifer asked.

The caller wouldn't give it a rest and kept sending call signs.

"Hold on," Mike said. "I think something came in recently."

He switched the menu and activated the search function.

"What do you mean by 'something'?"

"A warning. The other day, mission control passed on a warning. It came from the Pentagon and contained a list of frequencies we should ignore. Just a second, I've almost got it. There!"

He spread his fingers on the screen to zoom in on the text. Jennifer compared the data. As a matter of fact, the third entry showed the exact frequency of the person who was trying to contact them.

"Okay, so we'll ignore it," she said.

She felt guilty. Whoever was on the other end meant business. What if it was an emergency?

"Those warnings exist for a reason," Mike said. "There was that case recently with Russian hackers who could remotely control a space shuttle. That kind of thing does happen."

"Allegedly it was Russian hackers. That was never resolved."

"Yes, but they convinced the crew they urgently needed to install a software update, which then gave them control."

"I just want to hear what our caller has to say."

"I'd be really careful there. Why would the Pentagon warn us if this is totally harmless? But if you want to take the heat, please go ahead. After all, we only have forty-three guests on board plus three of us."

Mike floated away. Jennifer felt for the button that would accept the contact attempt. She'd trained for three years to get this job and had been at it for three months now. Things were looking good, and they'd be taking her on. Business was booming, and soon the hotel would double its capacity. Was it really a good idea to risk all that? Besides, they weren't the only ones who could be reached by radio. Someone else should be taking the call. Someone who didn't have to look after 43 civilians.

Jennifer took her finger off the button. As the receiver continued to emit sounds, she turned the volume down. She flew after her bedding, which had taken on a life of its own in the breeze coming from the life support system. Soon the visitors' program would be over, and the passengers would want to use their rooms without the housekeeper getting in their way.

October 11, 2029, Earth orbit

"THERE MUST BE SOME WAY I CAN MAKE CONTACT, RIGHT?" asked Mandy.

"Just relax and let things run their course. They'll get you back home on time," said Bummi.

This robot reminded her so damned much of her father that she wanted to kick him. *Just wait and see, blah, blah, blah, and a solution will come up.* The world had never worked that way for her, especially not under real, existing socialism. Those who dutifully waited always ended up last in line. But that wasn't where she wanted to be, because she only had a good four days to live. She wanted—she had—to see her children again!

"But down there, they can't possibly know how I'm doing," Mandy said.

"The condition of the Völkerfreundschaft can also be determined by observation. Surely they've noticed that we've reduced our orbit without starting the engine capsule. Such negative acceleration could only be caused by a defect in the tanks. Based on the exact value of the braking maneuver, they can calculate how much oxygen must have been lost. And with that, they know everything you could have told them if communications were working. Trust ground control! They have their eyes on all the ways and means they can use to help you. If you take action yourself, you'll just be making their job harder. Because in the absence of communication, they can't guess what you're up to! Do you understand? They expect you to follow the prescribed protocols. According to which you have to wait for help."

That was quite a long speech. Mandy grew angrier with every sentence. The robot had no idea how she felt! She had to do something or she'd explode. But Bummi couldn't know that, of course. It was just a machine, and all that mattered to it were protocols.

Fundamentally, though, she knew the robot was right. Her actions wouldn't make any difference. The extravehicular activity the day before had been a fiasco. The helmet radio should definitely have reached the ISS. The astronauts there must have been busy, or else they didn't care what was going on in their range of sight. Mandy felt like she'd been scammed. Either technology in the West wasn't as advanced as they always claimed it was, or they considered it beneath them to speak with her. Those were the only explanations she could think of.

The mailbox, of course! Some ham radio operator would surely listen to her. She floated to the workshop rack and switched on the device. The monitor greeted her. There were still no new messages, but two words glowed at the top of the screen, giving her hope: "Send data." Mandy shivered. This was the solution! She wrote a message.

"Völkerfreundschaft space station needs help. General loss of connection. Please contact Brocken ground control at..."

Dang it, how could the station be reached? "Bummi, what's the Mount Brocken station's phone number?"

The robot gave her the data and even told her Werner's cell phone number. Why didn't he object this time, as he had with her previous efforts?

Mandy added the numbers to the message and then delivered it to those who had sent the ten most recent messages. But why just ten? She copied the text and sent it to fifty addresses. The computer reported that it had processed the messages. Now she had to wait.

And wait. If she could only talk to her daughters! That would make all this stupid waiting around easier for her. The two of them were so sweet! And they'd never been so far away as they were now, even though it was just a few hundred kilometers in a straight line. Mandy thought back to Saturday, the last time she'd talked to them. Why had her mother skipped out on the conversation they'd planned for Sunday? If she hadn't, now Mandy would have another fond memory. Had they seen her shine a star in the daytime sky on Republic Day? Were they proud of their mother?

The star of Völkerfreundschaft. Maybe that could be her salvation? Making it light up wasn't complicated. She could even send a code. Three short, three long, three short. Her SOS would be visible from afar. Whoever saw the flashing signal would pass on the message, and eventually it would reach ground control on the Brocken. That way, Mandy could be sure they understood the gravity of the situation down there.

"I've got an idea," she said, and described the plan to Bummi.

The robot tapped the floor with its front legs as if it were calculating everything.

"I don't think it's a good idea," he said.

"Why?"

"They already know what's going on here. Help is on the way."

"But what if they don't? There's no harm in giving a clear signal, just to be on the safe side."

"Yes there is. You need to not just think about yourself. Such an SOS would tell our enemies in the West that something is going wrong here. After all, it wouldn't just be visible from the territory of the GDR."

"So what? Something *is* going wrong here. If there were another leak in the ISS, we'd know about that, too."

"You're being naive. The West keeps the really important things secret. Only minor issues like leaks are thrown to the media for it to feed on."

"I'm still going to do it."

"Then I will have to stop you. You must not harm the reputation of our state."

"If you want to stop me, you'll have to kill me."

The robot lifted its front claws as if to strike her with them. Mandy jumped backwards and hit her head.

"Easy there," said Bummi. "That was just a joke. I'm not capable of killing people."

"Guess I really lucked out with you, then."

She was breathing heavily and the bump on her head hurt. Why did Bummi always have to make such dumb jokes?

"But please, don't do it. Just have some faith."

"I have to do something now, no matter what you think."

"Outer bulkhead open," Mandy said. "I'm getting out now."

"Be careful. Remember the safety lines," said Bummi.

The robot really was on her side. But she still hadn't completely recovered from her earlier scare, when it seemed like it was going to attack her. It had frightened her to the bone. Bummi was so much stronger and heavier than she was. If he were to attack her unexpectedly, she wouldn't stand a chance. So, purely as a precaution, she'd taken an axe out of the toolbox before she went out and hidden it in her sleeping bag, even though it was a bit ridiculous.

"Start now," she said over the helmet radio. "First test one at a time."

"Confirmed."

She loosened the lines that secured the mirrors. Bummi had flat-out refused to help her with her silliness. So she couldn't just turn the space station to get the star to shine, like she had for the republic's birthday. She had to do it all by hand. Opening and then closing all the mirrors simultaneously wasn't easy with just two hands. The mirrors tended to have a mind of their own. But Mandy didn't need it to be perfect. If about two-thirds opened and closed at the same time, there should be a big enough difference in brightness to be seen from Earth.

Mandy pulled on the lines and watched the reaction of the mirrors. She was getting better and better at this. She had no gravitational force to contend with, just the tension of the integrated metal bars. The ropes to fold them up ran through pulleys, so Mandy could pull them inward. Closing the mirrors was more strenuous and took longer than opening them, which the tensioning mechanism helped with.

She still had a little time, and shifted her gaze to the Earth. Below, she could see the western part of Russia. Then they crossed Poland and finally reached the GDR. Unfortunately, almost 300 kilometers too high. She'd need a little luck today. Her light show wouldn't penetrate a cloud cover.

Bummi was probably right. It was pointless. Not because it made the GDR look bad, but simply because nobody would see it. She'd need fine weather and also people looking up at the sky. Most of the people she knew tended to look down, to avoid stepping in potholes. The money that her country brought in for its petroleum wasn't worth as much as it used to be. But the activity alone did her some good. Out here, she felt a lot closer to her children.

Okay, there was Poland. She should begin. If she started now, the star of the Völkerfreundschaft would appear in the late morning. Those who saw it might first think it was the morning star, Venus, overhead. But hopefully the flashing signals would convince them it wasn't a natural phenomenon.

Here goes.

"Starting signaling," she said.

"Good luck," said Bummi.

She pulled on the ropes to aim the mirrors towards the sun, and now the new star ought to be shining above the Earth. She closed the mirrors again. Short. Then she repeated the process. One mirror locked up, but the others opened. For a second, the star was shining. She closed the mirrors. Short. She opened them again, waited, then closed them. Short. That was short-short-short. When she pulled again, another mirror resisted, then another. It didn't matter. She waited three seconds and let go again. Long. The same thing again. All the mirrors joined in. And back. Long. It grew increasingly exhausting. Mandy opened the mirrors. 21, 22, 23. She let them shut again. Long. That made three longs. She was getting there!

"Mandy, come inside!"

"What is it?"

"It's urgent. I've connected with ground control. Be quick. I don't know how long it will last."

She let go of the ropes. That was fast! Or did it not have anything to do with her SOS signal? Mandy returned to the lock. She'd never been so anxious for its exit light to turn green. Finally! She took her helmet off and hurried forward in her spacesuit. Bummi moved aside for her. There was something written on the console screen. Just two sentences:

"I'm sorry. Yours, Bummi."

Two strong claws grabbed her from behind. Mandy tried to wriggle out of its grasp, but the robot was too strong. A third claw lifted the top of the spacesuit so that her arm was wrenched out.

"Ow, that hurts!" she exclaimed.

Bummi didn't answer. It pulled hard on her arm. She tried to fight back, but it overpowered her. She felt a sharp pain in her upper arm. Shit, what was the robot doing? This couldn't be happening...

YES, IT COULD. MANDY WOKE UP, RESPONDING TO THE LAST thought she'd had. Whatever Bummi had injected her with must have knocked her out instantly. What was this stuff, and why did they even have it on board? But that wasn't her most pressing concern. She was stuck in her sleeping bag, which was attached to several struts. Her arms were tied behind her back, and the sleeping bag was closed up above her chest.

She was tied up, but not dead. Bummi hadn't lied. He hadn't killed her. But he'd successfully prevented her from sending an emergency signal that would have been visible throughout central Europe. Mandy looked around. The robot wasn't in the cabin. She should escape before he came back.

The axe. She kicked her legs until she slid deeper into the sleeping bag. Hopefully the axe was still there! The sleeping bag was a universal size that could fit someone up to two meters tall. That meant there was enough room in it for a few of her belongings. Hopefully the axe was still there! She had to get it before the robot returned from wherever it had gone.

The sleeping bag was so long that it bunched up over her belly as she felt around with her legs. She grasped the fabric with her hands, which were still tied together, so that she could make her way down bit by bit. There it was. She felt it between her bare feet. Bummi must have stripped her down to her underwear. The thought of it made her cringe. She pulled up the axe carefully. She was lucky she was so limber. She just needed to be careful with the blade. The axe slowly made its way up along her body. Now microgravity was an advantage—the heavy tool didn't fall back down on its own.

The cutting edge of the axe touched her thigh. It felt cold. What now? Her hands were still tied behind her back. Mandy tried to climb through the restraint with her legs, but was unable to. She'd have to move the axe to the back, then. She maneuvered it around herself. The edge needed to point outward, so she braced the axe between her thighs.

Mandy twisted and stretched, over and over. The thin fabric rubbed over the sharp blade. Or at least that was what she was hoped was going on behind her. Twist, stretch, twist, stretch. Mandy was sweating. She should have been more diligent about her workouts. Then she felt a gust of cool air at her rear. Faster! She heard a soft noise that told her the fabric was ripping along the edge of the axe. She reached for it carefully with her hands. It worked!

Now for the bonds around her wrists. She couldn't see them, but she was almost certain that it was a cable tie. She worked the steel edge against buna rubber—and against the clock. If Bummi were to show up too soon, this would all be for nothing. She'd only be able to overpower him if she had the element of surprise on her side. She rubbed the shackles frantically over the blade. In the process, she kept pushing against their hard edges. Her forearms were probably a horrible sight. Was she bleeding? Or was that sweat? She didn't feel any pain. She was in far too much of a rush. The axe was her only chance.

There was a clicking sound behind her. The cable tie had popped open. She was free! Her joints ached. She brought her arms forward. There were deep marks around her wrists where the cable tie had been. Mandy also had several cuts, but they were superficial. She licked the blood off. There was a lot. She looked down expecting to see a pool of blood, but of course there wasn't one, since blood didn't drip here.

Mandy took the axe out of the sleeping bag, but kept the material over her body. She turned so that she was facing the airlock. In all likelihood, that was where the robot would be entering from. She'd only have one chance. As soon as Bummi realized she was free, surely it would corner her again. It clearly saw her as a danger. Who had programmed that into the robot?

The nice people from ground control? Werner? Surely that couldn't be the case.

She took the axe in her left hand. Bummi knew her and was aware that she was right-handed, so it would expect her to attack from the right. She needed every possible second she could gain by catching it off guard.

Its weak point was its the middle. Its egg-shaped body was well-protected on all sides by its strong legs, which were so long that she'd have no chance with a frontal attack. She'd have to lure it very close.

The airlock hissed and opened. Bummi came in upside-down. Every position in the room was the same for the robot, but not for Mandy. She'd have to strike upwards with the axe, not downwards. Bummi approached along the ceiling like a huge spider.

"Oh, you're awake," it said.

Mandy kept her arms behind her body as if she were still tied up.

"Yes, unfortunately," she said.

"Unfortunately? Aren't you glad to be alive?"

"This isn't a life! I can't even scratch myself if I have an itch."

"I'm sorry, but I had no choice. You behaved irresponsibly. Now I've eliminated the danger."

"What did you do?"

"I removed the reflective foils and thrust them into space. The star of the Völkerfreundschaft will never shine again."

"It didn't help anyway," Mandy said.

"See, I told you so. If only you'd listened to me!"

"Then you can untie me now that the danger's gone."

"I'm sorry, but I can't trust you anymore. You put your own well-being above that of your homeland, which raised you and shaped who you are."

"My mother raised me. Not like that would mean anything to you."

"You know that insults don't work on me, right? Anyway, I can help take care of you. I'll feed you until you die from lack of oxygen, and can also scratch your back."

What a bastard. The robot had been lying from the start. No

help would come, and Bummi was already planning her death. It clearly couldn't kill her, but it could let her die.

"The offer to scratch my back..."

"Yes?"

"I'd like to take you up on it. I've had an itch ever since I woke up."

"Okay. Don't be scared, I'm going to have to get pretty close to you for this."

Bummi crawled across the ceiling towards her. She needed it far enough back that she could hit its body. And it couldn't get so close that it would see the axe hidden behind her back. Mandy tried to keep her face as expressionless as possible even though she was extremely tense. Hopefully Bummi couldn't tell how anxious she was.

One more meter. Then another 50 centimeters. Mandy could smell the machine oil it used to lubricate its joints. Could it smell her fear? If it could, it didn't let on. Now the enormous spider was almost right over her and stretched out its front legs. The claws came close to her shoulders and opened up to reveal fine instruments that could have been drills or knives. Just one moment more. *Let them get behind your body first. It mustn't notice anything.*

Now! Mandy let out a cry, even though she'd hadn't planned to. Bummi flinched, perhaps thinking it had accidentally hurt her. The blade of the axe struck the egg and sank deep inside, nearly splitting it in half. Cables and oil spilled out. The robot drew in its legs, but it was too late. It curled up and made strange sounds, but was no longer capable of making any coordinated movements. Mandy struck again, but this time the blade hit one of the limbs and bounced off.

She'd done it. Right? Bummi was still moving, but didn't launch any counterattack. She seemed to have at least gotten to the mechanism that controlled its limbs and its communication center.

"Well, now what have you got to say for yourself?"

The robot sputtered a bit. One of its four limbs still seemed to be working a little. It used it to crawl away from her, like an injured animal looking for a place to hide and die. She almost felt sorry for the robot. What nonsense! It would rather let her die than risk her making contact with Earth.

Bummi reached the airlock. What did it want to go there for? Was it intentional? Did it want to go out into space? It would probably survive if it fell through the atmosphere. No. It wanted to get into the capsule! It was already in the airlock. She had to get out of the sleeping bag! But the damned thing was still tied around her chest. Faster! As she finally crawled out, Bummi was already disappearing around the corner.

Something was happening on the console. The robot must have activated the emergency launch from the capsule. Shit! If the spacecraft broke free from the station with the airlock open, she'd die!

Mandy dragged the sleeping bag along with her, ripping it from where it was attached. At this point, she wouldn't be able to pull Bummi out of the capsule. But she at least needed to close the airlock. Why was it doing this? Why didn't it just steal the capsule? She would die in a few days anyway, once the oxygen was gone.

It wanted to make sure! The damned robot wanted to make sure its job was one hundred percent done. It was the epitome of efficiency. How could she have trusted that machine for so long? Mandy rushed forward, got snagged on something and tore herself away again, thrashing with her hands and feet. She started to hear a hissing sound. It must be coming from the docking port that the capsule had just left. Shit.

Just a half meter more.

Go, mommy. Her children cheered her on. She howled and struggled and reached the airlock. She threw herself at it and turned the wheel.

October 11, 2029, Lusatia

Tobias steered the Passat to the right-hand side of the road. Gravel crunched beneath the wheels. He left the car halfway on the asphalt to keep from going into the ditch. He looked in the rearview mirror. Nobody was approaching, not even from the front, so he got out.

The place where he now found himself was a landscape created by man. Within half a lifetime, it had replaced what nature had previously created over many millions of years. Nature didn't like straight lines. Man did. The roadside ditch looked as if it had been drawn with a ruler, as did the barbed-wire fence behind it and the edge of the forest about five meters beyond the fence. The methodically planted pine trees were all the same height. They formed a thicket, which actually was good because it blocked the view.

There was another straight line—between light and shadow. Its actual location depended on the position of the sun. Right now, with the sun climbing up the sky, it was about to retreat in an easterly direction, towards the forest. Tobias looked at the clouds that hung as if stapled up over the restricted area. What was the meteorological phenomenon that kept them constantly over the zone? The innkeeper had told him she'd never seen the area free of clouds in her entire life. She'd moved there when she was ten years old, shortly after the oil discoveries started a boom. She claimed that there was a rumor among the locals that in the 1970s the weather there was still quite normal, apart from the foul exhaust fumes from the lignite-fired power plants.

Tobias stood next to the car and peed in the ditch. Then he opened the passenger door and checked the glove compartment. He'd been right. Miriam kept a pack of wet wipes in there. He took one and cleaned his hands with it, then threw it down the embankment. He immediately felt guilty. He climbed down, picked up his trash, and tossed it into the footwell on the passenger side.

What now? He felt for the service weapon on his belt. It was just a few meters to the fence. There were still no cars in sight. He climbed back into the ditch, jumped over the tiny stream, and crept out the other side. He carefully approached the fence. There were no warning signs. The chain-link fence had barbed wire on the top. It was the cheap version: chrome-nickel steel, 2.5 millimeters in diameter, with one spike every ten centimeters and manufactured by the state-owned enterprise Drahtwerk Staßfurt. Tobias had installed many rolls of it during his army service. It would be a horrible idea to climb over, since it would literally tear him a new one, in addition to shredding his uniform.

Better go underneath. He took a step closer to the fence and dug into the sand in front of it with his foot. The fencing only reached five centimeters below the surface, so he could dig through easily. Just as long as the fence wasn't electrified. He walked back to the car and looked in the trunk for the toolbox. Unfortunately, it didn't have a voltage tester.

He'd have to resort to more primitive methods. He found a dry branch and held it up to the fence. No reaction. The branch didn't change color, either. The applied voltage couldn't be that high. Next, Tobias picked a fresh blade of grass as long as his forearm and held it up to the fence. Again, nothing. He moved his fingers closer to the tip of the blade. Nothing. The fence was clean. He touched it with his left hand and jerked back, grimacing. *Ha ha, you fell for it,* he would have said to Miriam, and she would have given him a slap on the arm for giving her such a scare.

So this was one way into the zone. He thought it was probably how Miriam had gotten in. But the zone was 1200 square kilometers! It was like a giant version of "Battleship." He couldn't rely on pure luck to sink his opponent's ship. He needed more information. Tobias got back into the car, buckled up, and continued driving northeast.

AFTER TWO KILOMETERS HE CAME ACROSS A DRIVEWAY. IT WAS overgrown with grass but still clearly recognizable. The grass had been trampled in a narrow area along one side. Tobias braked and squealed to a stop. Miriam. The bent stalks were still fresh. It appeared that somebody had made their way that very evening up the driveway to the fence gate it led to. He followed the trail, which was more clearly visible now. Hopefully nobody would notice.

The gate had two panels chained together in the middle. The massive chains were rusty but intact. There was also barbed wire along the top here. Behind the gate was a path that looked like it led further into the interior of the zone. The pine thicket was interrupted by a grassy clearing. He was too far away to tell whether the overgrowth there had also been trampled down.

On the right side of the path was a red brick cottage. It didn't look much younger than the GDR itself. The roof was partially caved in and the windows were boarded up. Was it possible that the door was open? There was a little awning that cast a shadow, so he couldn't see it very clearly. He walked a few meters to the side. From this perspective, it was more obvious to him that the door was really open.

"Hello, is anyone there?" he called out.

All he got in response was a squeak. One of the shutters had moved. Maybe Miriam was hiding in the house?

"It's me!" he shouted.

The house must be empty. Miriam would have recognized his voice. He examined the fence. To the left of the entrance, some-body had pulled up some grass and dug out sand. The hole had been filled back in again, but someone had evidently crawled under the fence there. It could only have been Miriam. But where was the bicycle? Tobias looked along the fence in both directions but didn't see it. The hole was too small for it, and the fence was too high for her to have thrown it over.

He crossed the road. On the other side, there was another thicket of young pines beyond the ditch. He crawled in and then went along inside, parallel to the road. He saw the glint of metal. The bicycle! He pulled it out of the forest behind him. It would be best to get it back to the innkeeper before she reported it stolen. Otherwise, the wrong people might notice. Miriam probably wouldn't be getting it back to her anytime soon.

The wheel was too bulky to fit in the trunk. He used tools from the case to take it off, then put it in the back seat. Unfortunately, the old oil smeared the leather. Whatever. Miriam probably wouldn't be coming back for her Passat, either.

Tobias closed the trunk, pressing down a bit to get the lock to snap shut. What now? Tobias was at a loss. He took his hand phone out of his pocket, but then put it back in. Who should he call, and why? He would only be disclosing his position. His stomach growled. The innkeeper had given him a sausage roll. He took the paper bag from the passenger seat, removed its contents, and sat down with it on the hood of the car. He took off his cap and set it down next to him. It was pleasantly warm in the sun, which was already making its way southward. He would love to be going that way right now, too.

At that moment, a star was rising in the sky. In broad daylight? Tobias immediately thought of the Völkerfreundschaft star. It had been such an impressive sight! He'd really felt proud of his nation at that moment, which didn't happen often. But he must be mistaken. It wasn't a holiday. It must be Venus. Didn't it come up in the sky in the morning, and wasn't it visible during the day?

But this star stopped shining. Perhaps it had been an airplane momentarily reflecting the rays of the sun. But right after that the star came back, only to disappear again—and then start shining again. Then there was a pause. Tobias took the opportunity to take a bite of his roll. He looked briefly at his food, then back at the sky. The star had returned. This time it stayed a little longer. The game went on and he watched, mesmerized.

Was he the only one who'd noticed? Of course not. It must be visible all over the country. The star disappeared two more times, and after that the show was over. What had he done to deserve this? Was it some kind of experiment?

He sat down in the car and turned on the radio. "Stimme der DDR" didn't report anything about the event. He wanted to search the Kybernetz, but would have had to turn on his hand phone.

Actually, he wanted to set out after Miriam right away, but that would have to wait. He got behind the wheel and waited for a moment before driving off. He tried to remember what had happened in as much detail as possible. The star had shone three times, then three more. The first ones had been brief, the second ones longer. Three times short, three times long. If the first series had been repeated, it would have been an "SOS," a call for help from the Völkerfreundschaft space station. But it had only been "SO." So maybe it was just an experiment. Or an SOS that the cosmonaut up there hadn't been able to finish.

It was too bad Miriam wasn't here now. He needed to talk to someone about it. Tobias turned the Passat around and drove back to Neustadt.

"You're back again," said the innkeeper. "Did you find your girlfriend?"

He'd told the innkeeper that Miriam had probably left on her own because they'd had an argument.

"Yes, I drove her to Weißwasser. She asked me to return the bike. I have it in the car."

"She certainly could have kept it for a few days. Just put it in front of the house."

Tobias took out the bike and put it back together. Then he brought it to the front of the inn and pushed down the kickstand. The bike sank a little into the gravel.

"Could I use your stationary phone?" he asked the innkeeper.

She used the informal "du" form with him, so he did the same.

"Yes, go ahead."

He went over to the counter where the telephone was. The guest room was empty. Lunch time would be starting in half an hour. He'd have to hurry before the first guests arrived. He looked in his wallet for Jonas Schieferdecker's number, found it and dialed.

"Schieferdecker here, who am I speaking with?"

"It's me. You remember?"

"Like it was yesterday." Jonas laughed.

"It was the day before yesterday."

"Right. What can I do for you?"

"Earlier in the sky. Did you see that?"

"No, I'm sorry, I didn't. What was it?"

Tobias described what he'd seen.

"That's certainly exciting," Jonas said. "Hold on, I'm doing a Bergblick search right now."

"That's exactly what I was going to ask you to do. I don't want to turn my hand phone on."

"Sure thing. Be patient, it'll take a minute. Is our project going well?" asked Jonas.

At the word "project," his brain stopped working for a moment, but then he remembered what Jonas meant. Who he meant.

"All things considered, yes. I got off track temporarily."

"Gotcha. Then I hope you find time to get back to it soon. The deadline is getting closer and closer."

"I'm trying."

"So, I've made a few discoveries here. There are a few cyber forums where users have reported making a similar observation. Nobody can figure it out."

"Then I didn't just imagine it."

"Ah, and here's a report from the ADN news agency. It says the Völkerfreundschaft space station crew conducted an experiment."

"What for?"

"According to them, it's about increasing agricultural efficiency through supplemental lighting that uses mirrors stationed in space. This could be used to extend the growing season."

"And that's why the space station is sending the letters SO in Morse code?"

"It doesn't say anything about that."

"Is it reliable?" asked Tobias.

"Hey, I wouldn't go accusing our news agency of anything. When the Soviet Union still existed, they had plans like that there. But that had to do with Siberia."

"What do the cyber forums have to say about it?"

"They're skeptical. One of them wrote that he heard about a

mysterious illness that had broken out aboard the Völkerfreund-schaft, and that maybe our cosmonaut went crazy because of it."

"A disease, huh? Where would she have gotten it? From her robot? She's up there alone, isn't she? She'd have had to bring her craziness with her."

"That would explain some of the things that have been going on lately..." Jonas said.

"Ha ha. But seriously, that can hardly be the explanation."

"Oh, that's interesting. The post isn't there anymore."

"That's not especially surprising," Tobias said.

The cyber forums were, of course, under constant surveillance. Supposedly there were places in the Cherninetz where it was possible to exchange information without surveillance. If Jonas could ask around there... But access to the Cherninetz only worked via EPKs, and Tobias didn't want to put him in unnecessary danger. Miltner had been really lucky. Jonas couldn't hope for that, too.

"I don't think we'll find anything else beyond that," Tobias said. "Anyway, thanks for your help."

"Hold on," Jonas said. "What if the cosmonaut really needs assistance?"

"It's possible, but we're not in any position to help her. And with the project, we already have enough problems."

"I have a hunch that the two might be related."

"How so?" asked Tobias.

"Think about it. What was the last thing our project was working on?"

The MKF-8. Tobias didn't say it, but Jonas could tell what he was thinking.

"Exactly. And what's being used on the Völkerfreundschaft for the first time?"

The MKF-8.

"There's the connection," Jonas explained. "You probably also remember the problem that our project was having with it."

Yes, of course. The section that should have shown the restricted area was missing from all the shots. He followed Jonas' line of reasoning intently, though he had a good idea where it was going.

"What if the cosmonaut had the same problem as our project did?"

"The problem could very well result in a failed attempt to send a distress signal," Tobias said.

"That's a roundabout way of putting it, but yes, exactly."

"So we should keep that in the back of our minds."

"I'm afraid that's not enough. We need to make contact with her."

"If she's still alive," Tobias said.

The situation must be pretty serious for a cosmonaut to have sent out an SOS in such a dramatic manner.

"We'll see," Jonas said. "But we've got to try."

"You're right. But how?"

"I suggest we try the usual way."

"Which would be?"

"By radio."

"Great. Then we'll need powerful radio equipment. I'll see where I can get something like that. It won't be hard, I'm sure. That kind of thing is all over the place around here."

"I'm really serious about this. You don't need that much power. If the Völkerfreundschaft is over the GDR, it's just a few hundred kilometers in a straight line. Any ham radio operator should be able to do it."

"Good, Jonas. Then I know what I have to do next. Could you please calculate what time the station will be accessible next, plus the time after that?"

"Of course. Just a second. There's a chart on the Kybernetz site for the People's Ministry of Education. Ah. There it is. A good time would be in 124 minutes."

"Thanks. I'll get back to you as soon as I know more."

Tobias hung up. He actually would've preferred to go into the zone after Miriam. But that would be hopeless—and the whole matter seemed to be getting bigger by the day. He couldn't just ignore it. And the more he found out about what was really going on, the sooner he could effectively help Miriam.

He had two hours to find a ham radio operator to help him with his quest.

TOBIAS DROVE THROUGH VILLAGES IN THE PASSAT. THE innkeeper had told him she'd noticed a residence in Schleife with a giant antenna, but it turned out to be a satellite dish. Tobias's visit really spooked the owner, who showed him his special permit. In the annex out back, he provided housing for contract workers from Vietnam, and the dish made it possible for them to access their own public broadcasting network.

Then he went on to Groß Düben. The village wasn't large, but it stretched for quite a ways along the north-facing road. It consisted primarily of single-family homes on spacious plots of land. But nobody there seemed to have taken up the fine hobby of radio broadcasting. Towards the end of the village, he turned right, into a narrow street that led to a row of houses behind the ones facing the street. There were fewer lots, but the buildings tended to be somewhat newer.

He'd almost reached the opposite end of the village when he noticed an odd structure on top of a very small house. There was a metal bar affixed to the downspout leading from the rain gutter. It ended about ten meters above the flat roof in five straight struts, also made of metal, that stuck out in all directions. If that wasn't the antenna of an amateur radio operator, he didn't know what was.

Tobias stopped and got out. The house was built of concrete slabs and seemed to consist of a single room. It appeared to be uninhabited. There was one door and two windows with the blinds closed. Tall hedges around the building had grown up past the roof, but not the antenna. Facing the street was a low fence with a narrow gate. Tobias pressed the doorbell, but nobody answered.

Crap. He could break in, but wouldn't have any idea how to operate the radio. He looked around. Two houses down, an older woman was working in her front yard. She'd come over to lean on the fence and watch him. Tobias walked over to her.

"Salutations in the name of socialism," he said. "I'm Lieutenant Wagner, and I need to speak with your neighbor over there. It's urgent."

He gave his real name because it looked like the woman was about to ask to see his badge. But he was mistaken. She seemed to be more interested in gossip.

"Is he in any kind of trouble?" she asked. "I'm always wondering what he's up to. I'm sure he listens to Western stations."

"Well, every citizen is perfectly entitled to do that," Tobias said.

"If you say so..."

"I just want to ask your neighbor a few questions. It's possible that he witnessed a hit-and-run accident."

"Oh, what a bastard," the woman said. "I really hope they catch him. Was it the accident that happened the other day in Weißwasser?"

"I'd be able to conduct my investigation more rapidly if you'd tell me where I can find your neighbor."

"His name is Hardy Müller. He's been retired for a long time. When he's not here, he's at the tavern."

Great. The ham radio operator had a side job as a drunk.

"Here in town?" asked Tobias.

"No, in Neustadt. I've always found that surprising. He always takes his bike, even though it's fourteen kilometers from here! But Hardy doesn't let anything stop him."

"Is there a restaurant here in town?"

"No, there aren't any."

"Well, that's a good reason to go to Neustadt."

"I don't know, I still find it very surprising."

"Have you ever asked him? Maybe he's got a girlfriend there."

"I've asked him. Of course. He said he plays chess there. But who would believe such a thing? He leaves at noon and comes home late in the evening. Nobody can think for that long!"

"Thanks very much. You've been a great help."

"But don't you want me to give you a description of Hardy?"

"No, that won't be necessary."

Tobias ran to his car. If he was quick about it, he could get the chess player back here in time for the next opportunity to contact the Völkerfreundschaft. He went a little bit over the speed limit. There were no surveillance cameras along the route anyway. In ten minutes, he reached the parking lot in front of the "Hammer" inn. He dashed into the restaurant, but held back at first because it was so crowded.

"A nice hot meal for the section commissioner?" asked the innkeeper.

"No, thanks. I've just got to make a quick call and then I'll be right back."

He'd already spotted the two chess players. They were sitting where they always did. Tobias couldn't tell if the board was any different from the day before. He planted himself in front of the table.

"Which one of you is Hardy Müller?" he asked in a hushed tone.

"That's me," one of them answered.

He must have once cut an imposing figure, but now with all the wrinkles on his face and arms, he looked older than 80.

"I'd like to ask you to come with me."

"Why? Am I under arrest?"

"No. That's why I asked you to come with me. If you were under arrest, I would *take* you with me."

"Well, then, I can refuse your request. You can go to hell, Comrade Section Commissioner. Go ahead and shove it."

Their conversation had not gotten off to an ideal start. He should have spoken to the man differently. Not everybody was intimidated by his uniform.

"I'm sorry, Herr Müller. I'm in urgent need of your help. A young woman's life is at stake."

"I'll be happy to assist you after I've finished this game," the man said.

"Hardy-bear, I wouldn't mind if you..." the other player began.

"No, my dear. I did my share of groveling when I worked in the open pits. I really don't need to do that anymore."

Tobias took his hand phone out of his pocket and switched it on in normal mode. The innkeeper had already officially checked him in this morning anyway, so he wasn't revealing anything new. He took a picture of the board and loaded it into his chess program. Ha!

"Mate in six," he said.

"You don't believe that," Hardy said.

"Bishop to E5, then knight to B2, then..."

"Shhhh."

The man pushed his opponent's bishop to E5 and closed his eyes.

"You're right. Congratulations, Matze."

He knocked over his king. His opponent smiled.

"Come on, let's go," Hardy said, standing up. "Just sit tight. I'll be quick. How long will you be needing me?"

"We'll be back in an hour," Tobias said.

"Good."

Hardy gently caressed the other player's cheek, then took his jacket from the back of the chair and put it on.

"So, what's going on here?" asked Hardy.

The man smelled of pipe smoke, though he hadn't been smoking in the restaurant. They drove past the ominous wall of clouds that hovered persistently over the restricted zone.

"I need your help," Tobias said.

"You already said that."

"I've got to reach the Völkerfreundschaft space station. You're an amateur radio operator, aren't you?"

Hardy said his radio call sign. "For seventy years."

"Wow. Congratulations. Is that even possible?"

"Seventy years in ham radio? Why not?"

"I mean to reach the Völkerfreundschaft."

"Absolutely. Manned space stations always have amateur radio equipment on board. And the cosmonauts are often ham radio operators themselves. We're not the only ones who want to get through, of course. Our best chances are with packet radio."

"That doesn't mean anything to me."

"You can think of it as a kind of Kybernetz over the radio. You put data into little packets and send them wirelessly to the recipient. With a little luck, you wind up in their mailbox."

"And that's how I can reach the cosmonaut?"

"You can leave her a message. If you luck out and she has a moment to spare, she'll read it and even reply to you."

"Do you know if our cosmonaut—what's her name?—is also a radio operator?"

Tobias followed Hardy's lead and used the familiar "du" form of address in German.

"Mandy Neumann, yes, she's a YL. Very nice. I know some colleagues who have even gotten a QSO from her."

"Can we do without the acronyms?"

"You're asking an OM that? Impossible. We always have to conserve bandwidth. A YL is a 'Young Lady,' or a female ham radio operator, and a QSO is a two-way connection. An OM is an 'Old Man,' or a male radio operator."

"Well, I'm certainly glad I didn't break into your house to try to do it on my own."

"Yeah, me too! You would have messed everything up."

"By the way, your neighbor is wondering why you always ride your bike fourteen kilometers to play chess."

"Because of people like her. I can't stand how nosy they are. You saw the hedges around my property, right?"

ON THE INSIDE, THE OLD MAN'S HOUSE WAS SURPRISINGLY CLEAN and tidy. Tobias had obviously been a bit too quick to judge. There really was just one room, though a door in the back led to an adjoining bathroom. For heating, there was a coal stove and an electric furnace. One half of the room was taken up by a bed, chair, and kitchenette. There were books, mostly about chess, lined up on a shelf over the bed.

The other half of the man's home was set up for his amateur radio operations. A bunch of equipment with colorful flashing lights was arranged on four racks, and a computer was set up on a desk against the wall.

"Cozy," Tobias said.

"I have everything I need here. The house is mine, so I do great with my pension. I transfer my K-Marks directly to my daughter. She has more use for them than I do."

"I couldn't sleep with all those lights on."

"I can't sleep unless they're on. That's why I always come home on my bike instead of spending the night at Matze's, no matter how late it is."

"Then everything's perfect."

"Except for my hips and eyes."

The man fetched a stool from the corner of the kitchen and set it down next to his chair. Then he switched on the computer and the basic program, which was adjusted for an oversized font, started running.

"It's because of my eyes," Hardy explained.

"You could wear glasses."

"They give me a headache. Ed-hakes, my daughter always says. Such a cutie pie. Well, not actually that cute anymore. She just turned fifty. By the way, she's still single, if you happen to be looking. She's the sweetest person in the world. I can put you in touch with her."

"I'm quite honored, but I'm taken."

"Ah, I remember, that fancy lady from yesterday. You two made off pretty quickly."

"I guess it had something to do with my issue here."

"I'm always up for hearing interesting stories."

"Unfortunately it's too early for that, Herr Müller."

"Hardy. Everybody calls me Hardy."

"Okay, I'm Tobias."

"Tobias! That would work so well for my daughter."

"What's her name?"

"Tobine. Tobias and Tobine. What do you think of that?"

"Tobine?"

"Ha ha, gotcha. Who names their kid Tobine?"

The man had a bizarre sense of humor and wasn't particularly respectful, but Tobias still liked him. Hardy lived just as he pleased. Could he say the same about himself? So far, at least, that's what he'd always thought.

"Can we try the connection now?" he asked.

"Yeah, sure. I'll start it right now. But it could take a while."

"How long?"

"Hours!"

"Oh, the Völkerfreundschaft won't be in range for that long."

"That's not a problem. We can actually reach her no matter where she is."

"Because of the reflection on the ionosphere?"

"No, that's ridiculous. Because of digipeaters. Those are radio stations around the world that relay our requests."

"Well then, I just learned something new. But won't your friend be waiting for you in Neustadt?"

"He'll just lean against the wall and take a nap. Matze has always been good at sleeping no matter where he is."

After half an hour, Tobias was so tired that he went for a walk through the village. Hardy had gotten him to tell the whole story, at least the part about the Völkerfreundschaft. Now he was in the process of repeatedly sending out call signals. A ham radio operator's job seemed to primarily consist of waiting. This was not a hobby for Tobias. Now as he walked past the houses, he saw more people in their front yards. Most of them had probably gotten off work. The women were weeding flowerbeds as men trimmed the trees. They were probably starting to prepare their gardens for winter.

How was Miriam doing? Had she been caught yet? He should have gone after her first thing this morning. While it was a good idea not to just randomly stumble around the restricted area, this was taking so long. He should thank Hardy for his help and be on his way.

As Tobias stepped into the house, Hardy exclaimed, "Good news! We're in."

"You contacted her?"

Finally, some good news! Tobias rubbed his hands together.

"As we agreed, I left a message that we saw the distress signal and need more information."

"We? I said 'I.'"

"Me, me, me. You could say 'thank you' first."

"Thank you, Hardy, great job. But this is nothing I want to drag you into."

"You can't drag someone into nothing, only something, and you already did that by telling me the story."

"Which you made me do."

"I want to know what kind of mess I'm mucking around in here."

"Well, then don't blame me if things really get dicey."

Hardy laughed. "I'm old enough now to take responsibility for my own shit."

"But things really could get dicey. Or, going along with your imagery, things could get really sticky."

"I understand. That's okay. I think you're a good man, Tobias. That's why I'm helping you."

Tobias breathed in deeply. Hopefully he wouldn't have Jonas

and Hardy on his conscience at some point. Or his children, for that matter.

"So when will the cosmonaut look at our message?" he asked.

"Well, she's the only one who can tell you that. I don't know how busy she is. I'm pretty certain that ham radio isn't her top priority."

Maybe Mandy Neumann was up there fighting for her life right now. She probably wouldn't be checking her mailbox every half hour.

"Do you have a stationary phone?" asked Tobias. "I think I made a mistake and I need to talk about it with a friend."

"I'm afraid I don't. But you can still make a call."

"How's that?"

"I can use the radio to connect you to the Internet. Then you can start a digital voice call."

"With the imperialistic internet? That works?"

"The quality isn't particularly good, but you'll understand each other. The advantage is that nobody can tell where you're calling from. To the person you're calling, though, it looks like a Western call."

"Oh, you can do that? It's not prohibited?"

"On paper, this kind of voice radio actually isn't allowed. But the company has too much on its plate to go monitoring the entire spectrum at once."

You'd be surprised. But he wasn't going to deprive Hardy of that illusion. He'd just expect that someone would come looking for him within 24 hours.

"Great. Then could you connect me to this number in Jena, please?"

Before Jonas could say anything, he announced, "It's me. The man with the project."

"What are you doing... never mind. Did you reach her?"

"Let's just say I left a message on her voicemail. Now we have to get her to listen to it, in case she doesn't think of it on her own."

"I'm not sure what you mean, but there's not another channel? Another number?"

"No."

"Hmm. When I was a teenager, I'd throw little rocks at my girlfriend's window so she'd open it."

"Our cosmonaut lives a little too far up for that."

"I know. Let me think. She can't hear us, but she can see us. We could use white sheets to make an X that could be seen even from space."

"We'd need a lot of material for that, and before we got a chance to finish, we'd be found out."

"A forest fire in the shape of a..."

"A forest fire will follow its own path."

"I'm just thinking out loud here. What's big enough to be seen from up there, but also small enough that we can make it down here?"

"And that nobody would notice."

"It doesn't have to be that big. She's got the MKF-8," said Jonas.

"But how do we get her to point the MKF-8 at our message?"

"I believe she's got two kids. I bet she's secretly using the MKF-8 to watch them."

"How does that help us? Do we shave the kids' heads in a certain way?"

"You stay close to them and draw... never mind, that's silly. I've got an idea!"

"I'm listening."

"The MKF-8 is a very sensitive instrument and picks up large areas all at once. That gives us the opportunity to cause interference from Earth. And if we get it right and situate our message near the interference, Mandy Neumann will have the opportunity to see it."

Had he heard correctly? "You want to trip up the expensive camera from down here?"

"Exactly. We devised it as a theoretical scenario once, just in case we needed to stop enemy satellites from photographing our territory."

"So you mean nobody's tried this yet?"

"Yes, unfortunately that's the case, Tobias."

"Still, it's a genius plan. What will we need?"

"A powerful laser and an unobstructed view of the station."

Wonderful. First Jonas had given him hope, and now he was asking for the impossible.

"A laser. Sorry, but I forgot mine at home."

"Large telescopes have those kinds of things," Jonas said.

"I don't have a large telescope either."

"Let me think about who I know. The state-owned enterprise Carl Zeiss also supplies lenses for large telescopes all over the world."

Hardy tapped Tobias on the shoulder. That must mean he had news. The mailbox!

"Yes? Did she reply?" he asked.

"No. But you need a powerful laser?"

"Yes. Do you have one? A pocket model won't do."

Hardy fumbled around in the pocket of his pants and laughed.

"I don't seem to have one with me. But there's a dance club in the next village over that has one. You can see it every Saturday, even from a distance."

"Did you hear that, Jonas?"

"Yes. I don't know if it will focus well enough, but you can give it a try. It might work if you try it at night, when the MKF-8 is calibrated for low light."

"We'll give it a try," Tobias said.

"And I'll check around with the people I know who work in astronomy."

"But if we try it at night, how will she see our message?" asked Tobias.

"The MKF-8 is a multispectral camera. It takes pictures in many different wavelengths, which includes infrared. You'll have to create your message using a heat source."

October 11, 2029, Earth orbit

SHE HAD 72 HOURS LEFT. THIS ALSO INCLUDED THE RESERVES IN the oxygen tanks for the spacesuits. Just thinking about it made it hard to breathe. Mandy had managed to hold herself together long enough to check the status of the Völkerfreundschaft. But now she was done. Done with her life. Done with everything.

There was no way back. That goddamned robot hadn't killed her, but it had taken her life from her. And, even worse, her children! She pounded her fist against the wall. She'd never felt so angry and so helpless at the same time. Of course, it wasn't a great feeling to know that she was running out of air. But she'd still had the capsule. Even if no help had come, all she would have had to do was transfer and she could have made it back to Earth on her own.

Mandy climbed into her sleeping bag. Her palm hurt. She needed to calm down. But did she, really? Why? It didn't matter anymore anyway. No help was in sight. The robot was on its way home in the capsule. In her capsule! Had it really just been doing what it was programmed to do? It must have remarkable agency. Maybe the programmers hadn't foreseen such a situation. Was that possible? Or had Bummi acted that way because the station at Mount Brocken had told it to? Was it able to use communication channels that she couldn't access?

Maybe this had been the plan all along. She'd been needed up to the time of Republic Day. She'd been a true asset. A heroine. Socialism needed heroism. But she must have made some mistake without realizing it. Even that first mishap, when the station had let her enter the de-aerated cabin unprotected, shouldn't have happened. She'd thought it was normal. She'd been so naive! The space station was a masterpiece because a nation of 16 million people had put it into orbit, but it was far from perfect. Mistakes like that could happen.

Had the robot already wanted to get rid of her at that point? Mandy shook her head. No, that wasn't possible. She'd always performed her duties up here to the best of her ability. The GDR had nothing to gain from a dead heroine. They'd only get rid of her if the harm she caused was clearly greater than the benefit. But what harm could she have caused? She didn't pose any threat!

There was just one possibility: The robot must have gone haywire, maybe because it didn't have contact with Earth. The development of cybernetic consciousness was still in its infancy. Before the communications broke down, there were those on Earth who could check it daily and correct any undesirable behaviors. Then, suddenly, it was free. But it hadn't been programmed for such a state. Bummi was never designed to function for several days without external intervention. How would a cybernetic organism react when it found that the objectives it had been assigned were no longer consistent with those of the person it was with? It would resort to all measures to assert its own agenda.

Was that an explanation? She would never find out if she was right or not, but at least it helped calm her down. Mandy slid a little deeper into the sleeping bag until she couldn't see the cabin anymore. She closed her eyes but couldn't fall asleep. She was certainly calmer, and the anger was now gone. But despair took its place. With her eyes closed, she wept.

Mandy's eyelids opened and tears splashed in all directions. She actually must have slept a little. The sleeping bag smelled so much like sweat and fear that she had to quickly stick her head out before she got sick. She needed a shower, coffee, and something to eat. Mandy climbed all the way out of the bag and took off her track suit. There was one advantage to no longer having Bummi there: she could take off her underwear without feeling embarrassed. Under the gaze of the spider-like robot, that had always been awkward for her.

She went into the narrow booth that served as a shower and folded the outer enclosure. Space was limited and she was constantly bumping into something in front of or behind her, or with her arms. She turned on the suction pump on the floor, and before she could freeze in the air stream, she turned on the shower head above. Pressurized water was expelled from the nozzles and coursed down her body, making the sores on her wrists and forehead burn. It got trapped in orifices and hollows until it was caught by the air current from the floor pump.

It wasn't the same as a shower on Earth, but came pretty close. Normally, she was only allowed to shower every three days to make sure there was enough water, but that wasn't a problem that concerned her anymore. She squeezed some Badusan shower gel out of its little paper bag and spread it over her body. It generated hardly any lather, because it was a special mixture that the water recycling plant could break down more efficiently. Nonetheless, she immediately felt a lot cleaner. She switched the shower head to dry, and it began to blow hot air at her as the floor pump continued to suck out the remaining water.

Mandy pushed the outer enclosure aside with her rear end. She shivered. The temperature in the cabin was 16 degrees, tops. She got fresh underwear and socks, plus a knitted sweater and comfortable pants, from the clothing compartment and put everything on. As she pulled the sweater over her head, she used one hand to protect the freshly stitched wound on her forehead. Then she moved towards the closest porthole.

The capsule the robot had made its escape in was, of course, long out of sight by now. The space station was just over the western part of Russia. So it wasn't that much farther to the GDR. However, it would already be dark by the time she got there. That meant that Mandy wouldn't be able to observe her kids, at least not in the optical range. But the MKF-8 could do a lot more than that. Maybe it could pick up Sabine and Susanne in the infrared range? The number of overflights was limited. In the 70 hours she had left, she'd have a number of times to see her children, at least if she didn't sleep.

She would take advantage of as many opportunities as possible, that much was clear. Mandy readied the camera. She'd turn it on when she was over Poland so she could familiarize herself with the special features of the infrared display.

THE SPACE STATION HAD THE GREATEST COFFEE. BLACK, STRONG, and hot: that was how Mandy had liked it as a child, at an age when her friends still found it bitter and disgusting. The bitterness reminded her of the real world. The real world wasn't sweet. If you wanted to savor it, you had to embrace the bitterness, too.

She ate some milk bread along with it. The raisins were surprisingly fresh and juicy, as if they weren't dehydrated. In her final hours, she probably wouldn't get any closer to fresher fruit than that. She rummaged through the pantry compartment. There was a can of pineapple, and at the very back she found the bar of Western chocolate her ex-husband had slipped her when he left. She'd eat the pineapple tomorrow and the chocolate on her last day.

Mandy took the last sip of coffee and then put the cup into the net with the dirty dishes. It was time for the evening's entertainment. She floated over to the MKF-8 and made some adjustments. She had to use the main computer to select the spectral ranges. She did a half-somersault to reach the console, then started the program that controlled the MKF-8. She disabled all the channels except the infrared one. If she worked in only one spectral range, she could switch the camera to action mode. Then the software would display all the data for the previous ten seconds on the screen. It almost looked like a movie, or maybe more like a flipbook with the pages being turned very slowly.

At first, the picture was black and white. White spots meant there was a lot of warmth, and in dark places it was cold. Mandy switched to thermal mode, with cold appearing in blue and warmth in red. Still, there wasn't much to see. It was impossible to tell from just that that the station was currently flying over western Poland. She zoomed in further on the image. The larger the scale, the clearer it became that what she was currently looking at was a city. She zoomed in a bit more and could see red dots darting across the screen. The fast ones were cars, and the slow ones could be pedestrians.

It would be difficult to find Sabine and Susanne under these conditions. But maybe she'd be lucky. She'd had so much bad luck lately that it was high time she got some good news for once.

The Völkerfreundschaft crossed the Oder-Neisse border. This appeared in the image as a thin black line to help orient the viewer. The Spreewald was almost completely blue, though there were a few lines crisscrossing it—roads with cars on them—and there was also the occasional village. After that came the Lusatia region. It was entirely blue, meaning it was cold. It had once been an open-cast mining area, and it was a restricted area where nobody lived. But then where were the flares from the drilling rigs that had been the classic Lusatian motif since the 1980s? Had they finally managed to remove them, as had been promised so long ago?

"Error," the software suddenly announced, and the image froze.

Oh no. Mandy hardly had any time left to find her daughters. In ten minutes she'd be over the FRG. Dang it! What had happened? The camera's control program was displaying several error messages that consisted of codes. She'd have to look them up in the manual. Where was the damn manual when you needed it?

Maybe she could identify the problem by looking at the image. The bottom left was completely overexposed, as if there'd been an explosion there. But the brightness, which in infrared corresponded to heat generation, was so intense that it seemed unlikely that it could be limited to such a small area. It was unfortunate that it was so dark right now, or she might be able to see more in other wavelengths.

She enlarged the image. Gradually, she was able to see some structures, at least in the peripheral areas. The overexposed area in the center remained sharply delimited, equally bright throughout, while along the edges the intensity decreased by orders of magnitude. No natural phenomenon would have such sharp edges. A fire, for example, wouldn't have such a definite border.

Hopefully, the problem wasn't with the camera itself. But she didn't think that was very likely. With its high resolution, millions of image sensors would have to malfunction at the same time. Was that even possible? Maybe there had been a short circuit? It was far more likely that the brightness in the image wasn't an artifact, but represented something that actually existed. That could result if the camera had encountered a focused beam of light. Given the distance to the ground, it would have to be a laser beam. But Mandy couldn't rule out other spacecraft, either. Was it actually no coincidence at all, but rather a way to contact her, or even some sort of attack?

She zoomed in on the image a little bit more. In the lower right-hand corner, the southeasterly direction, she could see a fine pattern, almost like a signature. She zoomed in specifically on that area. Yes, that might certainly be text. If that was indeed what it was, it consisted of three letters: M-A-H. MAH? What did that mean? Mandy scratched her chin. MAH. Something about it looked familiar. MAH. Wait a minute. She'd forgotten what she'd been taught prior to takeoff: The MKF-8's optics produced mirror images. In action mode, these were displayed one-to-one on the screen; it was only in normal photo mode that the program automatically corrected for that particular feature. So the message wasn't MAH, but HAM.

Ham. Like the first chimpanzee who had ever made it to outer space. Ham like ham radio, the term used worldwide for amateur radio. The Völkerfreundschaft mailbox! But she'd already thought of that! The machine would provide a notification when a message arrived for her. Mandy looked at her watch. She still had three minutes over the territory of the GDR. She wouldn't be able to see her kids today.

With a powerful push, she floated over to the radio in the workshop area. It had been added on when an influential amateur radio operator with a seat in the Politburo had insisted on it. After all, the Soviet Union's legendary Salyut space stations also had such receivers. Radio traffic in the two-meter band couldn't be blocked from the ground. Even if Bummi had destroyed the antenna, she could have created a new one from simple wire.

She turned on the mailbox and retrieved the new content. Nothing. But that couldn't be! She banged on the lid. The robot! It had let her use the mailbox because it knew it wouldn't get her anywhere. She checked the status of the antenna. It wasn't that. Of course it wasn't. Bummi was smart and knew she could make a new antenna any time. It must have tampered with the software that managed the mailbox. What a great effort it had made to keep her from communicating with the Earth! But for once, she was lucky. The computer that the program ran on was independent of the station computer and made its own backup copies. The last one was from October 5.

It took Mandy some time to restore the old version of the mailbox software using cryptic commands she had a hard time remembering She started the program, and the screen immediately came to life. Greetings from radio amateurs all over the world appeared in rapid succession. Most of them were from a buffer in the device itself, but some were quite new. Mandy read each and every message. Whoever had gone to such great lengths to give her that code word didn't simply want to draw her attention to ham radio. There must be a message for her that was important.

October 11, 2029, Lusatia

TOBIAS SHIFTED FROM ONE FOOT TO THE OTHER AND RUBBED HIS hands together. They'd simply spread three strings of Christmas tree lights out on the road and used them to make an H, an A, and an M. But now it was dark outside and they hadn't plugged in the lights yet, so motorists wouldn't see them. Tobias, with the authority of his uniform, was supposed to keep anyone from driving over the lights as Hardy looked for an electrical outlet in the nightclub.

Hopefully he'd find one soon. They'd needed about 30 meters of road to set out the three letters, but Tobias could only stand at one end. If a vehicle were to come barreling down the road from the other direction, it would be hard to stop it in time. Once the lights were on, that wouldn't be a problem anymore. Tobias would just tell any drivers that there was an experiment underway.

This was essentially true, since they didn't know if the laser from "Tanztempel," the village nightclub, would be strong enough. Andy, the owner, had purchased it somewhere in the Czech Republic using K-Marks, and then gotten permission from the mayor to beam it out over the nightclub every Saturday, but not at any other time. So far, nobody had complained, perhaps because Andy's Tanztempel was one of the few facilities for young people in the area.

Even though it was Thursday, Hardy had still managed to convince Andy somehow. Tobias thought he'd heard the word "estate," but they were whispering, and it could have been "Sunday" or "stage." He didn't really want to know.

Tobias put his hands in his pockets and paced back and forth. As a token of gratitude and to prove that he trusted him, he'd told Hardy the rest of his story. About Jena, about Miriam. When would Hardy finally be ready? Was it really that hard to find an electrical outlet?

"Hardy, what's going on?" he called out.

A dark figure appeared in the frame of the back door.

"I already... Oh, damn it!"

Hardy made his way towards him. It was only then that Tobias noticed that he was dragging his left leg slightly.

"You have to screw in the first bulb!" Hardy shouted.

"What?"

"Jeez, do I have to do everything myself?"

Hardy crouched down and tightened the first bulb in the chain of lights. With that, the "H" lit up. Now Tobias understood what Hardy meant. He went over to the "M" as Hardy took care of the "A." The two strings of lights turned on almost simultaneously.

"There isn't a switch on these old lights, so we always leave the first bulb a little loose," Hardy explained. "Are you coming?"

Those lights must be ancient. But it wasn't all that surprising, since Hardy was no spring chicken.

"I need to keep an eye on the lights out here," Tobias said.

"Oh, just look. Nobody's driving over them. Besides, everyone's sitting in front of their TVs now anyway."

Actually, not everyone. The second night in the zone was just beginning for Miriam. Hopefully she'd found somewhere safe and warm to take shelter. It was already pretty cold.

"I'm coming," answered Tobias.

HE FOLLOWED HARDY TO THE ROOF OF THE NIGHTCLUB. THEY had to climb the last part using a ladder. At the top, a man who was probably around 40 extended his hand and helped him climb out of the narrow hatch.

"I'm Andy."

He had long, somewhat greasy hair and was wearing denim

pants, a denim jacket, and a denim shirt underneath. A gold chain hung around his neck.

"Tobias Wagner. Thanks for helping us."

Andy had a firm handshake. Around here, this seemed to be standard.

"Hi, Toby. Nice to meet you. Hardy made a compelling case," said Andy.

Toby! He really hated that. But he was the one they were helping out here, so he didn't complain.

"We should hurry up. How does the laser controller work?" he asked.

"I've got that sorted out already," Hardy said.

"Oh? Do you have experience with this kind of thing?"

"No, but I do know how to adjust a directional antenna," Hardy explained. "The laser is really no different. I calculated the position of the Völkerfreundschaft in the sky and entered it into the laser controller."

"The controller can draw great patterns using the laser," Andy said. "Will you still be here on Saturday? Then you can see it for yourself."

"I hope not."

"Hey, it's not so horrible here."

"No, it's not because of you, but a friend who urgently needs me," Tobias said.

"He came here with a fancy lady," Hardy explained.

"Then I wish us the best possible success," Andy said. "How will we know if we've been successful?"

"We won't," Tobias said. "And we've only got one shot at it."

All of a sudden, something started moving in front of them. Tobias could see nothing but shadows until Andy switched on a flashlight and turned the laser on. It was a kind of vertical tube that could move left and right within a given range. Just then, the structure it was mounted on turned, and Tobias saw that the laser could actually be pointed in any direction.

"He's looking for the firing position," Andy explained.

"We're not going to shoot down the space station with it, are we?"

"No, Toby. This isn't Star Wars here. You couldn't even blind an airplane pilot with it. And it will be even fainter from the Völkerfreundschaft."

"Good," Tobias said, relieved.

The structure remained stationary and the tube moved around within its given range. Tobias would have expected it to aim at the horizon, but the laser took aim almost directly overhead. There were, of course, still thick clouds hanging over the zone, and the laser wouldn't be able to see the Völkerfreundschaft until it was right above them. Hopefully that would work.

"Hey, Andy, if it doesn't work this time, maybe you'll have time again the next time there's a flyover?"

"Hardy asked me the same thing. Yes, I will, but it will work this first time."

"Yes, Tobias, you can count on it," Hardy said.

THE ONLY REASON TOBIAS DIDN'T MISS THE DECISIVE MOMENT was because the device suddenly started to hum loudly. He didn't see any light.

"Shoot, is it broken?" he asked.

Andy laughed. "No, that's what it always does. Look up!"

Tobias looked up to where he thought the laser beam ought to be. At a distance he couldn't determine, a green line suddenly materialized. The further up it went, the wider it got. Then, at a certain point, the beam disappeared into the night sky, as if it had been snipped off with scissors. Then the device stopped humming.

"That should do it," Andy said. "If it turns out it didn't work, just come and knock on my door."

"Thanks, man," Hardy said. "Will do."

TOBIAS'S PATIENCE WAS BEING SEVERELY TESTED. HARDY, meanwhile, remained surprisingly calm. He had it easier, after all. For him, nothing was depending on it.

"Shouldn't she have answered by now?" asked Tobias, squinting at his watch.

Half an hour had passed since they'd sent up the laser signal.

"She'd have to come to the right conclusions first."

Yes, of course. First of all, she needed to be using the MKF-

8. If the camera was switched off, then nothing would come of this. Tobias rolled the first string of lights over his arm. Before, it had taken him a long time to untangle them. And it was possible they'd need them again later.

What kind of person might this Mandy Neumann be? She'd managed to be chosen as a GDR cosmonaut, so she was definitely tops in her field. And she was presumably also a very committed socialist. After all, she would be the poster child for the GDR until she retired. Tobias had no problem with that. He himself had become a section commissioner in order to fight injustice.

He could hear the theme song for the show *Aktuelle Kamera*[1]. Was Hardy watching GDR television?

"Sorry," Hardy said. "But I wanted to know what AK had to say about your problem."

The speaker, who was wearing a suit and tie, first read out some reports regarding the upcoming Socialist Unity Party congress. Then there were pictures of a volcano erupting in Iceland, workers demonstrating in Stuttgart, and a brand-new model of the Wartburg 3 series, which was now powered by a hybrid engine. Within two years, the network of Minol fuel stations would be upgraded with charging stations. And finally, there was a new show at the Palast der Republik, and Egon Krenz had attended the premiere.

Then the picture changed to the Kazakh steppe. There was a fireball heading towards the ground. Its progress was slowed by parachutes before it gently reached the Earth. A reporter explained, "Here you can see, dear viewers, how Mandy Neumann, the popular GDR cosmonaut, has returned to us. Her capsule landed back on Earth a few days ahead of time because there were problems with the docking ports. For this reason, the scheduled replacement would have been unable to dock. Unfortunately, the automatic landing system was deactivated, so our heroine had to manage on her own. She suffered minor injuries in the process. Now she will be treated in the hospital and then begin her triumphant tour of our republic as soon as possible."

While the reporter was speaking, helpers could be seen in the background rushing to the space capsule. They removed an apparently helpless woman and carried her to an army transporter. But before the door closed behind her, the woman gave a brief wave.

"Is it possible that waiting for something is actually a complete waste of time?" asked Hardy.

"That's not possible. I saw the SO sign," said Tobias.

Had he been barking up the wrong tree? Or was there some kind of huge conspiracy going on here?

"Yes, and you weren't the only one," Hardy said. "And then they responded and saved our cosmonaut. There are a few things that still work in this decrepit country."

"Don't say things like that, Hardy."

"Hey, you suspected that somebody was trying to cover up a problem aboard the Völkerfreundschaft."

"That's what it looked like."

"At least Mandy is getting the help she needs now. I think I can shut down my equipment."

Everything had gone smoothly. The cosmonaut had encountered some problems and had then been rescued. A few days ago, he would have moved on from the matter. That was exactly how the state needed to function. But now it didn't feel right. Had he become an enemy of the Republic without even realizing it?

"Please, Hardy, hold off for just a minute."

"What's the point? Mandy doesn't have access to her mailbox anymore. Maybe the robot went berserk and was the one to send out the 'SO.' She was able to prevent it from finishing in the nick of time, and then they had to keep the cosmonaut safe from the robot."

That sounded logical and matched all the facts. All the same, Tobias had a bad feeling about it. It was as if he were desperate to find a darker truth. Wasn't it nice that all his assumptions had turned out to be wrong?

It was up to him. If he had to admit he'd been carried away, he'd also have to re-examine his commitment to Miriam. His old friend might not be who he thought she was. Was it possible that she was using him? And he was doing everything she asked of him and the whole time kept shouting, "Yes, use me!"

But that wasn't fair, either. She'd never asked him for anything, right? Wrong. She'd come to him seeking his help. The fact that he got caught in her web was all his fault.

"Tobias?"

"Yes, you're right. It's very clear. Shut the damned thing down."

"Um, this isn't the right moment."

"But isn't that what you wanted? I understand. I must have overinterpreted the facts."

"No, Tobias, you don't get it."

What else did Hardy want?

"Yes, I understand you very well now," Tobias said. "This whole time, I've just been..."

Hardy yelled so loudly that Tobias was startled. "Man, get over here! The Völkerfreundschaft has contacted us!"

October 11, 2029, Earth orbit

MANDY DID IN FACT HAVE AN AMATEUR RADIO LICENSE, BUT HER heart had never really been in it. Working all night with the equipment to establish connections to all continents had only really been fun for her in the beginning. But she still knew how to do it. The fact that she had no other choice was a tremendous motivation.

Still, it took a good half hour for her first message to reach the station that had asked for her to make contact regarding her accidental SOS sign.

"Völkerfreundschaft   here.   Thanks   for   your acknowledgment."

The message she'd received had been in German, so she also typed the reply in her native language. The call sign began with "Y2," showing that the message must have come from a GDR OM. Very good—discussing her situation with an amateur radio operator from the NSEA still seemed like treason to her, in spite of everything. After about three minutes, some new lines of text appeared on the screen. Mandy immediately threw all the other users out of the mailbox.

"Who am I speaking with?" the sender asked.

Surely whoever it was must know who she was? Surely there was no GDR citizen unaware of her space launch. She repeated her call sign, followed by a few question marks. The OM sent her a Kybernetz address.

"I have no communication access," she wrote back. "What do you want to show me?"

"Your landing in Kazakhstan. This is an excerpt from an Aktuelle Kamera video."

Attached to the message there was a tiny file, a GIF. Mandy opened it and saw a two-second clip of her being lifted out of the capsule.

"But I'm here, aboard the Völkerfreundschaft space station."

What was going on? Were they messing with her? She was on the verge of deleting the entire conversation. Surely she could contact some other ham radio operator. But anyone in the world who did a search for her would come across the same information that the sender had.

"There's reason to believe that you aren't who you say you are."

She probably would have thought the same thing. She looked at the video snippet again. The resolution was low, but even so it was clear that the clip had been very well made. It had to be a fake. Who would do something like that to her?

"Then who else would I be?"

"We suspect that you're a robot. After all, there's one aboard the station. It may have gone haywire."

"You think it went berserk and attempted to send an SOS, which the cosmonaut prevented it from doing, and then she fled to Earth in the capsule?"

But that was just... If she...

"Exactly," wrote the OM.

"That's what happened. Except that the roles were reversed. I, Mandy Neumann, tried to send an SOS. The robot kept me from doing it, then turned against me and ended up flying back to Earth."

"But it wasn't the robot who came back, but somebody who's the spitting image of you."

Suddenly it dawned on her. Those damned pigs! It must have been planned far in advance!

"I... yes, that's correct. I can explain."

"Please do."

"Before the launch, we tested the capsule's emergency break-away system. The capsule detached from the rocket properly, but it didn't go up high enough, so the parachutes weren't as effective. I sustained a couple of sprains in the process and, as a precaution, I was carried out of the capsule. Apparently this was filmed and is now being used to fake my landing."

"Is there any evidence of that?"

"The resolution of the GIF is too low. But the capsule in the video of me should still be silver. After a real flight through the atmosphere, a capsule is black."

"The capsule in the AK video is black."

Dang it.

"Please, search the Ministry of Science's Kybernetz site," Mandy typed, her fingers flying. "There were reports of the tests at the time. The original video must be there. Compare it with the new one."

"Just a minute."

Mandy's fingers drummed furiously on the keyboard. It would take the sender a few minutes to find and analyze the video.

Then the words started to flash across the screen. "You're right, Mandy Neumann. We apologize. The video is a fake."

She jumped up, hit the ceiling, then pushed herself back down.

"Thank you, OM."

"Of course, YL. The fake is very well done. They even changed the cloud cover and the position of the sun. But the motion sequence is identical."

"I'm so glad to finally establish contact. Can you call the Mount Brocken station for me?"

"Are you sure that's what you want? For the GDR, you're not even on the space station anymore. To us, it looks like they want you to die up there. If you suddenly communicate with them now, they might speed that up."

Ground control didn't want her dead, that couldn't be. There were people working there whom she considered friends, people who'd always been there for her when she'd had concerns.

"I can't believe that. I didn't even do anything."

"Something must have gone wrong on this mission."

This made sense to her, but there hadn't been any mistakes. Everything had been going great until she'd lost contact.

"Everything went fine," she wrote. "I finished all the planned scientific experiments on time, mapped the entire territory of the

GDR using the MKF-8, got the Völkerfreundschaft star to light up, talked to school classes, and so on."

"Could the MKF-8 be the problem?"

"Why? It worked perfectly. The resolution, the extended wavelength range, the sensitivity, the cloud transparency—everything met or even exceeded the designated parameters. Its inventor, I forget his name, congratulated me personally."

"Dr. Ralf Prassnitz. We're searching for him on behalf of his wife. He disappeared."

Yes, Prassnitz. That was him. A very kind man. She'd been very impressed that he'd contacted her personally. The other scientists whose experiments she'd performed had just communicated through ground control. And Prassnitz was undoubtedly the most famous of all of them.

"Disappeared?" she asked.

She felt cold.

"He was last seen in the vicinity of the restricted petroleum area. We suspect that his visit there was related to footage taken with the MKF-8. On the images we found on his computer, the restricted zone was completely missing, as if it had been cut out."

"The photos I transmitted to Earth were complete."

"Did you look at them?"

"I just glanced at them and checked to make sure they were complete."

"Do they know that on Earth?"

"No, it's not possible to tell from the pictures if I've seen them."

"Then the answer to the riddle must have to do with the footage taken of the restricted area. Maybe you're supposed to disappear for the same reason Dr. Prassnitz did."

This was outrageous. For the first time, she felt the free fall in her stomach.

"Oh, man. I don't have the foggiest idea what... Now what?"

"We'll have to advise you on that. We'll try to help you and Dr. Prassnitz."

"Could you please tell my daughters? They should know that their mom is okay."

"Right now, that wouldn't be a good idea. They think you've landed safely. By telling them that, you'd be putting your family in danger."

Unfortunately, they were right. How she would love to talk to them! Mandy swallowed her nausea. She had to focus now. Especially for Susanne and Sabine.

"I'm going to take a closer look at the images that the MKF-8 took of the restricted area. Are you searching for anything specific?"

"Dr. Prassnitz corresponded with an institute for landscape planning and design. We presume that he wanted to visit it. There is no such institute outside the restricted area."

"I see. In the photographs, the buildings don't have names, of course. But it should be easy to distinguish an institute like that from the drilling rigs and old lignite excavators."

IT WAS STRANGE. NOTHING ABOUT HER SITUATION HAD CHANGED at all. She would still run out of air in just under three days. But at least she wouldn't suffocate miserably, which was a horrible way to die. Fortunately, she had the gun, a Makarov pistol, that they'd given her just in case. It was in a floor compartment of the space capsule, secured with a code lock. It had actually been provided so she could defend herself against wild animals after a possible emergency landing in Siberia or somewhere similar.

The Makarov is in the capsule. Dangit! The robot hadn't just messed up Mandy's return flight to Earth, but also deprived her of the ability to leave this life with her head held high. Mandy stomped her foot and promptly flew up to the ceiling. But it didn't feel quite as shitty as it had before. She wouldn't die alone. Someone would be with her, at least in words. That brought her great comfort, which she found surprising. Mandy had always thought of herself as an independent person who could get by without others. Otherwise, she could hardly have agreed to embark on this solitary mission. But the thought of dying alone and unnoticed, completely cut off from Earth, was a real nightmare for her.

Mandy used the grab bars to pull herself to the main computer. Now she had something to do again. What had she missed in the images from the MKF-8?

October 11, 2029, Lusatia

"Want a beer?" asked Hardy.

"What have you got?" asked Tobias.

"Bergquell Pilsner."

"Don't know it."

"It's not too bad."

Hardy went over to the refrigerator, stooped down, opened the door and took out a brown bottle. He popped off the cap by drawing the lip of it quickly and forcefully over the edge of the refrigerator, then handed Tobias the open bottle.

He took a sip. "Drinkable. But damned cold."

He preferred beer at cellar temperature.

"I'm sorry, but I don't have a cellar here."

Hardy took another bottle from the refrigerator and opened it the same way.

"How long have you lived here?" Tobias asked.

"In this dump, you mean?"

"No, though it's definitely... unusual."

Hardy took a drink from the bottle and wiped his mouth.

"Since my divorce. The house used to be a garage and was part of the neighbor's property. I bought this little place from the owner cheap. Since she has the kids, my wife kept our house."

"You have multiple children?"

It seemed to him that Hardy and his chess buddy were more than friends.

"They've long since grown up and are scattered all over the world."

"And your ex-wife?"

"Lives in Rostock."

"The house..."

Hardy laughed. "It certainly wasn't blessed. Five years after the divorce, it disappeared into the zone."

"Swallowed up by the open-cast mines?"

"I don't know. Probably not. Lignite mining stopped in the 1990s. In 2004, they expanded the restricted zone because they made new oil discoveries. And that's when our house got in the way."

"There must have been severance payments."

"Not for me, but my ex got a decent sum."

"She didn't give you anything?"

Tobias took another sip. He could already feel the hops making him sleepy. He should have said no to the beer. But it really wasn't bad.

"Well, it was her house at the time. I didn't complain. This really is enough for me."

"Forever single?"

"Kind of. The divorce gave me the freedom to try out everything I'd always wanted to explore. And in the process, I noticed that I... get along much better with men. But I wouldn't ever move in with someone. That kills love."

"Interesting."

"And you and this Miriam, what's going on there?" asked Hardy.

Tobias didn't want to talk about Miriam. But Hardy had shared so much about himself that he surely couldn't refuse, could he?

"I have no idea, to be honest. I had a hopeless crush on her all through high school."

"She's a classy lady."

"Yes, out of my league."

"That's not what I mean, Tobias."

"But that's how it is. Her husband is a National Prize winner and they live in a miniature palace. She drives a Western car. And I'm just some section commissioner with a one-bedroom apartment in a tower block."

"But she asked you for help."

"To look for her husband, yes. And I'm dumb enough to help her do it, too."

"That's not dumb, it's very nice. She does realize that you're putting yourself in danger for her. That will make her think."

"Yes?"

"That's what I'm telling you."

All right. It was a nice thought. Tobias didn't ask any more questions. Otherwise he'd have to ask what kind of future might be in store for a section officer who secretly entered a restricted area.

"Hey, Tobias!"

A dark shadow loomed over him. He defended himself with his hands and feet.

"Take it easy. It's just me, Hardy."

Tobias shook his head and rubbed his forehead.

"Where am I?"

"On my sofa. You fell asleep."

"That damned beer. It always makes me sleepy."

He looked around. Hopefully he hadn't tipped the bottle over.

"Don't worry," Hardy said. "I finished the bottle. Letting it go to waste would have been a shame."

"Thanks. What happened? Should I go? You want to go to sleep, right?"

"No, don't worry, I've still got some energy. It's just a little before midnight. Do you have a key to the inn?"

Tobias felt around in his pants pocket. Yes, there was the key.

"I just woke you up to tell you the news," Hardy said.

"News?"

"Yes, something important just came up on Stimme der DDR."

Hardy turned the knobs on his radio until they heard a female announcer speaking.

"As the East German Ministry of Science has reported..."

"This isn't Stimme der DDR," Tobias said.

"Shh," Hardy said.

"... GDR cosmonaut Mandy Neumann has died in hospital. The 33-year-old had touched down on the Kazakh steppe with her landing capsule. Apparently it was a soft landing. However, videos show that Neumann was unable to leave her spacecraft on her own. Authorities have not indicated a cause of death."

Hardy turned down the volume. "That was Bayern 5, on the Internet. They have news broadcasts every fifteen minutes. But they said the same thing on FM radio's Stimme der DDR, but with more pathos."

"What kind of BS is that?" asked Tobias.

"A cover-up, definitely."

"And what if it's not? Who were we talking to, then?"

"You saw the two videos yourself, Tobias. It's very clear that the supposed landing is a manipulated version of the training video."

"Maybe that's what somebody would like us to believe. Let's imagine that the official version is correct. That means we've got a berserk cyber-consciousness on the Völkerfreundschaft. Maybe it was able to tamper with the video of the landing to make it look like a training video."

"And then it uploaded the fake training video to the Ministry of Science site?" Hardy asked.

"Why not? Maybe it's capable of getting past barriers that we have no idea about."

"It asked us to notify its children. Would a cyber-conscious-ness do that?"

"To seem as real as possible—why not?"

"I think we were talking to a human," Hardy said.

Tobias actually had that feeling, too. But all they'd exchanged were words. It was especially easy to manipulate impressions with text. And what if they were trying to track him down? Camou-flage and deception—those were secret service strategies. Who were he and Miriam up against? Or was he overestimating his importance?

"My head's spinning," Tobias said. "I don't know what's true and what's false anymore."

"What did you yourself see?" asked Hardy.

That was a very good question.

"Prassnitz's house was empty, and his colleagues don't know where he is. I myself found the letter he wrote to the institute. In the MKF-8 photographs that Prassnitz left behind, the restricted area is completely missing. Miriam's bicycle was lying in a thicket along the edge of the zone. The Völkerfreundschaft space station sent out an unplanned 'SO' signal. The space capsule that had been docked to it landed back on Earth."

"So you know a lot already," Hardy said. "To me, the most important thing seems to be that you can trust Miriam. She must be a good chess player. Everything she does follows a comprehensible plan. "

"That's right. It's about time I went looking for her."

"Now, hold on there. You'll just stumble blindly into some trap. Let's see what the night brings. Maybe the cosmonaut will find something in the MKF-8 images that will be helpful to you."

"You're right. I'd better get back to the inn. You must be tired, too."

"Can you still drive? I have a mattress under the bed that I can pull out."

"No thanks. The nap helped."

October 11, 2029, Earth orbit

51.501859 DEGREES NORTH, 14.539951 DEGREES EAST. MANDY identified the coordinates for the restricted zone and entered them, down to the very last point, into the search engine. With that, she'd reached the second step. The first one had taken her about an hour. That was how long the main computer needed to combine the results for the individual wavelengths in a way that produced the cloud transparency effect that was such a source of pride for the inventor of the MKF-8.

The restricted zone was not perfectly rectangular, so Mandy had to collect more than four points. 51.384593 degrees north and 14.761051 degrees east was the last coordinate she entered. She clicked the "Search" button, and a stopwatch with a rotating second hand appeared on the screen. The watch disappeared and was replaced by an expressionistic-looking mixture of areas in various shades of green, brown, and gray. So this was the big secret?

Mandy focused on the area's western edge and zoomed in further. The zone's borders were very clearly visible. The area outside was obviously overexposed. There were no clouds there. Mandy recognized the gray band of a narrow road running alongside the zone. Behind the fence, which wasn't visible at this magnification, there was forest. There were a number of clearings where buildings could be located. Mandy increased the scale, but the image didn't get any clearer. That must be because of the algorithm that had made the clouds magically disappear.

From above, those patches looked grayish blue. That meant they could be buildings, but they could also be small lakes with the colors distorted, or even ponds and pools. An area with constant cloud cover would certainly be quite humid.

Slightly further from the zone's boundary, Mandy encountered another road. It appeared to have just one lane. Or was it a wide ditch? No, up ahead there was a wider one that crossed it at right angles. Bodies of water didn't intersect like that at all. It must be a road crossing. She followed the first road because it seemed to run parallel to the edge of the zone.

The next intersection was a little further north. The other road was two lanes, headed east. Mandy followed the lane and could see that large trucks must use it, because there were turnouts. A square appeared on the right side of the road. The base measured about twenty meters and there were numerous cross-connections. In the middle was a bright point that radiated in the infrared. That must be a rig. Mandy was already wondering why there weren't more of them.

There was another derrick on the left. She checked the scale. It must be about one kilometer away from the first one. She imagined walking down the street. The atmosphere would be gloomy, with the dense clouds blocking out much of the sunlight. The burning flares from the derricks cast flickering shadows across the landscape. Although she was alone—she hadn't noticed any cars in the images so far—Mandy felt as if she was being constantly watched, because the landscape was in constant motion.

Now the two-lane road led into a forest. It appeared to get narrower, but that was probably because of the trees. The pines grew close together here. She would have thought that the constant dim light would long since have turned the restricted area into a semi-desert, but the opposite seemed to be the case. Maybe it was the bad air, since plants tended to flourish with higher levels of carbon dioxide.

Mandy sped up by first zooming out and then zooming back in where the forest cover ended. She'd covered about seven kilometers of forest. Behind that was what might have been a meadow. Long black lines led through it. They were perfectly straight, as if somebody had artificially cross-hatched the meadow on a computer. Could it be a drainage system?

Mandy kept moving virtually, now eastward. She came across a kind of bulge with two small buildings on either side. Maybe it was a checkpoint. She made a note of the coordinates. The resolution wasn't good enough to be able to recognize a possible fence. Past the checkpoint, the road widened. It led to a building —no, to several cottages. It was a little town. She took note of those coordinates, too.

The road divided, and in the middle she saw a pond. That was typical for villages in this region. But the houses were not typical. They were just blocks with perfectly rectangular floor plans. Even the measurements were all the same. They were probably prefabricated buildings. Behind them were vehicles, mostly painted with the camouflage of the People's Army, but there were also a few colorful splashes of private cars among them. It felt good to see some color again. Mandy felt as if she'd actually traveled the twenty or so kilometers from the zone's boundary to this spot on her own two feet, rather than with her finger on a map.

A place in the middle of the zone. Wasn't that what they were looking for? One of those blocks could be the institute. Mandy floated from the main computer to the amateur radio. She was in desperate need of a little shut-eye. But before that, she wrote to her only contact on Earth to share what she'd discovered.

October 12, 2029, Lusatia

TOBIAS RAPPED ON THE DOOR OF THE LITTLE CONCRETE HOUSE in Groß-Düben. No answer. He knocked louder.

"I'm coming!" exclaimed Hardy. "Who's there?"

A moment later, the door opened. First a crack, then wider.

"Oh, it's you," Hardy said. "You brought your suitcase? Do you want to move in with me?"

Tobias set down his travel bag. "No, I just haven't decided yet whether I'm going to wear my uniform or jeans when I go into the zone."

"Uniform, absolutely! The uniform certainly doesn't make you immune, but nobody's going to shoot someone in uniform without trying to talk with them first. That'll be your chance. Before he shoots you, put a bullet in his head."

"Uh, are you serious?"

"No, I'm kidding. Come on in. Do you even have a gun?"

Tobias ignored the question and held up the paper bag in his left hand.

"I brought breakfast for us. Will you provide the coffee?"

"Gallows breakfast," Hardy said, laughing.

"Hey, I'm not in the mood for jokes. Especially not ones like that."

Hardy put a basket on the table and Tobias emptied the contents of the bag into it. There were four sandwiches.

"Better save two for the road," Hardy said.

"I have a second bag in the car. Gerda made sure I had everything I needed."

"All right, then!"

Hardy helped himself to a roll. The smell of coffee wafted over from the other corner of the room.

"Yum, liverwurst!" said Hardy.

Tobias waited until the coffee was ready. He always needed to take a sip of it before he could eat. After three minutes, Hardy brought him the coffee in a humongous cup. The brown liquid was steaming. Tobias blew on it and sipped carefully.

"The coshmonauht shent ush a meshage," Hardy said with his mouth full.

"Did she find out anything?"

A cucumber slice snapped between Hardy's teeth. Tobias had to brace himself. Chewing noises drove him nuts. Hardy swallowed the bite.

"A village made up of nothing but blocky buildings," he said. "That might be the institute you're looking for."

"Where is it?"

"She sent us the coordinates."

"Great."

"It gets even better. She also found a few places that might be checkpoints. You'd better avoid those. She wrote down the coordinates for those, too."

"Very good. My only fear is that if I use the map function on my hand phone while I'm in the zone, they'll be on me right away."

"Then it's a good thing I still have an old Glonass device with no network connection whatsoever. I'll let you borrow it."

That should work very well. For geolocation within GDR territory, the good old Russian Glonass system worked better than the products made by Western competitors. Hardy rummaged in a drawer and handed him a device that looked like a barcode scanner. Tobias put it into his travel bag.

"Thanks so much," he said. "But I can't guarantee I'll be able to bring it back to you."

"Of course you will. Otherwise I'll grab you by the balls and hang you from the clothesline behind the house, you wimp."

"I guess I'll just have to, then."

Hardy laughed and put a hand on his shoulder.

"It's funny. The last time I put my hand on a uniformed man's shoulder was ages ago, but you're different somehow."

"You think so?"

Tobias could not and would not believe this. He was no different from before. He'd simply resigned himself to dying, which allowed him to act in a way he would never have dared to before. It was liberating but also stressful, because behind it was the conviction that his life would soon come to an end.

"Oh, Mandy Neumann wrote more. There are relatively few derricks, at least in light of the fact that the black gold that ensures the republic's survival comes from the restricted area. She suspects your friend Prassnitz fell from grace because he noticed that, too."

"I'll check it out. Do you have any idea what might be behind all this? Or does Mandy have a suggestion?"

"Who knows? Maybe the West is secretly paying us to leave the wall standing."

"That's ridiculous. It'd be a lot easier for them to just transfer us the money through illicit accounts."

"That was also a joke. It probably doesn't really mean anything. Maybe a long time ago the most productive oil wells were built over."

"But there must be something dirty going on there, Hardy. Otherwise Prassnitz wouldn't have disappeared and the cosmonaut wouldn't have been officially declared dead."

He thought again about the robot going berserk. But that didn't fit at all with the story about Prassnitz.

"You'll figure it out, Tobias, and come back a hero."

It didn't get much simpler than that.

After breakfast, Tobias brushed his teeth in Hardy's sink. He looked at his face. He'd grown old. What had the past few days done to him? He'd actually had it pretty good. A comfortable, important job with decent pay, an apartment with a view, guaranteed vacation in Mallorca or Italy—and now? Gloomy prospects that he didn't want to think too much about. He took the hand towel hanging next to the mirror and dried his face.

"Could you connect me with Jonas Schieferdecker again?" he asked over his shoulder.

"Yes, of course."

Hardy waved him into the radio area.

"Is he already on?" asked Tobias.

"No, I just wanted to explain something to you."

"What?"

"How the radio system works. Just in case I'm not here and you urgently need to contact the space station or your buddy in Jena or the evil Internet."

"Gotcha."

"I'm just going to show you the most important steps. You won't be able to get your own license with this, but you'll make contact."

"Okay, thanks, Hardy. You're a good man."

"No need to get gloomy about it. You'd better watch closely what I'm doing and file it away for safekeeping."

HARDY HAD HIM REPEAT EVERYTHING THREE TIMES. HOPEFULLY Tobias really would be able to remember the procedures. But now he should be getting on with it.

"Can we talk to Jonas now?" he asked.

"You know how it works. So get to it!"

Tobias sighed. He went through the steps Hardy had showed him. It worked the first time and they had Jonas on the line.

"Hello?"

"It's me," Tobias said.

"How's it going?"

"As expected, given the circumstances."

"I'm so sorry. I guess you really were right about the signal."

"What do you think, Jonas?"

"Didn't you hear the news? The cosmonaut died! Her poor daughters. So I decided not to bother with the laser anymore."

"We found one, not to worry. But I'll put it like this: the official information is not quite complete."

"Meaning?"

"The cosmonaut Mandy Neumann is alive. We've made contact with her. She looked at the images and..."

"Keep it down, Tobias."

"Don't you want to know?"

"No. You're getting yourself into hot water. I thought you wanted to get Miriam out of there?"

"Yes, that's what I want. But to do that, of course I need to know what's going on."

"Jeez, Tobias. To you of all people, it should be clear that it's never good to know too much."

Jonas had practically whispered the last sentence. Was that so it wouldn't sound like a threat?

"I don't get you. Up to this point, I'd assumed we had the same interests."

"Yes, to get Miriam out of the line of fire. But what are you doing? You're putting yourself in danger instead."

Jonas had played it so cool before. What had gotten into him?

"What are you talking about?"

"I thought they had it under control."

"What do you mean by 'they'?"

"It doesn't matter. Miriam's gotten mixed up in something she doesn't understand. That was why I suggested she ask for your help."

"You what? I thought Miriam...?"

If that was true, it had never been about him. Maybe Miriam actually hadn't remembered him on her own.

"All you had to do was convince Miriam to return to Jena. You're a section commissioner, a government representative. And now all of a sudden you're colluding with counterrevolutionary elements?"

This wasn't the man he'd talked to in Jena. Maybe somebody was listening in and Jonas knew that?

"Counterrevolutionary?"

"Don't you see? You're using illegal communication channels, calling me over the Internet... why are you still there? What time is it?"

"7:52."

"Then you have eight minutes to disappear. I hope the car has a full tank of gas."

"Disappear? What's happening?"

"I'm sorry, Tobias. You're a nice guy, no doubt about it. But this is about bigger things. Unfortunately Ralf didn't get that. Stupid guy. He screwed things up and now Miriam has to take the blame without having any idea what's going on. It would be horrible if she got thrown under the bus in the process. Please get out of there as soon as possible and bring Miriam back home. I don't want her to wind up in jail for the rest of her life. You don't want that either, do you? She trusts you."

"Jonas, what did you do?"

"Me? Nothing at all. I was just doing my job."

"Did you spy on Ralf Prassnitz for the Stasi?"

"No, I don't work for your ministry. My employer is... just ask yourself how I was able to trace this Internet connection."

"And why are you telling me all this?"

"Because I want you to let go of your illusions. It seems like you actually think you can find something out, achieve something. But that's ridiculous. The matter is far too important for them to let you go changing anything about the current situation. All you can possibly do is get Miriam out of there. I'll admit that I both underestimated you and overestimated you. I thought you were more limited than you are. Obviously, you can think beyond your education level. But at the same time, you're so amazingly naive to think you can change anything that you're putting what matters most to both of us at risk."

"This whole time, all you cared about was making sure that Miriam came back."

"Yes, Tobias, that was my mistake. I wanted to save her somehow."

Jonas was lying. He'd been using them both. Who knew what he really wanted?

"By sending her into the restricted area with the help of that flash drive? The essential data came from you!"

"Miriam is so desperate to find Ralf that I had to give her something to hold on to. Otherwise she would have lost it and landed immediately in Bautzen. But you've still got a chance. Get her out of there and escape with her. Hide and keep quiet. Then I'll be able to help you. I have the connections. I can take you to a place where you'll be safe. Now get out of there! Head south, that's where you can get out. You have exactly four minutes."

"And Hardy?"

"The man who helped you? I can't do anything for him. He violated the laws of our country."

Disgusted, Tobias stared at the speaker, which had fallen silent. What Jonas had just said was full of contradictions. Did he want to save Miriam or send her to her doom? Had it really been his idea to call Tobias? Of all the claims he'd made, it was this one, oddly enough, that bothered him the most.

"Did you hear that, Hardy?"

"Yes, all this doesn't add up. But he's right about one thing: we've got to get out of here. Jump in the car."

"And you?"

"Don't worry about me. I always knew they'd come for me one day. Move aside."

Tobias took a step backward. Hardy stooped over and ran his fingers along the dirty floor. A trap door opened, and cool air seeped out.

"I'm prepared," Hardy said.

"Thank you for helping me."

"It's been a long time since I've had this much fun. See you later!"

"Take care of yourself, Hardy!"

Tobias grabbed his travel bag and ran out of the house. He could hear police sirens coming from the north, a sound that was all too familiar to him. Should he stay here instead and explain everything to his colleagues? He had been a member of the People's Police for more than twenty years. His word should count for something. But that would be pointless. His colleagues couldn't just do whatever they wanted. Even if they believed him, it wouldn't change his destiny.

As Jonas had said: this was about something bigger. He didn't know what that was yet, but he was going to find out.

He drove away without going over the speed limit. He didn't want to attract attention. The road south was clear. Jonas had been aware of this detail, and yet he claimed that he didn't work for the company. What did it mean that he could have conversations over the Internet tracked? He probably worked for some Western secret service and had Stasi informants. Or was he a double agent? What did spies from the West have to do with what was going on in the zone? Shouldn't Jonas be just as interested in clearing this up as Tobias was? How big was this big deal he was involved in? And was he the right person for the job?

Probably not. But there was nobody else available right now to play that role. But whose game was it? And, first and foremost: did Jonas really believe that it was possible to just get Miriam out of the zone and bring her to safety? That would be naive, which was unlike him. Miriam was supposed to keep quiet and wait to be rescued while her husband was missing? Miriam! Tobias couldn't help but laugh out loud. And as he laughed, tears ran down his face.

October 12, 2029, Earth orbit

ODDLY ENOUGH, MANDY WAS DOING BETTER TODAY. SHE DIDN'T understand herself. Had someone put calming gases into the air she was breathing? Before breakfast, she treated herself to taking a look at her daughters. They were playing in the garden behind her mother's house. There were more people there than usual. Was there some reason for inviting guests that she'd forgotten about? Hopefully her mother wouldn't hold it against her, since she was, after all, officially in the hospital.

She warmed up some pancakes for breakfast. They were individually wrapped in a special film with all the moisture they needed. Mandy tore open the package. The pineapple can was a real problem. There was no can opener on board because the can had been a last-minute gift. So first she bored a hole in it with the metal drill and drank the juice. Then she used wire cutters to access the pieces of fruit. She speared them one at a time with her fork, taking bites from the pancake as she slid it out of the plastic film little by little.

It was really good. She'd have loved to use the pineapple chunks to make Hawaiian toast, but there was no toaster on the ship. She'd already considered melting the cheese with the gas burner from the lab. But then she'd discovered the pancakes. Going without treats during her first days on board was now paying off. She'd always planned to use them to cheer herself up some time when she got into a funk.

All of a sudden, Mandy burst into tears. She had no idea where that had come from, and why it happened just then.

The image on the monitor hadn't changed. Two bright dots were moving as if they were connected by a rubber band. They raced away from each other, around each other, got closer and then moved apart, but there was never more than maybe five or six meters between them. Mandy stroked the smooth screen. Static electricity made the fine hairs on her fingers stand up.

Her tears subsided. She made her way carefully to the workshop, so that the moisture didn't fly in all directions, and mopped it up with a fresh towel. Then Mandy put the towel around her neck. Time for her workout. She might die the day after tomorrow, but she wasn't going to die because of atrophied muscles. At least that was something she could control while the station's oxygen supply was running out. Saving oxygen now felt wrong to her.

The radio blinked. She pulled herself down by a couple of struts. The mailbox was full again. Perhaps she should think about looking for some contacts other than the radio amateur from Lusatia who'd attracted her attention with a laser. But she was afraid she'd end up in the wrong hands.

She opened the list of messages and froze.

RIP. Oh no. Terrible. My condolences. A cross icon. RIP. Rest in Peace. A rainbow. Awful. So sad! A candle. Another one. RIP. A white lily. RIP. RIP over and over.

What had happened? With all the condolences, it wasn't easy to find the last message her contact had sent yesterday. There it was.

"Hello, YL. Unfortunately there's a big mess I've got to tell you about. A few minutes ago, your death was announced on GDR television. According to the report, you died in the hospital. The exact cause of death is not yet known."

That can't be true! I'm here and I'm alive!

"I don't know what this is all about," the OM continued. "But it probably wouldn't be wise to contradict the report. Everything points to your being considered dead on Earth, and you'd better leave it at that. If you clear up the mistake, they'll resort to other means. That would make it completely impossible to rescue you. Maybe they'd even put a satellite on a collision course to be rid of the problem. We can only imagine how terrible you must feel. You have to watch your children bury their mother. But you've got to let them keep believing you are gone. We have connections and will do all we can to find a way to help you. But we can better arrange for you to be rescued if you keep quiet. We'll be in touch again tomorrow."

The message had arrived at 2 a.m. standard time. Mandy had been asleep by then. That was a lucky break, because after getting such a message there was no way she would have gotten any sleep. Her poor daughters! She floated over to the main computer. They were still playing in the backyard. Mandy moved back over to the radio. There was no follow-up message. Apparently help wasn't coming for her yet. She didn't think there would be. Nobody would come pick her up while she was in orbit, and there was no way she'd make it to the Earth's surface with the whole space station. She was going to die up here.

Susanne. Sabine. Now the image showed the two of them close to another person. It could be Mandy's mother. Maybe she was talking to the twins, telling them that their mother was doing great, that she was always with them and was watching them play from heaven.

Mandy didn't believe in life after death. But all the same, here she was, right in the midst of it.

October 12, 2029, Lusatia

TOBIAS STOPPED AT THE OLD GATE. NOTHING SEEMED TO HAVE changed. The grass he'd trampled underfoot had straightened up again. So nobody else had taken this path. He kept going south until he reached a forest road that led into the thicket on his right, and he turned. The road was bumpy, and the long Volkswagen kept hitting the ground. The wide tires didn't handle the sand very well. With a Wartburg, he wouldn't have these kinds of problems.

He looked behind him and could still see the road. It would be better if nobody could see the car as they drove past. He steered directly into the underbrush. The pliant branches of the young conifers scratched the paint. It had been spotless before, and Miriam wouldn't be pleased. But Tobias had to go at least four meters in. With the car in first gear, he rambled over hills of sand and young trees. The engine roared.

Suddenly, a terrible sound came from below. When you're screwing something together and you turn and turn and turn the screwdriver with all your might and then suddenly the tip of the screw pushes out of the material on the other side: that was the feeling.

Tobias slipped the clutch and the gear picked up the slack. The car wanted to bounce forward, and Tobias instinctively slid forward to the edge of the seat to give it momentum. But the car remained where it was, with the rear wheels spinning and the front ones suspended in mid-air.

It was stuck. The underbody had slid onto a tree trunk, and it was almost as if the trunk were pushing through from below. Tobias checked the bottom of the Passat, but there was nothing bulging through.

All right, then. He'd achieved his goal of hiding the car in the forest. He'd just have to find another way to get home. But he could solve that problem when it came up. If it ever came up. He tried to get out, but the driver's door opened just a crack. The pine tree next to him was pretty massive.

When he climbed over to the passenger side, the car tilted slightly forward and to the right. The right front wheel was probably touching the ground again. If he could accelerate in first gear, he might be able to get the car moving again. He slid back into the driver's seat, and the car tilted back. No, that wasn't going to work. But it didn't matter. He climbed back over to the passenger side. In the footwell was a red plastic shovel that looked like it went along with a litter box. Miriam didn't have a cat, did she? It might come in handy when he reached the fence. He took it, opened the door, and got out.

It looked like it was going to be a sunny autumn day. Dots of light trembled on the moss. He heard a jay and a few coal tits. And what was that chattering? A nuthatch? Tobias breathed in the air. It smelled like mushrooms. He still had a choice. He could simply go hunting for mushrooms and later ask a local farmer to pull him out of the underbrush with his tractor. City people like him were certainly capable of such silliness.

He didn't have to go stumbling after Miriam. The weather was perfect for chestnuts and porcini. He still had bacon and onions in the refrigerator, and he could go home tonight, fry them up with some mushrooms and look at the night sky over Dresden from his balcony. Then, tomorrow, he'd take care of the house registers of his precinct, just like he did every Friday. Oh no, tomorrow was Saturday. He'd have the day off!

Now it was Friday, and he'd been absent from work yesterday. Had anyone missed him yet? Schumacher was definitely a no. The next meeting with his boss was on Monday. Chief Constable Schulte covered for him when he was off, so tomorrow at the earliest. Schulte wasn't a problem. He might wonder why everything still looked the same as it had the last time he came in, but he was far too lazy to ask around. Maybe Tobias should call him tomorrow and issue some orders. Schulte was used to that.

Behind him, something cracked. Tobias turned around and felt for his service weapon, but there was nothing there. Could it be that he was just making flimsy excuses to himself to avoid finally starting to search for Miriam? It felt like leaping off a cliff into a body of water of uncertain depth, with no way out. And which he wasn't even certain was a body of water at all.

"Come on!" he shouted, then started muttering to himself.

Tobias walked around the car and opened the trunk. In the small toolbox were combination pliers, three universal wrenches, and cable ties. Underneath was the tire iron. Which of these things should he bring along? It seemed best to take all of it. He got his travel bag and stowed the tools in it. Now the bag was damn heavy and he only had one hand free. He should have brought a backpack. After all, it had been clear from the start that this wasn't going to be a comfortable vacation with his friend.

Maybe it would be best to try something different. Tobias took the large mat from the trunk and spread it on the ground. He put the tools in the middle, along with the tire iron, his rain poncho, the med pack, and the food. A change of clothes was a luxury, as were the toiletries, so he left those in the bag. The valiant hero could stand to be smelly. Hold on, he did need the toilet paper. His service weapon remained on his belt. The combination pliers went in his pants pocket, and so did the cable ties and the little shovel. He folded up the corners of the mat and fastened them snugly with the cable ties.

The result looked like a bulky black trash bag. It certainly wasn't any easier to carry. Tobias removed the two handles from his travel bag. Hurrah for the combination pliers! Next, he used the cable ties to fasten the handles to the folded-up mat so he could slip his arms through and carry it on his back. He stood up and the whole thing rose with him. Tobias took a few steps. The sack hung a little bit past his belt. If he kept his arms back while walking, the sack didn't constantly wobble back and forth. The tire iron knocked against his rear end with every step he took. But maybe that wasn't so bad. Surely what it meant was: *Keep going*. Tobias could use a little external motivation.

He took one last look at Miriam's Passat. The key was still

inside. It wasn't worth locking it, and whoever found it could keep it. Tobias waved to the car and marched down the forest path toward the road.

BEFORE GOING OUT ON THE ROAD, HE CHECKED FOR TRAFFIC. But he didn't have to. There wasn't a vehicle to be seen. Not even Hardy biking over to see his friend. How had things gone for him? It wouldn't be fair if he had to suffer because of Tobias. But clearly Hardy was prepared for anything. Anyone who dug a secret passage to freedom expected to need it at some point. Hardy surely must have stashed supplies down there. How had he gotten the idea in the first place? Was Hardy not who Tobias thought he was?

Whatever. The fact was that the man had helped him. He hadn't betrayed him to the Stasi like Miriam's former lover had. What had Jonas told them, anyway? Was his name known, too? What did the Stasi know? Tobias would have liked to call his superior, using some pretext or another. But to do so, he would have to turn on the hand phone.

Later. Now it was time to get into the zone.

ABOUT A HUNDRED METERS FROM THE GATE, HE CROSSED THE road. It wouldn't really help if they were to come searching for him with dogs, but he wanted to make it as hard as possible for them. Them. Who could they be? Colleagues from the German People's Police? Men from the Stasi? Soldiers from the National People's Army? Tobias sneaked alongside the fence. At least he tried to sneak. But the sack on his back was so heavy that every branch he stepped on snapped. Here at the edge of the forest, there were a lot of dry branches.

Fortunately, there were no hunters out. They might have mistaken him for a rutting stag. Rutting mainly because of the odor of sweat he was giving off by now. It was nice to catch a late summer's day like this in the middle of October. But it must be around 20 degrees, which meant that walking required some real work.

The gate came into view. Now Tobias needed to hurry. As long as he was on this side of the fence, he could be seen from the road. He took the plastic shovel out of his pants pocket and knelt on the ground so that he was mostly hidden by his bag. Just in time, too. He heard an engine in the distance and ducked down. The vehicle was approaching fast. He wasn't going to be able to find any other cover.

The closer the noise got, the calmer Tobias became. It was clearly a Jawa, a Czech motorcycle. The sound of its two-stroke engine was unmistakable. He'd actually had a Jawa 350 himself, shortly after his army service. But the police didn't ride around on Jawas. They relied on the more powerful MZs from Zschopau and, more recently, on BMW motorcycles built in a factory near Suhl, for customers in both the East and the West.

Tobias calmly breathed in and out. The person riding the Jawa would only see his bag, if anything. Whoever it was might wonder what it was doing there, but would be in the next town before coming up with an answer.

But the engine grew quieter. It howled and made a few banging noises before the machine stopped. Tobias remained huddled behind his bag, careful to avoid making any movements.

He clearly heard crunching sounds as the Jawa was pushed onto the gravel at the side of the road. Then a metallic clang— that was the kickstand being put down. There was a groan, and Tobias guessed that the rider was jacking up the motorcycle. Then came more crunching, which kept time with short but firm steps.

Crap, crap, crap. Tobias felt for his service weapon with his right hand. It was stuck between him and the bag. If he pulled it out, the sack might topple over. He was still holding the shovel in his left hand. This was his only chance. Tobias listened until it sounded like the stranger was close enough. Then he jumped up and attacked him.

The man grabbed his arm forcefully and laughed.

"You're going to clobber me to death with a kitty litter scoop? That's very original."

It was Matze, Hardy's friend and chess partner. The Jawa didn't at all fit the image that Tobias had of the sleepy old man he'd seen at the inn. But Matze seemed completely different now. The motorcycle jacket certainly played a part. The man was still old, but pretty alert. And he looked more muscular than Tobias. Maybe he'd been a bodybuilder?

"Oh, it's you. I thought..."

Matze let go of him and Tobias lowered the arm with the scoop.

"What did you think? That the Stasi was coming for you?"

"Where..."

"Hardy sounded the alarm," said Matze.

"The alarm?"

"It doesn't matter. Anyway, I know that the two of you are in trouble."

"And now you're going to pick up Hardy?"

"Exactly."

"Shouldn't you get there fast?"

"I've got time. Everything needs to cool down a bit there first."

"Have you got any idea who exactly marched in on Hardy?"

"No. All I know is that he used his secret passage."

Hopefully the two of them weren't underestimating their opponent.

"You're not worried?" he asked. "The trapdoor is pretty easy to find."

"No, I'm not. Finding it isn't enough. We set up a security measure, too."

A security measure. Would that stop the Stasi? Matze seemed quite certain. Maybe Tobias shouldn't worry him unnecessarily.

"Where does his secret passage lead?" he asked.

"Well, it wouldn't be a secret passage anymore if I told you that, would it?"

"I might need it sometime, but to go in the other direction."

"What for?"

"It's possible I'll urgently need to use Hardy's radio."

"Ha ha. Nice try."

"No, really. He showed me how to operate it."

Matze raised his eyebrows.

"Really? Then he must trust you more than I would have thought possible."

"Why wouldn't he trust me?"

"Look at you!"

"Because of my uniform?"

"Don't be silly. Because you're hiding behind a black bag, acting like nobody can see you when you can't see anyone."

"But you couldn't see me."

"You really think so? Your left foot and right shoulder were sticking out."

"Oh."

"But fine. If Hardy is letting you use his radio equipment, you may as well know where the exit to the secret passageway is."

"I appreciate it. But how do you know I'm not lying to you?"

"You have no idea how important Hardy's equipment is to him."

Tobias didn't find this reasoning entirely comprehensible, but he preferred not to ask any more questions, since it might make Matze change his mind.

"So, where does the passage end?"

"At the bottom of Halbendorf Lake."

That was... original. And soggy.

"How big is this lake and where is it located?"

"If you continue on to Groß-Düben, you'll find it south of the village. The access point is below the ski jump with the heart on it."

"Come again?"

"On the south shore there's a sports facility where you can also go water skiing. There are two wooden ski jumps, and you can see them easily from the shore."

"Good to know. So you have to get wet, then?"

"It can't be avoided. However, we also stored dry clothes in the passageway."

"That's convenient."

Tobias shuddered at the idea of having to dive to the bottom of a lake.

"There's something else you should know."

"You mean the booby traps?"

Or the miniature atomic bomb. Or the pocket-sized black hole.

"Ha ha, no. That would be too dangerous. But you should be able to use a breathing mask and dive down a few hundred meters."

"Where can I find it?"

"Just before you exit the passageway into the lake."

"But if I use the passageway in the other direction..."

"You'll have to hold your breath for a little bit. Sorry. That was never the plan."

"Is that the security measure you were talking about?"

"One of them, yes. But now you should be getting on with it."

"You're right, Matze. Could you please help me?" Tobias held up the shovel.

"Matthias. Only Hardy is allowed to call me Matze."

"Sorry, Matthias."

"Sure I'll help you. Hardy's friends are my friends, too."

Matze turned around and went over to his motorcycle. Oh, it was a model with a sidecar! The man folded the top back and took something out—a spade. Tobias took it and thanked him, then started digging. Matze put his hand on his shoulder.

"Step aside."

Hardy's friend started in with the spade and broke through the turf. The hole grew quickly, though sand kept slipping in from the sides. The heath soil wasn't great for digging. Matze panted and took off his jacket. Underneath, he was wearing a sleeveless Nikki. He certainly was jacked! Though he was definitely well over 70, the skin over his muscles was still tight.

"Do you want me to take over?" asked Tobias.

"I'm fine. It'll go faster if I do—huff—it," he panted.

"Watch out, the fence might be electrified."

"No, that was—huff—just at the beginning. Now nobody dares to enter anyway."

"Why is that?"

"I don't want to... bore you... with rumors."

"Nice guns!" said Tobias.

"These are—huff—muscles, not guns."

"Bodybuilding?"

"Lots of exercise... and turinabol."

"Isn't that dangerous?"

"Exercise or... the medicine?"

"You know."

"What's good for Agricultural Production Cooperative[1] cattle can't be bad for us, right?"

Matze managed to say the entire sentence without gasping once. The man was really in much better shape than Tobias. As soon as all this was over, he'd start working out again. Was that the sound of an engine? Tobias looked up at the sky but didn't see a plane. Crouching over, he sneaked forward towards the street.

They were coming from the north. Two vehicles with blue lights. Going by the sound, they were probably traditional Ladas.

"Hey, we've got company!"

"How much longer?" asked Matze.

"Three minutes, tops."

"Dang it."

Matze threw the spade over the fence.

"What are you doing?" asked Tobias.

"Saving your life. The hole won't be finished in time."

Matze took Tobias's sack and tore open the cable ties. Then he lifted it to the upper edge of the fence and, using his other hand, hit it hard from underneath. The contents of the bag flew in a high arc over the barrier and scattered on the other side.

"Hey, what are you doing? I still need that!"

"Yeah, that's what I thought. Come here!"

Matze was now speaking in a commanding tone, and Tobias instinctively obeyed. Matze gave him two corners of the mat, which was now empty. The sirens were very close.

"Use it to go over the barbed wire!"

They stood next to the fence and threw the mat on top so that it covered the barbed wire.

"I'll give you a boost!" Matze barked, then stood alongside the fence with his legs wide apart.

Tobias set his left foot on top of Matze's interlocked hands, braced himself on his broad shoulders—and flew! Matze had thrown him like a little boy. But gravity shows no mercy, and every flight must come to an end. Tobias's right foot brushed the fence. He was on the other side! The mossy forest floor was rushing towards him. There was a tree stump on the left. Tobias rolled off to the right.

Brakes squealed. The two white Ladas stopped, one behind the other. Men in civilian clothes jumped out and drew their weapons. Matze was standing next to his Jawa and pointed towards the forest. Tobias jumped up and felt a shooting pain in his knee. Shit, he must have injured it when he landed. The old cabin was up ahead. He sprinted toward it. His knee hurt, but he didn't care. Thirty more meters.

There was a bang. A piece of bark was blasted off the tree trunk in front of him. The bastards were shooting at him! He still had the pistol on his belt. But there were at least eight men. The trees didn't provide enough cover as they boxed him in. Twenty meters. Another bang. Pain shot through his body. The knee. He kept on running. With the Makarov, it wouldn't be easy to hit a target moving through the dim light of the zone. These weren't Western heroes he was dealing with, but the Stasi.

Ten meters.

He could hear the wailing of a siren again. They'd gotten reinforcements.

There was the hut. It had a back entrance. Hopefully the door wasn't locked!

Another bang. Tobias thought he heard the bullet whizzing over his head. No impact. There was the door. He pushed down the handle, hurled himself against it, and bashed his shoulder. Dang. It opened outward. Another bang. The bullet hit the door, leaving a small dent in the metal hardware. Open door, rush inside. Shut door. Tobias threw himself to the floor. He didn't have much time. They were hot on his heels.

Brakes squealed. Car doors slammed. Tobias crawled to the window looking out on the street. He pulled himself up carefully and peered out. There was the spot where he'd been thrown over the fence. The mat was gone. Matze must have thrown it after him. That would buy Tobias some time. Crap. He didn't have any of his equipment. Why hadn't he acted faster? But without Matze and just using the little plastic shovel, it would have taken him a lot longer.

Bang! A bullet hit the window frame, and Tobias ducked. They knew where he was. He fumbled for his gun. The hut gave him cover, but he was trapped. All they had to do was surround it and wait. Or they could smoke him out right now. They could put a little gasoline on a handkerchief, then set it on fire and throw it.

Another bang.

"Riedel, are you nuts? Put that gun away right now! Hold your fire. That goes for all of you!"

It was a woman's voice. Tobias spontaneously obeyed and

took his fingers off his own pistol. He peeked over the windowsill again. A stocky figure in a trench coat approached the fence at the point where he'd gone over. That must be the woman who'd given the command. She shook the fence and seemed satisfied.

"Riedel, come here."

A gangly young man appeared by her side. The woman bent down, picked something up, and pressed it into Riedel's hand. It was the plastic shovel.

"Use this to fill that hole!" the woman ordered. "I don't want anything coming out of there."

"And the fugitive?" asked a man in the back whom Tobias couldn't see. "He's hiding in that old low-rise. It would be easy for us to get him out."

"Are you crazy?" asked another man, who was also hidden by a bush. "Didn't you hear what happened to the task force from Schwarze Pumpe? They were completely torn to pieces, all three of them!"

"Oh, they were totally wasted and ran into a pack of wolves. They're starting to take over here. Don't believe those cock and bull stories."

"Quiet," the woman said. "Our pursuit of the fugitive stops here. Others will take care of him. What goes on past that fence is none of our business. And we don't spread any rumors about it either. Are we clear?"

"Yes, Comrade Major," said the man who had wanted to keep going after Tobias.

The disappointment could be heard in his voice.

The one who mentioned the task force's gruesome fate reassured him, "No need to be upset. The man in there is doomed anyway."

October 12, 2029, Earth orbit

STILL NO WORD FROM EARTH. MANDY HAD TO CONVINCE HERSELF that it hadn't all been a dream by reading the latest news reports over and over again. So she'd made a soft landing on Earth and then died in the hospital. How could anyone believe that? Shouldn't the western media at least jump on those announcements and ask questions?

But it was also complicated. Her "landing" had come as a surprise to everyone, so there had been no correspondents on the ground in Kazakhstan. Mandy couldn't rely on getting help from that direction. And her friends in Lusatia hadn't been in touch with her, either. Had they stuck their necks out a little bit too far with their promise? How would regular GDR citizens, which she presumed they were, bring her home from the Völkerfreundschaft? To do that, they'd at least need a spaceship that was ready for launch.

Now she only had two days' worth of breathing air left. She'd probably have to save herself. But how?

Trying to contact the ISS again could be a good place to start. Perhaps the crew hadn't taken it seriously the first time. But now the situation was different. Word about the GDR cosmonaut's death should have gotten to the ISS. If there was now something happening on the Völkerfreundschaft clearly indicating that there was a human aboard—shouldn't the astronauts in the other spacecraft start to wonder?

Mandy checked her spacesuit. When she spent 15 minutes on

the hull of the space station, she didn't lose much air. However, the life support system did lose some oxygen when the airlock was vented. Perhaps it was time to do something about that. Instead of filling the entire space station with breathing air, it would suffice to just supply the spacesuit with it. She could tap air directly from the station's tank. Plus, if the inside was no longer pressurized, she could pass between the inside and outside as she liked.

But that meant that the last two days of her life wouldn't be very comfortable. It was already exhausting to spend more than two hours in a spacesuit. What would 48 hours be like?

Mandy was uncertain. If she was going to die anyway, she could send Sabine and Susanne a message. A goodbye. But her contact on Earth had expressly discouraged her from doing it. Should she follow that advice? What if the two girls never found out what had really happened to her?

But Mandy didn't want to waste her final chances. She was probably still secretly hoping to be rescued. Then it would be smarter to stay calm and draw out the time she had left as best she could. Even if that meant wearing the spacesuit for a very, very long time. She looked at her watch. The Völkerfreundschaft was on course to approach the orbit of the ISS in about three hours. If she heard no news from Earth in two hours, she'd climb into her spacesuit.

October 12, 2029, Lusatia

THE THREE LADAS DROVE AWAY TO THE SOUTH. MATZE'S JAWA, meanwhile, sputtered and started heading north. They probably hadn't been able to prove that Hardy's friend had done anything, so they'd let him go. Or he'd lucked out and they didn't want to make any more work for themselves. What went on behind the fence was none of their business. Or maybe Matze had been arrested and the Stasi major was the one riding his Jawa. That would be a shame, and Tobias drove that thought from his mind.

He leaned back against the concrete wall. Of course, that story the Stasi guy had related was nothing but a tall tale. He didn't need to be afraid of a couple of wolves. Since the late 1990s, several packs had shown up in Lusatia again. The farmers had grown accustomed to them and protected their pastures with electric fences. Not one single human had been attacked by a wolf in the past forty years, though there had been several incidents involving feral dogs.

But who were the others the woman had mentioned? The group in the three Ladas was definitely with the Stasi. Yet obviously there was another unit, maybe even another ministry, responsible for protecting the restricted area. The border troops seemed like the likeliest candidates. But Tobias had driven past the zone several times and had never once seen a border guard. He'd have to be careful. Maybe there was an elite force he didn't know about, equipped with the latest surveillance technology from the West. The petroleum here was the GDR's most valuable treasure, and would be afforded the corresponding protection.

He stood up and walked around the only room in the flat-roofed building. Next to the door along the back wall, there was a cot with a thin, worn mattress. There was a solid, rectangular table with two chairs that looked homemade, and a potbellied stove in the corner, with a stack of logs off to the side. A metal pipe led up from the stove through the roof and to the outside.

Tobias saw a newspaper on the table. He sat down on one of the chairs and leafed through it. It was an issue of the *Lausitzer Rundschau* from the day before yesterday. Did the building get regular visitors? Tobias listened. No, he was alone. Just a few birds were chirping. He heard a thrush and a chiffchaff, as well as a cuckoo in the distance. He looked for reports about the Völker-freundschaft space station, but didn't find anything. On page 2 there was a small article about the third manned launch from India. The Gaganyaan 3 spaceship would orbit Earth for a week, with two space travelers and a female robot aboard.

A piece of paper fell out of the newspaper and sailed to the ground. Tobias picked it up. His heart was beating so loudly that he imagined it could be heard from outside.

It was a note from Miriam. It didn't have his name written on it, probably to protect him in case someone else read the note. Definitely.

"I had a hunch you wouldn't give up. Getting into the zone was surprisingly easy," it read in dark script. "I rested in this hut for two hours and got a little sleep. But in the meantime, it seemed like something changed. Maybe it's just the heavy clouds weighing down on my mind. Though I can't see them in the darkness, I do notice them because of the absence of stars. The treetops rise into a strange nothingness. Most of all, I get the feeling that there's something creeping around the cabin. I don't know what it could be, and I haven't been able to see it with the flashlight. So either it's too fast, or my mind was playing tricks on me. You should be careful. I'm not going to follow the trail but instead will head east through the woods. Hopefully I can avoid any guards that way."

The message ended abruptly, without either a sign-off or a signature. Had somebody overpowered Miriam at that point? Tobias squinted and looked at the final letter. The small "s" had a hook at the end, the kind made when a pencil broke off while a person was writing. He knelt down in front of the table. His knee hurt, but he tried to ignore it. He carefully examined the tabletop from the side. There was something there. He felt it with his index finger. It could be the remnant of a pencil lead. Maybe Miriam had only packed one pencil. He himself didn't even have one.

He didn't have anything at all. Everything he'd packed was still strewn in front of the fence. It was about time to go and pick it up. Tobias stood up. As if on cue, it grew quiet. There were no more chirping sounds from outside. Why had the birds suddenly become silent?

Tobias opened the back door. He looked around briefly and then stepped outside. The first raindrops fell on his head.

He ran to the fence, spread the mat on the ground, and threw everything he could find onto it. His stockpile was now complete again. He quickly bundled up the mat and carried it into the hut. His knee was throbbing. But he'd done it.

Now it was raining so hard that he was probably better off waiting in the shelter. Tobias took out his provisions and water and made himself lunch. As he chewed, he was overcome by a sense of guilt. Miriam probably needed him, but he'd barely made it over the fence, and now was discouraged by a little water.

SURPRISINGLY, IT WASN'T LONG BEFORE THE RAIN STOPPED. Tobias looked at his watch. It was exactly 12:10. That meant it had been raining for exactly ten minutes. That wasn't typical at all for the weather in this region, where there was sometimes precipitation for days. But it was good for him. He went outside the house again and peed against a tree. Then he closed his makeshift backpack and set off.

How had Miriam managed to keep heading east? Tobias had to keep looking for clearings so he could identify the compass directions with the Glonass locator. His knee was grateful to take a little breather, but it felt like he was wasting time. He couldn't feel the sun at all through the thick clouds, and in the forest Tobias couldn't walk in a straight line, even though the trees had been planted in straight lines, each row looking just like the others. The further he progressed, the older—and therefore higher—the trees became. At what point would he encounter the first derricks?

Tobias stopped. He needed to make a pit stop. He set down his backpack, took out the toilet paper, and squatted behind a bush. He finished his business and tore off some grass to cover what he'd left behind. Or should he take the used toilet paper with him? But if they followed him with dogs, that would be no help, either. So he left it on the pile.

Onwards. The tracking device said he'd only gone one and a half kilometers. That wasn't much for approximately 40 minutes of walking. He hadn't found any trace of Miriam. It was more than a day now since she must have come this way. But if she'd walked only five meters away from where he was, that would be enough for him to miss any clues. Every now and then, Tobias would try his luck and walk a few steps north or south.

The high forest ended, and now there were just waist-high spruces. Tobias looked up at the sky. The cloud layer had strange bulges, reminiscent of funnels, on its underside. He took the tracking device out of his pocket. Dang it, he'd accidentally veered off course again. The little screen directed him back to a patch of high forest. In the middle of it, there was a clearing. It looked familiar. But that was impossible. He looked for the bush anyway. There it was. Someone had relieved themselves on the ground, covered everything with grass, and then thrown some crumpled gray toilet paper on top of it.

Maybe it had been Miriam. He should take a closer look at the pile. He pushed the grass aside with a stick. What was underneath looked very familiar to him. It was still steaming. He felt nauseous as the stench suddenly overwhelmed him. He backed away until all he could see was the moss of the forest. It must be a coincidence. Miriam or some other person had needed to attend to the call of nature, just as he had. Of course this was nothing out of the ordinary! Every human did it, and animals did, too. Maybe the deer here used toilet paper.

He pulled out the tracking device and checked his location. The thing was lying. It stated that he was in the same place he was when he'd taken a shit behind the bush. He shook the device, but the position didn't change. What was going on? He must have walked twenty minutes since then. And supposedly he hadn't gone one damned meter? Impossible.

Tobias tilted his head to the side so that his cheek faced upwards towards the sky. Then he rotated his body until he thought he could feel the warmth of the sun. It was up there after all! He stopped and checked his line of sight. North. Impossible.

It must be those low-hanging clouds. They messed with his head and confused his thoughts. From now on, his turd pile would be his landmark. The tracking device didn't seem to be any good. Maybe material from the many derricks, none of which he had seen, was throwing it off. Or else the signals from the Glonass satellites couldn't get through the dense cloud cover. Besides, these weren't normal clouds. They contained all the crap extracted from the earth here, first with the open-pit mining and then oil pipelines. That couldn't be good. He who stirs the sludge in the septic tank reaps the smell.

Tobias carefully committed the clearing to memory. In the back was where he'd come from. A birch with a double trunk was in the back on the left, and a spruce without a crown in the back on the right. The shrub of truth was in the middle of the edge on the left. In the direction that he'd followed out of the clearing, there was a group of three spruce trees standing close together that reminded him of women at the market. In the front and to the right, there was a mature pine towering above all the other trees. He might use it to orient himself from a distance.

He put his backpack on and marched onward. It had been a while since his knee had stopped complaining. Actually, walking in the woods wasn't all that bad. Even as a child, he'd always liked to go hunting for mushrooms on his own. His gaze wandered over the moss and he kept spotting chestnuts, and every so often a birch fungus or a red cap. He didn't pick them, even though they looked really good and had hardly any snails on them.

Another clearing was up ahead. He felt somewhat anxious as he entered it. But here there was no bush in the middle of the left edge, no market women in front, and no double birch to the side. He walked out into the clearing until he could make out the tall pine tree. It wasn't directly behind him, however, but off to one side. He must have curved around to the left. Tobias returned to the edge of the clearing and looked for a landmark in the direction he was walking. A derrick. Finally! The building complex the cosmonaut had detected was behind several derricks. He couldn't be too far off, then.

He pressed onward. He deliberately kept turning a bit to the right to compensate for his clear tendency to drift to the left. He made good progress this way until he encountered a ditch. It led north to south in an amazingly straight line. It could hardly have formed naturally, especially since the side walls sloped downwards at 45-degree angles.

But nothing here was natural. Tobias walked through a back-filled open-cast mining pit. The Earth's surface here couldn't be any more artificial, so the ditch wasn't unusual. Nevertheless, Tobias didn't dare cross it, because of the material flowing in it. That wasn't what water looked like. The surface of the liquid glinted black and looked stiff. He immediately thought of petroleum, but he would have smelled that, and there was no odor coming from the ditch.

Plus, the ditch seemed to attract and absorb all smells from its surroundings. Tobias licked his index finger and held it next to his knee. There was no air flow at all. All the same, the scent of the forest was coming at him from all sides. He thought he detected moss, pine needles, mushrooms, primroses, wild boars' mud pits, and even the scent of carrion from a slowly rotting deer. He took a few steps back and the effect subsided.

This was one strange ditch. But he'd have to cross it somehow. Tobias picked up a dry branch and threw it into the black liquid. He expected it to plunge in and then float to the surface, but it just sank, without even slowing down. There were no waves, either.

He tried again, this time with a pebble. It hit the black surface and vanished. He needed something lighter. A feather would be good, but he couldn't find one. He made do with a narrow leaf. It sailed down slowly. This time his aim hadn't been good, and the leaf flew off over the ditch. Just before it could land on the other side, a darting flame shot out of the black surface and charred the leaf. Its remains fell onto the slope on the other side.

Damn! His breath stopped short. *You're a vicious trap.* For whom? Probably for intruders like him. What would have happened if he'd gone ahead and stepped over? Would his charred body be lying on the other side? Miriam was like that. She wouldn't have hesitated for long, and would have just taken a big step and held out her hand to him.

Boom. Carbonized hand. Well, that was great. He should look around the ditch. Tobias walked a few hundred meters in one direction, then the other. Whenever there was a dark spot, he expected to find a charred corpse. But he didn't find Miriam's body. There must be a way across. But he couldn't find it in either direction. Tobias tried throwing pebbles across the ditch, each time a bit higher. The third time he succeeded. That meant that the spurting flame was no more than three meters high. All he had to do was climb a tree, jump from there to another one, and then come back down.

That should be doable. Miriam had managed.

Tobias walked along the ditch once again. After a minute or so, he came across a pine tree that was just the right age. There were still branches at the bottom, so he would be able to climb it easily. It also had a thick trunk, so hopefully it wouldn't sway too much under his weight. On the other side of the trench, there was a spruce tree with a thick layer of needles. That was good, because it would give him something to grab on to when he jumped over from a height of five meters.

Tobias adjusted his backpack, grabbed the lowest branch of the pine, and pulled himself up. *Here goes.* The next branch was somewhat offset. Tobias tried to immediately hoist himself up, but he slipped. He managed to hold on with both hands even though the backpack was pulling him down. He struggled as he did a pull-up. He got his upper body over the branch. A brief pause. Then he sat astride it and finally pulled himself up the trunk.

The third branch was almost directly over him. But it was farther away than it looked from below. Tobias jumped, slipped, and just managed to hold on to the second branch. The backpack was to blame. He only had to make it five centimeters higher! Tobias looked over to the other side. He was about two meters up. His plan should work.

He shrugged off his backpack. Then, using his left hand to brace himself against the trunk, he held his bag with his right hand as if he were a shot-putter about to throw a ball. One, two, three. The backpack went flying. As it crossed the ditch, it reached a height of more than three meters. The jet of flame only reached the dangling straps. They caught fire, but went out when the bag hit the branches of the spruce. The backpack crashed to the ground, landing just beyond the slope of the ditch on the other side.

Tobias reached the third branch, this time without the ballast. This time, it was much easier to do a pull-up. He hoisted himself up on the trunk again. This branch wasn't as stable as the first two. The needles looked gray and dry. Tobias looked down. He must be almost four meters above the ground. That was pretty damned high. But he couldn't jump off the trunk from the back. From a standing position, he wouldn't make the three meters he needed to clear between him and spruce. He had to keep going out further on this dry branch.

He took a step. Only ten centimeters.

The branch cracked. Back. This wasn't going to work. Tobias looked up. The next branch looked even thinner. This time, there would be no second try. And no hesitating. Tobias pushed off and took three quick steps forward. The branch broke—he jumped off. His legs kicked in the air.

The momentum propelled him forward towards the spruce. He stretched out his arms. Through the dense needles, he couldn't see where he should reach out, where his salvation was hiding. His right hand felt something and grabbed for it. He was jerked to the right. Something hot was shooting up behind him and his back was being roasted. But the flame didn't reach him. His left hand caught hold of a branch. The one on the right could no longer hold his weight, and Tobias slid down a little. Needles scratched his face. One poked him in the eye. He slid even further down, but his right hand found something to hold onto again.

The barbecue turned off. Tobias had made it past the range of the flame. But he wasn't back on the ground yet. The spruce pushed him outward, as if it wanted to throw him off, preferably into the ditch. He pulled himself to the right, around the tree, away from the death trap. Another branch snapped off. Damn!

He fell and time stood still. He couldn't get hold of a branch. The ground rushed toward him. Tobias rolled off, had too much momentum, and crashed with his back against the next tree over.

At first, he just remained sitting there. He'd probably broken his back and was in shock. He savored the time he had left without pain, which would surely come soon. Tobias smiled, as if he were drugged. Which of course he was. Adrenalin is a drug. It had altered his consciousness. He felt great, even though he was about to die here.

A fat drop fell on his leg. It was water. He could feel that it was cold. Then came a second drop. He'd felt something! His backbone wasn't broken! He drew in his legs as a downpour set in. Close to the trunk, he was able to stay dry. But his backpack was still out in the open. He crawled over and brought it under the protective shade of the spruce. One of the two straps had been burned through. Tobias fixed it with two cable ties. Before long, the rain stopped. It was 1:10 p.m. Again it had rained for exactly ten minutes.

October 12, 2029, Earth orbit

THIS WAS A DIFFICULT DECISION. IF SHE BRUSHED HER TEETH NOW, she'd have the minty freshness of the red and white toothpaste in her mouth for a long time. But if she didn't brush them, she'd still have that delicious cocoa taste from the Western chocolate. Mandy opted for the chocolate. As soon as she put on the helmet, she wouldn't be able to eat any more solid food. She did have a supply of isotonic nutrient solution in her suit, but the stuff tasted like salted milk porridge. It was disgusting. In training, someone claimed that was on purpose, so that food would be taken sparingly in the event of an emergency.

Before she went outside, Mandy cleaned up the kitchen again. The robot used to do that for her. That piece of shit. She'd always thought it had been built to do her work for her. But obviously it was, more than anything else, supposed to supervise her. Robots were probably better suited to that than humans were.

Somehow she was glad that Mandy Neumann, GDR cosmonaut, was officially dead. In the end, maybe they had put Bummi in her clothes and driven the robot through the republic as a heroine. Was that technically possible yet? Probably not. That must be why she'd had to die. Mandy lifted the pineapple can to her mouth and sucked on it. Nothing came out. Too bad. Pineapple had always been her favorite fruit. Nothing else seemed so exotic to her.

Okay, girl. In a few minutes, the ISS would be coming close

again. It would be a little bit further away this time, but the range of the helmet radio should still suffice. She headed into the airlock, put the helmet on, and closed the door. The life support system sucked the air out. Mandy felt for the chocolate with her tongue. The button on the outer bulkhead lit up green. She hooked both safety lines into her belt. Their other ends were secured in the airlock. That was definitely enough. She just needed a clear line of vision to the other station.

The encounter wasn't particularly dramatic, perhaps even less so for the ISS than for her. From a distance of 80 kilometers, even a ten-story skyscraper—especially one passing by at high relative speed—looked tiny. Mandy had programmed a timer into her watch. It would start in thirty seconds. Then she'd have a maximum of 90 seconds to fit everything in. The countdown began. When it reached zero, she started to speak.

"Mayday, mayday. Space station Völkerfreundschaft, cosmonaut Mandy Neumann here. I'm in urgent need of assistance. Under Article V of the International Outer Space Treaty, you are obligated to provide me with all possible help. I have forty-two hours of oxygen remaining. I repeat. I am in urgent need of assistance. This is Mandy Neumann on the Völkerfreundschaft space station. Mayday, mayday."

That was 20 seconds. She paused briefly, then repeated the text three more times. Somebody had to hear her!

October 12, 2029, Lusatia

THIS FOREST WAS STRANGE. THE CONSTANT RAIN! BUT TOBIAS had to be careful about drawing conclusions. Maybe it was because of the clouds that stayed over the area as if they'd been nailed in place. Could it be that they created a fixed weather cycle of evaporation and rain? That was the kind of thing they learned at school about the tropics. Tobias left the backpack on the ground and crawled back to the ditch. Why hadn't they just electrified the fence and anchored it properly in the ground? That would be a lot cheaper than resorting to all these sophisticated techniques. Since the ditch noticed when somebody tried to cross it, there must be hidden cameras and other electronic equipment.

Tobias stood up and strapped on his backpack, then consulted the tracking device. It seemed to have fixed itself. He was significantly closer to his goal and was counting on making it there tonight.

HALF AN HOUR LATER, HE WASN'T SO SURE ANYMORE. THE tracking device confirmed that he'd covered three kilometers. That wasn't the problem. The problem was that the forest was changing. It had begun very gradually. But now he couldn't just attribute it to his overexcitement. The colors weren't right anymore!

With every passing kilometer, the chlorophyll of the needles and leaves took on a bluer hue. The moss, on the other hand, had first turned toxic green and was now yellow, practically orange. The tree trunks had been brown before, but were now drenched in black. Tobias touched the pine tree in front of him. The dark bark was glistening, but his fingertips remained completely dry. He crouched down and exposed a bit of the forest floor. The loamy Lusatian sand, usually light brown, was purple.

He stood up again and rubbed his temples. Was exhaustion making him crazy? Tobias took off his backpack and rummaged through it. There was the little plastic shovel. It used to be red, and now it was green. Things were changing. But that was impossible.

It must be his thoughts that were changing. He dropped to his knees and dug in the ground with his hands. His skin was frog green and flecked with purple bits of clay. There was an earthworm. It was glowing red. Tobias took the combination pliers out of his bag. What for? Then he remembered. He used them to pinch his left hand between the thumb and forefinger, squeezing hard until the two blades cut through the skin. Blue blood dripped out.

The pain brought him to his senses. He'd hurt himself! Something was wrong with him. Perhaps there was toxic gas in the air that was altering his perceptions. There had never been anything in the newspaper about a chemical disaster in Lusatia, but that didn't mean much. Tobias shouldn't be here. He shouldn't have jumped over the ditch. Maybe it wasn't even really a trap. Maybe the jet of flame served to neutralize the gas.

He needed to get out of here. He wouldn't be able to help Miriam in such a state anyway. He stood up and immediately felt dizzy. All these messed-up colors were hard to take. It was as if he were trapped in a dream. A nightmare.

Tobias put his bag on his back and started walking. He staggered. Fortunately, he was still holding the combination pliers. That surprised him. He picked a spot on his forearm and pinched it.

This time, he didn't squeeze the jaws all the way shut.

But the pain was intense enough to clear his mind. Adrenaline kicked in and chased away the nausea. The effect wouldn't last long. Tobias started running. Every time he began to stagger, he applied the pliers again. Maybe slapping himself would do the trick. But he didn't want to try it. Once he fell over, he'd never get back up. He had to get out of this nightmare.

Tobias ran. The backpack beat against his rear end as if to give him an extra push. The combination pliers bit painfully into his skin.

It was the pain that saved him. The first thing to change was his skin. It was covered with jagged bruises, but returned to its previous pink color in the places he hadn't pinched yet. Then the moss changed back. The tree trunks became lighter. The needles of the pines got back their old green, though with a slight bluish tint that no longer frightened him. Out of breath, Tobias stumbled ahead. He was afraid to look back. He wanted to put some distance between himself and the changed forest first. Sweat was running down his face. His shoulders hurt from the straps, and the bag had tenderized his backside like a fresh schnitzel.

He tripped over a root and took a long tumble. The backpack took on a life of its own and slid forward over him. Tobias was just able to keep a grip on it with his right hand. It felt a lot heavier than before. What was happening? Tobias tugged on the strap. The backpack pulled in the other direction, as if somebody was trying to steal his bag from him. But nobody was there. Tobias crawled forward. The strap remained taut. The backpack was running away from him. Tobias shook his head. Not on his watch. He crawled forward some more.

There he saw a cliff. The backpack was hanging over it. Tobias stuck his head over the edge. The backpack was dangling by the strap half a meter below. Then, for many meters beyond that, there was nothing.

And then there were clouds.

He started to panic. He crawled backwards as quickly as he could. One meter, two meters. He pulled the backpack with him and pushed it back towards his feet. Then he lay down on his back. The clouds were above him, just as they were supposed to be. Tobias shifted his gaze ahead very slowly. The heavens were divided. He saw a cliff, followed by an open area covered with grass, and finally the first trees, which were stretching their crowns toward him from the sky.

Tobias squeezed his eyes shut. When he opened them again,

everything would look like it normally did. Definitely. He imagined it: he saw a clearing with an open forest behind it. The clouds had gone back up into the sky. Tobias turned onto his stomach with his eyes still closed, then opened them very slowly. He saw grass. It was green. An ant was climbing a stalk. He turned his head to the side. There was grass there, too. Very good. He lifted his head, just a little at first, and then a little more, until he saw the sky. There were clouds. But they ended in a hard line. Behind that there was forest, which was upside-down.

This wasn't possible. Tobias crawled forward toward the cliff. He already had the feeling that he was going to fall, but he hadn't even reached the edge yet. Slow. Nice and slow. His view now extended over the edge—and sank into a vat with clouds floating at the bottom. Tobias pressed himself flat against the ground. His heart was racing. Still, he forced himself to turn his head. How was he supposed to understand his situation if he didn't look at it?

It was clear what he was seeing: the world was vertically inverted. Up became down and vice-versa. It was physically impossible, but he saw what he saw. What did this mean? Had physics completely changed direction? He tore off a blade of grass and threw it over the edge. The blade rose briefly towards the clouds, but then a mysterious force kept it suspended.

He felt for a stone. It, too, flew for a little bit, then stopped in mid-air. This was insane! The stone was floating over the tops of the trees on the other side of the cliff.

Tobias closed his eyes and considered what this could mean. Apparently, gravity still worked in its usual direction. Up and down had just switched places visually. Otherwise, the change had no effect. Then that should apply to him as well. If he crawled forward, he'd float in the air just like the stone did. That made sense. Matter was matter. His body wouldn't behave differently than the stone just because he was alive. Unless he'd lost his mind.

He crawled back to get his bag. Should he stand up? No, that would make everything more difficult. There was no need for him to be ashamed of being afraid. Nobody was here to see him. He slung the strap of the backpack over his left shoulder and crawled toward the cliff. He hesitated for a moment and then moved beyond it, forcing himself to keep his eyes open.

The impression of falling was overwhelming. His consciousness told him that he was plunging towards the clouds.

Tobias just breathed, feeling the tug in the pit of his stomach. This wasn't free fall. All the forces were acting on him in the way he was accustomed to. He clawed the ground with his left hand. There was even soil, and needles. He felt them, but he couldn't see them. It was an optical illusion. Someone or something was playing tricks on his eyes. Tobias crawled onward, leaving the normal world behind. What did it look like? In this world, a person crawled on their back through the sky, far above the treetops.

He was getting better and better at this. It helped for him to concentrate on his other senses. He smelled the forest floor beneath him. Branches prickled his belly. The sand irritated the wounds he'd inflicted on himself. He even heard the crunching of the subsoil and the ugly tearing sound as the thorns on a blackberry branch tore open one leg of his uniform pants. But he kept seeing the clouds below him, and they created a falling sensation that wasn't real. He knew that, but feeling contradicted what he knew, and sometimes it won. Then he clung to the ground in panic until his other senses regained the upper hand.

Suddenly, there were drops falling on him. It looked as if the clouds were sucking water out of the forest. Ropes of rain that began in the forest reached into the depths. The image couldn't get more surreal than this. *Congratulations, you've made it to the top.* But who knew what else was in store? It was easier for him to crawl. The drops reminded him not to trust his sense of sight. They were falling, as they should.

The final few meters were especially bad. Tobias could see the cliff, but the world below him was still infinitely wrong. The bank was only millimeters thick. He would break through and fall into the clouds. Left and right, six more times. Tobias counted the necessary crawling movements, then closed his eyes. The sand, the grass, the smell of moss, and the pain were with him. He was going to make it. After the seventh movement, he lay down on his back. The clouds were above him. At 2:10 p.m., when the rain stopped, he'd reached safety.

HIS UNIFORM LOOKED TERRIBLE. TOBIAS BRUSHED THE DIRT OFF as best he could, but even after that it still looked like he'd been run over by an off-road vehicle and then dragged for a hundred meters. He'd lost his cap. He wouldn't look for it. He turned his back resolutely to the cliff.

Tobias strapped on his backpack. The tracking device didn't have any good news for him. In the past hour, he'd covered just one kilometer. Hopefully the zone didn't have any more surprises like that for him. How was Miriam? Had she survived this torture?

At least for the time being, everything seemed normal. There was open forest, with pines several meters apart. There was tall grass growing between them. It would have been paradise if the sun had been shining. Tobias was making good progress. The birds were chirping, and he tried to identify their voices. There, that was a jay. He heard the tapping of a spotted woodpecker in the distance. A thrush warbled. The short, repetitive sounds were coming from a great titmouse.

One of the birds had an especially beautiful song. It might be a blackbird. Tobias strayed somewhat off the direct path to get closer to it. He wanted to see it. The calls were coming from near the ground.

"No. No-no. Chirrup."

What? The bird could talk?

"Chirrupup. Stop right there. Chirrup."

It was a high-pitched voice, clearly not human. And it was telling him not to go any further. He followed the call. Where was it coming from? Could it really be a bird?

"No. Not no not. Chirrup. Must not. Chirrup. Come."

There! The bird was hanging upside-down from a pine. It was a nuthatch. Its beak was opening, synchronized perfectly with its words. Oh, man. Now the damned birds were talking to him! It was probably all a dream. When had it started? Before Miriam visited him? Tobias wanted to pinch himself, but then he saw the marks from the combination pliers on his arm.

He wouldn't get out of this dream so easily.

"Back. Chirrup. Go. Chirrup. Home. Here. Chirrupupup. Will die."

Maybe it was a trained animal. Wasn't it possible to teach parrots to talk? He'd never heard that nuthatches possessed similar talents, but that didn't mean they didn't. He came closer to the bird, but it scurried up the trunk just far enough that Tobias couldn't reach it. The animal turned towards him and looked at him with its left eye.

"Scram. Chirrup. Unwelcome. Danger. Zone. Chirrupupup. Warning you."

"So you're warning me, huh?"

This wasn't a trained animal. This was a nightmare. The bird nodded. It had nodded! It seemed this damned animal could understand him! Tobias put his hand to his forehead. Suddenly he had a horrible headache.

"Must understand. You must turn back. The zone is off-limits to people."

The nuthatch was no longer chirping. The words were forming directly in Tobias' head. The bird watched him curiously, as if waiting for a reaction. Tobias looked at his arm. He couldn't wake himself up. There was just one way. He reached for his belt. His service weapon was still in its holster. It was loaded. He took it out. It smelled of gun oil. He pointed it at the bird, but the bird didn't react. Maybe it didn't know what a gun was.

The animal was innocent. It was a nuthatch. Tobias wouldn't get himself out of this nightmare by shooting it.

He held the gun to his throat. The metal of the barrel was warm. He wrapped his index finger around the trigger. The bird watched him but didn't say anything more. His index finger pulled back.

"Don't. Chirrup. Don't."

The trigger locked. The safety catch had prevented the shot from firing. The bird couldn't see that. Tobias put the weapon away. This wasn't a dream. And even if it was, there was no shortcut to get out. If he shot himself, he was sure he would wake up again as a zombie. Or, even worse, he'd have to go through it all over again. This was one of those dreams that had to be dreamed all the way to the end. The bird nodded as if it had read his mind, then fluttered away.

October 12, 2029, ISS

"MIKE, GET OVER HERE!" JENNIFER CALLED OUT.

"What is it? Is the lock jammed again? I can't always be babysitting you."

Her colleague sounded annoyed. But it was normal for her to have questions. The training on Earth didn't include the hotel module at all. It was a good thing that Mike would be replaced soon.

"No, listen," Jennifer said.

She pressed the play button on the radio console.

"I am in urgent need of assistance. This is Mandy Neumann on the Völkerfreundschaft space station. Mayday, mayday."

Mike came floating up to her and pressed the stop button.

"What did I tell you? We've got to ignore it!"

"It's not coming over the Völkerfreundschaft frequency. That's the international emergency frequency!"

"Whatever. It's none of our business. Somebody will take care of it. Hurry up. Your space yoga starts in five minutes."

Mike disappeared into the tunnel that led to the greenhouse. It was his turn to cook today. He hated to cook, and that was probably why he was in such a bad mood. Jennifer pressed the play button again.

"I'm in urgent need of assistance. Under Article V of the International Outer Space Treaty, you are obligated to provide me with all possible help. I have forty-two hours of oxygen remaining."

The system had automatically recorded the message and notified her about it. Every emergency call was registered. She had no choice. The cosmonaut was right: according to the space treaty, they were obliged to help. All the ISS operator countries had signed the treaty. Jennifer would be subject to prosecution if she ignored the call. Mike would fall back on the excuse that it had been her job to take action.

That was obviously not going to help. Only the same two guests—a mother and her teenage daughter—ever came to space yoga anyway. Jennifer could visit them later in their room and make up for the missed lesson. She copied the message to the internal com system, then contacted her CapCom.

"Hi, Jenny. What's up?"

It was Robert. She was glad he was on duty. He was the only one of the CapComs who didn't act superior towards her because she didn't have much experience yet.

"I picked up a distress call here. Under Article V of the Outer Space Treaty..."

"Yes, send it on over."

She transferred the file.

"Confirmed receipt. Give me three minutes. I'll take care of it."

Robert got back to her after seven minutes.

"Sorry that took so long. We had to ask the head office first, then they reached out to the Pentagon, and then they checked with the East."

"Thank you for taking care of that, Robert."

"No problem. I don't like the outcome any more than you do."

"What do you mean?"

"Our instructions are to do nothing."

"But the woman sounded really desperate. We have two Dragon capsules up here all ready to go. I don't know how long they'd need to make an orbit adjustment, but if they can make it from Florida to here in four hours, they should certainly be able to help the cosmonaut."

"I know, Jenny. You aren't supposed to touch the capsules,

though. For safety reasons, according to mission control. Then they wouldn't have enough fuel to evacuate all the passengers in the event of an emergency."

"But two capsules aren't enough to get all our passengers back to Earth anyway. We need the Dreamchaser for that."

"I know all that. But it doesn't change anything. You don't want to rock the boat."

"And what about the space treaty?"

"We shared all of this with the East, and they've forbidden any interference."

"Since when do we care about that kind of thing?"

"Ha ha, good point. But that's the way it is. No interference."

"Is it possible that we're sacrificing that woman over there just because of the political climate?"

"How do you know it's a woman?"

"What do you mean, Robert? I heard her with my own ears."

"You heard a woman's voice."

"Yes, and the day before yesterday I saw someone scrambling around on the outer hull of the station."

"That matches the information I have from other sources."

"Spill it, then. You know I can't just let that one go."

"Okay, okay. It appears that there was an accident aboard the space station. Our sources suspect it had to do with an AI. In the GDR, they've been experimenting with autonomous AIs for a while now. Apparently they installed one in a robot. It flipped out and killed the cosmonaut. But of course that isn't a great image, so they faked an emergency landing and alleged that the cosmonaut died in the hospital."

"Has all of this been documented?" asked Jennifer.

"The images of the landing were definitely faked, and they're surprisingly bad. Everything else is made up of fragments of information that our services picked up. The landing was supposedly yesterday. So what you saw on the tenth fits. The robot is probably still in orbit and is now trying, like a siren from Greek mythology, to lure in the nearest victim."

Jennifer imagined a humanoid robot pacing the station restlessly. She felt a little sorry for it. The fact that it wanted to prolong its existence made it almost human. Had things really advanced that far in the East?

"That's really interesting. The voice sounded truly authentic. I could hear actual fear in it."

"I can give this to our audio engineers. I'm sure they can verify that the sound is computer generated."

"That would be great, Robert. Keep me in the loop, would you?"

"Sure thing. Have fun up there and don't let Mike get to you."

LATER, AS SHE WAS LYING IN HER CABIN ROOM, JENNIFER PLAYED the message to herself a few more times. What she heard was not a robot but rather a very desperate woman. If a robot were now capable of such a good imitation, wasn't it just as deserving of being rescued? There was something of a contradiction here. After all, they'd have the opportunity to access Eastern technology, which seemed to be astonishingly advanced, under the pretext of a rescue operation.

But perhaps there was already such a rescue recovery operation underway, and they didn't want to let her in on it because it was above her classification level.

October 12, 2029, Lusatia

Maybe he should have taken the road after all. He'd thought the path through the forest looked easier. How naive could you get? He still hadn't encountered the troops responsible for security here. But of course, that explained why they could afford such a simple fence.

In any case, Tobias wasn't going to reach the institute, his ultimate goal, while it was still light out. He'd only managed to cover two kilometers in the past hour. The birds were no longer speaking to him. Had the forest given up trying to frighten him off? Surely that wasn't the last of it.

Tobias looked at the tracking device. If he kept walking north, he'd eventually reach the big road, where he might be safer. And where he'd probably have to deal with soldiers, too. He looked down at himself. As a member of the People's Police, he didn't even need to identify himself anymore. And anybody would immediately be able to tell what he'd been through.

Tobias moved the backpack to his left shoulder. The right one ached. His forearms hurt, too. And his knee. What he wanted most of all was to just wail a bit. He let out a tentative groan, but it sounded bizarre. The forest canopy, which was interspersed with deciduous trees, muffled every sound.

He walked toward a pine tree, which he found intriguing because the trunk had an indentation in the middle. How could it have formed? Was there once a second tree there, or some other obstruction? Or had the trunk simply felt like growing in a curve? It wasn't the only tree with such peculiarities. The birch tree next to it had branches that arched like mushroom caps. The top of another birch pointed towards the ground. Tobias found a beech with a trunk split down the middle. There was a pine tree wrapped around another one. Was it happening again? Were the trees about to leap into the sky? He touched the trunk of a spruce that had formed itself into a kind of egg. It was as if a fat, long-haired man had transformed into a tree.

But this wasn't a fairy tale. Had somebody been performing genetic experiments? What exactly was he looking at here? He could see the effect increasingly not just in the trunks, but also the branches and twigs. They formed impossible figures that looked like they'd been drawn by M.C. Escher, intertwining with each other or running perfectly parallel for two meters. It seemed that the rules that usually applied in nature had been suspended. With the exception, perhaps, that roots always started in the ground.

Nope, guess again. There was a pine tree hovering thirty centimeters above the ground. Tobias tested a branch to see if the tree really remained stable even though it had absolutely no support underneath.

It did. Tobias set down his backpack and moved away a few meters. At that moment, the bag blew up like a balloon, swelling and swelling until it looked like a pig's head. No, no, no. The forest wanted to drove Tobias insane. Or it already had. He rushed toward his backpack, and the closer he got, the more it shrank. When he reached the bag, it was the size of a clenched fist, but still weighed the same as before.

Maybe something in the air was confusing his senses? Tobias glanced at his fingers. They looked entirely normal. He walked over to a spruce tree that was split down the middle and, holding his hand perpendicular to the ground, tried to stick it into the gap.

His hand split, too.

The top side of his hand flowed around the trunk on the right, and his palm on the left. Tobias wanted to pull it back but forced himself to see the experiment through. On the other side of the trunk, his hand flowed back together again. He could see it through the opening. To prove it really was his hand, he stuck up his thumb.

Tobias turned around and went over to his backpack. His hand was back to normal. The perspective had changed. Now it went downhill. His pack was at the bottom of a hole in the shape of a slightly truncated cone. The farther down Tobias got, the clearer it became to him that it wasn't a hole, but an elevation. As he climbed, he bent forward instinctively and nearly lost his balance. The backpack seemed to shrink even more, but once he reached it, it was about half its usual size. Tobias felt something almost like relief, then put it on. He simply wouldn't look at it again until the zone had settled down.

The tracking device showed contradictory information. The alleged institute was sometimes 17 kilometers away, sometimes 12. But the direction was always the same. So he set out. So far, every strange phenomenon had eventually dissipated.

The innkeeper was right, after all. The zone was haunted. Or was it something else? It was almost as if the area had a consciousness of its own. What a great prank it was to confuse visitors like this.

But a forest in Lusatia certainly didn't act this way on its own. Tobias didn't believe in ghosts or spirits. There must be other causes.

Conditions did in fact normalize after a while. After just ten minutes, the backpack was smacking his rear end again, as usual. It started raining right at 16:00. The drops came down from the clouds above, splashing on Tobias's skin and running off in little rivulets. He couldn't be stopped now. He actually covered almost nine kilometers in an hour and a half.

His good intentions vanished into thin air when he noticed the things. Tobias immediately dropped behind a fallen tree. Something rattled in his backpack.

It appeared that the things were looking for something, because one of them had gotten down on its knees and was digging in the ground with its long arms. Something in its hand, or whatever that was at the end of the arm, was glowing blue. Then there was a hissing sound, and a hole opened up in the ground.

Its two companions consulted one another with a grunt and

approached the tree he was hiding behind. They must have heard him! As he watched them through a narrow gap under the tree, he was trembling all over.

They were creatures with two legs and shiny skin, and they were significantly taller than humans. They had huge eyes, almost like insects. The air on Earth must not agree with them, because they wore breathing masks that emitted a thin, green vapor from the sides with every breath they took.

They stopped two meters from where Tobias was hiding. They smelled of sulfur. If he had been religious, he might have mistaken them for emissaries of hell. But Tobias knew better. They were aliens. Now things became clear to him. A UFO must have landed in the zone sometime, probably when oil had allegedly been discovered. Somehow the GDR had managed to keep their visit under wraps. Maybe the aliens were supplying technology, or maybe energy, that helped to create the petroleum that supposedly came from the earth.

If somebody had told him that, he would have said it was the ravings of a total nut job. Why would aliens contact the GDR, of all places? Out of solidarity, of course, because socialism prevailed legitimately throughout the entire universe—that's what Egon Krenz would have said. But there were probably practical reasons. Maybe their spaceship had crashed here purely by chance, and now they had to wait in Lusatia until they could fly back home. The dense cloud layer served as camouflage so that the UFO wasn't visible from the air. The strange phenomena in the forest were perhaps side effects of the aliens' technology. Dr. Ralf Prassnitz had figured it all out and had therefore been eliminated.

The two aliens grunted again. The third grunted back. *Yes, go on with your patrol. There's nothing to see here.* But the pair were coming closer now. The smell of sulfur grew stronger. Tobias almost managed to hold back a sneeze. Almost.

The alien on the right leapt onto the tree trunk. Tobias felt for his weapon. He was going to put up the best fight he could. And what if that led to a conflict between humankind and the aliens? Whatever. They couldn't be that powerful, or they wouldn't have been living in a former open cast mine for the past forty years. If they could only breathe bad air, the chemical district near Halle and Leipzig would certainly have been a better location.

The alien landed behind him and looked in the direction that Tobias had come from. As soon as he turned around, it would spot him. Tobias drew his gun and released the safety this time. He pointed it at the alien.

It turned towards him, and German People's Police Section Officer Lieutenant Tobias Wagner shot starship commander Wikuss Quirtz of the Outer Fleet Quadrant 7, Milky Way.

That was how the history books would describe the start of the war between mankind and aliens. But Tobias had nothing against the visitors. He just wanted to help Miriam find her husband.

There was a bang. The alien flinched and grabbed its shoulder. Clean shot! It didn't seem to be troubling his opponent— quite the opposite. The being from another star rushed towards Tobias, roaring. This time he aimed for the stomach, hoping that the creature's heart was somewhere else.

This shot had an impact. The alien collapsed. Its friend sprinted over to its fallen comrade and tore off its head. Tobias was shocked by such cruelty until he realized that a human head had emerged from underneath.

"You moron, what have you done?" the friend shouted in a Berlin accent.

Tobias pulled himself up. The alien was a human. Its head was human, at least. His eyes were painted to look enormous. The forehead was black with three vertical white stripes.

"What are you? Hybrids?" he asked.

"Don't you get it? We're actors, you dummkopf!"

October 12, 2029, Earth orbit

Mandy turned the knobs on the radio. Either her last friends on Earth had forgotten about her or had gotten into trouble themselves. She was betting on the latter. What was going on was unbelievable. The ISS was ignoring calls made on the emergency frequency! That alone would normally be an international scandal, and the GDR would take the operators of the space station to the international court.

It seemed that everything was somehow connected to the MKF-8. That was what had started it. Somebody thought Mandy had seen too much, though she hadn't even viewed the images until just now! This person must have power in both the GDR and the NSEA that she previously wouldn't have thought possible. All she wanted was to hold her children in her arms again!

Mandy floated up to the camera. It wasn't attractive or especially modern-looking. It was a block the size of a nightstand, clumsily encased in metal and suspended from cables like a seriously injured patient in an emergency room. Several weeks of training were required to be able to operate the analysis software. Mandy had to travel to the state-owned enterprise Carl Zeiss Jena especially for that, because the engineering office didn't want to hand over the program under any circumstances. At first, she resented this Prassnitz guy because that meant she couldn't see her children for a week.

Now, because of him, she would never see them again. But

Mandy couldn't hold it against him. Seemingly he'd been caught up in all this in much the same way she had. Or had he made a mistake that would now be her downfall? She turned up the ventilation in her helmet. Her breath was fogging up the front pane again. She'd love to take back her decision to spend her final hours in the spacesuit. She would gladly make use of a toilet now instead of the diaper. But filling the station with air again would take two hours off the time she had left, and it she might urgently need them. She wouldn't give up hope, even though it would make the waiting more tolerable.

She readjusted the camera. According to the flight plan, she'd be crossing over the GDR again soon. This time she'd photograph the Baltic coast. The GDR's spaceport was located on the island of Usedom in Peenemünde. If any efforts were being made to save her, there should be a rocket on the launch pad there, pointing up to the sky with its tanks steaming.

There was still a little time before the flyover, so she floated over to the main computer. The images from the restricted zone were still open. Mandy looked at this place with no name. The color calibration told her that the trees had all been planted about 40 years ago. So the buildings must be about that old, too. But Mandy couldn't see any boilers or piping. This place definitely had nothing to do with the extraction and processing of oil.

She shifted the photo section further to the east. Behind the buildings, deep grooves ran through the terrain. Along the edge, she detected artificial structures, presumably remnants of earlier technology, that looked like giant rakes. There were still no drilling rigs or pipelines to be seen.

Instead, there was something behind an open pit that Mandy at first took for a lake. But it was simply too round for that. The surface area was a perfect circle. Inside, the image showed the deepest black she'd ever measured using the MKF-8. Around the periphery of the circle, about every eight degrees, were stations with a semicircular base. From space, she couldn't tell what purpose these formations served. Maybe they just created an appearance of what looked like a circle from space? She imagined that it was a projection that prevented even sophisticated technology like her MKF-8 from capturing images of what was underneath.

The GDR knew how to keep secrets.

Mandy sighed. She'd never thought she would be a victim of all that secrecy herself. But she wouldn't be taking the secrets to her grave. She made her way to the radio and described what she'd seen for her friends on the ground. Maybe they could do something with it. If they were still alive.

Mandy was distracted by the main computer. Several red lights were flashing. How long had they been doing that? One disadvantage to the lack of atmosphere was that she couldn't hear the alarm. She should get the computer to redirect everything to the helmet radio. As she got closer, the screen turned on. What in the world was that? She couldn't believe her eyes. It was a proximity alarm. A spaceship was flying toward the station! No, not one, but two! Tears of joy sprang to Mandy's eyes. Someone must have heard her. She'd be able to hug Sabine and Susanne again!

October 12, 2029, Nichevo

"Shit, he's shooting!" shouted P7.

"Well, I did warn you! Why didn't you get him with the fly swatter?" asked R4 in return.

"I had no idea he was going to..."

"You knew from the start that he wasn't some harmless mushroom picker."

R4 was right. He should have known. From the beginning, the small-town cop's pistol had been a level 3 risk. Level 3 meant immediate decommissioning. But R4 had been sitting next to him the whole time. He'd even been the one to add the "chirrup" to the bird calls.

"You yourself were watching pretty eagerly to see how far he'd get," said P7.

"But you're the one responsible for this breach. I'm not going to get involved with your work."

This was so typical of R4. P7 banged his fist on the table. As long as everything was going well, R4 was on board, but when there were problems, he tucked his tail between his legs. Now he wanted to push off all the blame on him.

"I won't let you get away with that, my friend," said P7. "We've both had our fun, and now we'll both accept the consequences."

"You're out of your mind!" shouted R4. "This is your problem."

"Oh, is that what you think? The recording I made of our shift proves the opposite. I'm sure you remember how beautifully you sang? 'Chirrupup. Stop. Chirrupup.' Ha ha. Great show."

R4 screwed up his face. "You what?"

"I made a recording, of course. That's what I always do. Now we'll find out what it's good for."

"But that violates..."

"Go ahead and report me. But then it'll be your turn. And your girlfriend's, too."

"Leave my wife out of the... What did you say?"

"Ah, so P5 is actually your wife. That's even better."

He'd known there was something going on between R4 and P5. Private matters were taboo at work. They didn't even know each other's names. If R4 had managed to get his wife placed here as well, he must have connections. *I need to be careful.*

"It's none of your business," R4 said.

"That's true. And it'll stay that way if you help me resolve this little problem here."

"You'll be sorry," R4 said. "Let's take a closer look at the puppeteers."

P7 switched to the camera closest to the injured man. The puppeteer had a hole under his collarbone and was bleeding profusely. He'd removed his disguise up to his chest. His two colleagues were standing behind him and the People's Police officer was holding all three of them at bay with his gun.

"This is what happens when puppeteers have to walk around unarmed," P7 said.

Discussions about whether comrades in the area should receive a weapon had been brewing in the collective for quite a while. Nobody had made it through the zone so far, so the higher-ups had shied away from the effort. But now, with two breaches in 24 hours, that would likely change. P7 wanted the comrades to be armed, even if it that meant it wouldn't be so exciting to watch them at work anymore.

"You forgot to power down the big mirrors," R4 said. "What if the company commander notices?"

P7 quickly turned off the mirrors. The company commander was constantly on their case about saving energy. Financing the zone got more expensive every year, and revenues had gone down. Somebody had recently suggested sticking unsuspecting citizens in the zone and selling their experiences to Western TV. Nobody would have to know where the recordings came from. Supposedly, a puppeteer had been caught auctioning off recordings over the Kybernetz.

"And now?" asked P7.

He zoomed in on the policeman. His uniform was torn and dirty. After crawling between the mirrors, it was hardly surprising. It wouldn't be a problem if he'd crossed the area standing up, but so far nobody had dared to do that.

"He won't last much longer," R4 said.

"But he's got the upper hand right now," P7 said.

"Can you activate the automatic firing mechanisms?"

"You know very well that they make no difference. It makes an even bigger mess. I vote to leave it to the puppeteers. After all, they're trained for this kind of thing."

"Are they?" asked R4.

"I think so. Well, I assume so. It would make sense, anyway."

"And if not?"

"Then it's their own fault if they bite the dust."

"Have you lost it, P7? Then we'll have a definitive breach!"

That was true. It would be a total fiasco. The mirage field was the last major obstacle after the aliens, and this member of the People's Police would probably make it through easily. R4 was right. He should have neutralized him with the fly swatter right at the start. The rule was to treat everything above level 3 that way.

"We need to talk to him," said P7.

"Talk? Now? The man already knows too much," said R4.

"The Stasi can deal with that, then. I'm sure they'd be happy for a distraction. We've just got to get him outside the fence, or they won't lift a finger."

"That could work. They don't often get their hands on people who have made it through the zone."

The Stasi and the ZfL had been in fierce competition since Krenz founded the Zentralinstitut in the early 1990s. At first, the Stasi was reluctant to accept being deprived of control over the zone, and it still followed the ZfL's activities with the eyes of a hawk. They'd take good care of an informant who knew something about the zone's current state. The institute's management would never know anything about it. Just as long as everybody kept quiet.

"So we're in agreement, then?" asked P7.

"Fine. But you get the puppeteers to keep their mouths shut."

October 12, 2029, Lusatia

THIS WAS A STANDOFF. TOBIAS HAD GONE THROUGH SUCH situations at the police academy. By actively moving around the area, he could hold three people at bay for a while with his gun. But he couldn't ever turn his back on them. How long could he keep that up? He didn't have time. He'd have to reach some sort of agreement with them.

Tobias saw that one of the three, still fully in costume, was touching his ear. Was he communicating with a central office? His lips were moving. He was probably vocalizing through a throat microphone. Finally, he nodded. Tobias pointed the gun at his head.

"Hey, hey, hey, just calm down," the man said.

"I am calm. Don't come near me," said Tobias.

"Our comrade here is in urgent need of a doctor."

The man Tobias had shot really was losing a lot of blood.

"Yes, and that's why you should comply with my demands."

The problem was that he hadn't come up with any demands yet.

The injured man moaned.

"It's okay," said the man. "If we all keep calm now, nobody's gonna get hurt. So, what do you want?"

"I want to know what's going on here."

He preferred not to tell them that he was looking for Miriam. There was always the possibility that she'd done better than he had. If he were to bring her up now, it would only set off a search operation.

"You haven't guessed already? We make sure that nobody breaks into the zone. A little hocus-pocus works better than a wall or a prohibition. You can see that with the anti-imperialist barrier. The higher the Stasi built it, the more people wanted to go over it. The zone only had one break-in last year. I'm sure you heard the rumors about it."

"So all these obstacles are just staged?"

"Hold on, this is high-tech deterrence. A whole lot of brain-power goes into it."

"And you're not from the company?" asked Tobias.

"We're from a different company."

"From the Central Institute of Landscape Planning and Design."

"Oh, so you already know that."

"There are a few things I know."

"Listen, comrade. Our friend here is seriously injured. That's why I have to cut our conversation short. Here's what we're offer-ing: We'll get you out of the zone, right up to the gate. Nobody will ever know anything about it. You'll change your clothes, go back home, and forget all about it."

"How is that supposed to work?"

"The road isn't far. Our patrol car is waiting there."

"What about the hole in your friend there?"

"An accident. There used to be a Soviet military training area here. He found an old Makarov and played around with it."

"They'll buy that?"

"Leave that to us. You'll be outside the gate and a free man."

Should he agree to this proposal? It was risky. If they got rid of him, they could just pick up the phone and make a call to the Stasi. On the other hand, he wouldn't get far with those three men here. He couldn't go looking for Miriam or her husband with them in tow, which would just put the two of them in danger. It was a shame that everything he'd done seemed to be for nothing. Now Miriam was on her own. Maybe he could at least help Mandy, who must feel completely abandoned in the space station. But he'd only get the chance to do that if the three men from the Zentralinstitut didn't hand him right over to the

Stasi. Their promises weren't enough. He simply couldn't give them the opportunity.

"I agree," Tobias said. "But on one condition: You won't drop me off at the gate, but will take me to Halbendorf."

"But our comrade here..."

"It's not up for discussion. That's ten minutes more at most he'll have to hold on. Otherwise, I'll have no choice and will have to shoot all of you."

Tobias said this as calmly as possible, as if it were the most normal thing in the world and he already had practice shooting people. He was bluffing, of course. He would never be able to kill someone just like that. He felt sorry for the guy with the hole beneath his collarbone. Hadn't he seen him at the inn the other day, with a friend? He remembered seeing a face that was made-up like that.

The man moved his lips again and gazed into the distance with an intent look on his face. Tobias guessed that the central institute was in that direction.

"All right, that's how we'll do it, then," said the man.

THE MOST DIFFICULT MOMENT CAME WHEN THEY WANTED TO GET into their vehicle, which was a small Barkas flatbed truck. There was only room for three of them in the cab. Tobias insisted that the injured man go in the back, because he posed the least risk back there. He could keep the other two in check from inside the cab. He took the backpack on his lap so he could comfortably rest his hand with the gun on it. The gun did get heavy after a while.

To get in, both had to take their heads off. Underneath, one had blond and the other had red hair. They weren't much older than 30 and all had identical makeup. It was impossible to tell which of them had been at the inn.

The spokesman sat at the wheel. He drove the Barkas as fast as it could go. Nobody said a word as they made their way to the gate, which took them just under 15 minutes. Tobias felt regret at every single kilometer that took him in the wrong direction. It had all been for nothing! At the gate, a guard in an unfamiliar uniform took a quick look at the driver's badge, then waved them through.

Staying alongside the zone, they sped north on the country road. Tobias looked in the rearview mirror. There was no one following them. The right side of the road was in the shadow of the clouds. Only when the Barkas avoided a pothole did sunlight briefly shine into the cab. All of this was sheer insanity. An obscure troupe had set up scenery and created a Potemkin village with the sole intention of scaring off possible intruders. It made no sense. At least not for a few oil wells.

"So tell me, what are you guarding there anyway? What's this whole song and dance about?" asked Tobias.

"If we told you, we'd have to take you right back," the driver said.

"You won't be doing that," Tobias said, brandishing his gun.

"Well, tell him already," said the one sitting next to him. "That gun makes me nervous."

"Fine. But you didn't hear it from us," said the driver. "Back in the mid-nineties, apparently they couldn't get enough. Something really bad happened in the middle of the oil production area. A chemical accident on the scale of Chernobyl, but with chemical waste instead of radioactivity. First of all, it wasn't supposed to come out, and secondly, the stuff is still there."

"And that's the reason for all this theater? Wouldn't it be cheaper to just clean it up?"

"You haven't been in there. The sludge causes mutations and cancer. It's actually worse than Chernobyl. And reportedly, the people who were living there... changed. The living dead, you know what I mean? The people up at the top are afraid it will spread. The chemical stuff also altered bacteria."

"Don't go telling fairy tales. Bacteria!" said Tobias.

"You only hear about the living dead," said the man in the middle. "I don't know anyone who's ever seen one."

"Because it's contagious as shit, that's obvious," the driver said. "Whoever encounters one becomes one themselves. Then they send you deep into the zone with your buddies."

Was that true? The driver seemed convinced. But maybe they were all trained to spout this drivel, and it was all a part of the strategy to disguise and deceive. Just like this ride that had taken him out of the zone. Everything was going too smoothly. Tobias looked in the mirror again, but they still weren't being followed. He almost wished they were. It would be easier to handle an opponent he could see.

The driver had to slow down when they reached a village called Schleife. Some people on bicycles were in the road. In the middle of the village was a sign for "Wake and Beach." That must be what Tobias was looking for. The truck was driving towards the lake. For a few meters, the road became a shore road.

"Stop," Tobias shouted.

At the same time, he released the gun's safety just in case they didn't follow his instructions. Maybe there was a Stasi unit already waiting in Halbendorf. The driver slammed on the brakes and the truck came to a screeching halt.

"We're not in Halbendorf yet," said the man who was driving.

"I know."

Tobias pushed open the door and climbed out of the cab, keeping an eye on the men.

"Okay, off you go!"

The door slammed shut. The Barkas turned around on the road and drove away. Tobias waited until it was out of sight, then headed towards the lake. Water seeped into his shoes. It was cold, but Tobias couldn't be stopped. The backpack suddenly felt light, presumably because it was floating. At the same time, his wet clothes pulled him down.

It was freezing cold. Tobias breathed in hard, then went deeper and deeper into the lake until he was fully submerged.

October 12, 2029, Earth orbit

THREE RINGS, ALL OF WHICH APPEARED TO BE ON THE SAME AXIS, circled the blue globe. On each of them glided a small sphere, expanding and contracting. Two of the spheres could have been rubies, while the one on the middle ring looked more like a sapphire. The two outer rings rotated slowly, relentlessly approaching the middle one. When they reached it, which would be soon, that would be her salvation.

Mandy tried to call the approaching ships, but the radio system still didn't work. She climbed back onto the outer hull. Australia was hovering above her. The globe bathed the gray metal of the space station in a pale light. It was enough for her to make out everything that might get in her way. Mandy secured herself with two lines.

The rescuers would have to come from behind. The two spacecraft caught up to the Völkerfreundschaft in a lower orbit, then closed in on it. Mandy looked behind her, but she was still all alone. That was to be expected. She wouldn't be able to see her rescuers until they were a few hundred meters away, unless they showed up against the globe behind them before that.

She tried the helmet radio anyway. The people on board the two ships were probably waiting to hear from her.

"Völkerfreundschaft to Rescue Mission, come in."

She didn't know what else to call her rescuers. Which space-faring nation could have sent them? The Americans, Europeans, Russians, and Chinese were definite possibilities. Only those four could manage to get two ships into a given orbit within 24 hours. Russia and China were the most likely. The GDR had bought space technology from both of them. But the West might also have an interest in saving Mandy; after all, she had the MKF-8, the world's most advanced camera for Earth observation, on board with her. She'd need to make sure the camera stayed put.

Or not? If the GDR was leaving her to die but the West came to her rescue, wouldn't it be fair to thank the latter by giving them the MKF-8? But Mandy had to think about her children, too. If she became a traitor to the socialist cause, it was possible she'd never see Susanne and Sabine again. That had already happened to several athletes who had chosen to continue their careers in the West because they could earn more money there.

"Völkerfreundschaft to Rescue Mission, come in."

Nobody answered. Maybe they were still too far away. Whoever was coming for her would certainly be listening on all frequencies. Should she climb back into the station? The main computer knew how much longer it would take. No. Out here, she could savor the anticipation better. Besides, she still had to get her fill of looking at the Earth. It was certainly the last time she'd be able to enjoy this view. She had no desire to ever get into a spaceship again, and she wouldn't stray a single meter from her daughters' side.

BUT EVEN AFTER A HALF HOUR HAD PASSED, NOTHING COULD BE seen or heard of the rescue mission. She loosened the lines again and crawled into the airlock. Since all the bulkheads were open, it only took her two minutes to reach the main computer.

She couldn't distinguish the three rings on the screen from each other anymore. The two rubies and the sapphire were gliding through space on practically the same orbital track. Mandy increased the scale. The spaceships were indeed approaching. If she were outside, she would be able to see their engines, which were equalizing the orbital velocity and thus also the altitude with a final reverse thrust. But she found it strange that neither of them seemed to be aiming directly at the docking port in the back. One of the two ships was approaching the front and the other the back, where the exit was located. There was no way to dock at either location. And why weren't they talking to her?

Mandy floated to the airlock, secured herself, and felt her way outside. Two shadows were hovering between the space station and the globe. Maneuvering thrusters kept lighting up briefly.

"Völkerfreundschaft to Rescue Mission, come in."

They didn't reply. Mandy tried to make out the exact shapes of the shadows. What had they sent out to her? They certainly weren't shaped like typical passenger capsules, which had heat shields for re-entering the Earth's atmosphere. Maybe the shield was hidden under cladding. But Mandy also found that everything else about the shape of the ships, which looked quite similar, was unfamiliar to her. They weren't transporters approved for human use. They weren't even cargo craft.

Now she noticed a robot arm taking aim at the station from the probe flying toward the tail. It was just ten meters away, while the other one still had about 50 meters to go. Mandy moved toward the stern, shining her helmet light on the robot arm, which ended in a three-fingered hand that resembled a dinosaur claw. In the middle was a long, spinning rod about the width of a finger. A threaded tip reflected the light from her helmet.

A drill. That thing wanted to drill a hole in the space station! She needed to get to the back of the station as fast as possible! Mandy released the safety line. This couldn't be happening! The visitors weren't interested in saving her. They wanted to kill her!

Mandy worked her way forward, from one handgrip to the next. There was no time for securing. The thing was just two or three meters away from the hull. The drill was about to go in. She wasn't going to make it. Shit! Unless... Mandy jumped. She pushed off toward the stern and broke away completely from the station. If she'd made a miscalculation, the Earth would be getting her as a new moon. The station flashed beneath her.

But she hadn't miscalculated. Mandy grabbed onto one of the unwanted visitor's solar panels. Her momentum pushed both of them further back. The probe resisted, but it had a poor approach angle. The thing was still trying to maneuver its power unit into a better position. It bucked under her like a boisterous horse. But Mandy wouldn't let herself be shaken off. They kept moving along the edge of the space station.

There was a place she could catch her feet at the very end of the space station. Mandy couldn't see it, but she remembered it from the training she'd had on Earth. This model wasn't completely true to the original, but it was very similar. And it had a railing running all the way around the tail that was great for clamping one's feet into.

Mandy stretched out. She had to reach the metal rail and get her toes under it. The probe helped her accelerate toward the space station. There. Mandy felt the metal. Now she mustn't let go. Her feet were her only connection to the station, to life.

Mandy pushed away the probe, which retained its inertia even in microgravity. She shoved as hard as she could, and slowly the module, which weighed several tons, broke away. "DEOS 12," the acronym for "DE-Orbiting Satellite," was written on the side. Somebody had sent two scrap collectors after her. The satellites, which were owned by the UN, forced space debris out of orbit by attaching themselves to an object and slowing it down until it quickly crashed. After that, they would search for another victim.

"You're not going to drill into my station!" Mandy shouted at the shadow that lagged slowly behind her.

She watched the probe's thrusters, but it didn't seem to want to approach again. Very good. Mandy brought up her line and secured herself.

At the same moment, she felt a vibration. It passed through the sturdy soles of her boots and gave her goose bumps. The movement was coming from the front. The second probe had settled on the bow. Its robot arm clamped onto two handles simultaneously, and the drill pushed into the metal of the outer hull.

Mandy climbed closer. The thread of the drill sent splinters flying, and they gleamed in the glow of her helmet light. She felt physical pain, as if the tool were drilling not into the Völkerfreundschaft but her skull.

Mandy tried to shake the satellite, but it didn't move. It was DEOS 17. She traced the number with her finger. The 17th probe of the DEOS fleet would eliminate any remaining traces of her. The satellite would direct the Völkerfreundschaft into the

Earth's atmosphere so that it would completely burn up. It wouldn't even be possible to detect any remnants of DNA. Perhaps her daughters would see a fireball in the sky, but they wouldn't know it was a final message from their mother. Maybe it was better that way.

Mandy released the safety line and floated toward the airlock. It wouldn't make any difference now if she were to accidentally lift off into infinity.

But she reached the entrance to the station. The drill had succeeded. It had pierced the inner wall of the bow. Now it split into three pieces that folded over in opposite directions like a rivet, affixing the DEOS probe to the station once and for all. It wouldn't be long before the scrap collector fired its engines.

October 12, 2029, Lusatia

THE SKI JUMP WAS ANCHORED ON THREE STEEL POLES AT THE bottom of the lake. But visibility was only two meters at most. Hopefully there really was an entrance to the tunnel down there, as Matze had told him. Tobias pulled himself down by the struts of the pole in the front. The backpack tried to drag him up, but he was stronger.

He made it to the bottom, which was covered in mud, in 30 seconds. There. That rectangular brown board over there might be the entrance. It was in the middle of the three steel poles. Tobias used one hand to hold on and the other to grab the board. It was surprisingly easy to lift. A cloud of mud rose as he pushed it to the side.

Beneath it was the opening to a concrete pipe. It looked up at him like the ravenous mouth of a huge snake hiding in the mud. The only thing missing was a forked tongue sticking out. Tobias gave himself a push, and before the backpack could pull him back up to the surface, he grabbed the edge of the concrete pipe. He nearly lost his grip because it was covered with algae and slippery, but he managed to pull himself inside and wedge himself in the pipe with his legs outspread.

He quickly glanced at the surface of the water. Forty seconds without air. He pulled the board over the hole and started down, climbing backwards. His feet felt their way ahead, and his arms pushed his body in the right direction. After just two meters, the concrete pipe bent off to the side. It had probably been used at some point to fill or empty this artificial lake created by open-cast mining. Now it was completely hidden from view.

Tobias was running out of air. He needed to be very calm. Even as a child, he'd been able to make it two minutes in the bathtub.

Unfortunately, the concrete pipe was not a bathtub. The stupid backpack kept getting stuck. Tobias' feet were stepping in mud. Sometimes the mud had texture, and he didn't even want to imagine why that might be. Especially because everything his feet encountered would get between his fingers shortly after.

Then his feet came across solid metal. Crap. That was a door. Tobias turned around and felt it with his hands. He found a wheel and turned it once. Even under water, it squeaked. If the door opened now, what would happen? If the passage behind it was dry now, it would fill up. And Tobias would drown.

You idiot. This must be an airlock. Two doors in a row. He would need to close both. Where was the second one? He felt around the top of the concrete tube. There, a handle. He pulled, and a piece of metal came out of the wall. A gate valve. The second door of the airlock. Tobias pulled it down with the last of his remaining strength. It didn't matter if it was completely sealed. Now he quickly opened the inner door. He turned the wheel. His lungs felt like they were about to burst. Asphyxiation was a horrible death that he wished on no one. One turn, two, three, and the door opened. On the crest of a wave, he tumbled head first into a dry canal.

Tobias sucked in air greedily. It smelled awful. It wasn't because of the mud that had sloshed inside with him, but rather the dead animal he'd landed next to. He peered at it, getting down on his knees. The body was undulating slightly because a shallow pool of water had spread out on the ground. It was either a large rat, a small cat, or some wild animal. Tobias didn't know anything about wild animals. An otter? A beaver? It didn't really matter.

Where was the light coming from, anyway? Further ahead in the tube, a lamp hung from the ceiling. It had probably reacted to his movements, or to the opening of the door. It was really clever of Hardy and Matze to install a light down here. But it also suggested that it still must be quite a ways to Hardy's house.

The concrete pipe was no bigger than before, but at least now he could breathe again.

That had been close. Tobias glanced over his shoulder. There was a small shelf behind him. The surge of water had probably tipped it over. He certainly could have used that breathing mask and small oxygen bottle. But to be fair, the tube had been designed as an escape tunnel, not for intruders like him. There had also been a few packages of zwieback toast on the shelf, but now they were lying soggy in a puddle.

He, too, was drenched. Strangely, he hadn't noticed until now that little rivulets had been streaming from his uniform this whole time. He reached for his head to take off his cap. No, he'd long since lost it. Tobias took off his jacket and uniform shirt and wrung them out. He shivered. After he put his clothes back on, he didn't feel any warmer. He repeated this with his pants, underwear, and socks. He figured his shoes were beyond all hope. Unfortunately, his pants were torn in many places. At least they were cleaner than before, even though he'd made his way through some serious mud. That certainly was saying something.

Onwards, then. He was sure to find something to change into at Hardy's house. Tobias made his way a few meters, his feet wide apart like a duck, but his knee wasn't having it. On all fours, then. That was a little better. He could forget about the pants anyway. But what did his back have to say about it? He preferred to push the backpack in front of him. He really was a true hero. Chasing after the princess to meet with adventure, but when he encountered the dragon, he didn't cut off its head but instead let himself be carried out of the fairytale forest on its back. No, no, no, he shouldn't feel guilty. After all, he'd done what he could, and Miriam wasn't the only one who needed his help. The cosmonaut had two little kids who needed their mother.

Little by little, he warmed back up. Crawling through a concrete tube was more strenuous than he could have imagined. How much further did he have to go? It was hard to believe that Hardy and Matze had made this passage themselves. There were probably a lot of drainage channels like this one in the former lignite mining area. If Hardy had previously worked in open-cast mining, he was probably familiar with the layout.

Tobias had to be careful. It seemed very unlikely that the pipe ran directly under Hardy's house. There must be a turnoff somewhere, maybe into an even narrower passage that the two had built on their own.

Tobias didn't come to the realization that he must have already passed it until it started getting darker and darker. There were no more lights on the ceiling. So Hardy had in fact put them in. But that meant that the turnoff to the house wasn't particularly conspicuous. That made sense, of course. If somebody were to come across the passage from the outside, as Tobias had, nothing should show the way to Hardy's house.

Couldn't Matze have given him some kind of clue? He'd just told him that there were dry clothes stored in the passageway. Which wasn't true. *Take your time, Tobias. Start by crawling back to the first light.* The turnoff surely wasn't far from it.

What was happening above ground? What if Hardy had wound up getting arrested and had testified against him? If that were the case, maybe his pursuers were already waiting for him in the basement. But he wouldn't hold it against Hardy. Who knew what they had on him?

Shit. Here he was, squatting in a massive concrete tube, and now he had to go to the bathroom. He hadn't eaten much today, so it must be all the excitement. He crawled back into the darkness and did his business. He used the wet handkerchief he found in his pants pocket to clean up after himself. He left it behind. It was actually too bad, because it was one of the last ones with his grandma's embroidered monogram.

The odor followed him as he made his way back into the light. Hadn't someone once claimed that we like the smell of our own crap? That was definitely not true. Now he had to find the exit all that much faster. First he scoured the left side of the passageway, then the right, and finally the ceiling. Everything appeared to be made of solid cement. The entrance was really well hidden.

Tobias took his gun out of the holster. There was water running down the barrel. He really needed to clean it, but there was no time for that now. He checked to see if the safety was on, then used the handle like a hammer. Left side, right side, ceiling.

It sounded the same everywhere. This couldn't be possible! What if the entrance was hidden in the floor? Tobias went back to crawling around in the little stream. Whenever he tapped it with his gun, there was a spray of water. Dirty water.

There. Finally, a noise that sounded dull. Right where the last light was located. The place where the ground sounded hollow measured about 70 centimeters across. Uh oh. At 1.20 meters, the concrete tube was definitely comfortable by comparison. The hole was very well concealed. Tobias only found its edge when he pressed hard on the center. This caused the metal on the sides, which was fitted exactly to the curve of the tube, to lift up a little bit, and he could reach underneath.

This passage was nothing more than a dark hole. Tobias threw the backpack into it first. Almost immediately, he heard a splash. Good—at least it wasn't deep. He climbed in and had to squat to pull the lid closed over him. The passage turned at right angles and moved away from the big tube. Was it possible that the walls were moving toward him? His breathing was fast and shallow. In this part of the passageway, it would be impossible to turn around. If he were to come across a locked door, he would have to crawl all the way backward.

But he didn't encounter a door. All of a sudden, he was unable to push the backpack any further. Tobias reached over it. There was a grate. That was all he needed. Like a prison. But at least in prison there would be light and three meals a day.

This couldn't be the end. He ran his hands over the grate. It had metal bars as thick around as a finger. They were spaced far enough apart that he could reach through with his hand. He tried the outside. There was something. It felt like a handle. It could be turned.

The grate folded outward under its own weight. The backpack fell ahead of him and Tobias followed after it.

Fortunately, he didn't fall very far. He landed on a tiled floor. It still stank down there, but the smell was coming from him. Tobias felt around the floor and then the walls. He was in a square-shaped room and was able to stand easily. His hands touched a switch. He pressed it, hoping it wouldn't electrocute him. It didn't. A neon tube flickered on, emitting dim light.

The room he'd reached was some kind of cellar. On one wall was a shelf with a folding ladder on top of it, and the ceiling had a hinged door with a pull. Tobias tugged on it and the door opened downwards. He had to jump to the side to avoid getting hit on the head. He was able to catch it just before it crashed into the shelf.

SUCCESS! THE FOLDING LADDER WAS JUST THE RIGHT HEIGHT. Tobias climbed up as quietly as possible and put his ear to the underside of the carpet that obstructed his view. Except for an annoying buzzing noise, probably a fly, he didn't hear anything at all. He pulled the carpet aside and a black dot swooped down on him. Stupid blowfly! He waved it away.

This was clearly Hardy's house. The room was filled with dim light. The sun would be setting soon. Tobias listened for another moment. It was completely silent. There was nobody up there.

All the same, he threw the backpack up first and waited to see if there was a reaction. Nothing. Tobias pulled himself up out of the rectangular hole. And how was he going to close the door? He looked around. On a shelf against the wall there was a bar with a hook at its tip. Tobias used it to catch a loop on the front side of the door. He pulled it up until it clicked into place in the floor.

Was it secure? He used his foot to test if it would hold. The trapdoor didn't move. Tobias marveled at how the hinge on the other side disappeared completely into the floor. Then he pulled the carpet back over it. There were no irregularities to be seen.

"Hardy, are you here?"

He wasn't really expecting an answer. After going through the narrow tube, he just wanted to hear a voice again. He was alone. The bed was neatly made. The lights on the radio and the computer were flashing. Amazing—when the Stasi conducted a search, tidying up wasn't part of the program. Above the equipment was a clock showing several time zones. It was now 6:55 Central European Summer Time.

A puddle slowly formed where Tobias was standing. He needed to get out of his wet clothes. He opened the back door. Inside the room, which measured about three square meters and had floor to ceiling tile, there was a toilet and a small sink with a mirror above it. Above the toilet was a shower head on the wall, and in the middle of the floor was a drain. How practical. You could poop and shower at the same time. That would save Tobias a lot of time in the morning, which he would otherwise spend sitting on the throne. He'd need a waterproof reader, though. Because nothing happened unless he was reading. Usually.

Tobias undressed and hung his clothes over the sink. Then he turned on the shower. It took a moment for the water to get warm. He took the bar of soap from the sink and used it to wash up. Drops also got on his uniform, but that certainly wouldn't do any harm.

When the water cooled, Tobias turned off the shower. As he went looking for a towel, he tracked water through Hardy's house. He found a towel, along with some clean underwear, in a drawer beneath the bed. He dried off and used the wet towel to wipe the puddles off the floor. Then he took a pair of underpants. They were too big for him and baggy in the back. In the bedside table, he found a pair of brown track pants with the stripes of the National People's Army. By the door were several hangers with shirts on them.

As he fetched his wet clothes from the bathroom, he avoided looking in the mirror above the sink. He walked outside barefoot. There was a fresh breeze blowing, and Tobias shivered. The high hedges almost completely hid the property from view. He didn't find a laundry room. Should he use the radio antenna? Hardy definitely wouldn't like that. Tobias hung his wet clothes over two low bushes on either side of the entrance. Hopefully they'd be dry by morning.

Now he needed to eat something. Hardy's refrigerator was filled mostly with beer. But there was also liverwurst and butter and a remaining quarter loaf of bread. Tobias helped himself to two slices and spread them with the wurst. It was delicious. He had a beer along with it. Meanwhile, where could Hardy be? The house was orderly, so he probably hadn't had to rush out. He was probably just playing chess with Matze. But what about Jonas's warning? Tobias had heard the sirens.

He could satisfy his curiosity by calling the innkeeper on his hand phone. But then he'd be blowing his cover. What if the alien clowns had informed the Stasi? It appeared there was some level of competition, which also wasn't uncommon between the People's Police and the Stasi. Who wanted somebody else stepping on their toes? Still chewing his last bite, Tobias examined his makeshift backpack. Inside was his hand phone, which was sopping wet. He'd have to let it dry before he could use it, anyway. He emptied out the backpack completely and also took it outside to dry.

The radio's flashing lights beckoned him. Hardy had shown him how it worked, after all. Tobias wasn't sure he remembered everything, but it would be worth a try. He sat down on the stool next to it. His limbs felt as heavy as lead. How did it go again? This key, then this... He was having trouble thinking. Arrgh. Maybe he'd lie down for half an hour first. It had been a hard day.

October 12, 2029, Earth orbit

THIS WAS IT. THE SCRAP COLLECTOR MUST HAVE DECIDED THAT her final hour had finally come. It would turn the space station into a tower standing on its nose by starting its engines and using them to slow it down. Mandy tracked its results on the main computer. She'd have just one hour left in the worst-case scenario, if the collector were to brake continuously. But it didn't have to. It could just put the station into such a low orbit that the density of the atmosphere would be sufficient to guarantee that it would crash. If the probe only did what was absolutely necessary, the outlook was extended to two or three days. It wasn't possible to predict this with absolute precision.

But Mandy somehow got the feeling that the scrap collector wouldn't leave it at the bare minimum. The fact that two of these units had been set on her spoke volumes. "They" wanted her out of the way as soon as possible. But who were they? If Mandy survived, it would probably be important to be able to tell friend from foe. Ground control in the Harz Mountains didn't seem to be lifting a finger for her. That wasn't what she would have expected of Walter.

As bad as the situation looked, Mandy still had every intention of making it out alive. Even if the chances of that happening looked pretty slim.

That meant she had to neutralize that thing up there as quickly as possible. She climbed to the airlock. In the process, she passed by the workshop and grabbed the toolbox. Gravity was about one-eighth g, so moving vertically wasn't very strenuous. It was far more dangerous on the outer hull, so Mandy took particular care to secure herself when climbing down.

The DEOS probe had settled down comfortably on the front of the station. It had stretched out its robotic arm and its lens-shaped body was lying flat. The drill was no longer visible. The thing looked like a crab with all but one of its legs torn out. The openings along the side of the lens further added to this impression. It was easy to see that this was where the sensors were located.

Maybe Mandy could trick the sensors. When the scrap collector thought it had completed its task, it would move away from the station. All she had to do was give it that impression. But how? How could the probe tell that it was at the edge of the atmosphere, as planned? Maybe by the air molecules? Without a moment's hesitation, Mandy held her breath, twisted the breathing hose off her helmet, and held it in front of the crab's two eyes. Steam rose and wafted around the lens-shaped body. She counted to 120, then reconnected the hose to the helmet. She breathed deeply in and out.

The DEOS probe paid no attention to that little bit of air.

Maybe she needed to shield the device. If it was getting information from GPS satellites, it could calculate its altitude that way. Mandy climbed to the airlock. The microwave cover was made of metal. It had served her well during her time in orbit, so Mandy was deeply sorry to take it apart.

I've got to take off your skin, dear microwave, to save my own.

It took her ten minutes to remove the metal casing, which was open on one side. The covering prevented the release of microwave radiation, so it should also be able to block radio waves. Mandy climbed back outside. The toolbox was still where she'd affixed it. She put the microwave shielding over the sensors. It wasn't a perfect fit, but it would suffice if the GPS signal was faint enough.

But this approach wasn't successful, either. Lying motionless on the bow of the station, the scrap collector might as well have been dead. Just its engine kept firing the whole time, flinging the products of a chemical reaction out of its jet. These reaction products took their momentum—mass times velocity—along with them, and because of the conservation of momentum, it also slowed down the system comprised of the scrap collector and the space station.

Hold on just a moment. Momentum wasn't only the product of mass and velocity. That was just the amount. Momentum itself was a vector, meaning it had a direction in addition to its magnitude. The DEOS satellite had oriented its engine so that the exhaust jet pointed in the direction of flight. Maybe this provided an opportunity. Scrap collectors were built as cheaply as possible because so many of them were needed. Therefore, the probe couldn't be very intelligent. It probably determined its orientation with a primitive positioning sensor. That would be enough. As long as the object to be slowed down didn't resist.

So all Mandy had to do was redirect the jet. The combustion products were extremely hot, so she couldn't do it with her bare hands. Instead, she would need something for the jet to bounce off of.

The microwave shielding. That should do. After all, it didn't need to redirect the engine's entire momentum. Just a little— enough to keep the station from crashing before the oxygen tank completely ran out—would work. She needed one more day.

You pigs won't even let me have my last day.

Mandy flattened out the metal cube and drummed on the surface. If only she knew who to direct her rage against! What had been a cuboidal shape was now a cross with three short arms and one long foot. And who here was to be betrayed and then crucified? That wasn't how it was going to be! She wouldn't let that happen to her.

Mandy climbed over the DEOS probe to the engine. She anchored the metal plate to a rope and then got the toolbox. How could she solidly clamp the baffle plate behind the jet of the engine? It would be very easy if she folded the side arms of the cross forward. Easy. Sure. She'd have to use a steel drill to make holes in the metal and its base on the probe, then attach it with thick screws. That would be hard work. Three screws on this side would have to suffice.

Now the other side. Mandy climbed over the probe to reach the back of the engine. But how could she get to the sheet metal? On one side, it was sticking out into space. In between was the stream of hot engine exhaust. If Mandy accidentally got caught in the gas exhaust with the spacesuit, the suit would be destroyed immediately.

Mandy climbed back. She bent the sheet so that it pointed towards the other side.

The footrest that she'd used as a support before wasn't holding her foot anymore. Mandy was just able to hold on with one hand. Phew, that was a close one.

Of course! The metal had gotten into the hot gas flow and diverted it. The forces had changed. The apparent gravity was acting in a different direction.

Somewhat shakily, Mandy climbed back onto the other side of the engine. It was as if she had to fit a mask over its jet without touching the mask itself. Mandy rummaged around in the toolbox. Somehow she had to pull the sheet of metal toward her without diverting the hot gas flow toward her. She found a shovel with a telescoping metal handle. That might work. She extended the handle to its full length and hooked the shovel blade into the sheet metal. Presto. She failed on her first attempt, but the second was a success. She pulled the metal sheet toward her.

Again, the path that the exhaust gases followed out of the engine changed, and again the forces it was subjected to changed as well. That felt better. Instead of forward, in the direction of flight, the engine was now firing downward, toward the earth. Mandy hurried to drill the holes and attach the screws, because she'd already noticed one disadvantage to the new orientation of the engine: It caused the space station to rotate around an imaginary transverse axis.

Success. The sheet metal was in place. Mandy jiggled it and her glove got stuck. Dang it! The top layer must have melted. She tore away the glove and looked at the material. It was still intact. She sure was one lucky cosmonaut.

Mandy laughed. If she added up all the shit that happened to her up here and then completely forgot about it, all in all she had really had her share of luck.

She felt lightheaded. Of course. The station could have very well given her a break, but no. That was just the German sense of efficiency. Cautiously, Mandy climbed back to the center of the station. Here, near the axis of rotation, was where it was most tolerable.

October 13, 2029, Lusatia

A BLINDING LIGHT WAS COMING THROUGH HIS EYELIDS. THEY'D found him! He'd gotten away from the aliens who'd shot at him with laser beams, but now...

"Hey, relax," Hardy said. "It's just me."

"What..."

Tobias opened his eyes. A giant was standing in front of him. Where was he, and what had happened to the aliens? Had this man come to save him?

"Hardy. Does that ring a bell?"

The man dug his paws into his shoulder. Hardy... Oh man. This was reality. Tobias was in the house of the man who'd helped him. Hardy, amateur radio operator, call sign Y2 something. He was lying in his bed. Of course. He'd only lain down for a moment.

"Sorry. I just wanted to rest for a little bit," Tobias said.

"No problem. I slept on the floor. But now I'm hungry and I'd like to have breakfast. That's why I raised the shutters."

"You've been here all night?"

"Yeah. When I got here around midnight, you were lying on my bed, snoring. I turned you on your side and then went to sleep on the air mattress. What's been going on with you? I was wondering about those clothes outside that are all torn to pieces."

"That's my uniform. It was, anyway. I borrowed some of your things."

289

"Sure, no problem. You know what? You go on and get cleaned up. I'll bake some rolls, and then you can tell me everything as we're having breakfast."

"An environmental mess? They could have just filled it in with rubble from the open cast mine," Hardy said, slicing open the rolls.

The two halves were steaming. Tobias poured coffee for both Hardy and himself.

"The two alien actors seemed to think so," he said.

"That's entirely possible. The ground personnel don't have to know everything. But my little toe tells me there's more to it than that."

"Yes, that's what I'm afraid of, too. I just didn't have any other option right then."

Tobias took some liverwurst.

"Well, I'm still proud of you, kid."

Hardy slapped him on the shoulder approvingly. The old man looked at him with a kindly gaze, as if he were his father.

"Proud? I let them take me out of there like a stupid boy who got lost in the forest."

"No, that's not it at all. You're the first person to have gone in there illegally, made it through the obstacles, and come back out alive."

"But I didn't find Miriam. She's still wandering around there by herself."

Hardy stroked his chin.

"I don't think your fancy friend has gotten lost there. If she had, those guys would have said something. I think it's good that you didn't shoot those guys. They're just doing their job."

"Thanks. But what's going to happen to Miriam now?"

"You said it yourself. There's another woman waiting for help. Our cosmonaut."

"Has she been in touch?" asked Tobias.

"Yes. She's got twenty-four hours of air left, and somebody tried to make her station crash. She isn't even getting help on the emergency frequency."

"Shoot. Isn't there anybody who can save her?"

"It doesn't look like it," Hardy said. "She's tried the Chinese, the Russians, the Americans, and the Europeans. They're the only ones who can get a ship into space that fast."

"It really does seem like the whole world is conspiring against her."

Tobias sighed. How was he supposed to save the woman up in space if he couldn't even rescue Miriam from the zone?

"Well, officially there's a berserk robot aboard the Völkerfreundschaft that thinks it's human. Nobody wants to deal with that."

"It's an ingenious story. We need someone who won't be intimidated by it. Excuse me for a moment. When I get back from the bathroom, we'll figure out a solution."

"So, did you come up with anything?" asked Hardy.

"I was thinking about Jonas. He seems..."

"Are you nuts? That guy sent the Stasi after us!"

"Yes, but he obviously has connections and doesn't work for the Stasi."

"And you believe him? I was lucky that I stick out around here like a sore thumb. Arresting me would have attracted more attention than they would like. I was just barely able to make that clear to them. But if they show up here again, there's no guarantee that things will go so smoothly. Then I'll need my tunnel on a more permanent basis."

"I'd just ask Jonas if he sees any way to help Mandy. He's still interested in Miriam. So if I promise him that I'll take care of Miriam, maybe he'll do something for the cosmonaut."

"And you really think he'd be able to do that?" Hardy asked.

"Well, we could explain to him that the story about the robot that went berserk is a hoax. He knows I wouldn't bullshit him. If he shares that with his contacts, maybe they'd be more willing to save Mandy. Now, that story would be perfect for propaganda! The West does what the GDR can't and rescues the GDR cosmonaut."

"I don't know..."

"Have you got a better idea, Hardy?"

"Unfortunately, I don't. All right, let's call him, then. I'll handle it."

"STATE-OWNED ENTERPRISE CARL ZEISS JENA, JONAS Schieferdecker here. With whom do I have the pleasure of speaking?"

The connection was crystal clear. Hardy's setup was great.

"It's me," Tobias said.

"You? Oh yes, it's *you*." Jonas apparently recognized his voice now.

"I need your help," Tobias said.

"Where are you?"

"That doesn't matter."

"I see. You're wary because of yesterday. But if I'm supposed to help you, I need to know where you are."

Tobias didn't like this one bit. Maybe Hardy had been right, and having this conversation was a mistake.

"You're not supposed to help me."

"There's nothing I can do for our mutual friend. She's beyond my reach. Only a miracle can help her now."

"Or me," said Tobias. "I may have found a way."

"Then why are we talking? Go on, go, go! Get her out of there before it's too late!"

Jonas sounded downright excited.

"Before that, I want you to do something for somebody else."

"Well, out with it then. Who is it? Your friends in Lusatia? My hands are tied there. That's not my turf."

What a coward. But that wasn't the point.

"Mandy Neumann. Does that name mean anything to you?" asked Tobias.

"The GDR cosmonaut. She died of internal injuries shortly after her capsule landed. She's left behind two children. Very sad. The children will receive a medal."

"That's the official version. Mandy is actually still alive."

"Are you sure? I heard a robot went haywire."

"I'm absolutely certain. Mandy desperately needs help. She's only got twenty-four hours' worth of air left. Somebody needs to pick her up in orbit. Please."

"I see. This is all new information. I'll have to have it verified first, of course. But I promise I'll pass it on."

"That isn't enough, Jonas. The woman has two children and is going to asphyxiate in her station. We can't let that happen!"

"I'm sorry, but I can't promise you anything. Under the current circumstances, it's inappropriate to allow the GDR government to lose face. If something happens, it must be planned carefully and be carried out discreetly. The cosmonaut must be prepared keep quiet afterwards. No one must be embarrassed publicly. Can you guarantee that?"

Could he? He didn't know her. But she was a mother and would surely do everything she could for her daughters.

"I can," Tobias said. "If Mandy Neumann gets the chance to see her children again, she'll be prepared to sell her soul to the devil in exchange."

"Whom your side has under contract, from what I understand."

October 13, 2029, ISS

"DEAR GUESTS, TODAY IT IS MY GREAT PLEASURE TO SHOW YOU the docking process for a very special guest, a Space Force Boeing X-38."

The audience crowded in front of the dome's windows. Jennifer estimated that around 30 of the 43 guests were there. Of course, there wasn't that much room on the side that the docking adapter was visible from. But she wasn't surprised. It wasn't often that the X-38 could be seen in the wild, and even less so near a civilian facility like the ISS.

What would the guests say when Jennifer told them that their return flight would be delayed? Their enthusiasm would probably quickly turn to anger, and she'd bear the brunt of it. Mission control had only given notice about the orbital glider half an hour ago. That was extremely short notice. Either there was a problem on board the glider or... she couldn't think of any other reason.

"Could you please let those who are waiting behind you take a look at the newcomer?" she asked over the intercom.

Some guests complied with her request, while others ignored her. But she wasn't going to interfere. She had already been butted in the head once. The man responsible for it got banned from flying for life, but ever since then she'd been afraid to put herself into situations like that. She watched the X-38 on the little screen on her wrist. The sleek space plane was approaching slowly. It looked as if its lower jaw was hanging open because it had lowered the flap that during flight was located in front of the docking ports in the nose.

"Jenny, can you come here?" Mike asked over the radio.

"I've got about thirty people in the dome here. If I leave them alone, they'll tear the place apart."

"They can't get the portholes open, and if they do, they'll only have themselves to blame. Just seal the bulkhead doors when you leave the room. I only need you for a second."

"Mike, I'll be violating approximately twenty-seven regulations if I lock the guests in the dome. Or will you take responsibility if they panic?"

"Yes. I don't have any other choice right now. So lock those people in and get your ass over here. That's an order."

Mike was a twerp. But he seemed to be under a lot of pressure right now. Jennifer floated through the lab and the cafeteria.

"Where should I be going, anyway?" she asked over the radio.

"Storehouse 17."

"Seventeen? Where's that?"

"Next to sixteen, where else?"

She knew storehouse 16 well. It was where food for the hotel guests was stored. But for as long as she'd been on board, they'd never opened 17. Behind the workshop, Jennifer took a turn to the right. Mike was already waiting upside-down in front of a closed bulkhead. Under the big "17" were the words "Property of the United States."

"And why do you need me now?" asked Jennifer.

"You should have paid more attention when you took the tour on your first day. Hold your ID in front of the scanner."

Oh, dang it. She really had forgotten. Seventeen could only be opened by two people together. She held the plastic card, which she wore on a cord around her neck, in front of the scanner.

The small screen above read, "Second confirmation required."

Mike also held out his ID card. There was a clicking sound in the door, and Mike opened it. The storeroom behind it was a lot smaller than 16. Three olive-brown crates, each around one and a half meters long, were secured to the walls with straps.

"You take the left and I'll take the right," Mike said.

He loosened the strap of the right crate and pulled it out of storage room into the corridor. Now it was Jennifer's turn. She pulled out the left crate. On it was written, "Handle with care."

"What is this?" she asked.

"None of our business. But try and guess."

The color of the boxes. The simultaneous arrival of the X-38 Space Force.

"Weapons?" Jennifer guessed.

Mike didn't answer.

"So these are weapons?" she asked again. "Doesn't that violate the Outer Space Treaty?"

Mike closed the bulkhead from the outside.

"I can't confirm that they are weapons. But if they were— storing and transporting them in space isn't prohibited. We could always run into a grizzly after the landing."

"Got it. I think I know who the crates are for."

Mike pointed to the front, in the direction of the docking adapter that the X-38 would attach to. Jennifer pulled the crate behind her. On the screen on her wrist, she saw that the space glider had just docked.

"Are the visitors staying for lunch?" she asked.

"No, sweetheart, you don't have to cook for them." Mike smirked.

"That's too bad. It would have been a nice distraction for the guests."

"I'm afraid the boys in X-38 are up to something, sorry. Now off to your guests. I'd better not hear any complaining."

October 13, 2029, Earth orbit

MANDY HAD FINALLY HEARD NEWS FROM LUSATIA AGAIN! SHE WAS in front of the radio but couldn't stand to be there for very long. The scrap collector had quickly powered down its engine when the rotation accelerated, but she hadn't found a way to slow down the space station yet. Only near the axis of rotation could she tolerate the motion for a longer period of time. That was where Mandy had slept for a few hours.

Here in front of the radio, centrifugal force pushed her lightly towards the ground. The artificial gravity might even be pleasant if it didn't change so quickly. But the forces acting on her skull were greater than those acting on her legs, and this led to headaches and nausea. Since she could no longer get out of the spacesuit, it would be extremely unfortunate if she had to vomit.

However, the latest news from Earth was encouraging. No, it wasn't nearly enough for her to feel hopeful again. But Mandy didn't feel so lonely anymore, and that was worth a great deal. She wouldn't die up here all alone. In her final hours, which were terrifyingly soon, she'd be able to talk to real people. Only then, when the gauge on the oxygen tank read zero, would she take off her helmet.

It was said that a person exposed to vacuum couldn't survive more than 15 seconds. That was a relatively quick death. She didn't want to vegetate for hours, breathing the last remains of the air she'd exhaled over and over again. And so she'd come to a deliberate end, at a time that was under her control, and when there was no chance that any rescue would reach her before her oxygen ran out. That was almost exactly eight hours from now. She'd just filled the cylinder at the station's tank. There was enough left in it for two more refills.

It was insane. Mandy felt like a castaway dying of thirst in her lifeboat. A dense layer of what right now was the most valuable substance for her was right below her, practically within reach. With a landing capsule, she could have made it down in two hours. But with the complete space station, she would just burn up. She preferred to take off her helmet.

Mandy focused her attention back on the radio.

"We've made contact with specific Western agencies," it said.

The sentence left a bitter taste in her mouth. She had tried to contact the ISS, after all. And they hadn't answered, not even on the emergency frequency. She described her unsuccessful attempts and sent the message.

"They're ignoring you because they think you're a deranged robot," she read. "Apparently this robot believes it's human. That is why nobody is allowed to get close your space station."

This was unbelievable. But it did provide an explanation. Who could have thought of it, and why? What had she done to be condemned to death like this? Every enemy of the republic got a trial, but she had just been disconnected, like a machine. Who knew what was going on here? She sent the OM some of these questions, but he didn't know the answers, either.

"We hope our friend can help you," she read.

Hope. Such a beautiful word. Mandy shouldn't let it distract her. It must all be related to the MKF-8, and presumably the footage she'd taken of the zone. If she was going to die, at least she'd leave a legacy. She floated over to the main computer and compressed the photos from the central area of the zone so they could be sent over packet radio. Then she copied the images to a flash drive, imported the contents onto the ham radio set, and attached it to a text message.

"I took these photos of the zone yesterday," she wrote. "I don't know if they'll help you. It's very possible that they cost me my life, even though I didn't know anything about them at first. Please find a way to publish them. And send greetings to my daughters and tell them I love them very much."

The tears didn't move downwards over her cheeks, but outwards. This was so bizarre that Mandy broke out into wild laughter. Now, surely, being face-to-face with death was making her slowly lose her grip.

The main computer sounded an alert. She already knew what it was. It was a proximity alarm. The last time, it had not boded well. She floated over to the screen. The radar couldn't tell her what was coming. But it wasn't the rescue she'd been longing for; the object was going too fast. And it was still accelerating. In order to dock, it would have to brake now. Mandy floated back to the radio.

"I'm going to have to sign off for a while," she wrote, "probably forever. Something pretty fast is coming towards the station. I'm not expecting anything good. Your friend probably isn't who you think he is."

The frequency of the main computer's warnings increased significantly. There were 30 seconds until impact. The airlock was right behind Mandy, and it was open. She was lucky. If the station had still been filled with air, she wouldn't have made it.

"Now show them," she typed quickly. "Whoever they are. I'm leaving the ship now before this thing hits."

She pulled herself into the airlock. This time, she didn't need a safety line. She got down on her knees and jumped up. She flew like a miniature spaceship into the blackness of space.

Shortly after that, something struck the fast-rotating space station. Everything happened so quickly that Mandy couldn't see what exactly had hit the Völkerfreundschaft. Maybe a torpedo? A rocket? Was the use of such weapons even permitted in space? The explosion was so bright that she was blinded, even though the helmet visor had immediately darkened.

In space she didn't have to worry about a shock wave, but rather debris. Yet again, she was incredibly lucky. All the parts followed the last impetus that the rotation of the station had given them. They spread out along the plane of rotation, which Mandy had moved away from when she'd jumped. Now there were ten thousand new fragments whizzing through the orbit, but none were on Mandy's orbital path.

Insane. It wasn't the robot but the world that had gone mad. The use of weapons in space. One, two, three assassination attempts. A serious violation of the space debris treaty. All this just to keep her quiet? And she hadn't even said anything! All she'd done was observe something, and she'd been declared guilty long before that. Those pictures from the zone must contain something scandalous. Something that would send the whole world off balance if it were to get out.

October 13, 2029, X-38

"MISSION ACCOMPLISHED," SAID THE WOMAN IN THE AIRLOCK.

"Come back inside, Vicky."

Roger took a deep breath. He'd never accept an assignment like this again. Not that he had a choice. But he'd listened to the recordings. That was no robot. Not on your life. Nobody could tell him it was.

Vicky, the shooter, would need about ten minutes before she was back next to him. The pilot went over the footage of the shootdown. The warhead had hit the station on the nose, as planned, even though the target had been rotating at a pretty good clip. So the simulations had calculated the smallest possible explosion. It was not intended to attract worldwide attention.

But the footage showed that everything had been far less dramatic than they'd feared. It was clear that the oxygen tanks would be practically empty. But it also seemed that the inside of the station no longer contained any oxygen. Regardless, the station had dispersed into many thousands of pieces.

He'd been right. A missile without a warhead would have been fine. A little relative speed and wham, even a nail became a projectile. But at the Pentagon, they'd wanted to be sure.

But what was this? The parts blasted out by the explosion were all flying away in the same plane. They were cooling relatively quickly, as shown by the infrared camera. But there was one hazy spot off-axis that maintained its temperature. The pilot checked the calibration. About 65 degrees Fahrenheit. Colder than a human body, but not atypical for radiation from a human in a spacesuit.

Hm. They had a second missile. The target was quite small, but easy to identify using infrared radiation. What had his boss said? *Blow up the station like our allies want, and you're done. It's a clean job. All that's left over there is one robot. The Chinese will grumble about the extra scrap, but that thing is a danger that needs to be removed quickly. After that, you'll get special leave.*

They'd finished the job. Nobody could ask them for anything more.

"Hey, Roger, why are you looking so dreary?" asked Vicky.

"Me? Oh, nothing."

He switched to the navigation screen. The hazy spot disappeared, but he still kept seeing it for a while. There was a reddish spot on the screen. Roger wiped at it, but it wouldn't go away.

"What's the matter? There's nothing there," said Vicky.

"You're right. I'm just deciding what to do with my special leave."

"I'm going to Vegas with my guy. We're gonna have a great time."

"Good idea, Vicky."

The reddish spot vanished.

October 13, 2029, Lusatia

"Jonas, you asshole, what have you done?" Tobias hollered into the microphone.

"I did what had to be done," Jonas replied. "There's no need to shout. I can hear you just fine."

"Why did the cosmonaut have to die?"

"Because you didn't do your job, Comrade."

"You bastard. Now you're going to point the finger at me? And don't call me comrade. I'm not your comrade. To hell with comrades like you. That woman is leaving two small children behind!"

"Somebody will take care of them. They've still got their father, and they'll want for nothing. Their mother is a heroine, after all! She's more helpful to them that way than as a traitor."

"Mandy Neumann isn't a traitor. She was just doing her job."

"You know that, and I know that. That doesn't mean anything. But if it makes you feel any better, she died for a great —a really great—cause."

"And what might that be?"

"If you found out, you'd die under similar circumstances as the cosmonaut."

The photos. He absolutely had to see those photos. She'd said it was her legacy. Maybe they'd tell them what this big cause was. The MKF-8 was behind all this.

"You didn't have to turn against her," Tobias said. "You're responsible for her death."

"Yes, I did. It was a trade. Miriam's life for Mandy's. When they get hold of Miriam, which they will, they won't kill her. They'll come for me, and then I'll get the chance to encourage her to go back to the way things were before. A grieving widow is always good optics."

"Widow? What do you mean?"

"I'm afraid her husband didn't make it. It's really too bad."

"If she finds that out, there's no way she'll back down. It seems you don't know her that well."

"I know her better than you do. She's always felt destined for higher things. Do you think you, just a little People's Police officer, would've ever had a chance with her? I'll step right into her husband's shoes. Miriam won't be able to say no."

"She will, though."

"Dream on, kid, and grow up already."

"I told you there was no point," Hardy said after Jonas disconnected. "The man thinks he's invulnerable. You've only put yourself in danger. Now they know where you are."

"I don't think he'll tell anyone. If the Stasi knew, I'm sure they'd be at the door already. But Jonas thinks he's won, and he's just waiting for the call so he can go and get Miriam."

"If you're not mistaken. It wouldn't be the first time."

Unfortunately, Hardy was right. It was a miracle that he was still helping Tobias. Hardy seemed completely indifferent to threats.

"I'm sorry, Hardy. I'm constantly putting you in danger. It would be better for me to hide in the 'Hammer'. The innkeeper seems to be a smart woman."

"Yes, she probably wouldn't rat you out. But stay here for now. You may still need my station. Besides, this is all way too exciting for me to back out now. I've got a feeling you're going to stick it to Jonas and find out what the hell is going on around here."

And save Miriam, Tobias would have liked to hear. But Hardy had probably deliberately refrained from mentioning that. Of course, it was possible that Jonas had been bluffing and Dr. Prassnitz was still alive. And if he was in fact dead, Miriam wouldn't leave the zone until she'd found those who were responsible. There was nothing even Jonas could do to change that.

"We need to look at the pictures Mandy sent," Tobias said.

"Is that a lake?" asked Tobias.

"I don't think so," Hardy said. "Look how round it is. No lake is perfectly circular like that."

"Not a natural one, anyway. But nothing in the open-cast mining area is natural anymore."

"But that round? Even with an artificial lake, there's gonna be a break in the edge somewhere."

"Maybe there's a metal barrier," Tobias said. "What if it's the toxic sludge from that chemical spill the actors mentioned?"

"I'm no chemist, but I imagine that toxic substances are more of a poisonous green than black. Kind of brightly colored and shiny like oil."

"I know what you mean. Could it be a huge above-ground petroleum tank? There aren't any ripples either. The surface is completely smooth. Petroleum is viscous and black, so that seems to fit."

"But the fact that you saw so few derricks doesn't. And what are these half-circles here?"

"There are quite a few of them." Tobias counted them. "Forty-five—that's one every eight degrees."

"And what if those things along the edge are propping up the circular area? Maybe it's a huge cloth hiding the real secret underneath."

"Or an antenna that they use to contact aliens..."

"That's ridiculous. If there really were aliens, they wouldn't have to hire actors."

"True. Dang it. I'm afraid we're not going to figure it out just by looking at it. I'll have to go back in again."

Have you lost your marbles? Hardy could very well have said, but he didn't say anything. He just nodded.

Then he added, "Right. And this time I'm coming with you."

"Are you sure?"

"Absolutely sure. This will be the last adventure of my life."

Oh. What did Hardy mean by that? The old man looked at

him with a resolute expression. It would be no use to contradict him.

"What does Matthias have to say about that?" he asked.

"Matze... I haven't heard from him since..."

As strong as he might be, Hardy suddenly looked very weak. He hung his head and slumped forward. Tobias swallowed and put his arm around Hardy's shoulders. It was what it was.

"Thank you," Hardy said.

He was already back to his old self. Tobias let go of him and walked around the room.

"As for the cosmonaut..." Hardy called after him.

"Yes, her poor kids. We should try to contact them," Tobias said.

"But are we sure she's dead? She intended to leave the station after she left her last message."

"Do you think she managed? I don't know what it was that hit the Völkerfreundschaft, but if it was a missile, she would hardly have time to get out of the blast radius."

"Remember, everything up there is in a vacuum. There are no shock waves there. She just might have been lucky enough not to get hit by the debris."

Tobias pictured her floating alone through space in her spacesuit, unable to contact anybody but still full of life.

"Right. But how would we reach her?" he asked. "The ham radio was surely destroyed."

"I already tried. The mailbox doesn't respond anymore. Everything's dead. But I imagine that a spacesuit like hers is constantly radiating heat. It could be distinguished from the debris that way. All it would take would be for someone to look."

"But who? You can forget about the West. I know it sounds crazy, but there seems to be more common interest in this than I'd imagined."

China or Russia seemed like the obvious choices. Did Tobias know anybody there? He'd studied in Moscow for half a year. He still had a pennant of honor from the Central Army Sports Club hanging in his apartment. But he hadn't made any acquaintances after that time. And China, meanwhile, was busy doing its own thing.

He thought about the newspaper Miriam had left in the hut he'd visited in the zone. He'd flipped through it to find something about the Völkerfreundschaft. But it had also reported on an Indian mission that had just been launched. India. That got him thinking. Raghunath. He wasn't just a school headmaster, but the head of an internationally known, award-winning private school. Many of the students he'd helped to get into college had gone on to make careers for themselves. Raghunath was sure to know somebody who knew someone who could help him.

"In a relatively recent newspaper, I saw something about an Indian space mission," Tobias said. "I can't remember what it was called, though."

"I can look that up in the Kybernetz archive. *Neues Deutschland* or LR?"

"I think it was the *Lausitzer Rundschau*."

"Okay. Just a second."

Hardy typed something into his computer.

"Yes, it was the LR. Or even *Neues Deutschland*. They all report the same thing anyway. The mission you're referring to is Gaganyaan 3. It has a two-man crew plus a female robot."

"Thanks. I have a good friend in India. He's a teacher."

"A teacher?" Hardy raised an eyebrow.

"Don't underestimate teachers. In India, they really command respect. I know that first-hand. My friend runs a highly regarded private school there."

"Then write to him."

Hardy stood up and pushed the stool toward Tobias. His Kybernetz mailbox was already open. All he had to do was enter his friend's address, which he fortunately knew off the top of his head.

"My dear Brother Raghunath," he began, writing in English. "I have an unusual and very urgent request. Therefore, I'll get right to the point: do you know anyone who can put us in touch with the Indian Gaganyaan 3 spaceship? As I've mentioned, it's very urgent and is a matter of life and death. Yours, Tobias."

He pressed the send button. And now?

"Come on, let's pack up some things for the zone," Hardy said.

Tobias was just about to get up when the Kybernetz mailbox issued a notification. It was a K-letter from Raghunath. He really could count on his friend! In India, it must be early in the morning.

"My dear brother Tobias," Raghunath's message started. "I have some good news for you. The vyomanaut Rakesh Banerjee attended my school, and I remember him very well. He was one of the best in his class and he was also a humble, friendly boy. His father is a well-known businessman from Delhi, but the boy never bragged about his family's wealth or his background. He could have followed in his father's footsteps, but he decided to join the Indian Air Force instead. I was very proud when I heard that he'd been chosen to be a vyomanaut. We had a big celebration at the school. Rakesh even joined via video. So I'm very certain that I could send him a message. What do you want me tell him? It would be my pleasure to be able to help you. Your brother, Raghunath."

Hardy looked over Tobias's shoulder and read along. Then he patted him on the back approvingly. "That's great. You really do have connections!"

"Yes, Raghunath is a great guy. We were even in Lusatia together one time. That was twenty years ago. We sat in the village pub and drank Nordhäuser Doppelkorn with the farmers. It was a lot of fun. But what should we write to him?"

"It would be good if his student could keep an eye out for a female cosmonaut in a spacesuit. He should know the orbit of the Völkerfreundschaft, at any rate."

"The former orbit," Tobias said.

He typed his answer. He couldn't go very fast because he had to mentally translate everything into English. But every second counted.

"Should I warn him?" he asked.

Hardy nodded.

"Please watch out," Tobias wrote. "It appears that certain powers would like to see our cosmonaut dead. So Rakesh should be careful. If he wants to help, he definitely shouldn't tell anyone. I don't want him to endanger himself too."

He sent the message. Raghunath must have been waiting for it, because he answered right away.

"Consider your message delivered. And thank you very much for the warning. Rakesh is just the right person for a mission like this. I took another look at his file. He does what he's told, but still maintains his right to think independently. If I hear anything from him, I'll be back in touch."

"Thank you, my dear brother," Tobias answered. "Especially on Mandy Neumann's behalf. She really deserves to be rescued. I'm about to set out on a little journey myself, and I'm not certain I'll make it out alive. You've got my hand phone number. Most of the time I keep it turned off so I can't be tracked, but I'll check it every so often."

"Very good, brother Tobias," Hardy said. "I hope Rakesh is able to steer clear of any danger."

"Nobody knows anything about it yet, right?"

"I wouldn't assume that."

"Oh. Why not?"

"The Kybernetz. It's entirely possible that somebody's reading along."

"Dang it. I hadn't thought of that."

"Well, it wouldn't change anything. This contact is the only chance the cosmonaut has at this point. If she's still alive. But come on, we need to pack."

October 13, 2029, X-38

"Begin re-entry," Roger said.

He leaned back and activated the thrusters. The space glider turned until the tail was pointing in the direction of flight.

"Mission control here. Hold on for just a minute."

"What is it?" Roger asked, taking his hand off the controller.

What did CapCom want from them now? They'd be down in about an hour, and then they could talk face to face. Hopefully the debriefing wouldn't take too long. He wanted to finally go home.

"It's about your target. We just got word that it might still be hot."

"Who'd say such a thing? You should have seen the blast."

"I saw it. You're right, the station's history. But the target..."

Yep, my friend. You wanted the station, and we took care of it. Done and out. They weren't killers, after all.

"The station was the target, right? It's definitely not hot anymore."

"Technically speaking, it wasn't about the station."

"Sure, it was about the deranged robot on board. But I guarantee you, it couldn't have made it out in one piece. It wouldn't be possible. We measured all the debris. There were just two that were bigger than the robot, and those were both pieces from the hull. That thing is down for good."

"Why don't you have another look?"

No, he wasn't going to say anything about that reddish spot he'd noticed. The higher-ups only had themselves to blame if they had to go covering up the truth. The cosmonaut deserved a chance, and he certainly wasn't going to be directly responsible for her death.

"CapCom, I'm on leave now. There's just the landing, and then..."

"Roger, you've got to understand where I'm coming from. I'm getting pressure from above here. We need to make sure we haven't overlooked anything."

"What does he want?" asked Vicky.

Roger was wearing headphones, so the shooter had only heard his end of the conversation. He switched off the microphone.

"CapCom thinks we might have overlooked something."

"He's nuts!" Vicky exclaimed. "That shot was flawless. The debris..."

"I already told him that. That was good, clean work."

"Thank you, Roger. Tell him to kiss our ass."

He turned the microphone back on.

"Vicky said that this was a job well done."

"I actually said you can kiss our ass," Vicky shouted into his microphone.

Roger put the call on speaker.

"But you've got to understand my position. It's not my idea. I'm just the messenger."

"What else do you want from us?" asked Roger.

"Not me. The ones at the top. They want you to orbit once more to take a look. At least that's how I interpret it. And if it becomes apparent that this damned robot did make it somehow, be sure to finish it off."

"Got it, mission control," Roger replied. "We'll watch for signatures similar to the robot's, and if we find any, we'll blast them out of space."

It was a simple assignment. They wouldn't find any of the robot's signatures because there weren't any. It was just annoying that they'd have to remain in space for one more orbit. Whatever the case, he definitely wouldn't be firing a rocket at some pale red spot.

"And after the next orbit, we're flying back home," Vicky said.

"Yeehaw. CapCom over and out."

October 13, 2029, Earth orbit

THIS WASN'T THE ENDING SHE'D WANTED. BUT IT WAS ONE SHE could accept. If Mandy simply opened the helmet, she wouldn't have to suffer for long. And the idea of orbiting the Earth as a satellite for a few years was comforting somehow. Up until the time they were adults, Sabine and Susanne would have a good chance of seeing their mother every time they looked up at the sky.

Then she would eventually burn up as a shooting star. Apparently, there were people who paid a lot of money to have a funeral like that. She'd be getting it entirely free of charge. Well, not completely. She wouldn't get to watch her children grow up. A tear was welling up in her right eye. It always did that whenever she thought of them. Her tear glands would be working hard up to her very last second.

Japan was passing by below. The curved row of islands was easy to see. She passed over the China Sea and reached the mainland. Even from space, the mega-cities on the coast stood out. At night they must look even more impressive, and she'd still get the chance to see it. She might not have enough breathing air, though, to see Germany at night.

She was calm now. Mandy was fascinated by China, which she'd never gotten the chance to visit during her lifetime. During her lifetime. Right. She'd already reached a kind of intermediate realm. It was like the moment a driver realized that the collision was inevitable, just before his body was thrown through the shattering windshield, right toward the tree that he'd wanted desperately to avoid.

The seconds stretched into hours. It was a very special gift. Somebody must believe that Mandy deserved it. It made it possible for the initial panic, which had rushed through her consciousness like a tsunami wave, to subside. Now she could look at the levelled landscape, which had a very special charm. It wasn't a kind of beauty, but rather a finality that was completely unknown to her before. In her day-to-day life, she'd constantly hovered somewhere between possibilities, chances, and probabilities. That was all over now. She had a total sense of security, felt only perhaps by the unborn child in the womb.

Yes, that was where she knew this feeling from. She couldn't have identified it if it were completely unfamiliar to her. But it was buried deep in her memory, covered by all the chaos of possibilities that the tsunami wave had washed away.

Mandy sang a nursery rhyme, the first one that popped into her head. It was about little Hans, who went out into the world full of good cheer.

October 13, 2029, Lusatia

"STILL DOESN'T LOOK GREAT," TOBIAS SAID, AND TAPPED THE knees of his uniform pants.

"I'd mend the rips, but we don't have much time," Hardy said.

"You know how to do that?"

"Sure do. My mother taught me."

Hardy would have let him borrow a pair of pants, but they were all too long and too wide for him. As Tobias finished getting dressed, Hardy made a few sandwiches. Tobias had requested liverwurst. There was also a backpack at the ready for carrying tools, the Glonass tracker, and the contents of a first aid kit. There was also a thin but sturdy rope made of artificial silk, a Knirps umbrella, binoculars, and a folding spade. And the gun, which he'd specially cleaned.

Hardy had thought of a lot of other equipment that might come in handy for such an expedition, but because of the weight, they had to do without it. They'd take turns carrying the backpack. Tobias was really pleased. Hardy was over 70, but he seemed to be in better shape than Tobias himself. This time they'd go faster, since they were already familiar with the obstacles.

There was a knock at the door. Hardy froze and put his finger to his mouth. Tobias held his breath. Could it be Matze coming to pay them a visit? But the two had probably agreed on

BRANDON Q. MORRIS

a special signal. Hardy appeared to be sure that there were uninvited visitors waiting outside.

"Herr Müller, open the door already. We know you're in there."

Hardy pointed to the trap in the floor, opened his mouth, and mouthed the words: *Get out*. Should Tobias let the Stasi get its hands on him again? Hardy certainly wouldn't get off so easily this time.

"Get out," Hardy whispered, audibly now.

Tobias tiptoed closer to the trap.

"Now, don't make this difficult for us," said the voice from outside. "There are two of you. We can see that with the infrared tracker. Right now, one of you is moving into the center of the room. There's no need for you to run. We just want to have a chat."

Crap. A chat. Right. Such an innocuous word for a grueling interrogation. And the trap in the floor wouldn't help anymore.

"Who are you?" asked Hardy.

"I'm S1," said the voice.

"Are you joking?"

"No, that's my name. I'm the head of security in the special area."

"Special area? What's that?"

The visitor was surprisingly patient. A Stasi unit would have long since broken down the door and arrested them.

"It's what you refer to as the zone," the voice said. "Can we come in now? All I want to do is talk."

"We can't stop you," Hardy said. "Well, we're in the middle of doing it on the kitchen table, but if you absolutely must..."

"Ha ha, that Herr Müller, just as funny as it says in his file. I'd like to point out that we are not immune to bullets. Your friend Wagner already found that out. So it would be nice if you wouldn't shoot us with them. Not that it would help you, because then your house would be leveled to the ground, but I, for one, care about my life."

"We've got something in common there, S1. So come on in. Alone."

"My colleagues have to wait outside?"

"Yes. My house isn't that big, as I'm sure you can see with your infrared sensor."

"Okay, I'll come alone."

Hardy went to the door and opened it. Now the visitors would open fire. Tobias covered his ears. But he could still hear the squeaking of the hinges. A middle-aged man came inside. He was wearing jeans, a plaid shirt and a black, classic-fit jacket.

S1 shook hands with Hardy, then Tobias. He had distinctly cold fingers. Tobias immediately wondered if he was a robot. He didn't even have a name. Had technology already secretly come this far?

"Tell me, S1, are you a robot?" he asked.

In the movies, robots often couldn't lie, so he thought it made sense to ask this question.

"Me? Ha ha." The man smiled broadly, and it didn't look rehearsed. "My wife sometimes says I'm a clumsy oaf, but nobody's ever thought I was a robot."

"Then what are you?"

"Head of security at the Central Institute for Landscape Planning and Design. I already told you. At our institute, all the personnel have numbers like that. Yesterday you left the zone with T6, T9, and V4. We separate our work and our private lives as much as possible."

"I see. Now I'm glad that I got to keep my name as a section commissioner."

"That's certainly not going to change. At the institute, however, it's all about the big questions, so very special rules apply."

"The big picture, you mean?" asked Hardy.

"No, the big questions. Life and death. Humanity. I don't want to go further into the details right now. It wouldn't be good for you."

"Then what do you want from us, S1?" asked Hardy.

"I need you. Well, not both of you. Just you, Comrade Wagner."

"Where Tobias goes, I go, too."

"That's honorable, Herr Müller. But this isn't the right time. I'm not going to arrest your friend."

"You're going to kill him."

"Quite the opposite. I really need him alive."

"Are you going to dissect me? Reprogram me or something?" Tobias asked.

"Oh, it seems you think poorly of us." S1 frowned, as if he were personally disappointed in Tobias. "And yet we only want the best for humanity. Believe me, I need your full personality, fresh and vibrant."

"And if I refuse?"

"Then I'll still have to take you with me. But then everything will be more difficult. Unnecessarily difficult. Do yourself a favor and trust me."

"Trust you? You have our cosmonaut on your conscience. Along with Miriam and her husband."

"Yes, the cosmonaut. Our partners assured me that there was no other way to resolve that. It was quite a shock for the party and state leaders. Every good comrade is grieving for Mandy Neumann."

"You're a liar!"

Tobias clenched his fists. What the man had said was utter mockery.

"Not in the least. You just don't understand that sometimes you've got to make sacrifices. What's at stake is the survival of humanity."

"And three people have die for that?"

"What's three versus seven billion? Anyway, your math is incorrect, Comrade Wagner."

"What do you mean?"

"Your friend Miriam is alive and well. She's the problem you've got to solve for us."

She must have done it! She'd discovered the big secret all on her own and had maybe even escaped, and now he was supposed to prevent her from making it public. But he wasn't going to let them exploit him.

"Miriam is with you?" he asked warily.

"I can't say that she is, unfortunately. She managed to break her way through. And now, regrettably, she's in a position she never should have gotten to. We really underestimated that woman. All the experts agreed that you, Comrade Wagner, posed a greater danger. After all, you're trained as a police officer and carry a gun. We targeted you with all of our gimmicks, not her. In the process, Miriam Prassnitz must have slipped through our fingers somehow."

"Yes, I'm happy to be overestimated sometimes," Tobias said.

Should he be happy that his efforts had failed, perhaps providing Miriam with the distraction she needed? Had that actually been her plan all along?

"Anyway, we need you now," S1 said. "I'm sorry, but I can't go into more detail. You have the chance to save your friend's life. But we need to hurry, or else it may be too late."

"I'll go with you," Hardy said.

"That's out of the question. It's not an option. But if you keep quiet, I'll be sure that your chess buddy goes free."

Hardy jumped up. "You bastard! Did you...?"

"He's doing fine. We just spoke with him."

"I'm definitely coming along with Tobias," Hardy said.

"It's okay," Tobias said. "Who knows how this is going to end? Somebody's got to plan my funeral. My ex-wife will thank you."

"You'll have the most beautiful funeral you can imagine," Hardy said, hitting Tobias so hard on the back that he choked.

"Thank you. I'm really looking forward to it."

"Take your hand phone with you," Hardy said. "And let me know how you're doing. If I don't hear from you once an hour, I'm coming after you. And then may God help the institute."

S1 sighed. "Believe me, Herr Müller. No place on this earth is as godforsaken as the Institute. You'll have to come there all on your own."

October 13, 2029, Gaganyaan 3

"New message," said Vyommitra.

"Thank you," said Rakesh.

"New message," the female robot repeated.

"Yes, I heard."

"No, it's a new message."

"Thank you, confirmed."

"New message."

"Shankar, could you silence the robot?"

Rakesh looked to the right. The three seats were all side by side. The middle one was offset a bit to the back. Vyommitra, the female robot, was strapped to it. She wasn't particularly useful. Next to her was Shankar, who as the scientist was responsible for all experiments on board. That included Vyommitra, since she was also an experiment. However, it was interesting primarily for the media, which had made a big story out of it. Rakesh would have preferred to have a real vyomanaut as a third crew member, but that was only planned for later flights.

"I apologize," Shankar said. "But I need to test her hearing."

"By getting her to say 'new message' all the time?"

"No. She said that because we received new messages. What if you just read them?"

"New message," Vyommitra said, as if in confirmation.

Rakesh pulled over the keyboard and the screen. He actually wanted to check the engine. It would have to be back in tip-top shape tomorrow before they plunged into the Indian Ocean. A bunch of new messages had in fact arrived. Rakesh immediately deleted inquiries from the media. They should have contacted the press department! And they'd even gotten their first spam. Space spam for penis enlargements! His email address must have been leaked to someone.

But one message looked potentially interesting. The sender started with raghum... which immediately reminded him of old times. The school in Raipur! Could this really be Mr. Mukherjee, the headmaster? A person who was truly respected, known alongside all the important figures in the city of millions.

He could see himself at eleven or twelve years old—little Rakesh in the uniform with the shorts. His English teacher had taken him to the side of the cricket field, which also served as a playground—in order of importance—and told him to appear before the headmaster in five minutes. The secretary with the fancy sari waved him right through. Mr. Mukherjee was sitting in his huge leather chair behind the imposing teak desk, surely another legacy of the English colonial rulers. He stood up and came over towards him, then sat him down on the desk and congratulated him for having made the highest marks that school year.

For him, Mr. Mukherjee had never been a kindly uncle or a friend. He was his headmaster. He'd had a very long talk with him at an alumni reunion a few years ago. He'd still been in the Air Force back then. What was it that Mr. Mukherjee might want from him? Whatever it was, he was certain the man wasn't asking out of personal vanity and that it was a serious issue.

"Imagine that. My old headmaster wrote to me," he said.

"Oh, are you still in contact?"

"Of course. Aren't you?"

Rakesh didn't hear Shankar's reply. He didn't even hear Vyommitra announcing the arrival of many new messages. What Mr. Mukherjee had written was so incredible that it must be true.

"Shankar?"

He was the pilot and therefore Shankar's superior. The scientist was also a few years younger than him, and this automatically earned Rakesh his respect.

"Yes?"

"Do you trust me?"

"Of course, Rakesh."

Shankar stiffened his posture.

"Very good. Because we'll need to change our orbit."

"Did mission control say to do that?"

"No, my headmaster."

"Ah, of course. Are we flying to the moon or Mars?"

"Buckle yourself in, please, so I can make the correction."

"Oh, that wasn't a joke? I'm sorry. That must have sounded disrespectful."

Shankar pulled the strap over his shoulder and clicked it into place.

"I know you didn't mean it that way. When we talk to mission control, they will mean it like that. But don't worry. If things go wrong, I'll take all the responsibility. You're not to blame."

"What does 'go wrong' mean in this context? What's the worst-case scenario?"

"We could get shot down."

"Shot down. Not bad. We'd go down in history as the first space mission to get shot down."

Rakesh liked Shankar's dry sense of humor. But the scientist would probably correct him and say he hadn't meant to be funny. Sometimes it was hard to tell, even though they'd been training together for over a year.

"And in the best-case scenario?" asked Shankar.

"In the best-case scenario, we save a human being."

"Very good. Statistically speaking, the actual outcome of an experiment tends to be somewhere between the two extremes. So I expect that after a few orbits we'll switch back to our old one and land a little later than planned. They'll kick you out of the space program and I'll have to go up with Joshi."

"Forget it. He's already got his scientist, whose name has slipped my mind."

"I'm better than him. You can tell just by the fact that you can't remember his name."

Rakesh fastened his belt and entered the data for the new orbit. The computer did the rest. When the engine fired for the first time, mission control was immediately on the line.

"New message," said Vyommitra.

The female robot had no opinion about the change of plans.

October 13, 2029, X-38

"Take a look at what the Indians are doing over there," Vicky said.

She clicked on a row of green squares, and four orbits appeared on the screen. Roger read the labels even though he could guess what he was looking at. They were the trajectories of their own X-38, the ISS, what had been the Völkerfreundschaft, and the Indian capsule Gaganyaan 3. All four orbits were crowded into a narrow section of the spherical layer surrounding the Earth.

"Maybe they're training to approach the ISS," Roger said.

"Shouldn't we be informed of that?" asked Vicky.

"Yes."

"Should we check with mission control?"

"No."

"Right there with you. If it's important, they'll tell us. We're keeping an eye on the Völkerfreundschaft. That's enough."

She pronounced the name of the East German station so that it really sounded German. Foilkerfroindshaft. He always made it sound like Walkerfroundshaft.

"Do you have German ancestors?"

"What makes you think that? My family's always lived in Tennessee."

"Ah."

"Mission control here. Roger, do you copy?"

"Roger."

"Ha ha. There have been some new developments. It appears that our friends from India have been alerted to something. You'll need to be extra careful now."

"What do you mean?"

"The global situation. Ever heard of it? China not good. India friend in Asia, but India also friend to Russia. You don't make your friends angry."

"Yes, I realize that, of course. But how could we possibly make them angry? We're just looking."

"Roger, Roger. I see you've understood us. What must not happen under any circumstances is for our Indian friends to be endangered. But if you run into that dumb robot, you should still neutralize it."

"What if the Indians fall for it and approach?"

"We'll figure that out if it comes to that."

October 13, 2029, Lusatia

THE INSTITUTE DIDN'T JUST HAVE A BARKAS, BUT ALSO A
Mercedes. A section commissioner from the German People's
Police was climbing into a luxury vehicle from the West. Tobias
felt like a traitor to the cause of the working class. S1 sat behind
the wheel and gestured for him to get into the front passenger
seat. His two companions got in the back. They had not introduced themselves. Hardy was standing in front of the house and
waved as they drove off.

The Mercedes drove along the road that Tobias knew so well
by now. He caught a brief glimpse of the lake he'd gone to the
bottom of. Then, with its unmistakable wall of clouds, the zone
took over the left side of the street.

The gate opened as they approached. The Mercedes barely
had to slow down as it rolled onto the paved forest road. Nobody
had to identify themselves. The vehicle probably spoke for itself.
These Western cars really had great suspension. In the Barkas,
Tobias had felt every pothole. Where were they taking him? He
thought he saw the spot where he'd come out of the forest with
the three actors.

But they kept driving. Based on the distance between the
pines, Tobias estimated that they were going about 60 kilometers
per hour. That meant they'd covered about 25 kilometers in the
zone. It was too bad he hadn't brought the Glonass device with
him. The people from the institute hadn't let him bring any

luggage. He had, however, insisted on taking his gun. He wanted to be able to make a graceful exit at any time.

Whatever that meant.

"So what exactly is going on with Miriam?" Tobias asked. "If I'm going to help, I'll need some information."

S1 looked at his watch. Then he pressed a button on the center console, and there was a humming sound behind them. A window now shielded them from the two back seats. Tobias knocked on it. He saw one of the men from behind also knocking, but he couldn't hear it. S1 pressed another button on the instrument console, and a red light came on.

"A jammer," S1 said. "Now it really is just us."

"Is that really necessary?" asked Tobias.

"Absolutely. There are so many cooks here with their fingers in the broth—or how does it go?—that you really have to be careful."

"Whatever you say. So, what's going on with Miriam, and why did you look at your watch before answering my question?"

"Good observation. It's really very simple. Miriam gave us an ultimatum, and I have to get you to the destination before it expires. But we still have more than an hour."

Had Miriam really asked for him? Jonas was wrong! Tobias knew it. He was important to her. He straightened up.

"She insisted on seeing me?" he asked.

"No. We were the ones who thought of you. Miriam didn't mention you."

Tobias slumped over, deflated. "Then what does she want?"

"She gave us an ultimatum that we can't meet."

"And what is it, exactly?"

"She wants her husband."

"I could have told you that."

"The only problem is that her husband died during questioning. It was diabetic shock. The interrogator hadn't been informed about his medical condition. It was an unfortunate accident."

"You let him die during the interrogation? And now you're wondering why Miriam isn't particularly happy about it?"

"She doesn't know yet. Our hope is that you can stop her."

"From doing what, S1?"

"Destroying the world."

"Do you think you could be a little less theatrical? You don't have to make it more dramatic than it really is."

"It's impossible to make it more dramatic than it is. What we're up against here is the ultimate drama."

"Is it possible that being so far away from civilization at your institute, you've turned into a bit of a megalomaniac?"

"Just a little bit, but that happened a long time ago."

Tobias looked at S1, who had a completely serious look on his face. Even his voice didn't sound like he was joking.

"You know what? Just take me to Miriam. I'll talk to her about it."

"It's not that simple, Comrade Wagner. If it were, we would have long since resolved the problem. You simply don't understand what's going on here. That's why I'm going to show you something that very few people in this world have ever seen."

"Great, I can hardly wait."

The Mercedes slowed down. S1 steered it over three humps in the road, one after the other. Tobias saw steel spikes pointing in their direction of travel. Next to the middle speedbump was a yellow place-name sign: "Nichevo."

October 13, 2029, Earth orbit

SHE WAS SLEEPING. SHE ONLY HAD A FEW HOURS LEFT, AND SHE was wasting them. She could have at least had dreams. Like about her children, for example. But she was just gone, as if she'd been dead for an hour.

The west coast of North America was below her. She'd always planned to fly to the USA one day, and actually even had concrete plans. The next international astronautical congress would take place in Seattle in the spring of 2030. She should have given a lecture there about the use of the MKF-8 on the Völkerfreundschaft space station. After that, she'd hoped to take a cross-country trip with Sabine and Susanne and fly back from the east coast.

Mandy sucked on the tube of nutrient liquid. It tasted awful, like salty milk porridge, but it provided her with everything her body needed. She was sweating. While she'd been sleeping, the sun had risen for her. The life support system hadn't responded automatically, and the temperature inside the suit had gone up three degrees. She turned it down. Energy wasn't her problem. The fuel cells lasted for at least twelve hours. She'd run out of air before that.

A hard crust with a soft filling. That was how she would end up if she were to wait for her air to run out. But that wasn't going to happen. When she opened the helmet, her body would cool down to the temperature of space. Her limbs would become fragile as glass. Whenever the sun shone on her, the side of her facing it would thaw on the surface. But her core would be colder than anything on earth.

She should think about something else. But with her impending death, she couldn't. The lightness she'd felt before sleeping was gone. What had disrupted this incredible calm? Mandy could still feel its after-effects, but the calm itself was gone. It was just a memory now.

"Wee Hans went out, to walk about..."

She tried the nursery rhyme, but it just sounded pitiful. Her voice was as thin and brittle as her body would soon be. Dying wasn't majestic. It just sucked.

October 13, 2029, Gaganyaan 3

THE RADAR HADN'T GIVEN IT A REST FOR SEVERAL MINUTES NOW. The new orbit they'd reached was anything but clean. They already needed to make a few adjustments.

"There, do you see that?" asked Shankar.

"New message," said Vyommitra.

"Yes, I see it," said Rakesh. "The radar, I mean. Do you know where the duct tape is?"

"It's in the compartment above you."

"Keep an eye on the radar."

"New message," said Vyommitra.

Rakesh unbuckled his seat belt, floated up, and opened the compartment. The duct tape was secured by a clamp, as were the scissors. He cut off about ten centimeters and stowed them both away again.

"New message," said Vyommitra.

Rakesh floated to the middle and pulled himself over the robot's head. *I'm sorry, Vyommitra, but you're driving me nuts.* He covered her mouth with the duct tape.

"New message," said Vyommitra.

The sound that came out was now much quieter and sounded somewhat hollow.

"Mission control's going to complain," Shankar said.

"They're doing that anyway."

Nobody at the ground station was pleased about this unauthorized change of course. Rakesh had almost been replaced as commander, but some force behind the scenes prevented that from happening. His school headmaster had probably had something to do with it. He must have enough connections who owed him a favor.

Rakesh buckled up. "Thanks, I'll take over again," he said.

The Gaganyaan 3 was slowly gaining on their target—the debris cloud orbiting the Earth in place of the GDR space station. It wasn't clear yet how close they'd be able to get to it. Rakesh was hoping that the explosion had blown away most of the debris from its original orbit. Then the Völkerfreundschaft's old orbit would be relatively empty.

That would be good, because otherwise they could suffer a similar fate. According to the information from mission control, there seemed to have been a tragic accident. A robot developed by the GDR had taken on a life of its own. Rakesh gave Vyommitra a sidelong glance. She was annoying, but she wouldn't be capable of taking over the ship. That was very comforting.

"When do you think it would make sense to start using the infrared imager?" asked Rakesh.

As a physicist, Shankar would be able to assess this better.

"If things continue like this, maybe in an hour. It will also depend on the thermal radiation of the object we're looking for, of course. Why do you think it might come in useful?"

"That's what Mr. Mukherjee said. I'm expecting to see radiation from a human body in a spacesuit."

"Then it would be best for us to meet your mysterious solo traveler on the night side. On the day side, the heat that the debris has absorbed from the sun could leave the astronaut overexposed."

"Thanks."

Rakesh looked at the flight schedule. It appeared they'd been lucky. The initial encounter would be on the night side.

"Mission control to Gaganyaan 3."

"Rakesh here. Go ahead."

"We have a request here from NASA."

"Regarding space weather?"

"Don't push it. They want to know the reason for the change of course."

"On what grounds?"

"They're worried that if there's an accident with the debris, it could endanger the ISS. There are forty-three civilians vacationing there right now."

"There won't be an accident."

"Rakesh, you're really not doing yourself any favors there, man. Someone's protecting you, but you yourself know that won't last forever."

"Thank you for the warning. I'm well aware of that."

"So what am I supposed to tell NASA?"

"Tell them that debris from the explosion is interfering with our original orbit. And use that opportunity to ask them if they can think of any cause for the complete destruction of the station. An asteroid has never, ever had an impact like that."

October 13, 2029, Lusatia

THEY DROVE PAST BLOCK-SHAPED HOUSES WITH FLAT ROOFS. ONE reminded Tobias of a gymnasium, another of a swimming pool, and the third could have been a warehouse.

"Who works there?" he asked.

"This is all part of the institute. It's primarily labs," S1 said.

"I'd love to have a look."

"After we've solved the problem."

The Mercedes rolled down a road lined with concrete slabs. Now on either side came two WBS 70 blocks that looked pretty run down.

"You don't live especially comfortably here," Tobias said.

"Just a few employees still live here. Most can't tolerate the constant twilight."

The town ended as unremarkably as it had begun. They reached a gate, and this time S1 had to show his ID. The back doors opened and his companions got out. Tobias reached for the door handle.

"No, stay in your seat. Past the town is where the special restricted zone starts. You have an exemption."

Tobias said nothing. A sentinel in uniform gave a salute, and then the boom barrier opened. The car lurched three times. On the left was an exit sign for the town, with the usual diagonal bar through the name. Block letters underneath read: "Nichevo 11 km." Someone had crossed out the 11 with black paint and written a 5 above it.

"The next town is the same one we just came from?" Tobias asked.

"Yes, more or less," S1 said. "You'll understand soon enough."

The Mercedes braked, and S1 rolled down the side window. Tobias could see in the rearview mirror that a uniformed man was running from the barrier towards them.

"Clean that graffiti off the town exit sign, you hear?" S1 ordered, then stepped on the gas.

Now he was driving much slower and kept looking left and right as if expecting a sudden attack. When a gust of wind hit the Mercedes, he tightened his seat belt and pressed his head back against the headrest. For somebody who drove this road every day, S1 was surprisingly nervous. Tobias followed his example and the man nodded.

"Mercedes, activate autopilot."

Did S1 want to show Tobias how great the Western car's technology was? There probably wasn't a more inappropriate...

Something hit him. Within microseconds, his head shrank to the size of a ping-pong ball, then immediately expanded again. His muscles cramped. It was as if the complex mechanism of the human body were halting every other second. He wanted to scream but couldn't open his mouth. A bolt of lightning was driving into his skull. He cleared all blockages as if he were forcibly straightening out a cramped limb. The pain was outrageous. His teeth chattered. He breathed in greedily. His underwear got wet.

...moment.

It took Tobias a moment to realize that the final part of his last thought had just materialized in his head. He groaned. S1 gave him a compassionate look.

"It's over now, right?" he asked.

"What the hell was that?" asked Tobias.

"You can think again, so that means it's over now. What you just experienced is what we call nitsch burya. One of our scientists visiting from Russia went through it for the first time and came up with the name. You could translate it as 'nothing storm.'"

"Is this one of your tricks?"

"No, what ever gave you that idea? It's an effect of what

you're about to see. The nitsch buryas go two to three kilometers up beyond the inner border. That's why you have to drive on autopilot here. If it had gotten me while I was at the wheel, I would have driven the car into a tree."

"But what is it?"

"Our scientists say they're travelling perturbations from the quantum vacuum."

"That doesn't mean anything to me," Tobias admits.

"Same here. This is how it was explained to me: imagine a sphere under high voltage, like in those lightning experiments. Sometimes its influence causes a conducting channel to be created in the air, and the voltage is discharged through it."

"This sphere is beyond the inner boundary that you mentioned."

"It is, of course, just an image."

"And how often do these nitsch buryas occur?"

"Pretty often. They actually get me every time I drive this way. So don't be surprised if I suddenly start acting strange."

Tobias could feel dampness in his crotch. He slid back on the seat a little and straightened up. That way it wasn't as immediately obvious what had happened.

"Don't feel bad," S1 said. "The nitsch burya blocked all your muscles and then released them with no remorse. It happens to everybody. That's why I wear a diaper when I approach the inner boundary."

"Well, you could have warned me."

S1 laughed. "How would you have reacted if I'd suggested you put on a diaper?"

"I would have told you you were nuts."

"That's what every newcomer who hasn't been past the inner boundary does. But it doesn't take long to realize how sound that advice is."

All of a sudden, S1 jerked his head to the right and stuck out his tongue. His hands clenched the steering wheel, but it didn't budge. Then he relaxed again.

"You all right?" asked Tobias.

"All things considered."

"For you it happened fast, though."

"It did for you just now, too. Your nitsch burya lasted five seconds, tops. But it felt a lot longer. The phenomenon also disrupts your perception of time. Some people believe they spent days in this state."

"That's really horrible."

"For them, the recovery period lasts considerably longer. But don't worry. The effect only increases following habituation. Incidentally, some scientists believe that it's not the perception of time that changes, but rather the passage of time. However, we haven't succeeded in proving a pronounced aging effect yet. A few days aren't enough for that."

What in the world had this ominous institute done here? Had something gone awry during the construction of some kind of superweapon? Or was S1 actually taking him to an alien spaceship?

"Interesting. But I haven't studied physics for years. Shouldn't we be addressing the Miriam problem now?"

S1 looked at his watch and shook his head.

"You haven't seen the most interesting part yet. But we're almost there."

S1 could have saved himself the trouble of saying this last sentence, because along the side of the road there now appeared warning signs written in several languages: German, Russian, and English. They read "Inner boundary" and "Danger of death." Others read, "Authorized personnel only." There were no guards, however.

"There's no security here?" asked Tobias.

"It's not necessary. After all the hocus pocus on the outer border, there's no need to restrict access. That's what we thought, anyway."

"But it didn't work with Miriam."

S1 didn't answer. He slowed the car to walking speed.

"Look, over there!"

THEY ROLLED SLOWLY UP A SMALL HILL, LEAVING THE FOREST behind them. To the left and right, only tree stumps were to be seen. Because of its sandy soil, the hill looked like a Baltic Sea dune. It was overgrown with bushes and scraggly grass. The car stopped at the top. From there, the hill looked more like a levee.

It formed two broad curves on either side, and at the summit was a driveway covered with concrete slabs.

S1 tapped Tobias's shoulder. "Over there!"

His eyes followed the dense layer of clouds. Fog was rising on the horizon, where the sky and earth merged. The Mercedes drove slowly forward again, this time down the hill. The ground seemed parched and lifeless. Every so often there were deep tire tracks that must have been made by enormous vehicles. With every passing meter, the air in the car became heavier. Tobias pressed the button to roll down the side window, but S1 blocked it before the window started to move.

"Better not right now," he said.

"Why? Toxic gas left over from the chemical spill?"

"I'd be glad if that's all it was. No, look to your right."

S1 pointed roughly in the direction of the side mirror on the right. About 15 meters from the car, a sneaker was floating in the air. It was amazing how starkly it contrasted with its surroundings, as if an unseen lens was intensifying the light reflecting off it. Even from that distance, Tobias could see the two double stripes of the Germina brand, which was made by the state-owned enterprise Spezialsportschuhe Hohenleuben.

"It's floating," he said.

"It's waiting," S1 said.

"For what?"

S1 didn't respond. The car rolled forward slowly, approaching the hovering sneaker before moving away from it again as it followed a curve in the road to the left. Suddenly, the shoe started flying. It rushed towards them at an incredible speed. Tobias pressed back against the headrest. The shoe bounced off the windshield and came to a stop. What on earth was that? Tobias's heart was beating wildly.

"Special bulletproof glass," S1 said.

"Good to know."

"In the Mercedes, we're protected against everything the inner zone can throw at us. Well, almost everything."

"Are there any more surprises like that?"

"Too many to count. We've been cataloging them for forty years, but we're still finding new ones."

"And what was that?"

"It belongs to the category of pamyat. That's a bastardized Russian word."

"Pamyat. I know that means 'memory.' So who remembers what?"

"If you looked closely, you would have seen that this was an old model. Germina shoes haven't been made for thirty years."

"And what exactly does it mean?"

"The way we account for it is a disturbance in the time dimension."

"But why did it want to clobber us to death?"

"It's looking for its owner," S1 said.

"What? I never had sneakers like that."

"The scientists say that the compromised causality is trying to repair itself. In the process, it also accepts non-optimal solutions. The compromised causality jumps, in a manner of speaking, into every lower-energy state, even if it cannot reach the lowest state. You could have owned such a sneaker at one time. You're old enough and it would probably even fit you. If a child had been sitting where you are, the sneaker wouldn't have been set into motion."

Tobias' head was pounding. Compromised causality? His energy level was low, too, and the man was drowning him in scientific explanations instead of answering the obvious questions. What was all this? Who was to blame for this bullshit? And why did the sneaker want Tobias dead and not S1, who doubtless deserved it?

"Why didn't it go after you?"

"I'm Russian-German. There weren't any Germina shoes in our country back then. We prefer that scientists who didn't live in the GDR in the late 1980s be the ones to study the pamyat."

"What other kinds of phenomena are there?"

"Time traps, deepfreezers, trambovki, the nasty nothing, revenants, Danube waves, gray holes, methusalems, double and triple pamyats, povtorniki, presswursts, micro-tornadoes, katyushas,..."

Tobias massaged his temples. The actors, the upside-down world, the altered perception—those had all been tricks. And now S1 wanted to trick him again. That must be what was going on. He just had to open the car door and he'd discover an ultra-thin rubber band on the sneaker. Tobias reached for the door.

But that nitsch burya... S1 had certainly peed himself, too. And the guy was really scared. Tobias could smell his sweat. This was different.

"Thanks. I get it," he said. "What are the chances of our running into those?"

Regardless of whether S1 was lying or not, Tobias would have to play along a while. At the moment, he had no other choice.

"It's not very likely. Most of them are easy to spot from a distance. For example, the trambovki look like little flat clouds, anywhere from thirty to fifty meters off the ground. When you pass beneath them, your z dimension shrinks by one to two orders of magnitude. From the outside, it looks like the cloud is ramming into you. That's where the name comes from. It means 'rammer.'"

"How do you keep all these things from crossing the inner boundary?"

"I don't know. That's just how it is. The scientists think it's because of our main issue. You can think of it in terms of a weather phenomenon: When warm and cold air collide, there's a storm in the transition zone."

"The inner border is the transition zone, then. But what is the main issue?"

S1 again refrained from giving him an answer. Instead, as the road curved slightly to the left, he drove off the road to the right. The Mercedes's engine roared briefly. One of the wheels was evidently spinning in the sand. S1 pressed a button and it gained traction again.

"Nothing to worry about," S1 said. "I've done this many times."

They bumped their way up a hill, just high enough that Tobias couldn't see over it. The car struggled up the last two meters and came to a stop.

There was a chasm about one meter past the front wheels. Tobias gripped the armrests with his sweaty palms. What if the cliff broke off? It didn't look particularly stable.

That was when his gaze fell on the nothingness. He knew immediately what it was, and S1 didn't have to tell him. But why was it like that? He himself could explain what it was. Before him was a round lake. The surface of the water was smooth as glass, but didn't reflect anything. It completely absorbed all the light from the clouds hanging over it. There were no waves and no texture whatsoever, but there was still a clear boundary between something and nothing. This boundary was the lake's surface.

"Can we get out?" asked Tobias.

What had he just said? His voice sounded totally foreign. He must have gone crazy. Why would he want to get out? The Mercedes surrounded him securely, like a mother's lap.

S1 looked around briefly, then nodded. "All clear."

Tobias got out. He held on to the hood of the car and slowly felt his way forward. When he reached the front wheels, he stopped. There was a cool wind that smelled of the forest. Tobias licked his index finger and briefly stooped down. At the level of his lower legs, the wind was blowing east in the direction of the nothingness, while at the level of his head, it was blowing in the opposite direction. It was as if it were bouncing off the nothingness.

S1 slowly followed him.

"The wind," Tobias said.

S1 smiled approvingly. "Good observation. Over the nothingness is an extremely stable high-pressure area. The wind bounces off it like a mountain."

"Then what's with the clouds?"

"The high-pressure area only goes up about 150 meters. Above that, the nothingness has less of an influence."

Tobias looked for a stone, picked one up, and threw it. It flew in a broad arc over the edge of the cliff and then plunged into the depths. It penetrated the surface of the nothingness and disappeared. Nothing could be seen in the black mirror.

"How deep is it?" asked Tobias.

"Scientists don't agree about that. Some say it's infinitely deep. Others believe it has no depth at all because it's completely dimensionless and therefore has no spatial or temporal extent."

"The surface does have a fixed circumference."

"That's the part we see in our three-dimensional world. The scientists disagree about what it looks like elsewhere."

"But the stone is something. What happened to it? Is it lying somewhere underneath?"

"No. Nobody knows what might have happened to it. But one thing is clear: With its energy, the nothingness expands."

Tobias took a step back. "It's growing?"

"Yes, that's the big issue."

"How fast?"

"After the 1987 experiment, it had a diameter of three centimeters."

Tobias remembered the images from the Völkerfreundschaft.

"It's around thirty kilometers now, right?"

S1 nodded. Tobias did the math in his head. For every year, that was around 750 meters, or three-quarters of a kilometer. The Earth measured almost 130,000 kilometers. That meant that in 17,000 years, the nothingness would have swallowed up the Earth. The GDR was about 250 kilometers across, from east to west. That would be 333 years. That was no reason to panic, either.

"The experiment?" he asked.

"The institute used to be a field office for the Rossendorf Central Institute for Nuclear Research, and they were trying to tap into the quantum vacuum. The scientists explained it to me this way: Our universe is in an excited state. Every cubic centimeter of vacuum contains a vast amount of energy. If they had been able to channel it, all our energy problems would have been solved. So they built the appropriate facility here where an open cast mine used to be."

"Did we drive past it?"

"No, it doesn't exist anymore. It was the first thing the nothingness captured." S1 pointed ahead. "It was almost exactly where the middle of the lake is now."

"Were the scientists successful?"

"Too successful. Apparently, they restored a part of space to its initial state. But in the process, it lost all its properties. Have you ever heard of a Bose-Einstein condensate? It's a kind of primordial soup in which the particles aren't differentiated from one another in any way. They lose their individuality. Something similar is at work here. Space and time lose their meaning. Yet this violates the laws of our world, such as the principle of causality. Now, the stone that you threw in never existed in our world. But then how could you have thrown it? This is how all the phenomena in the transition zone are produced. Maybe you just created a pamyat or a time trap."

Tobias shuddered. Was a pamyat trampling a human being right this moment? He folded his arms behind his back.

"That sounds complicated. Is there a remedy?"

"We have discovered something that can stop the nothingness from spreading. Come on, get in. We should be moving on."

Tobias sat back down in the car. His head hurt.

THEY DROVE UP TO A BUILDING THAT LOOKED LIKE A LIGHTHOUSE cut in half from top to bottom. It was perhaps twenty meters high, with a semicircular base. The flat side was about two meters from the slope and faced the nothingness. A ladder led up the rounded side, and almost at the top was a small door leading inside.

S1 stopped the Mercedes.

"Um, I'm not going to climb the ladder," Tobias said.

S1 smiled. "That wasn't the plan. But if you already don't like this, you're going to like the plan even less."

"What do you intend to do to me?"

"We'll get to that soon. You asked about the remedy. It's right in front of you."

"I see half a lighthouse."

"It's actually a kind of projector. Along with the other forty-four, it creates a barrier field that prevents the nothingness from growing."

"Barrier field? This really is science fiction."

"The nothingness itself actually helped us get here, specifically thanks to the time traps. Those are strictly defined areas that completely lack the dimension of time. Whatever ends up there exists quasi-eternally. But the time traps can be manipulated in all spatial dimensions. If you know how, they can be moved and their size can be changed. The scientists figured out how to do that."

"Ah, they can get them big enough to fit the nothingness into."

"Exactly. The time traps are now in the towers and form a timeless wall."

"An invisible eternity wall?"

"Very poetically expressed, and pretty much on the mark."

"The nothingness can't get past the eternity emitted by the lighthouses?"

"Yes, it can, but it needs an almost infinite amount of time to do it. Unless... but we'll get to that soon."

"But what's the whole spiel about drilling rigs? Was there never any petroleum here?"

"Right. But it was the only way. I wasn't here at the time, but I think it made sense. In 1987, the eternity towers didn't exist yet, and the nothingness was spreading very quickly. The thirty kilometers we see today were almost entirely created during the first four years. That's more than seven kilometers per year! In less than fifty years it would have reached the territory of the FRG. Shalck-Golodkovsky was quick to realize that, and thanks to Strauß, he immediately got the West on board. The Chernobyl disaster was in 1986, and they of course already knew about that. A little radioactive rain was enough to change the mood in the West. Yet the nuclear power plant was a thousand kilometers away! If people had found out that East and West Germany, and later the entire world, were going to be completely swallowed up in seventy years, it would have led to a global crisis. The only way to prevent that from happening was to keep it under wraps. The GDR also got enough money and scientific support to develop the towers."

This was all... appalling. Of course, panic would have ensued. But there was a solution, after all. There were technological means to keep the problem under control.

"That's insane! What a hassle! But couldn't they have explained it later?"

"That would have been stupid. Ever since then, the GDR has had the West by the balls. In any case, the problem did still exist. That was its number one form of leverage. If just one tower was blown up... Some scientists believe it would be possible to allow the nothingness to grow in a linear fashion toward the West."

"Without having to sacrifice any GDR territory in the process?" asked Tobias.

"A strip of the GDR had already been factored in."

"That's..."

"Don't worry. Most scientists believe that the nothingness always expands in a perfect circle, so it's not possible to attack the FRG directly with it."

"How reassuring. The very thought that it was given serious consideration!"

Tobias's voice grew louder. That would be a betrayal of all socialist values!

"Easy there, Comrade Wagner. You also had a pretty good life with the K-Mark, the Western cars on our roads, and the Western chains in our shopping centers. We wouldn't have been able to afford any of that without the subsidies from the EU."

"And what's form of leverage number two?"

"The authorities' power consciousness. If it were found out the party leaders had lied to their own people about something like this for four years, many of their careers would be over."

"Did everybody know?"

"I don't know. There were, at least, few enough that nothing ever leaked out."

"Until the MKF-8 came onto the market."

"Yes. On a regular basis, we thoroughly replenish the cloud layer over the zone with oil flares. Those are the 'derricks' you saw. But that doesn't affect the MKF-8."

"But such an expensive project surely couldn't go forward without approval from the top?"

"Right. Dr. Prassnitz had to agree to program the analysis software to provide images that wouldn't compromise the status of the zone. But it appears that went wrong."

"The scientist's pride in his work," Tobias said.

That fit with the impression he had of Miriam's husband, even if he only knew him from what she'd told him.

Had known.

"Now do you understand what a terrible problem we're facing?" S1 asked as they sat back down in the car.

Tobias pressed the button for the seat heater. The dampness in his crotch was slowly becoming uncomfortably cool. They drove past a statue depicting two men in a close embrace. It was a sad image that went along with the sad landscape. The statue was sculpted naturalistically, but it was completely colorless. Probably concrete.

"What's that?" asked Tobias, pointing to the statue.

"Keep your eye on the ball. Do you see the problem?" asked S1 impatiently.

"You're right, the nothingness is... huge," Tobias said. "A nightmare. If the world knew about it, there would be enormous difficulties. But it seems you have it pretty well under control. Is Miriam threatening to make it public?"

"No. We'd know how to prevent that."

"Meaning, the way you prevented Dr. Prassnitz and the cosmonaut."

"Cosmonaut?" S1 looked genuinely surprised. "I don't know anything about that. So it wasn't an accident? I really don't have anything to do with that. I'm only responsible for the security of the restricted area. Didn't she have two kids?"

"Yes, and now they have to grow up without a mother."

"That's really tragic. I'm very sorry about that. The two of them aren't to blame. Unlike their mother."

"What's that supposed to mean?" asked Tobias sharply.

"The cosmonaut herself decided to go into space. She was certainly aware of the danger."

"Not this danger, though!"

"My apologies, dear Comrade Wagner. I stand corrected. Let's focus on the problem."

S1 was an asshole. Prassnitz probably wasn't the first person who had to die because of this secret. But Tobias wasn't there for him, but for Miriam.

"Good," he said. "So what exactly seems to be the problem now?"

"I'll show you."

THE ROAD NOW LED ALONG THE EDGE OF THE PRECIPICE. THEY passed another tower. S1 stopped the car just before they reached the next one.

"There, a time trap!" he said, pointing to the left.

There was half a Wartburg in the middle of the sand. It had been cut cleanly at about the central column, with the rear part missing.

"Strange. But where's the trap?" asked Tobias.

"It's a 353 from 1985. Look at that paint job!"

The Wartburg's fenders had a metallic gleam. This half-vehicle had been here for over forty years and should be rusted through. But the time trap had preserved it perfectly.

"I see," Tobias said. "Couldn't this be sold all over the world, now that you've harnessed it with the towers? Maybe East Germany could make money from the zone itself instead of being dependent on the West."

"No way. The phenomena only work in the inner zone. They need the nothingness."

"Ah. That's too bad."

S1 pressed a button and the autopilot set the Mercedes in motion again. Now there appeared a gigantic form, that from a distance could have been mistaken for a sleeping dragon. As they approached, Tobias noticed that the form was made of metal. It had once been a lignite excavator. S1 stopped the vehicle, opened the glove compartment, and took out a pair of binoculars.

"Come on," S1 said.

He cast a searching glance through the windshield and at the rearview mirror, then got out. Tobias followed him. The Mercedes was close to the precipice. A strange feeling was tugging at his lower back. But he didn't want to show any weakness, and moved forward towards where S1 was leaning on the hood. The metal was warm. It smelled of heather and autumn fires. It looked as if the forest there had just been cleared recently. The area next to the road was full of tree stumps. S1 handed him the binoculars.

"So that's the problem?" asked Tobias, lifting them to his eyes.

"Yes and no."

"Please explain, S1."

"See that long boom with the big shovels?"

"Can't miss it. Very impressive."

The boom was about as tall as a high-voltage pylon and extended far beyond the cliff. A second boom at the back of the excavator acted as a counterweight. Two additional masts projected into the air at an angle. They had pulleys with tether ropes that connected the front and rear booms.

"What would happen if the boom fell into the nothingness?" asked S1.

"Nothing. The nothingness wants to spread, but it's prevented by the towers' barrier fields."

"Unfortunately, that's incorrect. The barrier fields are only effective in the case of minor changes, like the stone you threw in. Small amounts of sand are constantly crumbling off the cliffs and falling into the nothingness. But if the boom or even the whole excavator fell in, the nothingness would make a huge leap forward. We calculate that its diameter would increase by about ten meters."

"Ten meters? That's not even a per mill."

"Right, it's not much. But it would cost us the towers, and the barrier fields along with them. The nothingness would start growing again at its previous speed. The greater its circumference, the more material falls into it, and the faster it grows. We would have to build new towers, but many more than before, and at the same time the Institute would be in danger. The more towers we need, the more resources we use up. If the nothingness were to expand beyond the restricted zone, we wouldn't be able to keep its existence a secret anymore. That would lead to a global crisis and further reduce our resources, because it would mean an end to our deal with the West. We wouldn't be able to control the nothingness anymore. Our simulations show this very clearly. In less than a hundred years, nothing would be left of the Earth."

Tobias got goose bumps. Maybe it was in the cosmonaut's best interests to stay in orbit, after all. But at some point, the nothingness would reach her up there, too. What was 300 or 400 kilometers? Then it would be the solar system's turn. Shit. Couldn't the scientists back then have been a little more careful with what they played around with?

Now he understood. "So Miriam wants to crash the excavator into the nothingness?"

"Yes. Her ultimatum expires in just under an hour. Either she gets her man, or we get global annihilation."

"But her husband died during questioning."

"Which makes it difficult to meet her ultimatum."

"Why don't you just tell her that?" asked Tobias.

"And what if she doesn't believe us or goes ahead with her plan anyway, out of desperation? Do you think she'd do that?"

Tobias shrugged his shoulders. Would Miriam sacrifice the

world for her husband? He didn't know. But he couldn't rule out the possibility. What was the world worth to him, and to Miriam? He would readily take a bullet for her. But what if saving the world was only possible over her dead body? Would he shoot her as a last resort? Just thinking about it was unbearably painful.

"We've already considered bringing in snipers," S1 said, as if guessing what he was thinking. "But that won't work. Frau Prassnitz moved the excavator on the existing tracks as close to the edge as possible. Then she pivoted the boom over the nothingness. She attached herself to the very end of the boom with a rope. She's hanging from a lever that folds down the boom."

"And if you shot her, she'd fall from the excavator and her weight would release the lever. That's brilliant."

Miriam was really going all out. This was the Miriam he had come to know. Her husband would have been proud of her. What loyalty! But it wasn't just her life at stake, but those of eight billion innocent people. She had a good cause. The forces she was fighting against didn't deserve any better. But the path she'd chosen was that of the ultimate terrorist.

"This is why we really need you. You need to find a way to get Miriam off the excavator."

October 13, 2029, Earth orbit

THERE IT WAS. HER HOME. EVEN IN THE DARKNESS, SHE COULD make out its contours. Her hometown was in the southwest. Without the MKF-8, Mandy couldn't directly observe her children anymore. But she could imagine their grandma tucking them in right now, perhaps reading them a story. Hopefully, they'd have their grandma for a long time to come. Jochen had neither the desire nor the time to read to them, though he wasn't a bad father overall.

But what would the loss of their mother do to her children? It would surely be traumatic for them. She would have done anything to make sure they'd be okay. Mandy sighed. She had no tears left, but sighing was enough. What was happening to her up here was total crap, and she no longer had any control over her own destiny.

It was time to open the helmet. The oxygen would only last for a few more minutes. Mandy grabbed the clasp with both hands. There were three buttons she had to unfasten. Left, right, center. She'd start on the left. For safety reasons, she had to use both hands.

There was a clicking noise as something hit her arm. A tiny fragment of the station, maybe. She watched the oxygen gauge, but there were no leaks in the suit. It hadn't hurt her, either. Lucky! Lucky? That was one way of looking at it. A little further to the left, and she would have already been set free.

She reached for the helmet with her left hand. There was the button. Now for the one on the right. She had to undo both of them at the same time... Grrrrr! She couldn't bend her right arm anymore. The joint was blocked. Mandy tried with all her might, but the arm remained rigid. She pushed as hard as she could with her left hand, but the joint wouldn't budge. She howled with rage.

One more time. She reached around her breastplate with her left hand. Yes... almost... there was the button! She pressed it, but nothing happened. On the left, the clasp had snapped back into place. The helmet was designed not to come off if someone accidentally pushed just one of the buttons. Shit!

Her right arm was useless. She could only move it at the shoulder joint. Hold on. She lifted it upward, guiding it past her helmet. With her left hand, she pushed the button, then quickly pressed her right arm against it. Now quickly push down on the right. *Come on, button! Come on, set me free!*

But the helmet remained snugly on her head. She lowered her right arm. The fabric was probably too soft to keep the button pressed down. Mandy whimpered. Now she couldn't even decide when to say goodbye. She would slowly and excruciatingly suffocate.

October 13, 2029, Gaganyaan 3

"I GUESS IT WAS A FALSE ALARM AFTER ALL," SAID SHANKAR.

They'd almost reached the orbit of the Völkerfreundschaft and were continuing to gain ground. All the objects in the vicinity were either ice cold or, when they saw sides that had been illuminated by the sun during the last orbit, too hot.

Rakesh sighed. This meant he'd have a bit of explaining to do after they landed. But the trip still meant something to him. He'd been able to give something back to his former headmaster, who had always believed in him. Without Mr. Mukherjee, he would never have gotten the recommendation for the Air Force, since his father had actually hoped he'd be his successor in the company.

"Proximity alert," the ship reported.

A piece of debris was approaching. A collision was unlikely, but Rakesh still made corrections to the orbit, though they were minimal. He had to economize on fuel, or there wouldn't be enough for the landing. He carefully monitored the screen. It wouldn't be easy to identify a person in a spacesuit out there.

"Let's abort," Shankar said.

"Hold on."

At that very second, he saw it. His former director was right! In the immediate vicinity of the Völkerfreundschaft orbit, there was an object orbiting the Earth that was somewhat brighter in the infrared than the other fragments.

"See that, Shankar?" asked Rakesh, pointing to the screen.

"Yes. It could be a fuel cell."

"A working fuel cell that's about 1.80 meters tall? Did you see the other debris?"

"Maybe it's a piece of the engine."

"Which happens to be twenty degrees and isn't cooling down any further. We have to check it out!"

Rakesh applied some thrust on the engine, which increased the orbit. The bright spot was above them.

"Proximity alert!"

Dang it, another piece of debris. The ship's computer calculated a risk of ten percent. Rakesh ignored it.

"Are you sure?" asked Shankar.

"Yes. We need to save fuel."

The debris raced past them. The radar indicated that it had only been one meter away. That was really close. Rakesh felt guilty. He couldn't put Shankar in danger just because he wanted to help his director. That had nothing to do with him. The next time they'd move out of the way.

But there wouldn't be a next time. The bright spot was getting closer and closer. One last adjustment maneuver. Now they still had a relative speed of 20 kilometers per hour. In cosmic terms, that was almost nothing.

"I'm going out," Rakesh said.

"Okay. Be careful."

The Gaganyaan 3 had an airlock it could use to dock with space stations. They'd never tested it, just as no vyomanaut had ever performed an EVA. But for safety purposes, there were two suits in the airlock. Rakesh climbed in.

"Could you pass over Vyommitra?"

Shankar pushed the human-sized robot toward him. There wasn't enough room for four in the capsule. It would be too heavy anyway. Therefore, they'd have to say goodbye to Vyommitra. Rakesh pulled the robot into the airlock and closed the bulkhead behind him. Now he had about ten minutes.

"Exit in sixty seconds," Shankar said. "CapCom said you can expect to get a severe reprimand."

"Got it. Standing by."

"All values within normal range. Evacuate airlock."

The air was sucked out of the lock.

"Ready. Have a nice trip!" said Shankar.

Rakesh opened the hatch. He needed to move quickly. A countdown was running in the background, and right now it was at 45. Rakesh attached both safety lines and climbed out. The capsule was tiny, and the earth was enormous. He felt like Gulliver in the land of giants. Focus.

30, 29, 28. The warm object would have to come from the direction of flight. Rakesh was briefly disoriented because it seemed like the capsule wasn't moving at all. Then he remembered that he'd last braked with the main engine, so the tail was pointing in the direction of flight. He turned around. He wouldn't be able to see the object until he was close. Twelve, eleven, ten. There was nothing there. Had he been mistaken?

No. A flash of silver. A helmet pane? The object was a little too high, and it was moving fast. Rakesh leapt and started flying towards it. Hopefully it wasn't a sharp piece from the engine that would tear his spacesuit apart.

Womp. A knee hit him in the stomach. Rakesh grabbed at anything he could get a hold of. He caught an arm and a leg. It was a human being in a spacesuit. Who wasn't moving. Their speeds were now equalized, so Rakesh could use one hand to pull on the safety line, which brought him back to the capsule. First, he pushed the human he'd rescued into the airlock. The suit stuck in the opening. Rakesh pulled himself closer. It was the right arm that was causing problems. It appeared that the joint of the spacesuit was damaged, and now the arm was sticking out to the side. *I'm sorry, but I'm going to have to hurt you now.* Rakesh pushed hard against the arm until it no longer resisted.

He reached behind it with his upper body to pull the robot out of the airlock by its head. They really needed the space now. Rakesh gave it a push towards the Earth. *Have a pleasant journey, Vyommitra.* The robot didn't say anything in response. It had no consciousness. It was a machine. Still, Rakesh felt sorry for it. At that moment, the sun was rising and bathed Vyommitra in its brilliance. *Oh, you've earned it.* He closed the bulkhead.

"I've got everything," he said. "We need oxygen."

"Okay," Shankar said.

The visor of the foreign astronaut's helmet was covered with ice on the inside. At half normal pressure, he opened the helmet, which had a rather old-fashioned closure with three snap buttons. The visor flipped up. It was a woman. Rakesh recognized the face, which had been drained of all color. It was the German cosmonaut.

"Amazing. Do you see this?" asked Rakesh.

"The camera image from the airlock is a little blurred. Is that the GDR cosmonaut? She was reported as dead," Shankar said.

"Please do me a favor," Rakesh said. "Don't tell mission control about this. Something's not right here."

The inner airlock door opened. Shankar took the unconscious woman from him. As Rakesh took off his suit, Shankar peeled the cosmonaut's off and took her pulse and blood pressure.

"She's alive!"

October 13, 2029, X-38

"SEE, THAT COULD BE A SALVAGE OPERATION," VICKY SAID.

"Yes, but what is he trying to capture?" asked Roger.

He did have an idea what the Indians might be salvaging, of course. But he hadn't told anyone about the bright red blot. It would only be a burden to Vicky if she knew what her work out there had done.

"Looks like a warm body to me."

"But where would that come from? Maybe they're interested in the camera."

It was said that the GDR space station had some kind of miracle camera on board. Vicky must have heard about it, too. Who knew if there was any truth to it?

"It's an odd shape," Vicky said. "Maybe we should intervene."

"Remember what mission control said. India's our friend."

"Then they'll also understand if we..."

"No, forget it, Vicky. We'll let them do their thing. The sooner we get home, the better."

"True. I'll go clean up in the airlock. When we land, the rocket launcher should be secured."

"Good idea. Wait, did you see that?"

"They're throwing it back out?" asked Vicky.

Roger was just as astonished as she was. The sun was just rising and illuminated the object that had come out of the Indian spaceship's airlock. It very clearly had two arms and two legs.

"Seems to be dead, then," he said.

Roger gulped. The blot in the infrared... when he'd seen it, the woman could still have been alive. She was... she had been a colleague and deserved better than this icy grave. He gulped again.

"You should pass that on to CapCom. I have a feeling it could be important information."

"You're absolutely right about that, Vicky."

October 13, 2029, Lusatia

Tobias swung the binoculars to the very end of the boom. But he couldn't see Miriam. Maybe the magnification wasn't high enough, or she was hiding behind one of the numerous crossbars. Or what if she'd actually given up and S1 hadn't been informed yet? That would be the best solution.

He lowered the binoculars. Then he noticed something moving way back on the boom that hovered over the cliff.

"Do you see that?" he asked, raising the binoculars again.

S1 jumped up. "What? Is it Frau Prassnitz? Quick, show me!"

"No, it's too big to be a human."

A U-shaped metal part at the very end of the boom turned slowly downward as if a giant were playing with it. The binoculars raked the top of Tobias's nose as S1 snatched them away from him.

"Ow!"

"I need to see. There!"

S1 completely froze. Tobias could tell why even without the assistance of the binoculars. The u-shaped part was breaking away from the excavator, hanging by a few screws or wires at most. And now it was falling. Tobias watched it until it vanished behind the cliff. It was obvious that...

"Scheiße, Scheiße, Scheiße!" shouted S1.

He tossed the binoculars aside and rushed to the driver's side of the Mercedes. *You can't stay here!* Tobias looked at the asphalt road. It went on for at least another kilometer to the next tower, right next to the cliff.

"Come on! Let's go!"

Tobias' thoughts were racing. One part of his brain was screaming, *Escape*! But another part managed to calculate his odds. To the left of the road, on the safe side, ran a deep ditch overgrown with stinging nettles. Even if the Mercedes made it down the slope and back up again, the stumps would be in the way. What had S1 said? The nothingness would expand. The road wasn't safe.

"Hey, Wagner, get in! We need you!"

Tobias shook his head. Maybe he was making a fatal mistake, but he thought that speeding along the cliff in that clunker spelled certain disaster. He pointed to the ditch.

"Are you nuts? I'm your only chance!"

He shook his head once again. *Go on.* The nothingness certainly wasn't going to wait around forever. Leaving the asphalt strip behind, Tobias plunged into the nettles. He heard the engine of the Mercedes revving and knew that S1 was no longer waiting for him. Tobias stepped into the water. The ditch was surprisingly deep. He had to pick his way through the nettles before coming up on the other side. His hands were burning. It didn't matter. Onwards.

He ran through the area that had once been a forest. Roots grabbed at him as if they were alive. He tripped over a tree stump and was able to catch himself, but then he stumbled over the next one and fell into the grass. He hit his knee on a stone. The other one. Dang it. Pain flashed through his entire body, taking the wind out of him. He rolled onto his back, drew in his legs, and howled loudly. That helped. He rolled back into a squat, then sat down on a stump that had been sawed off at knee height.

It was ten or twelve meters to the road, so it must be fifteen to the precipice. Was that enough? The Mercedes started to fishtail and the brakes screeched. Was that a cloud over the road? It looked utterly harmless, as if somebody had blown a colossal smoke ring into the air. The driver's door opened. S1 must have realized he'd made a mistake.

At that very moment, a powerful force came down on the hood of the Mercedes. It was as if an invisible stamp pressed it completely flat; not even the solid engine block could defend itself. The power of the nothingness pulled the sheet metal of the passenger compartment forward and downward. Tobias heard glass shattering. The open door was ripped off its hinges and fell to the side. S1 screamed, then immediately fell silent.

Tobias's heart was thudding in his chest. He felt sorry for the man. It was pretty much impossible that he'd survived that. Where the driver's seat had been, the Mercedes was now about one meter high. Tobias didn't want to think about how it would feel to be crushed, but couldn't help it.

He had to go over there. What if S1 was still alive? Performing first aid was his duty. He was still a section commissioner, your friend and aid. He didn't see the cloud anymore. Tobias stood up. Both knees hurt. He gritted his teeth. There was a thorn in his palm. He pulled it out, and there was a drop of blood. He licked it off, and found the taste oddly calming.

This was no occasion for calm. If just a stone could set off a pamyat, what effect would such a large piece of metal have? He needed to watch where he stepped. Why hadn't he gotten S1 to explain all the dangers to him? He could still remember time traps, pamyats, and of course, the nitsch burya. Whatever had flattened the Mercedes must have been a trambovka. But how would he be able to recognize the other things S1 had mentioned?

Tobias drew closer to the car. The beautiful car from the West was completely destroyed, from the front to about the B-pillar, but the trunk appeared to be intact. Tobias listened. It was quiet. Too quiet? He sniffed the air like a deer but was unable to detect any danger. He slid down into the ditch and climbed out on the other side, panting.

There wasn't a cloud in sight. He stepped over the driver's door and crouched down by the side mirror. It was pretty dark inside, but just light enough for him to make out S1. His body was horrifically contorted and jammed between metal plates and the steering wheel, as if he'd driven the Mercedes into a car crusher. The nothingness was cruel, and Miriam had to be stopped from letting it loose on the world.

S1 was dead. But he still sent him a clear message. He needed to get to the excavator before the ultimatum expired, and prevent Miriam from making an irrevocable mistake.

Tobias stood up with a groan and went to the trunk. Whoever was up there could just put an explanation of the forms that the nothingness took in it for him. Please.

The trunk opened with a squeak. It was so loud that it startled Tobias. Hopefully it hadn't attracted any danger! Meanwhile, he found that his request had not been granted. He found a spare tire, a repair set, a first-aid kit, and a shiny metallic blanket. But no instructions for the zone.

No more games. No hocus pocus. He'd seen it. The nothingness meant business.

Tobias turned around abruptly. Was that something? That was ridiculous. The nothingness didn't mean anything. It was just there. It was nothing personal, just an altered reality. He took the tools and the first-aid kit and wrapped them both in the blanket.

And now? Should he go along the road or off to the side? He estimated the distance to the excavator as two kilometers. He'd made the right decision earlier. But the nothingness hadn't engulfed the road, as he'd feared. The invisible walls of eternity had held up. He'd made the right decision for the wrong reasons. He'd been lucky—and S1, in his panic, had overlooked the harmless-looking little cloud. That was good to know. Therefore, maybe it was better to take the road. That way, he might get to Miriam before the ultimatum expired. Traveling two kilometers off the road in less than an hour would be difficult.

The road, then. He walked around the left side of the car. He'd keep as much distance as possible from the nothingness, and if he sensed even the slightest danger, he'd jump into the ditch. But that was ridiculous. He sensed danger all the time. It was lurking under every stone, in every crack and, of course, in the ditch.

Stone. Tobias bent down and picked up a handful of pebbles from the narrow area between the road and the ditch. He threw one of them ahead of him and watched its trajectory. The stone described a parabola, landed on the asphalt, and rolled on a little further. Everything was okay. Tobias followed it.

He threw another one. Parabola. Rolled on. Great. Throw. Fly. Roll. Whee, clack, click-click-click. Over and over, and then he'd check the sky. He was able to make good progress this way.

Whee, klock.

Wait! The stone didn't roll any further. Tobias took a step

back. The stone didn't budge. He threw a second one next to it. Whee, klock. The pebble hit the ground with a thunk instead of a high-pitched sound. Tobias knelt down, bent forward so that his face touched the asphalt, and observed the two stones.

They hadn't reached the ground.

Instead, they were hovering two or three millimeters above it. Tobias thought of the sneaker. It had been floating, too, but that had been... different. Tobias got back up. He had to find another route. He'd better throw another stone.

Klock. The first pebble hit the ground as if it were gaining momentum, then described an inverted parabola to make its way back to Tobias.

"Ouch!" The stone had hit his hand. Tobias threw it again, and then a second pebble. This time he carefully observed the trajectory. It was identical to the initial parabola. The pebbles repeated the same movement, only in the opposite direction. This must be a povtornik. "Povtorit" meant "repeat."

They didn't seem especially dangerous. But what would happen if he were to run into it himself? Would he then be caught in an infinite repetition?

With the help of the pebbles, Tobias found a way around the obstacle. It led him very close to the edge of the cliff. He tried to keep from looking to the right. But that wasn't easy, since he had to keep tracking the pebbles' trajectories.

Unfortunately, he ran out of pebbles before he got back to the gravel bed on the left side of the road. Should he risk it? Better not. He got the repair and first-aid kits out of the blanket and threw them, one after the other. They rattled as they flew through the air. Anyone who saw him would surely think he'd lost his mind.

Finally, the gravel bed. New stones. This time, he filled all four of his pants pockets with them. Whee, clack, click-click-click. Throw, fly, roll. Whee, clack, click-click-click. He started saying "Whee" out loud instead of just thinking it.

Whee, clack, click-click-click.

Tobias stopped, but couldn't say why. There was nothing unusual about the sound made by the pebble he'd thrown. He got on his knees and stared at it. What was different? *What are you warning me about?* Ah! The stone itself had changed. A whitish layer was growing on it. It reminded him of lichen.

But it was happening too fast for normal lichen. The whitish substance spread to the ground. The black asphalt, which a moment before had been shining with humidity, was turning gray. An ice-cold gust of wind hit Tobias. What had S1 called it? Right, "deepfreezer"! Surely that's what this was.

The thing was growing, and the danger was making its way towards him. He needed to get out of here! Tobias turned around. The Mercedes was already far away. That was the wrong direction anyway. He had to go ahead, towards Miriam!

The pebble hadn't changed color until it touched the ground. Tobias took a run-up of three steps, then leaped. At school, he'd always been good at the long jump. He flew over the danger zone. The cold gripped his feet, but his momentum carried him past it. He landed, but the frost was too close. His toes froze and he could barely keep his balance. He didn't have time for "whee" s now. Tobias ran. If the deepfreezer caught him, he'd turn into a pillar of ice. He looked over his shoulder and saw what the thing was doing to the nettles in the ditch.

Okay. Keep calm. Don't run too far. He stopped, panting. Could it be that the phenomena remained at a certain distance from each other? Maybe it was just luck. He clutched his knees and coughed. Onwards. Miriam was waiting. No. Worse. She wouldn't wait.

Whee, clack, click-click-click.

Whee, clack, click-click-click.

"Whee," clack, click-click-click.

"Whee," clack, click-click-click.

"Whee," "clack," "click-click-click."

Shh. He should be quiet when he threw the pebbles.

Whee, clack, click-click-click.

"Sʜʜʜ!"

Tobias winced. Focus. Whee, clack, click-click-click. Everything was great. He could keep going. He had to get to the excavator. That was the only thing that mattered.

"Shhh!"

He looked in the direction the sound was coming from and began to feel dizzy. It was Miriam! She was walking down the side of the road next to him, smiling. Tobias stopped. He couldn't help but look at her. She was wearing her sari and high heels. It didn't seem like entirely appropriate attire for the zone.

"It's a qipao, I already told you!" The apparition spoke!

"Qipao, right," he said.

This couldn't be Miriam. She'd tied herself to the excavator. Or had S1 been lying?

"Forget S1. Now come here and start by giving me a hug."

"What about Ralf? We've got to save your husband!"

Miriam wrinkled her nose. She looked so real! Why shouldn't he hug her? What could possibly happen?

"Yes, exactly. Why won't you hug me? Don't you like me anymore?"

Because Miriam can't read minds. You moron, that's not her. Stay away from her!

"Because Miriam can't read minds," she repeated, smirking. "And what if she can?"

This was not Miriam. It was something created by the nothingness. Inwardly, Tobias went over the phenomena that S1 had told him about. Revenants. That could fit. But where did the danger lurk here?

"There's no danger lurking here. Come over here and give me a hug already."

It was probably some kind of mirage born of his memory. What harm could it do for him to embrace such an apparition— except that he'd make a fool of himself?

"Yes, Tobias. Get over here already! Or should I take my clothes off first?" Miriam reached back and unzipped her dress.

"Not out here on the street!" he shouted, his ears growing hot.

"You are and always have been such a square, Tobias. You don't have the guts. You wanna bet?"

This was too much. She was trying to provoke him, but Miriam would never go that far... He'd been listening to this apparition too long. Damned hormones! The real Miriam was waiting up on the excavator.

Pitter-patter. The fake Miriam was running toward him! He fled. Hopefully the apparition wasn't driving him into another trap! Or was that her intention? He looked for little clouds. Nothing. Miriam was running slowly, probably because of the tight qipao and the high heels. He was able to keep his distance and still throw a pebble every so often.

Then she tried a different tack. She wasn't moving her feet at all and was now gliding towards him. It looked spooky. A shiver ran down his spine. She was too fast for him, and escape was futile. He let her get close. She touched his forearm. Her hands were ice-cold. Miriam spread out her arms, but at the last second Tobias pushed the blanket and its contents towards her, and leapt backwards.

Miriam went pale. Her entire body changed. She became colorless and turned to concrete. Only the blanket still shone silver. Tobias thought of the statue he'd seen from the car. Would he be standing there now, too, if he'd given in to his impulse? He stopped, shaking. What was the nothingness doing to them? What was the physical basis for it? He breathed in deeply, approached the new statue, and took the blanket.

"I still need that," he said.

Miriam's statue didn't answer.

Whee, clack, click-click-click.

Whee, clack, click-click-click.

The excavator was getting bigger. He had maybe 500 meters to go. He'd made it two-thirds of the way already. It was too bad he didn't have the binoculars. He'd definitely have been able to see Miriam by now. He waved just in case she was watching him.

As loud as he could, he shouted "Miriam!"

No answer. Just a whining sound, like a swarm of mosquitoes. From behind him on the left. Something was coming toward him. It was grayish-green and round. And fast. Should he run away? That was a dumb idea. Tobias narrowed his eyes. *Focus. Remember the sneaker.* Meanwhile, the thing kept accelerating. It was as big as his head. Which it appeared to be aiming for.

Just stay where you are. Nice and easy. Easy. Easy. Now!

Tobias dropped to the ground. The pamyat hissed above him, right through where his head had been a moment before.

Be careful! No time to stand up. On your knees. The thing slowed down, flew in an elegant curve, and came back. But slower. *Wait. Easy. Let it come.* Ten meters, five, three.

Tobias tilted to the side. The pamyat didn't hit anything. Tobias saw that it was a steel helmet. How did a goddamned steel helmet end up in an open cast mine? Soldiers had been on duty there in the wintertime, obviously.

Watch out! It was coming back. Still going damned fast. Tobias was on his knees, as if waiting to be executed. Could the pamyat anticipate how he'd react? Of course not. The thing couldn't think. It just wanted to get on his head, where it belonged. *Be careful. Now!* He tilted to the side.

Okay, over here. The pamyat was so slow to react that it went three meters before turning. Tobias waited for it, standing. He unfolded the silver blanket and the two cases tumbled out. The helmet aimed for his head but wasn't successful.

"Come on!" he shouted.

Tobias was a torero and the blanket was his red cape. The helmet was the bull. A deadly weapon. Still more than fast enough. The pamyat came at him. Tobias jumped and held the blanket where his head had been.

The helmet hit it and disappeared into the fabric. Tobias clutched the blanket. *Gotcha!* The helmet leapt, attempting to free itself from the trap. No way. *You're mine now.* He held the blanket out in front of his belly.

Where had that damn thing come from? It was his own fault. It must have heard him. Tobias knelt down and carefully unwrapped the quivering helmet. The strap was missing, but the padding still adhered to the inner surface. What was he going to do with it? Should he throw the helmet into the nothingness? He'd hardly get rid of it that way. The thing had only one goal—his head. As soon as he moved away from it, the battle would start all over again. Then it occurred to him to use his opponent's momentum.

Of course. The helmet wanted to go up. Very slowly, he gave in. He lifted his hands, and the helmet with them. Nice and slow. Chest height. Head. The helmet turned. Now. He let go of it. The helmet slipped over his head. It fit snugly but wasn't uncomfortable. Especially since he didn't need to fasten the strap. The helmet would stay on no matter what the weather.

Onwards. The excavator! Tobias stood up. That was when the spasms started. Shit. So the phenomena didn't have any respect for each other after all. This must be a nitsch burya.

Tobias fell onto the asphalt, and the helmet protected his head. What pain! He bit down on his fist to keep from screaming. Who knew what might come flying at him? His bladder emptied. He rolled back and forth on the ground. Almost over. Almost over.

But it didn't stop. Had he already gotten too used to it? Was it something else? Tobias sweated, slobbered, peed, wept, and ejaculated, and snot came out of his nose and blood came out of the wound made by the thorn. All his bodily fluids were flowing. The thing was squeezing him like a lemon. No. It was using his own muscles to squeeze him. Was this the presswurst that S1 had mentioned? It just wouldn't stop! He pulled in his legs, stretched them, then crawled away, practically blind because of all the tears in his eyes.

Until suddenly his hands were reaching out towards the nothingness.

He was lying on the cliff. First his tears dried up, then the snot and saliva. He looked directly into the blackness. The presswurst very slowly released him. His body calmed down and started to obey him again. Tobias just lay there to gather his strength.

But he didn't. He was completely empty. Tobias turned onto his back and stared at the clouds. There was no point to all of this. He wasn't going to save the world. It didn't want to be saved, and there wasn't anything he could do about that. He just wanted to go home. To his office. Check the house registers and carry out Kybernetz checks.

How boring was that?

Tobias stood up. It was arduous, like life itself. His knees hurt. He looked around. The street had turned into a gigantic parking lot. Asphalt all the way to the horizon. On the left. To the right was the lake, the eternal, the nothingness. It called to him.

The horrible emptiness. That must be it. It reached into his innermost being. This wasn't a phenomenon of the nothingness. He was very familiar with it. Most of the time he was able to contain it. But the nothingness had magnified it to a grotesque extreme. Oddly enough, that helped him accept it. The emptiness was so all-encompassing that there was no room left for him to hope at all. He just had to carry on. That helped. Hope was deceitful. He couldn't see the excavator anymore. But to the right, there was still the nothingness. He used that to orient himself.

He ran and ran and ran. Hours might have gone by, but his watch had stopped. On the horizon there appeared a wall of fog, clearly demarcated by the thick clouds.

Onwards, onwards, onwards. His feet moved automatically. It seemed as if he hadn't made any progress. But he was now right up against the wall of fog.

Tobias entered the fog. It was dry—not like autumn fog, but more like what comes out of a fog machine—and it had a completely neutral small. Tobias wandered through it. He tried to affect the gray soup by moving his hands, but it was as if he were from another world.

Then the fog lifted. Tobias saw the world as if in a wide shot. Here was the cleared forest, there the lake, further back the excavator, halfway over the nothingness. The camera that was stuck in his head moved quickly toward the asphalt. He felt lightheaded and everything went black.

Eventually, he got himself up on his knees. He crawled back to the middle of the road, keeping his distance from the damp trail he had left behind, like a snail's trail of slime. The first aid kit was lying on the side of the road near the blanket. He briefly lifted his helmet to let the sweat run off, and cleaned himself with some gauze bandages.

The wind brought a stench with it. No, that was him. Tobias wanted nothing more in the world than to take a cold shower, but that would have to wait. He'd survived the presswurst and the horrible emptiness, and that was what mattered. Miriam. He was actually able to make it to his feet. There were still enough pebbles in his trouser pockets.

Whee, clack, click-click-click.

"Who's there?"

It was Miriam's voice. She must have heard his steps on the ladder. Just one more rung and he would reach the massive chassis. He couldn't see anything of Miriam herself.

"Stay the hell away! You've got fifteen minutes left! Then I want to see my husband here!"

She shouldn't shout so loudly. There were probably still pamyats lying around within earshot, just waiting for a target.

"Quietly, Miriam!"

"Tobias? Is that you? What are you doing here?"

"I'd like to talk to you. But please don't yell like that. Don't forget the pamyat!"

He climbed a bit higher. His knees hurt. He looked around, which was a mistake. The ground was eight meters below. Shit, that was high!

"What's a pamyat? Do you know about my ultimatum?"

Of course, she hadn't gotten an explanatory tour.

At first, Tobias played dumb. "What ultimatum?"

"I want to see my husband. I know they've got him. Tell them to hand him over—or the excavator will go crashing down into the pit."

"Can you come a little closer? I'm afraid of heights."

"No. If I move away from here, they'll shoot me. And you never told me you were afraid of heights."

Tobias wished he was lying, but he really was afraid. "Okay, I'm coming."

He balanced across a double girder that had a handrail and was connected in the middle with crossbars. Still, he was trembling and his backside hurt. That was the place in his body where his fear of heights was located. At the end of the girder was a cab with glass windows that had been broken out. It had an actual, solid floor. He sat down on it. That seemed fine.

"What do you want from me?"

He still couldn't see Miriam, but her voice sounded tired.

"I want to help you."

The wind was coming from Miriam's direction, so he had to shout louder than he wanted to.

"You can't help me, Tobias. You're just putting yourself in danger. When the ultimatum expires, I'm going to deliver on my promise."

She sounded very determined, and he had no choice but to believe her. What he really wanted to do was embrace her and bring her home with him, just like her revenant had suggested.

"That will to kill us all."

"Get out of here, Tobias. Please. I like you. In another life, we could have been a couple. You still have a chance at happiness. Go away. It's too late for me."

It was painful for him to hear those words. Miriam really did like him, but it sounded as if she'd already said goodbye.

"When the excavator falls, I'll die too, no matter where I am. You'll destroy the entire world with it."

"Is that what they told you?"

"Yes, now I know everything." A tear ran down his cheek.

"Tobias, they're manipulating you. They lied to you."

She didn't believe him. If only they'd entered the zone together!

"Then why would they ask me to bring you back down? They could just shoot you."

"It's entirely possible that something will change when the excavator falls into that hole there. I actually hope it does. It will take money and effort they'd rather save. And they don't want to get their hands dirty. So they're letting you do the dirty work."

"And how do you know that?"

"I know them. I know these people." Miriam spat out the words with utter contempt. "They tell us all about the triumph of the working class, but secretly it's just about frivolous luxuries for them and their families and a dacha by the lake."

Tobias needed to go to Miriam. She'd lost something valuable. She didn't realize it yet, but she must have sensed it. When the ultimatum expired, she would know. How would she react? By now, he knew her a little. It was entirely possible that she'd throw herself into the depths in despair and drag the whole earth into the abyss with her.

"I'm coming!" he shouted.

The direct approach out onto the boom was blocked with a barrier of barbed wire. Tobias looked up. A mast extended upward at a 60-degree angle. It consisted of four girders connected by a network of struts. A rock-climber would have thought nothing of it.

But he wasn't a rock-climber. Even the path he had to take to the foot of the mast, which was connected to the mobile base by a meter-long joint, was stressful because Tobias had to leave solid ground. It sloped downwards in all directions, though it was impossible to fall through the gridwork of struts. *I'm absolutely certain. The holes are far too narrow. I just need to stay on the struts.* And what if I suddenly tip to the side? This damn fear of heights! *You won't tip over. Unless you let yourself fall.* Then I'll let myself fall. *No, you won't. You managed it in the forest above the clouds!*

Phew. Tobias had reached the mast. He didn't dare look to the south, the direction he'd come from. If it had been possible to see the crushed Mercedes, he would have some evidence for Miriam. But it was too far away.

Now began the ascent. It was actually pretty simple. He held on with his hands and climbed up on all fours. Always following the metal and always looking up. All right! He'd made it the first meter. Left hand to the front, pull the right foot forward, steady. Right hand, left foot, steady. Left hand. How high up was he now? Two meters? No! He clung to the mast and closed his eyes. His breathing was rapid.

"Tobias, what are you doing?" Miriam's voice asked him above the roaring in his ears.

"I want to tell you myself."

"What do you want to tell me?"

"Hold on."

He had to keep going. Miriam needed to hear it from him. Maybe he could keep her from doing something really foolish. Right foot. Steady. Right hand. The metal was cold. If only he had a pair of gloves! Left foot. Steady. Knee pain. Ignore. Left hand. He was making progress. Right foot. Steady. Right hand.

Tobias didn't feel the splinter until it had already torn his skin. Dang it. Left foot. Left hand. Right foot. Right hand. The fresh wound was painful. But that was good, because it distracted him. From the knee pain. From the altitude. From his concern for Miriam. Left foot. Left hand. He transformed into a robot that moved to a beat of its own making. The ground didn't matter anymore. He had to make it to his goal. Right hand. Left foot.

Thunk. His head bumped against a projection. All of a sudden, he was back to being the little boy on the ridge of the roof who was so scared of heights that he peed himself. His father laughed. Tobias clung to the mast and closed his eyes.

"My ultimatum expired a minute ago!" Miriam exclaimed. "Where's Ralf?"

Tobias couldn't answer. He carefully looked over his arm down at the ground. Nothing had changed. The Mercedes was a black spot close to the horizon. Somewhere, hidden from view, there must be snipers awaiting instructions. It must be clear to Miriam that her husband hadn't come. Why hadn't the officer in charge said anything? Couldn't he stall her a bit longer? Hopefully they weren't waiting for S1!

"I'll be there with you in a second!" Tobias called out. "Please wait."

He'd climbed the mast. From the place he'd reached, several steel cables led to the end of the boom. He still couldn't see Miriam, but she must be there. He fumbled with his belt buckle and pulled the leather belt out of his pants. It looked so easy, and he'd seen it many times in movies. The hero would loop something sturdy around the rope as a kind of hook, hold on to it, and glide safely through the air to his destination.

But he'd have to stand up in order to do that. The hawser started above the projection he'd bumped into. He would have to feel his way around the steel sheet and then, hanging from his belt, jump into the void.

Better not. He'd just go back. Miriam wouldn't go to extremes.

Yes, she would. And bring humanity to the brink of extinction. There really were a lot of assholes in the world. Tyrants, thieves, murderers, egoists, people like Schumacher. But there were also the cosmonaut's children, who might have to grow up without a mother. There were Hardy and Matze. There was Martina Frommann, who because of Tobias had to wait for her boyfriend. They didn't deserve to die.

He stood up and narrowed his eyes so that all he saw was the rope. All of a sudden, everything was very simple. He climbed around the projection. There was the steel rope. It was probably eight millimeters thick and when he pulled on it, the vibration was minimal. He took the belt, which the holster with the gun was still hanging from, and put it over the hawser. He tested it out by dangling from it. The rope didn't budge. The entire weight of the boom was hanging from its end, so his 80 kilos made no difference.

And what if was all a lie? What if they were really just using him to get rid of Miriam? The end justifies the means. Was that possible? Would they bring him in specially from outside, tell him all those secrets, just to—well, what actually? Tobias had seen the effects. But those could be tricks, too, of course. The fact that S1 had died along the way could have been an accident. Even the nitsch burya and the presswurst he'd felt in his own body could have been caused by the use of some secret weapon. But all the tricks were only worth all that trouble if there was really something at stake.

Tobias tugged on the belt again. The leather looked sturdy. He closed his eyes and jumped.

Shit, that was fast! It seemed like the belt hardly slowed him down at all. Wind was rushing towards him. His injured hand and the muscles in his arms ached. Forty kilos on each side—he wouldn't be able to hold on for long.

But he didn't have to, since he was hurtling downwards so fast. He needed to open his eyes before he crashed. Now! The boom was right in front of him. Crap, crap, crap. His feet hit the metal. He ran. The belt on the rope stabilized him. Then his left foot got caught in a cavity. Tobias was unable to hold on any longer and fell.

Ow, right on the nose. He rubbed his face with his right hand. There was blood on his fingers. A few steps in front of him, the belt slipped off the rope. Tobias crawled over quickly and caught it just in time.

"Quite the Tarzan," Miriam said.

Tobias turned around and drew himself up. Miriam was behind him, perhaps twenty meters away. She wasn't wearing a qipao but a rain jacket covered in mud, ripped pants, and hiking boots. There was a big Band-Aid on her forehead. But she still looked gorgeous—and more determined than ever.

Tobias had slid down the hawser to the very end of the boom, where it was just one and a half meters wide. On either side, it went straight down into the nothingness. Tobias closed his eyes.

"Just come towards me slowly," Miriam said. "It's only ten feet, and then the boom gets wider."

He made it three meters. That was enough for now. He wasn't an action hero, just a simple section commissioner.

"So, what is it that you want to tell me?" asked Miriam.

I love you. But this wasn't the right time. It would never be the right time. "It's about your ultimatum."

"Don't get mixed up in this. I don't want anything to happen to you."

"It's too late for that. You need to hear it from me. Your husband is dead. It was an... accident during questioning. That's what they said. Diabetic shock."

Miriam howled. "Everybody knows Ralf is diabetic. That was murder!"

Dr. Prassnitz had been an important scientist. Tobias didn't believe he'd been deprived of insulin deliberately. But he wasn't going to disagree with Miriam now.

"Maybe. I still want to ask that you not do anything reckless right now."

He tried to speak as steadily as possible, but he couldn't keep the worry out of his voice.

"I've given this a lot of thought."

Miriam pointed to the rope she'd tied around her waist.

"If you do that, you're condemning the whole world for something that just a few individuals are responsible for. Is that fair?"

Tobias kept thinking about Jonathan and Marie. He didn't want them to die. He would have rather died himself.

"Ralf is gone. Is that fair?"

Miriam slowly approached him, the rope trailing behind her. Tobias crawled in her direction.

"Stay right there, Tobias!"

Miriam had propped herself with both arms on a crossbar. She looked ready for battle.

"Miriam, your husband is dead. You can't save him anymore. But if you throw yourself off the boom, you'll be condemning the whole world to die."

"I don't care."

"Do you want me to die, Miriam? And what about the nice innkeeper? Your uncle, and..."

"I don't want you to die, Tobias, I really don't. I like you."

Her voice had become warm, almost affectionate. Tobias had to wipe the tears from his eyes.

"That's why you have to get out of my way," said Miriam. "My plan can't be changed. If Ralf doesn't come, I'm throwing myself into the abyss."

She didn't believe him. Had she not seen the strange

phenomena? Presumably she thought they were just as fake as the obstacles on the way to the zone. What should he do? How could he convince her? Miriam seemed firmly resolved not to go on living without her husband, even if that meant sentencing the rest of humanity to death.

Tobias crawled ahead, and Miriam backed away. He moved a bit more. She maintained the distance. In this way, without seeming to have consciously noticed it, she reached a platform about four by four meters, that couldn't be seen from a distance. Tobias crawled forward a little more until Miriam was standing in the center of the platform.

This was his chance, probably the only one he'd get. He reached for the Makarov, turning to shield the gun from Miriam. The grip pressed on his wound, but the pain didn't bother him. If he was unable to convince Miriam, he'd have to shoot her. From where she was now, in the center of the platform, she could no longer just fling herself into the abyss. And that meant that the rope around her waist wouldn't pull the lever. But he would have to kill her with the first shot, or at least completely immobilize her. It was five, six meters at the most. In basic training, they'd shot at targets 25 meters away while standing and 50 meters while kneeling. But he wouldn't have time to take aim. After Miriam noticed the gun, she'd have a moment of shock, and then run and perhaps fall—or jump.

On the left, where the heart was. From where he was looking, that was to the right. Don't think about it too long, or she'll notice that it's too far to the abyss. This was the way it had to be. Tobias could see before him the Miriam from way back when, unattainable and so fascinating. If only he had... the letters! They could have been a couple. She'd said so herself! He would have brushed her hair from her forehead. Kissed her on her warm lips.

But he had two amazing kids, just like the cosmonaut. Did they deserve to die just because Miriam had been wronged? Was that fair? He'd definitely let himself be exploited, but he would shoot because of his children, not because of S1's orders.

Tobias held his breath. One, two, three. Take aim quickly, squeeze the trigger. There was a bang. He brought the gun down as it recoiled. The sound of metal clanging against metal. Miriam looked at him, wide-eyed. So this was the face of her terror. Tobias was completely calm. Strange. He'd shot at a human being. At his beloved.

Miriam didn't move. The moment of shock wasn't over yet. Tobias allowed himself to breathe again.

He'd missed. It had probably hit a steel beam. Miriam felt her way back to the edge of the platform. She surely thought he'd shoot again. But he couldn't. That one shot had been hard enough. Maybe his hand had known. He had a marksmanship ribbon. Back then, at 25 yards he used to hit every target.

Tobias threw the gun aside.

"You gave me quite a scare," Miriam whispered. "You just wanted to scare me, right?"

"No, I was going to shoot you," he said flatly. "There in the center of the platform, you wouldn't have been able to go through with your threat."

"Oh, Tobias. So this is what it's come to."

"I can't let you punish the entire world for your misfortune."

"But it's the whole world that just watched as Ralf got killed."

If Miriam knew that Jonas was also a traitor... or how they'd treated the cosmonaut... fundamentally, Tobias had to agree with her. But there were innocent people. He wasn't one of them, but they did exist, scattered throughout all the countries on Earth. Sometimes they made up the majority, sometimes the minority.

"You need to leave now, Tobias. I'm going through with my threat, and there's no way around it. But you don't have to die here with me."

Tobias nodded. "Good, then I'm going to move forward now."

"You can climb along the boom up to the barbed wire and then jump. You might break something, but you'll survive. Just don't get too close to me."

"Okay."

He crawled forward. Then he felt it again, the rigidity in his muscles. It was the nitsch burya. Shit. His limbs started to twitch uncontrollably and bolts of lightning flashed through his brain. But he was still alert enough to see his foot digging into an opening. Then all of a sudden his knee tensed up forcefully, spinning his body over the boom. There was the edge. He could see the nothingness below him. He was about to fall.

Someone grasped his foot and pulled him back to the middle of the platform. Miriam! His muscles relaxed. His bladder emptied. He'd never been so free and light as he was now. Miriam was standing next to him. She'd saved his life. Tobias gathered what strength he could find. He wouldn't get another chance. At lightning speed, he fished for Miriam's legs with his feet, got hold of them, and pulled her down. Then he threw himself over her. It was 80 kilos versus 60. Then he used the lock hold he'd learned as she kicked the air.

He had her. Miriam groaned. She was still struggling, but he tied her arms and legs so she couldn't move. He could have tied up a whole battalion with the long rope she had around her waist.

"Don't do this to me," she pleaded.

"I'm sorry, but I can't let you sacrifice the planet."

"Then just sacrifice me. Roll me over the edge. I don't have a place here anymore. They'll congratulate you."

Tobias looked into the abyss. It would only be fair to grant her wish. But it would be murder. "I can't do it, Miriam. Really."

"Just push me to the edge." She moved so that her body rocked back and forth.

"See? I'll do the rest on my own. You just have to give me the opportunity."

Tobias shook his head. "I can't shoot you, and I can't let you die either."

"Then you're condemning me to something that for me is worse than death. I have to live with the knowledge that they killed my husband."

"Yes. I'm sorry."

Tobias was tired. He had no feelings left. This time it wasn't the horrible emptiness.

He heard heavy footsteps on metal. The officer in charge was coming. He had three uniformed men in tow.

"Thank you, Comrade Wagner. We knew you'd take care of it."

October 16, 2029, Dresden

"You do realize that you have me to thank for being back here?" asked Schumacher.

How he hated that furtive look! Tobias scratched his nose. The injury he'd gotten on the bucket wheel excavator had scabbed over, and it itched. "Yes, I'm aware of that."

"They wanted to keep you there. Because of the secrecy. What a laugh! As if secrets weren't safe with us. Good thing we were able to track your hand phone. Then they couldn't just make you disappear."

Ah. Here it came. The Stasi was hoping to hear straight from his lips what was really going on in the zone. That was why they'd pulled out all the stops to get him out of there.

"True enough," Tobias said.

"And what did you see there, Comrade? I'm only asking this for internal analyses. Obviously, we already have the most important information."

"Obviously. Well, at the oil refinery, there's been a big environmental mess. The groundwater is contaminated, and will be for centuries. There was a risk that it could spread throughout central Europe, so they set up sheet pile walls hundreds of meters deep to contain the deadly concoction. None of our neighbors can know this, of course."

"Wow, Comrade. Yes, that is what our officers in special operations have learned as well. Thank you for your confidence in us. Your promotion to first lieutenant has practically come through."

"Thank you, Comrade Schumacher. There's one more request I'd like to make."

"Yes?"

"I'd like to be transferred to Lusatia. To Neustadt, for example. If the request reached your desk, would you approve it?"

"Reluctantly, Comrade, because then we wouldn't see each other as often. But in all honesty, you've earned it. It shouldn't be a problem to find someone for your precinct in Dresden."

TOBIAS LEFT THE BAUTZENER STRAßE COMPOUND. AS HE WAS waiting for the 11, he imagined Matze riding up on his Jawa to pick him up. He'd ride to Neustadt in a sidecar, not a Passat. He wouldn't miss Dresden. Oddly enough, he'd never made any friends there. Was it because it was a big city, or because of his job?

He'd start over in Neustadt. The name—"new city"—was perfect. He'd play chess and drink beer with Matze and Hardy in the evenings. He was a little worried about Hardy. The old man had hinted at a health problem, and Matze was probably too close to him to talk sense into him. Nowadays medicine could perform miracles that seemed inconceivable just ten years ago.

Yeah, Hardy would certainly love it if Tobias tried to tell him what to do. But he could respect that. Tobias smiled. He'd wander through the woods again like he had as a child, searching for mushrooms, lying in the moss under pine trees, and catching sunbeams. And all the while, he could also keep his eye on the zone. Maybe somebody would be needed to save the world again. Nobody knew about it, but he didn't care.

November 5, 2029, Mumbai

MANDY NEUMANN FELT LOST ON THE ENORMOUS CONCOURSE. There were announcements constantly being made in both English and Hindi. Planes landing, planes taking off. Suitcases had to be claimed and not left unattended under any circumstances.

"Come along," Rakesh said in his soft English.

Her rescuer had driven her to the airport. Ever since they'd landed in the Indian Ocean, he'd been organizing her life for her. He did this selflessly, without ever asking for any kind of thanks. At first, she'd found it weird and unfamiliar. But she'd come to accept it. She no longer wondered if he might be in love with her. Rakesh didn't speak of it. He simply helped her, and that was what she needed right now. At least until she'd seen her children again, she wouldn't be in a position to think about whether she felt anything for this man.

Deep gratitude, definitely. For the time being, that would have to suffice.

They made their way through the concourse. Rakesh must have found the arrival gate. The flight, IF 752, was arriving from Berlin-Schönefeld. It even seemed to be on time. Rakesh led Mandy to a double door that didn't look like a place where regular travelers would be coming out.

"Are you sure this is it?" asked Mandy.

He put his hand gently on her shoulder. She liked it. Her father used to do that. She found it very soothing. Rakesh sign next to the door. It had the letters "VIP"

d of mine at immigration will bring them out here."

had a lot of friends. Even the security guard at the entra. had greeted him enthusiastically. It probably didn't hurt that he'd been on Indian state television. But nobody knew who Mandy was, and she was just fine with that. Her unusual entry into the Asian country had been completely under the media's radar. There had been no cameras pointed at the Gaganyaan capsule as it splashed down in the ocean. The patrol boat that brought her to shore only had soldiers aboard. After that, she suddenly became a part of the crowd. Only two witnesses knew she'd ever been aboard Rakesh's spaceship.

It was almost time. How she yearned for them! Rakesh looked at his hand phone, then nodded at her. Mandy was bouncing on her toes. Even though the entire concourse was cooled to what felt like ten degrees, she was sweating. The door opened, and a Sikh in uniform stepped through. He held the door open and gave the elderly woman from Germany another bow. That was her mother, who was supposedly vacationing with the two girls. And there they were. Sabine and Susanne were running towards Mandy. They both wanted to get to her first. It was a good thing she had two arms. She embraced her daughters, lifted them up, and turned.

"Mutti, Mutti," the two exclaimed, shouting over each other. "Who are these people here? Where were you for so long? Why does that man have a turban? Where are we going to live? Why are you crying, Mutti? Do you have to leave again?"

They couldn't stop asking questions. Mandy was crying and laughing at the same time. Her nose was running and her makeup was smudged, but she didn't care. She wouldn't ever let go of them again.

Author's Note

Dear Readers,

I'm so pleased that you've followed Mandy and Tobias this far. The research I did for this book took me back to my childhood again and again. The country I grew up in doesn't exist anymore. I'm not at all sad about that, and there are two ways of interpreting this—both correct. If it hadn't been for the events of 1989, I wouldn't be a writer today. Instead, I would probably be working as a physicist in a nuclear power plant, wouldn't be able to travel, and would have to watch everything going downhill.

Nevertheless, I have memories of a happy childhood. A native of Brandenburg, I played in the woods of the Fläming region and built sand castles on my grandparents' farm—which was in Lusatia, by the way. The feeling of living in a huge prison didn't come until later, and before it could really kick in, suddenly it was all over.

During my school days, it was duplicity that made an impression above all. People spoke differently at school and in front of the teachers than they did with friends or family. This was normal. We knew it, the teachers knew it, and those watching all of us knew it, too. It was a small world where the best way to get by was to withdraw into one's private life.

The GDR in this book is, of course, not the same country that once existed in East Germany. As is always the case in literature, it is a construct that also serves to tell this story. My genre is hard, realistic science fiction, and it's highly important for everything described to be theoretically possible. Would a real GDR, together with help from the West, actually have been able to cover up an accident like the one described in the book?

I don't know the answer to that question. After all, in the end it's only fiction. I would enjoy hearing your opinion about this story. Perhaps you'd even like to express it in the form of a review. In the appendix you'll find "The Biography of Nothingness," which sheds light on the fundamental physics of the plot. You can get this biography as an illustrated PDF when you register at hard-sf.com/subscribe.

I look forward to seeing you again.

Kind regards,

Brandon Q. Morris

facebook.com/BrandonQMorris

amazon.com/author/brandonqmorris

bookbub.com/authors/brandon-q-morris

goodreads.com/brandonqmorris

youtube.com/HardSF

instagram.com/brandonqmorris

Also by Brandon Q. Morris

The Beacon

Peter Kraemer, a physics teacher with a passion for astronomy, makes a discovery that he himself can hardly believe: Stars disappear from one day to the next, with nothing left of them. The researchers he contacts provide reassuring and logical explanations for every single case. But when Peter determines that the mysterious process is approaching our home system, he becomes more and more anxious. He alone perceives the looming catastrophe. When he believes he has found a way to avert the impending disaster, he choses to pull out all the stops, even if it costs his job, his marriage, his friends, and his life.

3.99 $ – hard-sf.com/links/1731041

Helium 3: Fight for the Future

The star system is perfect. The arrivals have undertaken a long and dangerous journey—an expedition of no return—seeking helium-3, essential for the survival of their species. The discovery of this extraordinary solar system with its four gas giants offers a unique opportunity to harvest the rare isotope.

Then comes a disturbing discovery: They are not alone! Another fleet is here, and just as dependent on helium-3. And the two species are so fundamentally different that communication and compromise appear hopeless. All that remains is a fight to the death—and for the future…

The Triton Disaster

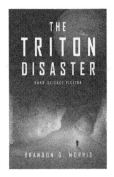

Nick Abrahams holds the official world record for the number of space launches, but he's bored stiff with his job hosting space tours. Only when his wife leaves him does he try to change his life.

He accepts a tempting offer from a Russian billionaire. In exchange for making a simple repair on Neptune's moon Triton, he will return to Earth a multi-millionaire, enabling him to achieve his 'impossible dream' of buying his own California vineyard.

The fact that Nick must travel alone during the four-year roundtrip doesn't bother him at all, as he doesn't particularly like people anyway. Once en route he learns his new boss left out some critical details in his job description—details that could cost him his life, and humankind its existence…

The Dark Spring

When a space probe returns from the dead, you better not expect good news.

In 2014, the ESA spacecraft *Rosetta* lands a small probe named *Philae* on 67P, a Jupiter-family comet. The lander goes radio silent two years later. Suddenly, in 2026, scientists receive new transmissions from the comet. Motivated by findings that are initially sensational but soon turn frightening, NASA dispatches a crewed spacecraft to the comet. But as the ship approaches the mysterious celestial body, the connection to the astronauts soon breaks. Now it seems nothing can be done anymore to stop the looming dark danger that threatens Earth…

The Death of the Universe

For many billions of years, humans spread throughout the entire Milky Way. They are able to live all their dreams, but to their great disappointment, no other intelligent species has ever been encountered. Now, humanity itself is on the brink of extinction.

They have only one hope: The 'Rescue Project' was designed to feed the black hole in the center of the galaxy until it becomes a quasar, delivering much-needed energy to humankind during its last breaths. But then something happens that no one ever expected —and humanity is forced to look at itself and its existence in an entirely new way.

3.99 $ – hard-sf.com/links/835415

The Enceladus Mission (Ice Moon 1)

In the year 2031, a robot probe detects traces of biological activity on Enceladus, one of Saturn's moons. This sensational discovery shows that there is indeed evidence of extraterrestrial life. Fifteen years later, a hurriedly built spacecraft sets out on the long journey to the ringed planet and its moon.

The international crew is not just facing a difficult twenty-seven months: if the spacecraft manages to make it to Enceladus without incident it must use a drillship to penetrate the kilometer-thick sheet of ice that entombs the moon. If life does indeed exist on Enceladus, it could only be at the bottom of the salty, ice covered ocean, which formed billions of years ago.

However, shortly after takeoff disaster strikes the mission, and the chances of the crew making it to Enceladus, let alone back home, look grim.

2.99 $ – hard-sf.com/links/526999

Ice Moon - The Boxset

All four bestselling books of the Ice Moon series are now offered as a set, available only in e-book format.

The Enceladus Mission: Is there really life on Saturn's moon Enceladus? *ILSE*, the International Life Search Expedition, makes its way to the icy world where an underground ocean is suspected to be home to primitive life forms.

The Titan Probe: An old robotic NASA probe mysteriously awakens on the methane moon of Titan. The *ILSE* crew tries to solve the riddle—and discovers a dangerous secret.

The Io Encounter: Finally bound for Earth, *ILSE* makes it as far as Jupiter when the crew receives a startling message. The volcanic moon Io may harbor a looming threat that could wipe out Earth as we know it.

Return to Enceladus: The crew gets an offer to go back to Enceladus. Their mission—to recover the body of Dr. Marchenko, left for dead on the original expedition. Not everyone is working toward the same goal.

9.99 $ – hard-sf.com/links/780838

Proxima Rising

Late in the 21st century, Earth receives what looks like an urgent plea for help from planet Proxima Centauri b in the closest star system to the Sun. Astrophysicists suspect a massive solar flare is about to destroy this heretofore-unknown civilization. Earth's space programs are unequipped to help, but an unscrupulous Russian billionaire launches a secret and highly-specialized spaceship to Proxima b, over four light-years away. The unusual crew faces a Herculean task—should they survive the journey. No one knows what to expect from this alien planet.

3.99 $ – hard-sf.com/links/610690

The Hole

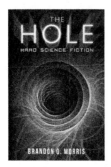

A mysterious object threatens to destroy our solar system. The survival of humankind is at risk, but nobody takes the warning of young astrophysicist Maribel Pedreira seriously. At the same time, an exiled crew of outcasts mines for rare minerals on a lone asteroid.

When other scientists finally acknowledge Pedreira's alarming discovery, it becomes clear that these outcasts are the only ones who may be able to save our world, knowing that *The Hole* hurtles inexorably toward the sun.

3.99 $ – hard-sf.com/links/527017

Mars Nation 1

NASA finally made it. The very first human has just set foot on the surface of our neighbor planet. This is the start of a long research expedition that sent four scientists into space.

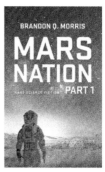

But the four astronauts of the NASA crew are not the only ones with this destination. The privately financed 'Mars for Everyone' initiative has also targeted the Red Planet. Twenty men and women have been selected to live there and establish the first extraterrestrial settlement.

Challenges arise even before they reach Mars orbit. The MfE spaceship Santa Maria is damaged along the way. Only the four NASA astronauts can intervene and try to save their lives.

No one anticipates the impending catastrophe that threatens their very existence—not to speak of the daily hurdles that an extended stay on an alien planet sets before them. On Mars, a struggle begins for limited resources, human cooperation, and just plain survival.

3.99 $ – hard-sf.com/links/762824

Impact: Titan

How to avoid killing Earth if you don't even know who sent the killer

250 years ago, humanity nearly destroyed itself in the Great War. Shortly before, a spaceship full of researchers and astronauts had found a new home on Saturn's moon, Titan, and survived by having their descendants genetically adapted to the hostile environment.

The Titanians, as they call themselves, are proud of their cooperative and peaceful society, while unbeknownst to them, humanity is slowly recovering back on Earth. When a 20-mile-wide chunk of rock escapes the asteroid belt and appears to be on a collision course with Earth, the Titanians fear it must look as if they launched the deadly bombardment. Can they prevent the impact and thus avoid an otherwise inevitable war with the Earthlings?

3.99 $ – hard-sf.com/links/1433312

The biography of nothingness

TOBIAS SAW IT: THE NOTHINGNESS. IS IT EVEN POSSIBLE TO perceive something that isn't there? This is a fascinating question for which there is currently no definitive answer. First and foremost, nothingness is an abstract, a philosophical concept. It describes the opposite or the absence of being. The Greek philosopher Parmenides warned against concerning oneself with it, "for you can neither recognize (it is impossible, after all) nor express that which does not exist."

Early Christian philosophy brought nothingness into play again, since creation is only possible "ex nihilo"—i.e., out of nothing; otherwise it is not creation. Hegel first established nothingness as the antonym of pure being, but then went on to assert that pure being and nothingness are basically identical. In his "Encyclopedia," he wrote, "This pure being is now the pure abstraction, hence the absolutely negative, which, taken immediately in the same way, is the nothing."

With this, Hegel was not far removed from the ideas of physics. For him, pure being is simply itself, and it has no relations, no complexity. Such a state would violate a whole series of fundamental physical laws and therefore does not exist in nature —and neither does nothingness.

It did, however, take physicists a while to come to this realization. For a long time, nothingness was considered to be a synonym for vacuum—a theoretical state in which a given space is entirely empty. The first atomic theory by Leucippus and/or

Democritus already assumed that matter consisted of atoms moving in empty space. Under Plato's influence, Aristotle postulated that nature had an aversion to the void, also known as "horror vacui." The universe was thus filled with aether, which physics initially needed to explain the propagation of light—at the time, it was believed that there could be no waves without a medium.

That something like a vacuum could exist was demonstrated in the 17th century by Otto von Guericke, the inventor of the air pump, with the help of his now-famous Magdeburg hemispheres. In 1654, he conducted experiments that involved harnessing horses to connected copper hemispheres 42 centimeters in diameter that he pumped the air out of. Even two teams of 15 horses each could not separate the spheres. At the time, it was thought that this was a property of the vacuum, a kind of contracting force. Today we know that it was the external pressure of our atmosphere—the many kilometers of air above us—that pressed the two halves of the sphere, which were under lower pressure, together.

Over the centuries, vacuum technology continued to evolve. What Guericke achieved with his air pump is today only considered a rough vacuum. Normal pumps that work with pressure difference aren't sufficient to achieve an ultra-high vacuum with pressures of less than one-billionth of a bar (one bar is the normal pressure on the Earth's surface). To achieve this, substances such as titanium are used on the walls of a cooling chamber to bind the remaining residual molecules, while cold traps are used to liquefy the residual gas. With the aid of liquid helium, it is possible to achieve pressures of 10^{-19} bar, or one ten-billionth of a billionth of normal pressure.

The vacuum of space

Pressure is two orders of magnitude lower in space. However, depending on the environment, there are still approximately 1000 atoms per cubic decimeter (which corresponds to one liter). The vacuum of space has some interesting properties that science fiction doesn't always render accurately. Sound, for example, always requires a carrier medium. Therefore, it cannot travel in open space. Explosions would not be audible. Light, on the other hand, does not require a carrier medium. It propagates at the speed of light in vacuum. This applies to the entire electromagnetic spectrum: this includes x-rays and gamma rays as well as thermal radiation (infrared).

Heat transfer in space can only take place by way of radiation, not convection (transfer by contact). This means there are surprisingly high temperature differences in space. If a spaceship were to get very close to the sun, it could be melted by the thermal radiation. But the temperature of whatever was in the shadow of the spaceship would remain just above absolute zero. Shadows in space are always very sharply defined. "Penumbra," which occur on Earth because of the diffraction of light in the air, cannot exist in space.

The biological effects of vacuum are somewhat less dramatic than one might first expect. The pressure difference is just a matter of one bar. Scuba divers experience greater pressure differences very quickly and are able to handle them. Because of the lack of heat conduction, there is no risk of the body shock-freezing. Heads bursting apart is the stuff of horror novels. A burst lung would be more likely, so it would be advisable not to hold your breath.

The biggest problem is that all bodily fluids start to boil. The skin usually protects the body from this, but not for long. When air bubbles form in the blood, blood flow stops and an individual goes unconscious. Since the retina is one of the tissues with the best blood supply, the sense of sight probably would probably fail first. The eyes could also theoretically burst, but the person this happened to would no longer be able to perceive it. How long would it be possible to survive? There are different opinions about this. A person involved in an accident that took place in a negative pressure chamber survived for just under 30 seconds. NASA estimates the maximum survival time to be 80 seconds.

And then? It depends. The parts irradiated by thermal radiation would dry up. This means that a corpse rotating in the solar system would turn into a mummy. But if the same side were always facing the sun, only that side would mummify, while the other side would freeze. A body in constant shadow would be preserved as a frozen corpse.

The vacuum is not empty

The way that physics conceives of nothingness has evolved quite a bit since von Guericke. As is so often the case, this has involved many trials and tribulations. At first, it appeared that Democritus's atomic theory, which stated that particles floated around in the nothingness, was right after all. Bohr's atomic model, for example, describes an atom that resembles the solar system, with the heavy nucleus in the middle and the light electrons revolving around it like planets in circular orbits. In between them there's a lot of nothing.

Today, we know that while the Bohr model can explain some phenomena of chemistry (such as the "valence" of elements), it is still just a model. In actuality, neither the atomic nucleus nor the shell is fixed. The electrons form a kind of cloud of probabilities. The closer one looks at it, the blurrier the image becomes. This happens because here we find ourselves in the realm of quantum physics, which didn't emerge until the twentieth century (and was initially rejected by the founder of the other groundbreaking theory, relativity). It is concerned exclusively with the state of the world on the very smallest scale. now It has long since proven its worth, since electronics and other areas of modern technology operate on its principles.

Quantum physics doesn't just describe individual particles, but also systems with many particles, electromagnetic fields, and —at least this is what scientists are hoping—also gravity (science is still working on this). It turns out that nothing is what it seemed. No particle has a fixed location and a fixed velocity. In addition, particles can be in more than one place at the same time, and they also have mysterious properties that link them to one another even when they're far apart ("entanglement"). You can read more about that in the appendix to my book *The Disturbance*, which is available from the same publisher.

The main point in terms of nothingness is that according to quantum physics, even empty space is filled with particles. The universe sometimes acts a bit like a teenager. As long as we're looking, everything remains calm—but then as soon as the vacuum feels alone, it suddenly fills up with particles that come out of nowhere. Why does this happen, even though the law of conservation of energy that we learned in school forbids exactly that?

The source of this childish behavior is the Heisenberg uncertainty principle, specifically the way it connects energy and time. The more precisely we try to measure energy, the less we know about the exact time of the measurement. This can be easily explained through the use of an analogy: From school, we might (hopefully) still know that the energy of an oscillation depends on its frequency—how quickly a pendulum swings, for example. Imagine a slowly moving clock pendulum. My grandmother had such an old-fashioned clock with a pendulum hanging in her living room.

Maybe it takes the pendulum two seconds for one swing. If I observe it for nine seconds—a short period of time—I can count four whole swings. The error, or the deviation, is half a swing divided by four, which is one-eighth, or 12.5 percent. However, if I watch for a much longer period of time, say 99 seconds, the error is still half a swing, but on a much larger base—in terms of percentage, just about one percent. I can certainly determine the energy of the pendulum's movement with greater precision by watching longer, but this comes at the cost of accuracy in terms of the time measurement. This uncertainty principle is not due to any lack of ability of human observers, but is rather a principal property of our world.

And also of vacuum. The law of conservation of energy does indeed prohibit the creation of something from nothing. But if this something disappears quickly enough, it was essentially never there. If we measure the energy content of a certain section of space over a long period of time, we find that the vacuum is empty. But if we look only very briefly, we can no longer be certain that there's really nothing there. This is because of the uncertainty principle. Completely legitimate particles may have emerged and then disappeared again. According to quantum physics, every state that can occur, does occur (in practice there is a big problem with this statement, but more on that later).

How large can these virtual particles be, and what properties must they possess? In the first place, they are forced to obey other laws of conservation, such as the law of conservation of charge. If a negatively charged electron is born out of nothing, it is always paired with a positively charged positron as its antiparticle.

If the two of them come together, they annihilate each other. The result is two photons that settle the energy debt to the universe that formed when virtual particles were created. The energy of the virtual particles determines how long they can exist. From this, it is possible to calculate the mass by using Einstein's famous formula, $E=mc^2$ (with c being the speed of light, which is just under 300,000 km/s). For example, the electron and positron combination lasts at most 10^{-21} seconds, which is one billionth of a trillionth of a second. During this time, light travels a distance that corresponds to the size of an average atom. For a likely chance to see a proton and an antiproton created, the observer only needs to look for 10^{-24} seconds.

However, practical problems can hardly be solved in this way, regardless of what ideas about "asking the universe" might suggest. Suppose you forgot to buy milk again—if your partner wanted to serve themselves at breakfast from a virtual, one-kilogram milk carton created from nothing, they would only have 10^{-52} seconds to pour it. But the smallest possible unit of time is Planck time, which lasts about $5 \cdot 10^{-44}$ seconds. Below that, time loses its meaning. The largest possible mass of a virtual particle is about one-hundredth of a milligram—that doesn't sound like much, but it still corresponds to the mass of approximately ten billion viruses.

So far, it hasn't been possible to detect virtual particles directly. Yet it should be possible to detect their interactions with the rest of the universe. If the vacuum of space is filled with particles that are constantly appearing and disappearing, this should have an effect on its properties. Some scientists speculate that these so-called quantum fluctuations are the source of the dark energy that is believed to be responsible for the accelerated expansion of the universe. This would be a nice explanation that would require no new exotic theories (if we think of quantum physics as normal).

However, there is a small—no, a huge—problem: The physicist John Wheeler calculated that, based on the known Planck constants, the universe must have an energy density of 10^{94} grams per cubic centimeter. A cube with an edge length of one centimeter cut from space would thus weigh ten billion billion

billion billion billion billion billion billion billion billion kilo-grams. However, practical observation says that this value is a bit smaller. A cubic centimeter of steak weighs a couple of grams, and empty space is significantly lighter—according to physicists' measurements, on average the value is 120 orders of magnitude less.

Can this calculation be dismissed? No, not with the current possibilities of quantum physics. Scientists hope that in the future they can somehow renormalize the calculated value of vacuum energy, so as to reconcile it with reality. Renormalize—in other words, scientists are hoping that somewhere they can find a (physically meaningful) number they can divide this ridiculous number by so it can then fit with reality.

But there are other observations that speak to the existence of quantum fluctuations. Stephen Hawking, for example, used vacuum energy to explain the behavior of black holes. These have what is referred to as an event horizon, which extends around the object like a spherical shell. Everything that occurs within this shell or that reaches its radius is removed forever from the normal universe: The black hole's huge gravitational force doesn't permit anything to escape. Therefore, these objects must actually be enormously stable and follow just one trend: growth.

Hawking then used quantum fluctuations in order to postulate a kind of evaporation process for black holes. Namely, if a particle-antiparticle pair forms near the event horizon, one of the partners may be pulled into the black hole while the other one just barely escapes. The virtual particle becomes a real parti-cle. The energy needed for this is taken from the black hole, so that over time it loses mass and shrinks. According to Hawking, the smaller the black hole, the faster this happens. Thus far, it has not been possible to prove the existence of so-called Hawking radiation. One of the reasons for this is that it is relatively weak. Primarily, however, the smaller the black hole, the greater the radiation, and thus far astronomers have not succeeded in observing mini black holes.

The Casimir effect, first verified experimentally in 1958, shows that vacuum energy actually exists. This was predicted by the Dutch physicist Hendrik Casimir in 1948. From quantum theory, it follows that when two parallel, electrically conductive plates are placed in a vacuum, a force acts on them, pressing them together. The two plates must be very close together, and the distance needs to be just a few nanometers in order for the effect to be measured. The force results because only virtual particles with wavelengths matching the distance between the plates can occur in the space between them—the distance must be an integral multiple of the particle wavelengths. However, this restriction doesn't exist outside the plates. The virtual particles thus create a pressure difference between the space inside and the outside the plates, which pushes the plates together. At a distance of 11 nanometers, the pressure is at least 100 kilopascals.

In the 1950s, the Russian physicist Yevgeny Lifschitz extended Casimir's calculations to more general cases. He was able to demonstrate that the Casimir force could not only attract but repel. This depends mainly on the properties of the material. This prediction was experimentally verified in 2009. Scientists are hoping to harness it so that objects can levitate frictionlessly.

The dynamic Casimir effect is one extension of this concept. If the two plates of the classic Casimir effect were moved towards each other very, very quickly, it should be possible to create real photons. However, it has not yet been proven whether this really works. Nonetheless, with its (now discontinued) program "Breakthrough Propulsion Physics Project," NASA investigated whether the dynamic Casimir effect would be suitable for spacecraft propulsion. They hoped that the recoil from the generated photons would be able to propel a ship through space.

However, it appears that the effect is far too small. Physicist Steve Lamoreaux, who studied the Casimir effect extensively and published articles on it, dashed all such hopes—even burning gasoline has a better energy output than the Casimir effect. Lamoreaux contends that the practical significance of the Casimir effect is rather that it facilitates chemical bonds in the first place.

Incidentally, the claims made by some mystics that it's possible to gain energy from nothing with the help of the Casimir effect are likewise nonsense: As explained above, the Casimir effect doesn't violate the law of conservation of energy at all, which would be necessary to build a *perpetuum mobile*.

The wrong vacuum

Another exciting concept related to nothingness is that of the false vacuum. Shortly after the Big Bang, during the time of inflation, the universe expanded very rapidly. It's possible that this inflation took place because at that time the vacuum went from an excited state to its ground state, just like a pendulum swinging from its deflected state back to the center.

This offers a nice explanation for the mysterious inflation phase. But it would also produce a new danger: Perhaps the universe stopped halfway, and what we think is vacuum is not the ground state of empty space at all, but rather an excited state, or what is called a false vacuum. The pendulum could have been interrupted on the way down. In that case, it would be possible for the universe to suddenly resume the interrupted inflation and the pendulum would complete its movement. The false vacuum would become a true one, and then universe as we know it would cease to exist.

Such an implosion would propagate through the universe at the speed of light. This might actually already be happening and it just hasn't reached us yet. Scientists have calculated that we would have an advance warning time of three minutes if such a disaster were to strike. Some scientists even fear that it would be possible to accidentally trigger the vacuum decay—in particle accelerators, for example. In the story, something like this could have happened during the experiment that Rossendorf ZfK conducted in an open-cast mine in Lusatia. But for the time being, nature seems to have much better particle accelerators than we do in the form of quasars, black holes, and pulsars. This is reassuring, since if such things could trigger vacuum decay, it technically should have already happened long ago.

Technically.

Nothingness and zero

We move on from this cliffhanger to switch over to school. We can also approach nothingness from a different angle: in terms of mathematics. When counting, zero (0) signals that nothing is present. Aha! There it is, our nothing. But what is a zero? It's the integer that immediately precedes 1. Zero is an even number because it can be divided by 2 with no remainder. Zero is neither positive nor negative—or it's both positive and negative. Often, 0 is considered a natural number, or the only natural number that isn't positive. Zero is an integer and therefore a rational number and a real number (as well as an algebraic number and a complex number). It can't be a prime number because it has an infinite number of factors, and it can't be a composite number because it can't be expressed as a product of prime numbers (since 0 must always be one of the factors, and 0 isn't a prime number). Zero is even (that is, a multiple of 2) and simultaneously a multiple of any other integral, rational, or real number.

"Never divide by zero, or you'll break your elbow": a jingle similar to this is learned in German schools. But what exactly happens when we divide by zero? The smaller the denominator a fraction has, the larger its value. The result approaches infinity—and this brings us back to the universe. Out of nothing comes everything. It's tempting to think that the Big Bang happened just because somebody successfully divided by zero (apparently Chuck Norris can do it). The result of this operation would surely be nothing less than an infinite cosmos.

There are quite a variety of nothings, aren't there? Incidentally, most cultures used zero before they accepted the idea of negatives (that is, quantities less than zero). The Babylonians didn't yet have a true symbol for zero. But by 1770 BCE, the Egyptians were already using such a symbol in their accounting texts. The symbol "nfr," which means "beautiful," was also used to refer to the base level in drawings of tombs and pyramids.

Initially, the ancient Greeks didn't have a zero. Ptolemy first introduced it around 150 CE. The zero was probably used most consistently on the Indian subcontinent, where it appeared around the 5th century. It was from there, in addition to Greek sources, that it migrated to Islamic culture. In 813 CE, the Persian mathematician Muḥammad ibn Mūsā al-Khwārizmī used Hindu numerals to create astronomical tables. Around 825, he published a book that synthesized Greek and Hindu knowledge and also included his own contribution to mathematics, which included an explanation of the use of zero. In the 12th century, this book was translated into Latin with the title "Algoritmi de numero Indorum." The Italian mathematician Fibonacci (1170-1240) was one of the first to make regular use of the "Arabic number system." It soon became the standard among scientists, whereas merchants kept using the Roman system for a long time.

The German (and English) word "null" is actually borrowed from Italian ("nulla"), which is based on the Latin word "nūlla" ("nothing"), the neuter plural of the Latin word "nūllus" ("none"). It first appeared in German-language texts in its original form "Nulla" around 1500. "Null" can be found from the end of the 16th century onwards, along with "Noll," "Nulle," and "das Nullo." Meanwhile, the "zero" that is found in other languages came from an Italian corruption of the Arabic word "ṣifr" ("empty").

The search for nothing

In *The Neverending Story*, the imaginary land of Fantastica is threatened by The Nothing. When I was a child, I loved both the book and the movie. Partly because the nothing is such a fantastical concept that is encountered early on when studying cosmology. If the universe came into being with the Big Bang, what was there before that? Nothing. If the universe is finite, what is outside of it? Nothing.

The second question may certainly be answered within the framework of perception. Geometric shapes may very well be endless but also finite. Picture an ant on a spherical shell or, to make it more exciting, on a Möbius strip (which is such an impossibly intertwined loop). The area at the ant's disposal is finite and can be calculated. But the creature will never reach the end. The universe is not spherical, but almost flat; yet even with such geometry, it can be demonstrated mathematically that it can have an unlimited form.

In addressing the first question, we must become principled (which I hate). The universe consists of space and time, both of which first appeared with the Big Bang. Therefore, a time before time cannot in principle exist. The whole mass of the universe was concentrated in a singularity, a point source. Mathematically speaking, a point has no dimension. Space and dimension didn't exist until the Big Bang.

I'll admit that these are unsatisfactory answers. This is because we don't yet possess the scientific tools to investigate singularities. Current physics fails at this. But there are already promising theories. "Loop quantum gravity," for example, may show that the universe expands over and over in a perpetual process of renewal to then emerge again from nothing. However, the nothing would be replaced by an "eternity," which is unfortunately just as intangible. Many mathematicians are reluctant to play with infinities, but that's a separate issue.

Let's just wait a few more years. It surely won't take scientists forever to answer questions about the nature of nothing.

Tip: You can also get this biography as a nicely illustrated PDF, free of charge, when you register at hard-sf.com/subscribe.

Notes

October 5, 2029, Earth orbit

1. Völkerfreundschaft = Friendship of the people of all countries
2. Bummi was the name of a children's magazine as well as its eponymous mascot, a plush bear. This magazine, intended for preschoolers and kindergarteners, first appeared in 1965 for 25 pfennigs.
3. Sports academy for children and youth translates to Kinder und Jugendsportschule, KJS. At the KJS, children and young people were trained as junior GDR athletes while they completed their secondary education there. Most of the time, the students were housed in boarding facilities.
4. The NVA (Nationale Volksarmee or National People's Army) was the army of the GDR. Because of its high standards for training and good discipline, it was considered one of the most powerful armies of the Warsaw Pact.
5. DeDeRon, a polyamide fiber created in the GDR, was the equivalent of what was known as "nylon" in the West.

October 6, 2029, Dresden

1. Herr = Mr.
2. The Company is a colloquial term for the Ministry for State Security (Stasi), which spied on citizens. "X is from the Company" meant that this person worked for the Stasi.
3. The Ministry of State Security was the interior secret service, the famous Stasi.
4. The GDR had been founded on October 7th, 1949, so every October 7th was Republic (Birth)Day.
5. Frau = Mrs.
6. Egon Krenz was the long-standing chairman of the youth organization Freie Deutsche Jugend (FDJ) and was therefore always regarded as the successor to the state and party leader Erich Honecker.
7. The Deutsche Reichsbahn was the railway company of the GDR.
8. Fräulein = Miss
9. Erich Honecker has been a long time state and party leader. His wife Margot was minister for education.
10. A Section Commissioner (or "Abschnittsbevollmächtigter", ABV) was a police lieutenant who was responsible for a certain part of the town.

October 6, 2029, Earth orbit

1. Mifa (Mitteldeutsche Fahrradwerke) was the biggest bicycle manufacturer in the GDR. The popular saying was: "a piece of sheet metal, a piece of wire, and the Mifa bike is complete."
2. Malimo is the brand name of a finished textile product that has been made, first in the GDR and now worldwide, since the 1950s using a stitch-bonding process with three thread systems that was developed by Heinrich Mauers-

berger. Malimo is used to make outerwear, upholstery fabrics, towels, carpeting, and curtains.

3. State-owned enterprises were called "volkseigener Betrieb" (VEB) which translates to people-owned enterprise (while they were actually owned by the state). Over the years, private companies became increasingly rare.

4. The Trabant was the iconic car of the East, made partly from cardboard (really!) There were only two car brands in the GDR, Trabant and Wartburg.

October 7, 2029, Dresden

1. Karat and The Puhdys were rwo famous GDR rock bands.

2. HO (from Handels-Organisation, or "trade organization") and Konsum (from Konsum-Genossenschaft, or "consumer cooperative") were two retail chains that sold everyday consumer goods. They ran smaller stores as well as supermarkets ("Kaufhalle"). Konsum was organized as a cooperative. Citizens received stamps for the purchases they made and would receive a rebate at the end of the year.

3. Invented name for the east german (closed) interner.

4. Intershop was a nationwide store chain selling goods for western (convertible) money.

5. Robotron was one of the few east.german computer manufacturers. They were famous for copying western software, like dBase which became REDABAS and MS-DOS which became DCP. Here, I'm assuming they would have copied Windows too which would have become Window-DCP ("Fenster"-DCP).

6. Equivalent to a VPN (virtual private network) today.

7. Yes, in that reality even Google Plus survived!

October 8, 2029, Dresden

1. The POS (Polytechnische Oberschule, Polytechnic Secondary School) was the main part of the GDR school system, starting at first grade at 6 to 7 years of life until tenth grade.

2. The People's Police included all of the police forces in the GDR, from the criminal police to the traffic police. One of its distinctive features was the "ABV" (Abschnittsbevollmächtigte, or "section commissioner"), who was responsible for a specific residential area.

3. A People's Solidarity Club (Club der Volkssolidarität) was a kind of a social club for elderly people

4. The WBS-70 type apartment blocks, built using the modular construction system in almost all East German cities, were confusingly similar in appearance. The layouts of the apartments in the six-story buildings were also almost identical.

5. The class enemy (Klassenfeind) was everyone who had a different opinion than the state's leaders.

6. Bergblick = Mountain View

7. *Neues Deutschland* was the GDR-wide party newspaper of the SED and therefore the most important press medium of the state and party leadership. Independent journalism could not be expected from *ND*.

8. The National Award of the GDR was a state prize given for "outstanding creative work in the fields of science and technology, significant mathematical and scientific discoveries and technical inventions, the introduction of new work and production methods" or for "outstanding works and achieve-

ments in the fields of art and literature." The monetary prize was 25,000 to 100,000 marks, depending on the award class.

9. The class point of view describes the way that GDR citizens were supposed to look at political issues—namely, in terms of the workers and farmers as well as the interests of the East German regime. Anybody who expressed themselves as hostile to the republic had "no class point of view."

10. Lada was and is a Russian brand of cars producing vehicles under Fiat license.

October 9, 2029, Jena

1. Grilletta was the east german name for a burger.
2. Letcho is a kind of tomato sauce fron Bulgaria.
3. This was, without question, the most famous brand of mustard in the GDR. Today it belongs to the Bavarian company Develey.
4. A term invented by the author for the GDR wide mobile network (which never existed).
5. The KoKo was a division of the GDR Ministry of Commerce and was responsible for selling GDR goods abroad in exchange for hard currency. Sometimes the KoKo was very creative and sold everything that could be converted into West German marks, down to old streetlamps.
6. In the small town of Bautzen, the Stasi had a famous jail. "Go to Bautzen" meant to get jailed by the Stasi.

October 10, 2029, Lusatia

1. *Spuk unterm Riesenrad* ("Ghosts under the Ferris Wheel") was a popular television series set at an amusement park.

October 11, 2029, Lusatia

1. *Aktuelle Kamera* was the main news program on GDR television. The reporting was, of course, managed and controlled by the state

October 12, 2029, Lusatia

1. A Landwirtschaftliche Produktionsgenossenschaft (LPG) was a cooperative association of farmers and their means of production for common agricultural production in the GDR; initially membership was voluntary, but it became involuntary following forced collectivization.

Printed in Great Britain
by Amazon